W9-BLD-087

The Inn at Angel Island

**Center Point
Large Print**

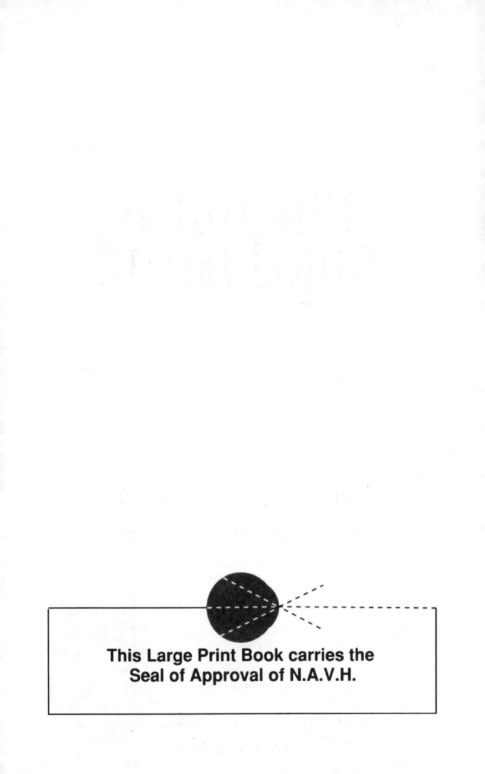

**This Large Print Book carries the
Seal of Approval of N.A.V.H.**

The Inn at Angel Island

THOMAS KINKADE
& Katherine Spencer

CENTER POINT PUBLISHING
THORNDIKE, MAINE

This Center Point Large Print edition
is published in the year 2010 by arrangement with
The Berkley Publishing Group,
a member of Penguin Group (USA) Inc.

Cover art: Thomas Kinkade
Cover design: Lesley Worrell

This is a work of fiction. Names, characters, places,
and incidents either are the product of the author's
imagination or are used fictitiously, and any
resemblance to actual persons, living or dead, business
establishments, events, or locales is entirely coincidental.

The text of this Large Print edition is unabridged.
In other aspects, this book may vary
from the original edition.
Printed in the United States of America
on permanent paper.
Set in 16-point Times New Roman type.

ISBN: 978-1-60285-745-2

Library of Congress Cataloging-in-Publication Data

Kinkade, Thomas, 1958-
  The inn at Angel Island / Thomas Kinkade and Katherine Spencer.
    p. cm.
  ISBN 978-1-60285-745-2 (libbrary binding : alk. paper)
  1. Islands--Massachusetts--Fiction. 2. Taverns (Inns)--Massachusetts--Fiction.
  3. City and town life--Massachusetts--Fiction. 4. Large type books.
  I. Halpern, Katherine Spencer. II. Title.
PS3561.I534I66 2010b
813'.54--dc22
2009051349

Dear Friends,

Some of my fondest memories from childhood are of summer vacations with my family. It was a long drive to the old Victorian inn that looked out on the ocean, and I couldn't wait to arrive. I would spend my days on the beach, happily building sand castles, collecting shells, and chasing waves. When evening drew near, we would return to the inn to watch the sunset from the porch. All the guests would then gather around the oak table in the dining room for delicious, home-cooked dinners, prepared with fresh ingredients that were grown on surrounding farms or plucked straight from the sea. It was, I now realize, a kind of paradise. Back then I believed that something so perfect had to be a gift from the angels. It filled me with a love of the wild beauty in the natural world and a sense of the truly divine. It has been a constant source of inspiration for my paintings—a place of light that my mind returns to again and again.

Even the sweetest things must one day end, and that particular inn, sadly, is no longer standing. In some way, I have been searching for it ever since. That is why Katherine Spencer and I have created *The Inn at Angel Island*, the first in the Angel Island series that captures the essence of that welcoming, homey inn—a place where all travelers find comfort and solace, a place to renew and restore one's faith in oneself and in God.

Come with me then and meet Liza Martin, who, along with her brother, Peter, has just inherited the Inn at Angel Island. For Liza, the inn is a far-from-welcome gift. She has too many conflicts in her own busy life—a high-powered job that may be at risk, an ex-husband who claims he still loves her, and a deep grief for the loss of her aunt Elizabeth. Her brother Peter comes to the island with his own troubles—precarious finances and an even more precarious relationship with his fourteen-year-old son, Will. The charming but dilapidated old inn seems to be a complication that no one needs, and Liza and Peter are determined to sell it—until Angel Island, with its white beaches, soaring cliffs, and quaint little village, begins to work its magic on them, opening their hearts to what they really need.

All you have to do to is cross the land bridge from Cape Light to Angel Island. There you will discover a wild, unspoiled, romantic haven, a place to reclaim one's dreams and one's faith. I hope that, like me, you will often return to the Inn at Angel Island, where you will find a soft, cozy bed, a home-cooked meal, and a warm welcome. May it always be your home away from home.

Thomas Kinkade

The Inn at
Angel Island

Chapter One

OF course, it was raining. Nothing about this trip was going to be easy. Liza Martin already knew that. Why should the weather cooperate?

The drive from Boston to the north shore was hard enough at the end of a workday, the traffic easily making it two hours or more. But the timing couldn't be helped. A client emergency had erupted at four, just as Liza was heading out of the office, trying to beat the commuter crush and the dismal forecast.

So here she was, on a Tuesday night at the height of the rush hour, driving all the way up to Angel Island in steady rain. She had turned the wipers to high speed and slowed her car to a careful crawl. At least it isn't snow, she reminded herself, which was not out of the question even in late March in New England.

She hoped the skies were clearer beyond the city. On a night like this, heavy rain and high surf could wash out the land bridge that connected the tiny island to the town of Cape Light, making it impossible to cross the harbor.

When Liza was a little girl, staying with her aunt Elizabeth and uncle Clive for the summer, visitors often came to the island for the day and were then stranded when a storm blew in. Aunt

Elizabeth never paid much attention to weather forecasts and never failed to be delighted by these unexpected overnight guests. Those stormy summer nights, with so many interesting people milling around the old house, were among Liza's fondest memories. Her aunt and uncle must have enjoyed it, too; Liza often thought those nights were what had inspired them to turn their rambling old house into an inn.

Liza slowed for a light, letting the sound of the storm outside bring back those rainy nights on the island when her uncle would play the piano and everyone would sing. They would even move back the furniture in the front parlor and dance when the mood was right, often by candlelight when the power went out or with Aunt Elizabeth shining a flashlight on the keyboard, swaying the beam to and fro in time to the rhythm. There would be card games and ghost stories and shadow shows on the big wall in the front parlor, her uncle's specialty.

Liza recalled how she would always feel disappointed the next morning to see the sunshine and the clear blue sky. But other charms of the island would quickly distract her, like an early morning beach walk, where she would sift through the odd treasures the wild surf had tossed on the shoreline the night before. She and her brother, Peter, would race each other to the best shells, arguing over the vilest remains of some defunct sea creature. Her aunt would follow, laughing at them and playing judge and arbitrator with endless patience.

How did Aunt Elizabeth manage to put up with us, Liza wondered. And do it so cheerfully? It couldn't have been easy, though her aunt and uncle always acted as if their season with Liza and Peter was the highlight of their year. They had no children of their own, so perhaps it really was, Liza reflected.

It was hard to believe her aunt would not be there tonight, waiting for her. It had been nearly two months since she had passed on. Liza had come up for the funeral and burial, of course. But she knew that the reality of the situation, the hard truth of it, had not yet sunk in. Some part of her still expected to see her aunt's tall, willowy form, silhouetted in the doorway, watching and waiting for her.

The memory made Liza feel sad. She knew that she should have come to visit more often. In some way it seemed pointless to go there now. Aunt Elizabeth was gone. It was too late.

A buzz from her BlackBerry cut into her thoughts. Liza quickly answered, speaking through her wireless headset.

"Hi, Liza, it's Charlie," a familiar voice replied. "Sorry to bother you, but something came up with one of your clients right after you left. I thought you should know."

Charlie Reiger, her former assistant and present office rival. She'd figured as much. A glance at the dashboard clock read half past seven. The office was empty by now with only the workaholics and mischief-makers left. Charlie fell into both categories.

"What is it, Charlie? Which account?"

"Berlinger Tires. Harry Berlinger sent back comments on the new ad proofs by messenger. He doesn't like the colors or the typeface. The boards landed on Eve's desk, so she passed them off to me. I put the art department on it, and we're working up a new version for him."

"That sounds like a good plan," Liza said in a reasonable tone, though she felt herself simmering. "You'll e-mail the revised proofs to me first, so I can take a look before they go back to Berlinger, right?"

"Sure thing. That goes without saying," Charlie insisted.

She nearly laughed at him. *Right, Charlie. As if I believe that for a second.* "Thanks. I'll keep my eye out," Liza answered. Charlie double-checked her address on the island, then said good night. Liza clicked off the call, fuming. She hated it when he got his sticky paws anywhere near her clients. It was like leaving a hungry dog alone with a roast beef.

Did he really think he could cut her out of the loop so easily? She would call the client herself as soon as she could. And why hadn't Eve just called her directly about the problem?

Because that was the way their boss, Eve Barkin, operated. Eve liked to fan the flames of rivalry to get the best work out of her top two account executives. She had even been dangling a promotion between them for months now. Liza knew that she was the obvious choice. She had more experience, the most important clients, and far more creative ideas than Charlie. Everyone in the office said she would get it. But Eve liked to keep life interesting, treating Charlie like a valid contender.

Eve had promised that nothing would be decided until Liza returned to Boston, but Liza hated leaving the office and giving her nemesis a clear field. She only hoped Eve could see through good old Charlie, with his five-hundred-dollar suits and two-hundred-dollar haircuts.

And she hoped the ordeal on the island—settling her aunt's estate and selling the inn—would be over quickly, so she could get back to her job and her life, which pretty much amounted to the same thing these days.

Liza would only be gone two weeks, but she felt as if she would be away for months. She had definitely packed a month's worth of work, stuffing her briefcase, a large knapsack, and a portfolio with layouts and sketches. Thank heavens for the Internet and all the high-tech contraptions she relied on. She only hoped the island had good reception.

Sorting out the inn and everything in it was going to be a nightmare, but at least she didn't have to do it alone. Her brother, Peter, would be here by tomorrow. He lived in Arizona now, a photographer with his own business, struggling lately to stay afloat. He had told her that he was taking on a lot of little jobs, the kind he used to sneer at in better days. These next two weeks were the only break in his schedule for months, which had determined the timing of their visit.

It was probably better for both of them to just get this ordeal over with. There would never be a good time to travel back to Angel Island. To sort through her aunt and uncle's belongings and put the gracious old Victorian up for sale. There was no good time to go back and be reminded of all the happy summers she and Peter had spent there as children.

Maybe that's why Liza had rarely returned. She didn't want to remember. Those memories were bittersweet, even painful at times. Especially now, when her life was not turning out anything like she had expected.

As she traveled farther north, the traffic thinned. Liza finally spotted her exit and turned off the highway, then headed onto a county road toward the village of Cape Light.

She felt half-relieved the awful drive was almost

14

over—and half wished the trip would take even longer.

Except for her last visit, after her aunt died, Liza had not been back to the island in a long time. Maybe once or twice in the last few years? She had felt bad about that and did call her aunt every couple of weeks to stay in touch. She and Peter had lost their parents in a car accident when they were both in college. Her aunt and uncle had been the only close relatives left. Still, once Liza graduated from college and got busy with her own life, it was hard to get to visit them except on holidays.

Once she really dug in at the advertising agency, Liza was always so busy; she almost never took vacation time. Work usually spilled over to the weekends, and her limited free time was always filled with other things. She had better things to do than travel out to this remote, barely inhabited little chunk of land. How her aunt and uncle managed to live here all those years—and seem so happy in this rough, primitive place—she'd never know.

Sure, she had loved it as a child, but as she grew older and her tastes changed, it seemed too quiet and downright dull. There wasn't even a good restaurant here—or any type of restaurant at all that she could remember.

That seemed selfish, now that she thought about it. But it was true. After Uncle Clive passed away, Aunt Elizabeth seemed to accept Liza's infrequent visits. She claimed to be busy, too, running the inn with just the help of one full-time employee, a woman named Claire North. Aunt Elizabeth was not the type to make Liza or her brother feel guilty about being inattentive to her. She had always been, and was to the very end, totally independent.

Liza did feel guilty now. Elizabeth had passed on in late January when a bout of bronchitis that had lingered all winter suddenly flared up into pneumonia. Her once-robust aunt was not strong enough to fight it and passed away very quickly.

Or so it seemed to Liza—as if there had been no warning at all. She had been very concerned when she heard that her aunt's condition had worsened into pneumonia. Still, she fully expected her aunt to recover; Aunt Elizabeth had assured her that she would. Before Liza could manage to get over to the Southport Hospital, the next call had been the worst news of all and a great shock. Leaving Liza stunned . . . and full of regrets.

There were so many reasons why it was hard to come back here.

Liza suddenly decided to turn down a road that led to Main Street in Cape Light, though staying on Beach Road was a more direct route to the island. She wanted to see if there were any changes in the small town.

Driving slowly and peering out the window, she did spot a few: signs changed over shops and a new fire station. But she had to look closely to notice the differences. For the most part, Cape Light looked very much the same as it had when she was a child.

The lights were still on in the Clam Box, she noticed. The bright red neon letters "OPEN" glowed in a window alongside a faded poster that read, "Try Our Famous Clam Rolls and Blueberry Pancakes—Box Lunches to Go." That poster had always been there, though Liza wasn't sure the clam rolls were famous beyond the town limits.

The town's landmark eatery had been Aunt Elizabeth's favorite dining spot. Liza didn't recall the food as anything special, but as a kid, she had loved sitting on the spinning stools at the counter, feasting on hot dogs or hamburgers and fries—or on a hot afternoon, a big, drippy ice-cream cone. She bet the place still looked the same inside, too.

It was half past eight and she was definitely hungry, but she didn't stop. The rain fell lightly now, and Liza knew that if the bridge to the island was still open, it might not stay that way for long.

When Liza arrived at the bridge a short time later, the yellow gate was up, signaling that it was safe to cross. The water on either side looked inky black and bottomless. The night sky was just about the same color, with thin, low clouds stretched like cottony threads across a glowing crescent moon.

She steered her car onto the two-lane bridge, which had a rail and a paved shoulder, edged by large gray boulders, on each side. A few tall highway lights lit the way, but she still drove slowly down the narrow black ribbon of highway. From the middle of the bridge, she could see the coastline curving around to Cape Light's harbor and the cluster of lights in the village.

Waves crashed against the rocks on either side of the road, threatening to spill over, and Liza felt a stiff wind push against her compact SUV.

Why the town didn't build a real bridge to the island, she had never understood. Maybe they wanted to keep it private and challenging to reach. It kept people out. Or maybe it was sheer economics: Because so few people lived out there, or even visited, it didn't seem an efficient use of taxpayer dollars.

But that was all supposed to change—and very soon, she had heard. Angel Island had just been designated a Historic National Seashore. Improvements were coming, including a ferry service from the nearby village of Newburyport, about ten miles north along the coast. The ferry would land on the beach at the north side of the island, which would be improved with bathhouses, a dock, and a boardwalk, all the amenities day-tripping tourists expected.

Predictions were very positive. More visitors would come, and real estate values would rise. Liza wasn't sure who would even be interested in coming here. The place still seemed so remote and out of the way. But that was another good reason to sell the inn now, while everyone was still so optimistic.

Fortunately, her aunt had put Liza's and her brother's names on the deed while she was alive, so the property automatically transferred to them upon her death and was not part of the probate process. At least they had been spared that hassle. There would certainly be more hassles to come before it was all over; Liza was sure of it.

The ride over the land bridge was brief, the winds stronger across the open stretch of water and just wild enough to hint at the island to come, which had always been rustic and untamed. Liza suddenly realized she hoped the island hadn't changed much since her last visit.

The inn was a short drive from the bridge. Liza found her way easily, though she had not made the trip in a long time.

She felt strangely excited, driving slowly down the dark, narrow roads. She rolled down the windows, feeling the moist breeze on her skin and smelling the salty air, sensations that brought back a wave of memories.

There weren't many opportunities to get lost out here. But she was surprised at how clearly she remembered the route. Everything looked exactly the same: the high marsh grass on the roadside, the dark shadows of houses popping up here and there, even the bent old trees that stood like sentinels and served as landmarks, directing her way. Straight on Old Dock Road, veering right on Mariner's Way, just past the huge willow at the crossroads.

The beach appeared on the left side of the road, at the bottom of a high bluff. Liza could see the water shimmering in the moonlight. The sky had cleared, and stars sparkled like pinpoints of light in the dark blue sky. There were always so many stars out here; it was really astounding. She could hear the waves rolling in, the sound of the surf muffled and distant, the way it had sounded every night when she fell asleep in her summer bedroom.

Suddenly, on the right side of the road, the inn came into view. Liza stopped a moment and gazed out the window before pulling up the drive. She had always loved this house, three stories high with matching bay windows on the first and second floors. The windows on the second floor were fronted by a balcony, and there was even a turret on the right side of the building not far from the front door.

When Liza was a little girl and had heard the extravagant Victorian called a Queen Anne style, she had instantly known the term was perfect for the house. It was definitely a place worthy of royalty, something right out of a fairy tale.

Set on a large piece of property that sloped toward the road, the house faced the bluffs and the expanse of ocean that stretched out below. In the summertime, the wraparound porch was filled with sitting chairs, Adirondacks, wickers, and straight-backed rockers. During the inn's busiest weeks, the seats would be filled with guests, from morning to night, sipping lemonade or ice tea, reading or knitting in the shade. Or just gazing out at the sea. But the big porch stood empty now, except for a few cardboard cartons and dark lumps covered with black plastic. The remaining chairs were stored for the winter, Liza suspected.

A light on the walkway leading up to the porch glowed. A sign swung in the wind. "Angel Inn— All Are Welcome." Her aunt Elizabeth had painted and hand-lettered that sign, Liza recalled, though the scroll of vines and flowers on the border was now hardly visible.

Up on the porch, there was another small light on over the door. Liza couldn't see too much of the building, but what there was to see was not encouraging. The roof sagged, and the paint was dingy and peeling. There were shutters missing, and others hung broken and dangling. The sight was painful to her. The day her aunt had been buried out here, Liza had driven past the inn without really seeing it, and hadn't had the heart to stop and go inside.

No sense lingering now, she reasoned. There would be time enough tomorrow in the daylight for a full, depressing inventory.

Liza drove her SUV up the curved drive and parked near the porch. The front door swung open, and Liza saw Claire North silhouetted in the doorway. With Claire's back to the light and her face in shadow, it was hard to see the older woman's expression. Was she smiling? Liza wasn't sure.

She had met Claire only once before, at her aunt's memorial service, which had been held in the old stone church on the green in the town of Cape Light. Liza knew that her aunt had depended on Claire a great deal and valued her friendship. But in their brief meeting and during a few recent phone calls, Liza found the woman very hard to read. Liza wasn't sure if that was simply Claire's personality or some reaction she should take personally.

Liza walked to the rear of the vehicle, pulled out her bags, closed the hatch, and started toward the house. For the first time, she wondered about Claire's expectations. Did she think Liza and Peter might keep the inn, running it as absentee owners with Claire in charge? Didn't she realize they would sell it?

Liza and her brother had agreed that it was only fair that Claire hear about their plans right away. Liza was hoping, though, that she could put off that conversation until Peter arrived.

She walked up the porch steps, forcing a smile and a friendly greeting, the one she used to win over difficult clients.

"Hello, Claire. You didn't have to wait. There was a lot of traffic. I meant to call and let you know I'd be late . . ."

But she'd forgotten, Liza realized. She had forgotten all about the housekeeper and had not expected her to be waiting here. Claire did not live at the inn, though she had a room on the third floor, where she stayed over in case of bad weather. Her real home was in a cottage on the other side of the island. Liza's aunt Elizabeth had told Liza that when Claire had first started working for her.

"I didn't mind waiting." Claire stepped forward and helped Liza with her bags. Her welcoming smile and warm tone caught Liza off guard. "It must have been a hard drive in all that rain. You must be very tired."

"It wasn't that bad." Liza downplayed the aggravating journey.

"Well, come on in and dry off," Claire urged her. "Any more luggage?"

"Not much. I'll get it later." For some reason, Liza didn't want Claire waiting on her. It made her feel uneasy and a little guilty.

Liza set her big purse and laptop on a hall table. Claire shut the door, then turned to face her. "Your coat is wet. I'll hang it up for you."

"Okay, thanks." Liza shrugged off her damp wool coat and handed it over.

Claire hung the coat on a coat tree near the stair-

23

case, then positioned the tree closer to a large old radiator.

Very efficient, Liza thought. Though without her coat, she felt a sudden chill. Claire quickly took notice of that, too.

"I'll turn up the heat a bit. It is a raw night."

As the housekeeper stepped away to adjust the thermostat, Liza glanced around, feeling a bit stunned by the sights that were so familiar yet, at the same time, almost forgotten. The wallpaper patterned with vines and flowers. The Tiffany lamp softly glowing on an Eastlake-style table. The blue and red Oriental rug beneath her feet. Such familiar and comforting sights. But all a bit faded and worn looking now—the wallpaper peeling at the edges and stained in spots, the rug almost threadbare.

The place even smelled the same, a mixture of sea air, cooking, and her aunt's special blend of lavender and rosemary. Elizabeth would gather the herbs from the garden and hang bunches in various spots around the house. Liza spotted a bunch, tied with a thin blue ribbon, just beside the doorway.

When she turned, Claire was standing nearby again, looking at her expectantly. Liza didn't know what to say. Aunt Elizabeth had been very loquacious. She talked enough for two, Uncle Clive always said. Maybe that's why Elizabeth and Claire had gotten along so well—her aunt had done all the talking?

"Well . . . thanks for waiting. But it is late. I'm sure you want to get home." Liza heard the forced, false note of friendliness in her voice. Claire was being so kind to her, it made her feel even more guilty about having to tell her that she would soon be out of a job.

If she leaves now, I won't have to tell her until tomorrow, Liza realized.

"Are you hungry?" Claire asked, ignoring Liza's hint. "I've fixed you some dinner, just in case."

Liza was hungry. As much as she wished she were alone and out of this woman's company, her stomach easily won out.

"I am. I didn't stop to eat. It was raining so hard, and the places on the highway have such horrible food."

Claire nodded, seeming satisfied by that answer. She headed down the long hallway to the kitchen that was at the back of the house, and Liza followed, aware of her heels clicking against the wooden floorboards. Had she ever worn heels in this house? They didn't seem right here.

"I made some rosemary bread and chowder with plenty of cod and potatoes. I used the tomatoes from your aunt's garden. We put them up together last fall, before she got ill."

By *put them up*, Liza knew Claire meant preserved them in glass jars. Her aunt had been a devoted gardener and a very practical one, too, cultivating both beautiful flowers and rows of vegetables and herbs, which she and Liza's uncle would pick and preserve, then eat throughout the winter.

Claire stood at the wide, black cast-iron stove with her back to Liza. Solidly built, Claire wore a long dark blue cardigan over brown wool pants and heavy brown shoes that looked waterproof. A practical outfit for a rainy day in this part of the world, Liza thought. The housekeeper's fair hair looked as if it had once been blond but was now blended with gray and white strands, all wound in a coil at the back of her head.

Claire lit a burner beneath a large pot. The flame sprung up with a whooshing sound that Liza suddenly remembered. The stove was the same one her aunt had used to cook on, so old it had probably come with the house.

Liza rinsed her hands at the sink and dried them on a towel. The big farm table was long enough to accommodate a houseful of guests. Tonight it had been set with one place: a blue and white cloth place mat, a white linen napkin, silverware, and a water glass.

Liza sat at the spot, which was obviously meant for her. She suddenly realized it was the very same seat she had always sat in as a little girl. Had Claire somehow known that? But how could she?

It seemed an odd coincidence, considering the size of the table and the place Claire had chosen. Not some obvious spot at the head or even a corner. Liza glanced at the housekeeper, who stood at the stove, stirring the chowder, and felt an uncanny chill. She marked it up to her damp clothes and to being so hungry and tired.

"That soup smells good," Liza said, mostly to break the silence.

"That must mean it's ready. Or you're ready to have some." Claire glanced over her shoulder and smiled briefly. Then she filled a large bowl with chowder and carried it, along with a basket of fragrant bread that had just been taken from the oven, over to the table.

Liza noticed a small dish of butter near her plate. This was the perfect kind of bread for butter, and Liza did want to indulge, knowing it would melt instantly and taste very good. But she resisted. This was not vacation, and she didn't want to go home bursting out of her clothes on top of every other inconvenience. She would stick to her usual diet, thank you very much. No butter, no sugar, no empty carbs.

She took a bite of the bread, which was still delicious on its own, then glanced at her dinner again. There was a lot more floating around in the chowder than just some cod and potatoes. Bits of celery—or was that fennel? Some carrot, onions, and herbs. Some shellfish, clams and mussels and even a few plump shrimp. The scent was rich and fragrant, hinting at saffron.

Liza dipped her spoon and took a sip, then

closed her eyes, savoring the mixture of flavors. It really was . . . divine. It was more like a bouillabaisse and very much like the chowder her aunt had made. Had Claire followed the same recipe? Liza wanted to ask her, but for some reason, she held back and simply took another large spoonful.

Claire set a mug of tea near Liza's place along with a jar of honey. Liza was a coffee person, an absolute caffeine addict, but for some reason, tea was just what she wanted tonight. Somehow, Claire had guessed without asking.

Claire took another mug from the counter near the stove and sat at the table across from Liza and a few seats away, so that they weren't directly facing each other.

"This soup is very good," Liza said between bites.

"Put it up this afternoon. The General Store had almost everything I needed. You can't be too particular about recipes here. You have to learn to improvise."

Her aunt used to say the same thing. You had to be flexible in the kitchen. If you couldn't find a potato, a turnip would have to do.

"Thank you for fixing it for me," Liza said politely.

"It was no trouble." Claire sipped her tea, then sat with her hands folded on the tabletop.

They had run out of conversation again. Liza took a few more spoonfuls of chowder and a bite of bread, then pushed the food away and sat back. Ten minutes ago, she had felt very hungry. Now she just felt tired, worn out.

Claire glanced over at her. "So, you'll be here two weeks. Is that right?"

Liza nodded. "That's right. Two weeks." *Unless everything is settled sooner,* she added silently. Meaning Claire North would be out of a job sooner, too.

"At least you'll have your brother. You won't be doing this all alone," Claire said.

"Yes, he's coming tomorrow." Peter had not been able to come east for their aunt's funeral, so he and Claire had never met.

Claire nodded. "Good. I'll get his room ready."

"Thank you. I appreciate that," Liza said honestly. She forced herself to smile back. Claire North was very kind—and making it even harder now to impart the bad news.

Liza sighed and took a long sip of her tea.

"Would you like anything else? There are some oatmeal cookies," Claire offered.

"No thanks. Not right now." Liza paused. She felt so tired. It was probably a bad time to talk to Claire about serious matters, but Liza knew if she didn't say something tonight, she wouldn't be able to sleep.

"There is something I need to speak to you about, Claire," she began.

"Yes?" Claire turned her head and met Liza's

glance. She didn't seem nervous, Liza noticed. Perhaps she already guessed what was to come.

"You must be wondering what my brother and I plan to do with the inn, now that we own it."

Claire's mild expression remained unchanged, her clear blue gaze serene. Liza was beginning to think that the house could come down all around her and Claire wouldn't bat an eye.

"We appreciate that you've stayed on here, after my aunt's death, and taken care of the place. But we've decided to put it up for sale. We've been in touch with a real estate firm in Cape Light, Bowman Realty. We're hoping to find a buyer and have everything settled within the next two weeks."

There. That was clear enough, wasn't it?

Claire calmly sipped her tea. "I thought that might be what you would do," she said at last. "I guess we'll see how it goes."

We'll see how it goes? What was there to see? The answer got under Liza's skin. How blunt did she need to be? Did she have to tell Claire that once they sold the place, she would be out of a job?

Unless someone came in and wanted to keep running the inn and kept Claire on. That was possible of course. Maybe that's what she was hoping and hinting at? It was extremely unlikely considering the condition of the place. Even Claire North must realize that, Liza reasoned.

"There really is no question," Liza told her. "The agent we spoke to already has a few clients lined up to see the property. It could happen quickly."

Claire didn't answer. But Liza still wasn't sure that her point had come across.

She's been here a long time, and my aunt's death was a blow. She must be in denial about having to leave, Liza realized.

I won't say anything more, she decided. *Not tonight. Maybe after Peter comes, we'll talk to her again and offer her some compensation or a gift.*

"Is that all you wanted to tell me?" Claire asked finally.

"That's it, I guess."

Liza rubbed her eyes. This first evening was not going at all the way she had planned. She had imagined meeting Claire and really being able to talk with her, asking questions about Elizabeth's last days. But you had to feel comfortable with someone for that kind of conversation, and Liza had a feeling that she had just ruined any possibility for that kind of ease. Instead, she was sitting in this cold, damp kitchen feeling awkward. And she was fairly certain that in two weeks' time, she would leave here without ever having asked those questions.

It was her own fault. She shouldn't have to ask a stranger about her aunt. She should have just

31

taken a few days off from work and come out here to visit once she knew Elizabeth was sick.

But it hadn't seemed that serious. And there always seemed to be some crisis in the office that she couldn't abandon. And then her marriage had blown up, right in her face. Like a balloon that looked so pretty and harmless one minute, then shocked you with a big bang.

And she was still picking up the pieces of that mess.

Elizabeth had promised it wasn't serious and she would be better by the time spring came. That's what her aunt had told her. But Elizabeth must have known something. She just didn't want to be a bother. Liza should have realized.

Liza suddenly felt she might cry. She pulled a tissue from her pocket and blew her nose.

"I think I'll have some more tea. I must be coming down with something." She stood up and carried her plate to the sink, then ran some water and filled the tea kettle. "Can I make some more for you, Claire?"

"No, thank you. I'm fine."

Liza set the kettle on the stove and sat down again at the table. She felt Claire gazing at her but didn't dare look up to meet her eyes.

"It must be hard for you, coming back here after all this time," Claire said quietly.

Liza nodded. "It is hard," she admitted.

"I would like to help you, Liza. Any way I can.

Just let me know whatever it is you'd like me to do. I promised your aunt Elizabeth that I would. So you must let me," Claire added, as if there were some argument.

"Thank you . . . I appreciate that. I'm going to need your help sorting this place out," Liza said honestly.

Claire smiled mildly and nodded at her, looking pleased that they had come to this agreement. "If you don't mind me saying, you ought to get a good night's sleep. Things might look a little bit better tomorrow." She rose from the table, her movements economical and surprisingly graceful. "If there's nothing else you need, I'll head on home. I made up the room on the second floor for you. Third room down on the right."

The third room down? Liza wasn't sure if she remembered correctly after all this time, but she was pretty sure that had always been her favorite room in the whole inn.

She remembered it with sky blue walls and white curtains, and wondered if the decor had changed in all this time. It had a big bay window with an ocean view and a padded window seat.

It was not the room she used to stay in, though. It was always reserved for guests. Though she did sometimes sneak in, when it was vacated, and stretch out on the bed and pretend it was her room. Her aunt would laugh and never got mad at her.

Odd that Claire had picked that room out of so

many, Liza thought. Maybe she thought Liza would enjoy the view. But all the rooms on that side of the building had good views.

"Do you know the room?" Claire's voice broke into her thoughts. "Does it suit you?"

"Sounds fine." Liza was almost tempted to ask Claire how she had made that choice.

Then the kettle whistled. Liza stood up and shut off the flame, then fixed herself more tea. Claire walked into the foyer and put on a thick parka and gloves, definitely dressing for protection from the elements, not fashion.

She briefly waved to Liza from the front door. "Good night, Liza. I'll see you tomorrow."

Liza waved back and watched her step out the door. "Good night, Claire."

The heavy door closed, and Liza felt a sudden stunning silence close in around her. She sipped her tea, conscious of the creaking sounds in the walls and of the wind rattling the windows.

Had she ever been totally alone here? She wasn't sure about that. She certainly had never spent an entire night alone in the inn. It was a bit . . . unsettling. Especially since she'd been away from the place for so long. It was familiar, yet strange.

Liza finished her tea, then went out to her SUV and brought in the rest of her bags. She carried the essentials upstairs and soon found her room. Claire had turned on a small lamp that stood on a table near the bay window.

The room looked cozy and warm, still decorated in the same blue and white color scheme, though the paint, curtains, and quilt had definitely been updated since Liza's childhood summers.

Liza put down her bags and gazed around. The room looked the same as the rest of the house—clean but worn out, in need of fresh paint and wallpaper, new rugs and furnishings. It would be a project to update this place, especially at the cost of things these days. Liza couldn't imagine taking it on and wondered what daring soul would. But there were people out there dying to run a bed-and-breakfast, who were saving their money and taking courses on just how it should be done. People who would see this house as a great opportunity, not the broken-down burden Liza saw.

She sat on the bed, giving a quick test to the bounce, then immediately pulled out her BlackBerry to check messages. There were several voice mails and half a dozen new e-mails. The e-mails were all from the office.

She checked the phone messages first. Her brother's voice came on the line. "Liza, it's me, Peter. I'm sorry, but I can't leave Tucson tomorrow. Something's come up. I'm going to be stuck here a few more days. Sorry, but I'll explain when we talk. Call me when you can."

Liza sat back on the bed. That wasn't what she wanted to hear. She needed Peter here to figure things out with her, but obviously, she would have to start without him.

The next message was from the real estate agent Liza had been speaking with, Fran Tulley at Bowman Realty. Her voice was cheerful, as usual. "Just checking in, Liza. I have you down for a meeting tomorrow at the inn at twelve. Call me if there's any change. I have some possible clients lined up who want to see the place. But let's talk first."

Another more familiar phone number came up, and Liza almost deleted the message without listening. Then at the last second, she couldn't resist.

"It's me, Liza," her ex-husband, Jeff, said. "I remembered that you were going out to the island tonight, and I hope you made it okay in the rain. I know it's got to be a rough trip for you. I hope you're not alone out there."

And what if I am? Will you run out and protect me from the creaky boards and worn-out wallpaper? From all the sweet and sad memories?

"Let me know if you need anything. I'll be around tonight. Well, all week actually. I don't have any plans. Just call my cell."

He didn't have any plans? What did that mean? Just like Jeff to toss out a tantalizing tidbit and leave her guessing.

Liza sighed. She wished she didn't care what Jeff was doing every night of the week or whom he was dating these days. But sometimes, she still did. He could be so sweet and thoughtful, and they had known each other so long. It was tempting to turn to him. Especially on a night like tonight.

But Liza forced herself not to cave in and call him back. She and Jeff were officially divorced. The last legal documents had been signed, sealed, and delivered. Funny how he was the one who had dragged it out when it was his infidelity that had broken up their marriage. An affair with one of his coworkers, a new hire in the law firm who had been assigned to his department and turned his head. How trite was that?

Liza wouldn't have known a thing if she hadn't come home unexpectedly early from a business trip—and found them together, about to enjoy a candlelit dinner that her husband had prepared.

He was quite a good cook; Liza had to hand him that. Good at cooking up excuses, too. But she had eyes in her head. She could see what was going on, though part of her still wanted to believe Jeff's spin on the cozy scene—that the relationship didn't mean anything to him and he still loved Liza.

The larger part of her felt hurt and betrayed. She had demanded a divorce, and Jeff had finally agreed, dragging his heels all the way. About two weeks ago, they had both received the final decree. But Jeff kept calling. She clicked off the phone before she let herself listen to his message a second time. She could feel his charm and tender concern wearing her down, making her confused, even at this late date. Here she was, once again, wondering if she had done the right thing after all by ending their marriage.

Liza washed up and put on her nightgown. Then she put a few of her things away, hanging up clothes in the empty closet. She found her notebook computer and a stack of client files and climbed into bed, making a mini-office of the space.

She was tired but wound up. Work was always the perfect distraction from too much emotion. She needed to tie up some loose ends and answer a few e-mails, especially the messages she had noticed from her boss and clients, before she went to sleep.

Angel Island might feel like a world away from Boston, but Liza knew she would be returning soon enough. She had to keep her eye on the ball and keep things running smoothly in her real life, even at this distance.

Chapter Two

LIZA woke to the sound of her BlackBerry, buzzing like an electronic insect trapped in a jar.

Groggily, she reached around the covers and nearly rolled over on her laptop before locating the device. She picked it up and squinted at the message. An e-mail from her assistant, Sara, marked "Urgent."

Was Sara in the office already? Liza checked the time.

Nine forty-five? She quickly sat up in bed. How had that happened? She barely slept past seven most mornings and rarely needed an alarm.

The room was pitch-black for one thing, the heavy shades and curtains blocking the light, except for a slim crack of sun that showed under the fringed edge. She had been in a deep sleep, tired from the drive in the rain, exhausted enough to sleep late, and already there was some emergency going on.

She quickly opened the e-mail, bracing herself. It was not good news. Liza's boss, Eve, wanted the sketches of the new logo that was part of a pitch for a new account. For some reason, which was not explained, Eve needed the sketches by one o'clock that afternoon.

The account hadn't signed on yet at the agency, and there was a call for all hands on deck to bring this one in. Liza was once again pitted against Charlie Reiger in a contest to see who had the best logo ideas.

Eve had originally said the sketches weren't due until next week, but it seemed she had changed her mind. Now Liza had to scramble. At least she had brought the sketches with her, though they weren't quite finished.

Knowing Charlie, he had probably given his ideas to the art department and already had four-color samples with complete, finished graphics ready to submit.

Liza jumped out of bed and pulled open the package of artwork she had brought along. She found the sketches easily, but her heart dropped when she looked them over. They were rougher than she remembered. She wondered if there was some sort of quickie graphics place or print shop she could find around here. Not on the island, of course, but back in Cape Light?

No, there wasn't time. It was nearly ten o'clock. She would never find a place, get the work done, and get the material faxed in by one o'clock. It simply wasn't possible.

She stared at the sketches again, then began to rummage through the art supplies she had packed. Quickly, Liza grabbed a pencil and some markers and added a few polishing touches. Hardly perfect, but better, she thought. They would have to do. She had to send them in and hope Eve would use a bit of imagination when she reviewed them. Well . . . more than a bit.

Liza hurriedly got dressed, placed the sketches in a large envelope, and ran downstairs. She wished now she had brought her printer along. She could have scanned the sketches and e-mailed them to the office in about two minutes. It had been dumb to forget the printer of all things. Now she had to find someplace where she could make a copy and send a fax.

She checked the kitchen, but it seemed that Claire had not arrived yet. The housekeeper probably wouldn't be able to help her anyway, Liza reasoned.

She grabbed her coat and purse and headed outside, having no real idea of where she was going. She got in her car and decided to try the General Store first. If they couldn't help her, then she would head into town.

The ride to the small village center was brief but scenic. The ocean stretched out on the left side of the road, and there were rolling meadows on the right. The inn had few neighbors, though there were some large old houses built around the turn of the century nearby—some, but not all, in better condition than the inn, Liza noticed.

There was also some farmland. There had always been a farm here on the island, but it seemed the ownership had changed hands since her last visit. What was once a nondescript farm was now an herb farm where she saw a flock of goats grazing. *"Gilroy Goat Farm,"* a sign read. *"Organic herbs, goat cheese, fudge, soaps & lavender."* There was a barn and several small outbuildings, one painted light purple, where she guessed the lavender was sold. Liza made a note to stop there when she had more time.

She drove on a bit farther, passing a few cottages and lots of open land, then finally came to the small commercial center of the island, the place where the two main roads met. There was an open area and space for cars to park around a small square with benches and a fountain. The fountain was not running at this time of year, but in the summer it was a nice place to sit, shaded by a large tree and edged with flowers.

Liza parked and ran inside. The store was wide and low, and she was immediately transported to the past by the very distinct scent of the place—a mix of wooden floorboards, fresh-brewed coffee, soap powders, produce, and who knew what else.

For a small space, the store held an amazing variety of stock, just about everything a person might need, from motor oil to mayonnaise, dog biscuits to diapers, tea bags to tent pegs.

She wondered if Walter and Marion Doyle still owned the place. Liza recalled seeing them at her aunt's memorial service, but that didn't mean they still lived out here and ran the store.

Liza glanced around and soon spotted Walter behind the deli counter, packing up an order for a big, burly man wearing high rubber fishing boots.

Marion was closer, stocking a shelf with boxes of throat lozenges. Liza walked over and caught her glance. "Hi. I'm looking for a fax machine. Do you have one here?"

"A fax machine?" Marion shook her head. "We don't have one of those. We have express mail delivery, though. Your package might get delivered by tomorrow, depending on the zip code."

Liza remembered now. The General Store on the island also served as the post office, with a section of PO boxes right past the deli counter. Marion Doyle had always been the postmistress, selling stamps and weighing packages. Now she had express mail to offer. But tomorrow was too late. An hour from now was too late.

"That's all right. I need to have some sketches at an office in Boston by one o'clock . . ." Liza glanced at her watch. It was already a few minutes past eleven.

Marion straightened up and frowned a moment. "Let me see . . . I think there is one around here. I just can't remember where . . ." She turned to her husband. "Walter? This lady is—"

"Doesn't Daisy have one? I don't think she uses it much," he added. "It might not even be hooked up."

"That's right." Marion nodded. "You can try her."

"Daisy?" Liza knew she was grasping at straws now. "Does she live somewhere on the island?"

Marion laughed. "Daisy Winkler runs the tea shop across the square. Just knock on the door. She's usually in there, even if the place isn't officially open . . . Hey, aren't you Liza Martin, Elizabeth Dunne's niece?"

"Yes, I am. I didn't think you'd recognize me

after all this time, so I didn't introduce myself," Liza explained, feeling a bit embarrassed at the lapse. She had easily recognized Marion and Walter, who had not changed very much since her childhood. Her explanation was partly true, but Liza had also wanted to avoid getting bogged down in small talk. Now she couldn't avoid it.

"It's good to see you, dear. I heard you were coming back for a visit," Marion confided. "Claire North mentioned it when she was in here shopping yesterday."

For the chowder ingredients, Liza realized. That figured.

"I almost didn't recognize you," Marion admitted. "You've changed so much since I saw you last."

Liza wasn't sure when that was. Or what to say. Was that a compliment or a comment on how little she'd been around to visit her aunt?

"It's been a while," Liza replied vaguely. "This place looks the same though, exactly the way I remember it."

Marion smiled widely. "Seems to work for us. If it ain't broke—"

"Don't break it," her husband finished with a laugh. Something about that was wrong, but Liza wasn't about to take the time to figure it out. "How long are you staying?" he asked.

"Are you going to open the inn this summer?" Marion added, before Liza could answer the first question.

They both looked at her expectantly. Liza was put on the spot. All she wanted was a fax machine. How had she gotten into this conversation?

"Actually, my brother and I are putting the place up for sale."

"Really?" Marion seemed shocked.

Walter wiped down the counter with a paper towel. "There'll be a lot of that going on pretty soon. Can't say I'm surprised."

With all the improvements on the north side of the island going on, he meant. But Liza didn't want to start in on that topic either. She had lost enough time and had to get back to the hunt.

"Well, guess I'll try Daisy. Thanks for your help," Liza said.

"I don't know that we helped you very much." Marion sounded genuinely concerned. It was very kind, considering that they were practically strangers.

"Good luck." Walter's expression made her heart sink.

Liza sighed out loud. Her head was pounding, maybe because she hadn't eaten a bite or even had a sip of coffee. Caffeine deprivation could be ugly. "May I have a pack of those pain tablets, please?" she asked, pointing to the brand she wanted.

"Sure thing. Here you go." Marion handed them across the counter.

"How much will that be?" Liza opened her purse.

"Oh, they're on the house. I hope you feel better. You're not having such a good day so far, are you?"

"No, I'm not," Liza admitted.

"Well, I hope it gets better. Just remember, don't sweat the small stuff—and it's all small stuff," Marion added in a jaunty tone.

Liza nodded but didn't reply. She really hated those cheery little inspirational slogans. People who said them either had to be in deep denial or were just plain lying.

She stepped outside and blinked at the strong sunlight. The day was chilly but fair. No sign of rain. That was a plus. At least the bridge would be open.

"Don't sweat the small stuff"? What was that supposed to mean? This wasn't small stuff. This was big stuff. Liza had worked so hard and come so far. She wasn't going to let herself be beaten out steps from the finish line. Not if she had to swim to the mainland with the sketches between her teeth.

Liza retrieved a water bottle from her car, downed her headache pills, and surveyed the tiny town center. Right next to the General Store, she spotted a storefront window covered by a red first aid symbol. The sign above read, *"Medical Aid— Walk-in Clinic. Emergency Services. Visiting Nurse."*

She wondered if they had a fax machine. Her

46

problem was definitely an emergency, though not of a medical nature. There was an automotive garage on the corner of the block with one lonely old-fashioned-looking gas pump in the small lot. That place had always been there, though if a vehicle needed serious repairs, it usually had to be towed to the mainland, Liza recalled. She doubted they had a fax.

On the opposite side of the street, she noticed another storefront office. This one had even more official-looking lettering on the window that read, *"State of Massachusetts Environmental Protection Agency."* And another sign below that read, *"Angel Island—Village Office."* Between the two bureaucratic offices, there must be a fax machine, she reasoned. But as she drew closer, she could tell both were closed.

She checked the hours listed near the door and saw that the state office was open only once a week, and the village office had limited morning hours three times a week. Though there was a number to call and a night court held once a month.

What in the world did people visit night court for out here?

Speeding tickets? Inappropriate trash dumping?

She passed another little shop that had colorful signs for homemade ice cream. Now that place was definitely new. If only it had existed when she was a kid. A hand-written sign on a sheet of notepaper was stuck to the inside of the glass door. *"See you in the spring!"* Liza wondered how the shop survived here, even in the summertime.

Finally, she ended up at Daisy Winkler's place, her last hope. The small cottage stood diagonally opposite to the General Store on the town square. Surrounded by a sagging picket fence, the building was two stories high but in dollhouse proportions. Painted pale yellow with a violet door and gingerbread trim on the roof, eaves, and porch, it looked like something out of a fairy tale, and she doubted that anything even remotely technological was going on within. But Marion had said there might be a fax machine here, and Liza had to ask.

Liza walked up to the cottage and opened the creaky wooden gate. She passed a painted sign that hung near the path. *"Winkler Tearoom & Lending Library—Books Are Our Best Friends."*

Liza remembered this cottage but didn't recall its present incarnation. When she was younger, it had been an antique shop, one that she was rarely allowed to visit with her aunt, in fear that she and Peter might break something. But the name Winkler definitely sounded familiar.

A brass bell with a pull chain hung near the door, and Liza rang it. The tinkling sound hardly seemed loud enough to alert anyone inside, but she soon heard steps approaching. A small face peered at her through the front window, then the

48

curtain quickly snapped back, making Liza wonder if she passed inspection.

The front door soon opened. A small, birdlike woman stood in the doorway, peering up at Liza through thick round glasses. Liza assumed it was none other than Daisy Winkler. Who else could it be?

She had wild, curly hair, a rusty reddish gray color. A bunch of curls gathered on her forehead, and the rest swirled in a haphazard upswept style around her head. She wore a golden-colored cro-cheted sweater over a dark burgundy skirt that nearly reached her ankles. Liza's gaze lingered on the skirt. Yes, it was velvet and possibly Victorian. A bit formal for a weekday morning, but this woman clearly had her own sense of style. She held a messy pad in one hand and a pencil in the other. There were also at least two more pencils stuck in her bird's nest of a hairdo.

The little woman smiled, looking pleased to see a visitor. "Can I help you? We're not open yet for tea, but you're welcome to browse in the library."

"I'm not here for the library . . . not this time," Liza amended, not wishing to offend her. "Marion Doyle at the General Store said you might have a fax machine I could use?"

Daisy looked suddenly and deeply concerned. Her smooth brow wrinkled. "A facsimile machine? Yes, I know what you mean. I do have one that I use occasionally. To send my poems to my editor," she added, catching Liza's eye. "But it's not working right now. Something is . . . funny. I have to get it fixed. Otherwise, I'd be happy to let you use it, Miss—?"

"Liza Martin. That's okay. I'll try to find one someplace else." Liza tried to keep the desperate note from her voice.

"I'm so sorry, Ms. Martin," Daisy Winkler said sincerely. "You might try the environmental office down the way. I think Mr. Hatcher has a fax machine."

"I took a look before coming here. The office is closed right now."

"What a pity. You'll need to go into town then, I suppose. There's a drugstore on Main Street in Cape Light. They might have a fax machine," she added.

Liza wasn't sure how reliable this tip was. Daisy looked a little . . . out there.

"Thank you. I'll check before I drive over," Liza said, backing away from the door.

Daisy started to follow her. "Good idea. Call and check. Please come back when you have a few minutes to spare and browse the bookshelves . . . Wait!"

She stared at Liza in alarm, and Liza stood stone still, wondering what the crisis could be. Daisy quickly riffled through her pad, tore off a sheet of paper, and stuffed it in Liza's front pocket.

"Here's a poem for you. I hope it helps."

A poem? How could a poem help? Liza decided the woman must be batty.

"Uh, thank you. Thanks for your help. Sorry, but I have to run."

"Any time. That's what neighbors are for," Daisy called after her, and waved from the doorway. "See you soon, Liza Martin."

Liza waved back but didn't answer. She quickly crossed the street, jumped in her car, and headed down the road the way she had come. She would drive into Cape Light and try her luck. The fax machine in the drugstore might be working. If not, someone there would surely know where she could go.

She passed the goat farm and rounded the next curve. The inn came into view, and she noticed a dark blue car parked in front. A woman stood on the porch. She had been peeking into the front parlor window, Liza noticed, but now took a cell phone from her bag and held it to her ear.

Fran Tulley! The real estate agent.

In the midst of her emergency, Liza had forgotten all about their appointment. That was not good . . .

Liza wasn't sure what to do. She had an impulse to hit the gas and speed past the inn, so she wouldn't have to waste time explaining her dilemma to some chatty real estate woman.

But she knew that was not very polite and a poor way to start off a business relationship. She

51

quickly slowed the car and then drove up to the inn. She heard her cell phone go off and realized who Fran was calling.

Liza got out of her SUV and trotted up to the porch.

"Ms. Tulley? I'm sorry to keep you waiting. I'm Liza Martin."

"Oh, there you are. I was just trying to call you," Fran said cheerfully. "Don't worry, I haven't been here long. I just wondered if there was some miscommunication."

"To tell you the truth, I'm in the middle of a work emergency. I'm not sure we can meet right now."

"What's the matter? Can I help you at all?"

Liza explained the situation and Fran nodded. "Don't worry, we have a fax and a scanner at my office. I can send the sketches for you."

"Would you?" Liza felt as if some superhero had just swooped out of the sky to save her. "That is so generous of you to help me like this—"

"No big deal." Fran patted Liza's arm. "It's different around here. We all sort of look out for one another. You'll do me a favor sometime, I'm sure."

Liza wasn't so sure about that. Unless Fran needed a big favor in the next two weeks.

"When did you say your office needs them?"

"By one o'clock," Liza answered quickly.

Fran checked her watch. "It's eleven thirty. Why don't we get started, and I'll make sure I leave for town in about an hour. That will give us plenty of time."

Liza wished she would go back to town immediately and send the sketches. But the plan made sense. And Fran had come all the way out here, expecting to look at the house.

"Fine. Where should we start?"

"Let's start out here, I guess," Fran replied. "I'm curious to see how the place has held up."

It had not held up that well, but Liza didn't want to sound negative. She smiled and followed Fran as she headed around the side of the inn.

Fran gazed up at the building, making the occasional note on a legal pad as she walked the property. It was cool and breezy outside, and the sun was shining. But the inn looked no better in the sunlight than it had last night in the rain, Liza thought. Maybe even worse.

"This was once such a beautiful place." Fran shook her head and tucked a strand of hair under her wool hat. "Such a shame for it to get run-down like this."

"Yes, it is," Liza agreed. "My aunt tried her best. But she was all alone at the end and in poor health."

"Oh, yes, I know. Elizabeth was a wonderful woman. I knew her from church," Fran added.

Everyone seemed to know one another around here. From church or . . . wherever. Liza wasn't surprised.

"Your aunt had a beautiful garden back here and one in front, too. She was famous for her roses," Fran recalled. She turned to Liza. "I don't suppose it was kept up? That could be a selling point."

"I'm not sure. I don't think so," Liza said honestly.

Unless Claire North had continued working on it. Liza would have to ask her about that. Claire had mentioned that they grew tomatoes last summer, but that didn't mean they still kept a big garden. Just a few plants could yield piles of tomatoes.

They went in through the back door and began to tour the rooms on the first floor. Fran didn't say much, though she made a few notes on the pad and used an electronic device to measure the rooms. She took photos of the kitchen and several of the large rooms downstairs, the front parlor and dining room.

Fran checked the condition of the pocket doors, which were solid oak. "Not bad," she told Liza. "They don't even stick much. And those plaster medallions on the ceiling are the real thing, not the plastic molds you can buy these days at the hardware store."

Liza hadn't known you could buy ceiling medallions at the hardware store. She hadn't even known what the ornate plaster carvings around the light fixtures were called until this morning.

They climbed to the upper floors, where Fran

took photos of a few bedrooms, those that were in the best condition and nicely decorated. She even took a few shots that showed the ocean views from different windows.

Liza found that encouraging. Some people didn't care what a place looked like, as long as they could see the water. You could see the ocean from nearly every room of the inn. That was one of the wonderful things about it.

They finished the tour and went out again through the front door. "I'm going to take this information back to the office and work up some figures," Fran said, pausing on the porch. "I want to have my broker, Betty Bowman, help with the asking price. She's very good at it. There's so little property out here for sale right now, it's hard to find anything comparable. But we definitely need to figure in the rising market value. We don't want to put it out there too low."

"No, of course not," Liza said quickly. "What about fixing the place up a bit? Will that help?"

"Some paint would help. You'd be surprised. Just the minimum to make it presentable. You can fix the shutters and those broken panes of glass—" She pointed out a window on the third floor that had been patched with cardboard. "You should clear out whatever you can inside. The less clutter, the better. Just try to stage the place with the nicest pieces of furniture."

Liza nodded. She'd heard that term before—

staging a property—and knew there were professionals who came in and did that for a seller. She would have to read up on the Internet and figure it out herself.

"I'm going to start cleaning up today," Liza promised. "How soon do you think you can begin showing it?"

"Not long. A day or so. It sounds as if you don't want to wait until the paint job is done."

"No, I don't," Liza said firmly. "I only have two weeks off from my job. I don't even want to stay here that long."

"We'll go as fast as we can," Fran promised. "If we don't get any offers, I'll keep showing it after you leave. Let's figure out the asking price and any conditions you and your brother might have about the sale."

"Conditions? What kind of conditions?"

Fran shrugged. "Oh, I don't know. Sometimes in this situation, people want to make sure the building will still be run as an inn . . ."

"We don't care. Someone might want to restore it to a private house. That's what it was originally."

"Yes, I know. And someone else might want to buy it just for the property. As a knockdown. Would you be comfortable with that scenario?"

A knockdown. Liza had never even considered that, but of course, it seemed so obvious. So definitely possible.

The wind off the water suddenly gusted up, and Fran grabbed on to her hat. Liza turned her back a moment, grateful for the chance to get her thoughts together.

"I'll have to talk that over with my brother," Liza said finally.

Peter's answer was easy to predict. He needed the money from the sale of the inn immediately. His divorce had made a big dent in his finances, and his business had hit a slump in the ailing economy. She doubted that sentimental feelings would win out over his checkbook.

"Yes, talk it over. I'm sure this is very stressful for you both, right on top of losing your aunt."

"Yes, it is," Liza admitted.

Not to mention the other dramas going on in her life right now: the tournament of champions at the office and her divorce.

"Well, I hope to guide you through the process as painlessly as possible. With all the action going on out here and all the articles in the newspaper, this island is becoming a hot spot. I just sold a little cottage on the north side, near the new beachfront. There were so many offers, we had to have an auction," Fran said proudly.

"Really?" That was encouraging. Would they need to have an auction for the inn? Liza wondered.

"If you have any questions at all, please feel free to call me, day or night." Fran handed Liza a business card and a thick packet of information about Bowman Realty. "I'll be speaking to you soon, once I come up with some numbers."

The two women said good-bye, and Fran headed for her car.

Just as Fran's car pulled out of the circular drive, Liza saw another car pull up and recognized Claire North behind the wheel. The battered dark green Jeep suited her. It was just the kind of car Liza expected her to drive. Sturdy and nondescript.

Claire parked and walked up to the inn, carrying a cloth tote filled with groceries. Liza stepped forward to greet her, feeling relieved that Claire had not been around to overhear the conversation with Fran. Especially the part about possibly knocking down the inn.

"That was Fran Tulley from Bowman Realty," Liza explained. "She's going to show the inn for us."

"Yes, I recognized her. We go to the same church, Reverend Ben's church," she explained. "Everyone knows her husband, Tucker. He's a police officer in Cape Light."

Liza should have guessed. It was such a small town. There were not even six degrees of separation among the residents around here, more like one—or even zero. She couldn't imagine living in a place like this, where everyone knew everyone else and their business. She wondered how her aunt had coped with it. Elizabeth, for all her innate hospitality, had always been such a private person.

"Have you heard from your brother? What time do you expect him?" Claire asked.

"Oh . . . he's not coming today. He's stuck in Tucson for some reason. I'm not sure when he'll get here. I haven't spoken to him yet."

"I see. I'll get his room ready, though. I have a feeling he won't be too much longer."

Claire sounded so definite. Liza wondered if she had some inside knowledge. Impossible, of course. The woman was simply eccentric.

Claire went inside, and Liza checked her watch. It was just past twelve. So just past nine in Tucson? She always got the time change wrong, but it seemed late enough to call her brother.

Liza walked up to the porch and sat on the steps, then pulled out her cell phone. The air was cool, but the sun felt strong. Spring was coming, even out here. In the daylight she could see that the lawn in front of the house was sprinkled with snowdrops, the first flowers of spring, and other promising bits of green seemed to be sprouting up as well.

Across the road in front of the inn, a stretch of vacant land sloped down to the beach. The land was unbuildable, her aunt had once told her, and their wide, wonderful view would never be blocked out by a new building there. Liza hoped it would stay that way, despite all the predicted development.

Well, she wouldn't be here to see what happened either way.

She took a deep breath of the cold, salty air and felt it seep into her lungs. She had heard that something about air at sea level was good for you, the positive ions or something. Or was it the negative ions?

Her BlackBerry buzzed, the vibration startling her. She snapped out of her reverie and checked the caller ID—Peter—Tucson. "Hey, I was just going to call you. What's going on?"

"Something's come up. Sort of a good news/bad news situation. Gail went away with her boyfriend, so I have some extra unscheduled time with Will. That's the good news," he added. "But it's the bad news, too. If I have Will here for the next two weeks, it means I'm stuck in Tucson."

Liza didn't answer. She didn't want to sound mad or upset, but did he really mean he wasn't going to come at all?

"Why don't you just bring Will with you?"

"Well, he's in school this week. Next week starts his spring break, and he's already got big plans. A camping trip with his buddies."

"I see," Liza said slowly. "Could he do that trip another time, and you can just bring him out here? There's the ocean and the beach, an entire island to explore. Wouldn't he like that just as well?"

60

"Who can tell what he likes? A mind reader, maybe. All I know is, everything I say is wrong or stupid. Or embarrassing."

"Ouch," Liza said sympathetically. "That must be rough. Still, I really think you should explain it to him, persuade him somehow. Tell him it's a family emergency and ask him to help you out."

"You don't get it, Liza. He barely takes off his headphones long enough for even a one-word conversation."

Liza felt bad for her brother. She knew how much he missed Will and worried about their relationship. Peter felt he hardly got to spend any time with the boy. But she felt even worse for her nephew. Watching your family split up had to be hard at any age, and adolescence was rough enough without having that monkey wrench thrown in.

"Well, he might want to come," she pointed out. "You never know. It might improve things between the two of you, taking a little trip together? Making him feel he's helping you solve a problem?"

"Or not," Peter said. Liza didn't answer. She heard him give a long sigh. She knew he was now stuck between that proverbial rock and a hard place, but she really needed him out here. Surly teenager and all.

"I don't mean to stick you with all the work, Liza. Honestly. It's just the way things played out this week. As usual, Gail didn't even give me any notice, just packed him up and dropped him off yesterday after school."

"I understand." She really did, too. "If I could rearrange things so we didn't have to deal with the inn this week, I would," she told him. "But I'm here now, because you said this was when you could be here. And the Realtor's about to start showing the inn, and there's a lot of cleaning up to do and—"

"All right," Peter said finally, "I'll persuade him somehow. Though this is definitely going to cost me."

Liza laughed. "We'll consider it a business cost and reimburse you after we sell the inn, okay?"

"I'm going to take you up on that," he said. "So what's been happening on that front? Any news?"

Liza quickly filled him in on the visit with Fran Tulley.

"She does think we should make some repairs. A coat of paint, fixing the broken shutters, and replacing some missing window panes."

"There are broken windows?" She heard a note of distress in her brother's voice as he realized the inn had fallen into disrepair.

"You haven't been here in a long time, Peter. Aunt Elizabeth just couldn't keep it up. I'm surprised she was able to keep it open and people still came here . . ."

"She had loyal customers," Peter said. "Everyone loved her. That's why they came."

That was true. There had been some very loyal guests who came every summer, as often as Liza and Peter did. Like old friends of the family, they came as much for her aunt and uncle as the ambience.

"Well . . . do whatever you think is necessary. We want a good price, and sometimes a coat of paint hides a lot. It can make a big difference in what a person might offer."

It would take more than a coat of paint to make a big difference here, Liza nearly answered. But she didn't want to make him too worried.

"Okay, we'll go for the paint," she said instead. "A quick job. I hope I can find somebody."

"I'm sure there are plenty of capable workmen out there. Just ask around. Ask that housekeeper, that Mrs. North," he suggested. "Did you tell her that we're going to sell the inn?"

"I told her last night. Right after I came in. I wanted to get it over with," she admitted.

"How did she take it? She must have guessed, right?"

"I really couldn't tell what she expected—or guessed," Liza said honestly. "She's very hard to read. Not exactly distant but . . . self-contained or something."

"Very Yankee," Peter filled in for her.

"Maybe." Liza knew what he meant but didn't

63

quite think that was it either. "She's been very kind to me. She said that she wanted to help us any way she could. That she promised Aunt Elizabeth she would. And that was even after I told her we were selling and she would be out of a job."

"That was nice of her," Peter answered quietly. "Someone else might have just quit and disappeared."

"I thought so, too. But she's not the type to act out that way. She's . . . different. I can't quite figure her out," Liza admitted.

She wanted to tell him how her dinner place had been set in her old spot, even though the table was as long as a bowling lane and Claire North had no way of knowing. And how Claire had chosen her favorite room. Not her old room but the one Liza had always coveted. But making something of those coincidences—for that's what they had to be—would have sounded silly.

"So how is everything else going?" her brother asked. "How did you manage to get away from the office for two whole weeks? Won't the building fall down?"

Liza ignored his jibe. He always teased her about being a workaholic. "I'll fill you in when you get here. Tell me when you book a flight, okay?"

"I will," he promised. "I hope you don't regret having Will around. It won't be pretty. You really can't imagine."

"I have some idea. I lived with *you* when you were fourteen, remember?"

Peter laughed, and they ended the call.

Liza's talk with her brother had put her in a good mood.

They had been very close growing up but had grown apart during college and even further when Peter moved out to Tucson right after he graduated. She was looking forward to spending time with him. Now that they were both divorced and had lost Aunt Elizabeth, their final link to their mutual past, it seemed to Liza they needed each other more than ever.

Peter was only two years older, but she still looked up to him. She admired the way he had stuck to his original youthful goals and become a photographer. While she had let hers fall by the wayside.

Growing up, Liza had always loved painting and drawing. She could entertain herself for hours with just a stick of charcoal and a drawing pad. Maybe she had inherited her artistic tendencies from her aunt—or maybe it was all the encouragement and instruction from Elizabeth that made her want to be an artist. Probably a little of both, she thought.

Summers at the island were like art camp, learning how to use watercolors or oils, to sketch, or to make sculptures from found objects or plaster casts in the sand. Even spinning clay pots and fiber weaving were not beyond Elizabeth's deft hands. Her aunt was not an artist who specialized; she saw creative potential in just about anything that came her way.

But her aunt had never relied on her artwork for a living. She had always had the inn, Liza reminded herself.

The sign for the inn blew in the breeze on its rusty hinges. The creaking sound shook Liza from her thoughts. She noticed again the carefully hand-painted lettering and the border of flowers and vines her aunt had painted so long ago.

Elizabeth had never given up on her talent, Liza thought. She simply practiced her art every day in everything she touched without seeking public approval or recognition. She'd had few showings of her work and had never made the big time. But she took great joy in expressing herself. She lived and breathed her talent—and seemed completely satisfied that way.

Liza could see now that her aunt had been a true artist through and through. No matter what the outside world might say.

Liza gave the ocean one last look, then rose from the steps and went into the house. She had a lot of work to do. Sitting around and thinking over the past wasn't going to get anything done.

She was in the foyer, hanging her jacket on the coat tree, when Claire came down the stairs.

"I just spoke to my brother. He won't be here for

a day or so," Liza reported. "He's going to call me when he's booked a flight."

"His room is ready," Claire said evenly.

"He's bringing my nephew, Will," Liza added. "So that will mean another room will have to be cleaned. Sorry," she added.

"No problem. How old is he?"

"Fourteen. He'll be starting high school next fall."

"Fourteen is a hard age," Claire remarked, her eyebrows raising a notch.

Claire sounded so knowledgeable, Liza suddenly wondered if she had any children. But that question seemed personal. Even though the housekeeper had been close to her aunt, Liza didn't see the point in encouraging a close relationship with her. It would only make things harder later when Claire actually had to go. Things were hard enough as it was.

"I want to start clearing things out," Liza said instead. "Fran thinks we should empty the rooms as much as possible." She glanced around at the parlor shelves, each one filled with books. "My aunt was a real saver."

"She liked to use things until they had worn out their usefulness," the older woman clarified. "She didn't buy something new if she didn't absolutely need it. She was a bit ahead of her time that way, wasn't she?"

"I suppose that's true," Liza admitted with a

smile. "I'm sure there are a lot of useful things around here that can be given to charity." And piles of stuff that can and should be tossed, she added silently.

"There are empty boxes in the basement. I'll go down and get some."

As Claire set off for the basement, Liza headed for the stairs. "I'm just going to run upstairs to change my clothes. Let's start in the front parlor."

Liza needed to change her cashmere sweater and wool slacks for a sweatshirt and jeans. She wondered now if she had brought enough old clothes for all these dirty jobs. Even her worst jeans or workout outfits from the gym were probably too new and "good" to wear cleaning out the attic or basement.

Well, she would figure it out. There were plenty of old clothes in this house to choose from, that was for sure. As she put on her comfortable clothes, she quickly checked the messages on her BlackBerry and saw a note from her assistant. The sketches had arrived just in the nick of time.

Great, Liza began to type back. *Make sure—*

"Drat!" The connection disappeared.

She retyped her message, then hit Send—and promptly lost service again. What was it about this island that made it impossible to send a complete sentence? The Internet and cell service out here were beyond spotty.

She tried to call her office instead and got an

"All circuits are busy" message from some robotic voice. She tossed the BlackBerry on her nightstand with a groan.

No choice but to face the closets. Claire was probably already in the front parlor, waiting for her. Liza truly dreaded tackling this job. Clearing this house out was going to be impossible. Like trying to dig your way out of an avalanche with a teaspoon, Liza thought as she headed downstairs.

THE closet in the front parlor was even worse than Liza had imagined. It turned out to be a black hole, a magic portal that couldn't possibly contain the amount of clothes, cartons, and miscellaneous items that seemed to be packed within. Once Liza and Claire began pulling things out, it seemed there was no end.

No end to the memories either—another hazard of the job, along with the endless dust.

Liza would have felt completely overwhelmed if not for Claire's quiet, calm way of sorting it all out. At times, the older woman seemed like the carved masthead on a ship, guiding Liza through the foggiest waters.

Whenever Liza would get off-track, lost in another memory, Claire would lift her chin and say, "Save, discard, or give away?"

Liza had started calling the query "the magic question," making them both laugh each time they had to remind each other to ask it.

"I don't know what's wrong with me. I'm usually so decisive," Liza despaired. "I'm not like this at all, especially not at the office."

"But this isn't your office. It's your past. It's your family history," Claire observed quietly. "Very different places."

Yes, they were. No argument there.

An unmarked carton emerged. Liza was the one who tugged it out. It was too heavy to be another box of mismatched mittens and moth-eaten hats. She opened the lid and found the carton was filled with photo albums and envelopes stuffed with snapshots. She didn't mean to detour and start looking at them, but once she started, she couldn't help it.

Claire had gone into the kitchen to make them tea. She came back with a tray and set it down on a side table near a wingback chair.

"Oh, wow . . . these are amazing," Liza said, leafing through an album of photographs that had once been black-and-white but were now yellowed with age. "Look at my aunt and uncle; look how young they were."

Claire walked over and glanced over Liza's shoulder. "Yes, they were a lovely couple."

Liza couldn't agree more. The photos showed them just about the age she was now. There were many pictures of them working on the inn, painting, or out in the garden. Pictures of her uncle in his woodshop or of the two of them relaxing at the beach, entertaining friends.

"They were a perfect pair," Liza said quietly. Her aunt always looked so pretty and full of life, and her uncle looked so handsome and strong. She glanced at Claire. "It was a pity they didn't have children. They would have made wonderful parents." She turned the page and looked away. "There was a child, you know. They lost her when she was about four."

"Yes, your aunt told me. That's when they came out here. Your aunt said it saved her life, coming to this place."

Liza glanced at Claire. "Yes, I think it did. She had her artwork, at least."

"And you and your brother," Claire added with a smile.

"For the summers, anyway," Liza agreed. Her aunt and uncle were like a second pair of parents. But it was funny, she had never really considered how important she and her brother were to them.

Some consolation for not having children of their own.

Liza turned the page, trying to turn away her more melancholy thoughts.

"Oh, my . . . who's that? The young Georgia O'Keeffe?" Claire pointed at a large photo in the middle of the page, then looked at Liza with a twinkle in her eye.

Of course they both recognized the little girl in a pink T-shirt and shorts, covered in paint. A child-sized easel stood nearby with a few small red and blue handprints on the otherwise blank sheet of paper.

"That was my random handprint stage. I was trying to express the deep yearning within modern society to reach out and connect with one another," Liza explained in a mock-intellectual tone.

"I can see that," Claire said, playing along. "A deep need for sticky fingers and stain remover as well, I'd say."

"Exactly," Liza nodded. "This place was like an art camp. Aunt Elizabeth always had us working on something messy and fun—pottery, painting, papier-mâché. That's why I wanted to be an artist, just like her."

"Is that what you studied in college?" Claire asked.

"My special area was painting. The Rhode Island School of Design . . . I tried my best after school, but I didn't get very far," she admitted. "Not far enough, anyway."

Liza had worked hard at her painting, never expecting easy success. For a time, she had believed that with persistence, dedication, and a thick skin, she would finally break through. She worked part-time in the art departments of advertising agencies to pay the bills and spent all her spare time in her tiny studio apartment, which was pretty much an artist's work space, with a stove, a fridge, and a bed shoved in one corner.

But time passed, and her successes were few. The rejections from galleries undermined her confidence more than she had ever expected. Meanwhile, her work at the ad agency was noticed and valued. She became the go-to graphic artist for the most challenging projects, where a creative flair and fine-art skills were needed.

Eventually, the part-time job that paid the rent and bought art supplies became full-time with benefits.

"Do you still paint?" Claire asked curiously.

Liza shook her head. "I don't even own a paintbrush or a canvas," she admitted.

"There's plenty of that stuff around here. You find it all over . . ." Claire tugged out a large roll of canvas from the closet as if to prove her point. "I mean, if you ever want to try your hand again."

Liza glanced at the canvas wistfully. It was true, there were enough supplies stashed around the house to open an art school. Maybe that's where she'd donate all of it, to a local school.

She glanced at the album again and felt her breath catch, her joking mood instantly evaporating.

Claire noticed her shift in mood. Her clear blue gaze searched Liza's face.

"Those are my parents," Liza explained, pointing down at the photo. "We were all at the beach, jumping the waves." Everyone looked so happy and excited—and wet. Her mother held

Liza's hand tight. Her father had one arm around her mother, and with the other he had hoisted her brother up above the water. Peter had been all skin and bones in those days.

"It's a beautiful photo. You ought to save that one in a special place," Claire suggested.

"Yes, I should," Liza agreed. "Elizabeth was my mom's sister. They looked so much alike, people thought they were twins."

"I can see that. You look a lot like your aunt and mother as well," Claire said.

Liza smiled briefly at her, taking the words as a compliment. She had inherited the dark brown hair, the gray eyes, and the same slim build, but she was a bit taller than Elizabeth—though not quite as tall as her mother had been.

She sighed and looked down at the photo again. "My parents died when I was in college. A car accident. They were just coming home from the supermarket one night. But it was winter, icy roads. They were hit by another car that skidded through an intersection . . ." Her voice trailed off.

Claire rested her hand on Liza's shoulder for a moment. "Yes, I know. Elizabeth told me. What a great loss for your family, you and your brother especially."

Liza nodded and softly closed the album. "At least we had Aunt Elizabeth and Uncle Clive."

Now they were gone, too. Nothing lasted, did it?

Certainly not happiness. You could grasp a moonbeam in your hand more easily, Liza thought.

She rubbed her hand across her eyes, and Claire handed her a tissue.

"I didn't realize this cleaning business was going to be so . . . heart wrenching. Pretty soon I'll be crying over the broken umbrellas and boxes of old magazines," she quipped through her tears. "My uncle had a thing for *Reader's Digest*, didn't he?"

"We'll both be crying if we have to lift another box of those. Come and sit down, have a cup of tea," Claire urged her.

Claire sat on the antique love seat covered with faded chintz fabric. Liza finally followed, taking the armchair. She was not the type of person who took a break while working. Once she started something, she went full steam until it was done. Tea time right in the middle of a task seemed positively . . . indulgent.

But this was not an ordinary job and not an ordinary day. She sat down with a deep sigh and stirred a bit of honey into her cup, then surveyed the row of boxes and black trash bags that had already accumulated.

"We won't get it done in a day, I guess," she finally admitted. "But we've made a dent."

"A good dent," Claire agreed. "Save, discard, give away. That's my motto."

"Mine, too." Liza nodded and smiled over the

edge of her teacup. There would be many more closets ahead and more weepy moments. But at least now she had a magic question to guide her through. Thanks to Claire North.

Chapter Three

THE next morning Liza silently repeated the question, though it did not always have its magic effect. She and Claire had finally emptied the closet in the front parlor, but that project was a mere warm-up compared to the next closet they tackled in the foyer, which was even larger and deeper.

Liza, perched on top of a ladder, wrestled with an antique hatbox and finally pulled it from one of the upper shelves. She knew that people collected these things, and it might be worth something. But it hardly seemed in collectible condition. She stared at it, feeling stumped, then glanced down, about to ask Claire her opinion.

But Claire was gone, along with several black bags of discards that had piled up in the hallway.

The brass door knocker rapped loudly on the front door.

Liza climbed down the ladder and headed over to answer it. It was probably Fran. They had spoken on the phone last night, and Fran was going to drop off some papers for her to sign, granting Bowman Realty the right to show the house to prospective buyers.

Liza pulled open the door, a friendly smile in place for her favorite real estate agent.

But it was not Fran Tulley on the other side of the door. Not by a long shot.

It was a stranger, a man about her age wearing a battered leather jacket and worn jeans. And an annoyingly amused expression as he looked her over.

"Can I help you?" Liza's tone was curt, trying to make up in attitude what she lacked in appearance. She had picked out some old, worn-out clothing last night from the bags marked for charity, and now looked like a pile of cleaning rags wearing sneakers.

"You must be Liza, Elizabeth's niece."

"Yes, I am . . . Are you here about a room? The inn isn't open for guests right now."

"Yes, I know." He seemed amused by her answer. "I'm Daniel Merritt. Claire called me. Something about a leak in the basement?"

"Oh . . . right. Come on in." Liza stepped back and pulled open the door.

Daniel Merritt was the handyman who usually worked on the inn, Liza remembered now. She had mentioned the leak to Claire last night, and the housekeeper had said she would call him. Liza had forgotten all about it.

And she'd also pictured the "regular handyman" around this place as someone much different.

Older for one thing. Balding. Paunchy.

Daniel Merritt was none of these.

Tall, dark, and . . . ironic was more like it.

Liza closed the door and turned. Daniel Merritt stared down at her curiously. She tucked a strand of hair behind her ear, as if that would help.

Skip it, Liza. Doesn't matter.

Uh . . . yeah. Right.

"Looks like you've been doing some cleaning up around here." He glanced into the big parlor. "Quite a project."

"No kidding. Know anyone who wants some sheet music from the 1950s? We have a nice collection from extremely corny Broadway musicals."

Daniel smiled. "I'll ask around."

"Thanks. You never know."

"That's true. Many people wouldn't own up too quickly to that passion."

She smiled back at him, surprised by the clever comeback. Okay, a handyman could have a sense of humor. Even out here.

"At least Claire is still here," he said. "I'm sure she's a big help."

A godsend, she nearly said aloud.

"No question," she agreed. "So . . . you came to check that leak? Do you need me to show you where it is?"

"Claire told me. I'll just go down and take a look."

"All right." Liza stepped back and watched as

78

he slipped off his jacket and hung it on the coat tree.

She didn't mean to keep looking at him. He had broad shoulders and a good build. It wasn't just the jacket. His black sweater was nearly the same shade as his thick dark hair; the collar of a denim shirt underneath peeked out from the neckline. Sort of stylish for a handyman, she thought.

He walked down the hallway and opened the door to the basement with an easy familiarity. He seemed very at home here. But her aunt must have called him frequently. The inn must have needed a lot of repairs. Still did, she reminded herself.

That was all going to be someone else's headache in a little while. It was one thing she wasn't going to inherit from her aunt. That was for sure.

Liza went to the big front parlor and started to work on a bookcase. She considered running upstairs to wash her face and fix her hair, which had more than half escaped from a ponytail, then rejected the idea. What did she care what Daniel Merritt thought of her? She wasn't here to win a beauty contest. She was here to work and get this house on the market.

She had loaded two boxes of books when Claire walked into the room. She looked like a real country woman today, Liza thought, wearing a long brown skirt, thick leather walking shoes, and a red down vest over a yellow sweater. Her long hair was pinned up in its usual style, parted in the middle and coiled in a big bun behind her head, emphasizing her round face and large gray blue eyes.

Liza thought Claire was a pretty woman for her age, which, if Liza had to guess, was probably late fifties. She had very smooth skin, almost wrinkle free, but otherwise seemed older. Perhaps it was her steady, quiet manner or the way she dressed. Her style was sort of a mix of hippie–Earth Mother and country bumpkin.

"I packed a load of bags in my car and brought them right out to the carting station," Claire reported as she walked in. Her round cheeks were red from the cold, and Liza felt guilty, knowing she had done all that work alone.

"You should have told me. I would have come to help you." Liza stood up and wiped some dust off her hands with an old cloth.

"It wasn't very heavy. Just bulky stuff. Besides, someone needed to be here for Daniel. I saw his car outside. Did he repair that leak downstairs?"

"He's taking a look at it right now."

"He'll fix it. He can fix just about anything."

"Does he paint?" Liza had meant to look for a painter today, but she'd gotten too busy.

"I believe so. Here he is. You can ask him yourself," Claire suggested.

"Hello, Claire," Daniel greeted the housekeeper with a wide, friendly smile. While he and Claire exchanged greetings, Liza took a moment to notice his impressive set of dimples.

Now, now, Liza. Handyman, remember? He's definitely not your type.

"So how's the leak? Can you fix it?" Liza asked abruptly.

"It wasn't much. It's already history."

"Oh, good. Thanks." He was efficient at least.

"Anything else you need me to check?"

Liza met his glance and looked away. His eyes were brown, a shade almost as dark as his hair, and were filled with a deep, serious light, even when he was smiling. It was an odd thing to notice about a stranger, but she instinctively felt it was true.

"I was wondering . . . do you do any house painting?"

"What did you have in mind?" He crossed his arms over his chest. She couldn't tell if he was interested in the work or not. He didn't act very eager like some contractors. He didn't act as if he needed work at all.

"My brother and I have inherited the house, and we plan on selling it. As soon as possible," she added. "The real estate agent suggested that we have the exterior painted—a quick job, just to freshen it up—and paint some of the rooms, too."

"A quick job on the outside of this place?" She could tell from his expression he was trying hard not to laugh at her.

"Why? How long will it take? I just mean a quick coat of paint. It doesn't have to be perfect."

"Don't worry. I'm sure you're in no danger of that."

Liza started to say something, then stopped. So he was the clever type on top of it. Did she really need that?

And he had never even told her if he did painting, she suddenly realized.

"If you don't take paint jobs or aren't interested in the work, just say so, Mr. Merritt. I just thought I'd ask you first, since you seem to do so much here."

"I never said I wasn't interested."

"You never said if you paint or not."

"I do paint. And I'm interested. And it's Daniel."

He smiled again, meeting her gaze. Liza intended to brush him off—the last thing she needed was a sarcastic painter—but she relented.

"Well, that's what we want. A quick coat of paint on the outside, just to freshen it up. The main rooms down here seem all right, but there are a few upstairs that need work. There's a big brown stain on the ceiling in one bathroom."

He nodded. "A leak last winter. Your aunt never got around to having the ceiling repaired."

"I have a list somewhere. But that's basically it."

He looked surprised. Then amused again. "That's it?"

She nodded, feeling off balance. "Why? Is something wrong?"

"That's a drop in the paint bucket, that's all."

"Well, that's all we intend to do. We just want to sell the property," she repeated.

"And leave the big headaches for the next owner," he finished for her.

She smiled at him. "Exactly."

So now he was questioning her ethics? For goodness' sake, it was done all the time. People didn't bring a place like this into tip-top condition before they sold it. It wasn't their responsibility. Buyer beware, everybody knew that.

"You know what this place really needs?" he told her. "A new roof and new windows. That will save money on heating and protect the whole building, especially with all the rain coming this spring."

Liza shook her head. "We wouldn't dream of doing anything that extensive." Expensive, she really meant. But he understood her. She could tell.

"Besides," she continued, "those kinds of repairs might be a waste. Somebody could buy this place and just . . . knock it down."

Daniel tilted his head. "That wouldn't bother you?"

She was taken aback by the question, by the way this conversation had suddenly turned personal. "I don't think it really matters if it bothers me or not. It could happen," she said, sidestepping the real answer.

"It would be a shame if it did, I think. This old building is a real landmark. It's one of only a few in this area built in the Queen Anne style. I'd hate to see it destroyed. But I guess there's going to be a lot of bad development around here now unless somebody steps up to stop it."

Liza sighed. "I don't want to see the inn knocked down. That's not what I'm saying at all. But this place needs so much work, it's amazing the building hasn't fallen down all on its own by now."

And how had she even gotten into this argument with him? She was just trying to find a housepainter, for goodness' sake.

"That much I agree with. Maybe the spring storms will do the job. Do you want to wait and see what happens? Or go through with the painting?"

"I'd like an estimate. If that's not too much trouble. By tomorrow?"

"I'll leave one off today," he promised.

"That would be great. Thanks." Her tone was flat and bland, though inside she felt anything but.

This guy was incredibly nervy. Maybe he was used to sounding off to clients since there were so few choices on the island? Or maybe he didn't care what people thought or whether anyone hired him back. Daniel Merritt was just proof that you had to be somewhat eccentric or a misfit to live out here in the first place.

A good-looking misfit, she amended.

She stomped back into the parlor and started on the books again. Claire was back at the foyer closet. Liza soon realized there were no more boxes. They had quickly used up all that they had in the house yesterday. Someone really needed to make a run to the General Store—or into town—and score some more. Liza stood up and rubbed the small of her back.

Claire, who was up on the ladder, glanced down at her. "Back stiffening up?"

"A bit," Liza admitted. Back in Boston, she worked out at a gym when she had the time, but clearing out closets and carrying boxes of books worked muscle groups that were just not included in the usual tighten-and-tone classes.

"Take a walk on the beach. That's the best thing for it."

Liza was surprised by Claire's suggestion. She would have expected something more in the line of a hot bath or even a heating pad.

"I'd like to, but there's still a lot to do here."

"It will all be here when you come back," Claire promised.

Yes, it would. This mess wasn't going anywhere.

"All right. Just for a few minutes. It did turn out to be a really nice day."

The morning had begun under a heavy veil of fog, as often happened on the island. But by noon the low layer of clouds had burned away and the sun had risen bright and high in a clear sky.

The foggy morning meant spring was almost here, Claire had told her. An odd sign, Liza thought, but it did make sense. The air had to be warm and humid to create a fog, so maybe spring was arriving.

Liza was already wearing a heavy fleece pullover. She grabbed a quilted vest and gloves before she went down to the water. She also wound a big woolen scarf—another find from the charity pile, a scarf her aunt had knitted ages ago—around her throat twice. Amazingly enough, Liza remembered the pale-yellow-and-cream-colored ribbon wool immediately when she saw it. It was a real treasure to her now.

She crossed the lane in front of the inn and headed down the narrow sandy path that led to the beach below. After all these years, she remembered the way easily. The path seemed so familiar, as if she had walked it yesterday.

The hill grew steep at one point, and Liza felt herself pulled down by the force of gravity, her feet moving beneath her faster than she wanted them to. She knew she had to just go with it or fall down. It was a freeing sensation to rush down the last few yards toward the ocean with the sound of crashing waves greeting her.

At the bottom of the hill, she slowed to a stop. She'd made it without tripping over a root or sliding on the sand. She stood still, giving herself a chance to catch her breath. She stared at the waves rolling in, tumbling one over the other, white-capped curls and foamy endings that rushed up the shoreline and were sucked back out again.

The waves were big today, making a loud crashing and booming sound. Liza had not been to the beach in a long time. She had forgotten how beautiful it was. This beach in particular. The sand was smooth and white.

The beach curved up around the cliffs, edged with huge reddish brown rocks, some covered with green moss and seaweed. Liza knew that if you examined those rocks closely, each one was like a little planet, supporting entire communities of tiny sea creatures that survived on the nourishment brought in with each wave or high tide. The same tides that left pockets of shells on the shoreline. Like a treasure chest casually emptied on the sand. The natural world was astounding, almost too much to get your mind around if you really sat and thought about it. Walking this beach had always made her feel humbled and distant from the rest of the world and all her worries.

It was working that same magic on her now. The cares that weighed so heavily on her shoulders seemed to melt along with the knots and aches in her arms and legs, and even those down in her back, as Claire had predicted.

The late-afternoon sun was sinking toward the horizon. The breeze off the water was colder than she would have liked, but Liza just tightened her scarf and kept walking. She had almost the entire beach to herself. Only one other hardy soul was in sight, some distance down the shoreline, a fisherman casting his line into the surf.

Liza drew closer to the fisherman, a man with a thick beard and wire-rimmed glasses. He was dressed in high rubber waders, a heavy sweater, and a down vest. She watched as he reeled in his line and checked the reel. He looked vaguely familiar, and she wondered where she knew him from.

He looked up at her suddenly and smiled. "Hello there. Beautiful afternoon, isn't it? If you don't mind the wind."

She smiled back. The sound of his voice triggered her memory. It was Reverend Ben Lewis from the old stone church on the green in Cape Light. He looked very different today in his fishing garb; she hadn't recognized him.

"I don't mind it, Reverend," Liza replied. "Though it must make your surf casting a challenge."

"Oh, I'm not very good at it," he admitted, "so it doesn't make too much difference to me. My family keeps giving me these expensive rod-and-reel sets. But the sport is a lot like cooking. It's not the equipment; it's the person using it, if you know what I mean."

He laughed, and she had to laugh with him. Then with a more serious expression, he said, "Aren't you Elizabeth Dunne's niece, Liza?"

She nodded. "That's me."

"I remember you from the memorial service. Are you visiting the island?"

"For a week or two. I'm meeting my brother, Peter, here. We're going to clear out the inn and put it up for sale."

"That's a big job. Serious business," the reverend replied.

"It is a big job. I mean, clearing out all my aunt's old belongings will be. I started yesterday, and I've hardly finished one closet. Claire North is helping me," Liza added, recalling that Claire was a member of the reverend's congregation.

"That's a big help to have. You're lucky." His blue eyes seemed to twinkle behind his glasses.

Everyone Liza met thought so well of Claire. Fran Tulley, Daniel Merritt, and now, Reverend Ben. Not to mention her aunt, who had loved Claire dearly.

"She's a very hard worker," Liza replied. "I know she did so much for my aunt. Especially . . . at the end."

When I should have been there, she nearly added.

"She and your aunt were very close," Ben agreed. "More like friends than anything else."

Liza suddenly had the urge to confide in Reverend Ben about her own relationship with her aunt, the way she had neglected Aunt Elizabeth and disappointed her when she had needed Liza most. But of course she couldn't say that. She hardly knew the man. "Did you see my aunt much last winter?" she asked instead.

"I came out and visited her once a week or so. I try to keep up with all the folks at our church who are shut-in for one reason or another. She didn't leave the inn much once she caught bronchitis. Then the pneumonia set in," he said in a somber tone. He looked up at Liza and caught her eye. "I will tell you that Elizabeth rarely seemed down or dispirited. She seemed to think it was just a passing thing, like a bad cold. Or at least that's what she kept telling me."

"That's how it was when we talked over the phone. That's what she told me, too," Liza replied. "Now I wonder if she knew more but didn't want me to worry."

"I don't think so. I don't think Elizabeth ever believed anything was seriously wrong. Or that she wouldn't be up and around by the spring, getting the inn ready for her guests again."

Liza took that in. Her aunt had never expected to die. *So don't beat yourself up if you didn't come out here to visit in time.*

Liza blinked. She felt her eyes tearing up and wondered if it was the wind or simply the conversation.

"Your aunt was a woman of great faith," Reverend Ben continued quietly. "She lived a full life and felt satisfied. I honestly don't think she feared death. I know that even at the very end she was resolved and at peace."

Liza swallowed hard to keep from crying. "Thank you for telling me that, Reverend," she said finally.

He gazed at her a moment but didn't reply. Then he turned his attention back to the fishing pole, which he had stuck in the sand for safekeeping.

"How long will you be staying at the inn?" he asked.

"About ten or twelve days more. Depending on how things go, I guess. Fran Tulley is our real estate agent. She seems to think she can find a buyer quickly. The island has become a hot spot, she says, with all the improvements going on."

"A hot spot, eh?" Reverend Ben smiled. "Well, maybe for around here it would qualify. But the inn is a beautiful old building. I imagine there are many fans of historic houses who would be interested."

"I hope so," Liza said simply. She yanked her gloves up a bit, so that they covered the cuffs of her pullover. The setting sun was almost touching the dark blue ocean, and the air had grown even colder. "I guess I'd better get back to the inn. Claire will be wondering what happened to me. It was nice seeing you, Reverend."

"Good to see you, Liza. Come by the church and say hello if you have time," he added. "If I can help you with anything during your visit, please let me know."

He was gently offering her a chance to talk more about her aunt and her loss, she thought.

"Thanks. Maybe I will." Liza smiled at him, then she turned and started back in the way she had come.

Reverend Ben was a nice man. She enjoyed talking with him, even though she had never been a big churchgoer. Her parents had not belonged to any particular church, only attending services on holidays like Easter or Christmas and choosing whichever church was most convenient. Her father liked the music and appreciated a good choir.

When she and Peter came out to Angel Island in the summertime, her aunt often took them to the church on the green in Cape Light. Liza vaguely remembered Reverend Ben holding the services there, though there may have been another minister before him. She couldn't recall now.

Either way, she had never gotten to know Reverend Ben. She only spoke to him briefly when she and Peter had planned the memorial service. He was intelligent and easy to talk to;

nothing like the impression she had of ministers —stuffy and even judgmental types. Even so, she doubted she would go out of her way to see him again, though it had been nice of him to offer.

WHEN Liza returned to the inn that afternoon, the house seemed flooded with a warm, buttery scent, an appetizing aroma she couldn't quite identify.

Liza tugged off her gloves, scarf, and vest, and walked back to the kitchen. Claire had the oven door open and was checking her work in progress, wearing a big blue oven mitt on one hand.

For some reason, Liza's conversation with Reverend Ben had made her feel more appreciative of Claire's presence. Claire didn't have to stay on here and help dismantle the house, Liza realized, even though she was being paid for her work. The entire process had to be hard for her. *Maybe even harder than it is for me.*

"What are you baking?" Liza asked. "It smells delicious."

"Chicken pot pie. Do you like that?"

Liza smiled. "I haven't had it since I was a little girl. But I did like it then. It was one of my favorites."

Her very favorite. Aunt Elizabeth would make it for her, even in the summer when such a hearty dish seemed out of season. She always used lots of vegetables from the garden; it was almost a vegetable pie, Liza thought.

Liza knew Claire was a good cook but doubted anyone could match her aunt's perfection of this dish. Her aunt seemed to use some secret ingredients to make it taste so good.

"I was cleaning out a bookcase and found your aunt's recipe book. One of her many recipe books," Claire corrected herself. "I think they're all over the house." She pulled off the mitt and set it on the counter. "The pot pie recipe fell out, so I decided to try it."

Claire nodded toward a piece of lined yellowed paper that lay on the kitchen counter. Liza recognized her aunt's handwriting immediately, a hurried, artistic scrawl. Thoughts always racing ahead of her pen; that was Aunt Elizabeth.

Liza looked the recipe over; there were a few smudges and food stains blurring the words. A tiny note in the margin read: *Extra carrots for L.*

That's about me. I used to ask for extra carrots, Liza realized, feeling touched.

Liza looked up. Claire had been watching her. Reading her thoughts, Liza guessed, from the expression on the housekeeper's face. Liza suddenly felt self-conscious. Too close.

"Do you need any help?" she asked.

"I think we're all set. Dinner is ready, whenever you are."

Liza suddenly realized that with everything going on around the inn—put dealing with Daniel Merritt on the top of that list—she had gotten so distracted, she hadn't checked messages from the office since that morning. She hadn't even brought her BlackBerry along to the beach. She must have a hundred messages by now.

"Let me just run up to my room a minute. I'll be right down," she promised Claire.

She found the BlackBerry on the small table near her bed and checked her e-mail. She scrolled down the addresses and subject lines quickly, guessing what most messages contained.

She was looking for one in particular, some word about the logo sketches that were sent via Fran Tulley's fax to the office yesterday.

Liza had her fingers crossed that her ideas would be chosen over Charlie Reiger's. If the prospective client, a national chain of discount shoe stores, preferred her take over Charlie's, it would tip the scales in her favor in regard to who was named account manager—and who was promoted to vice president.

If only she'd had a chance to send the ideas in as a more finished presentation. But that couldn't be helped. Sometimes the best ideas just won out, even scrawled on a paper napkin.

There was one message from her boss, and Liza quickly opened it. It was a question about some other project. No mention of the logos.

That worried her a little, but Liza tamped down her anxiety. If she didn't hear by tomorrow, she would send Eve a note and ask directly. Better to know than wait in limbo.

Liza opened another e-mail, this one from Peter.

Liza—

I've worked out time off from school for Will, so we're trying to get a flight out tomorrow. See you soon.

Love,
Peter

Well, there was some good news. Liza shut down the device and put it in her pocket. Peter and Will were on their way. She would definitely see them by tomorrow night.

That was a relief. For a while there, she had wondered if he was going to make it at all. She felt sorry now for doubting him. Peter could be scattered at times, but he wasn't going to let her down. They would get through this mess together.

Liza washed her face and hands, and went down to dinner. She had read somewhere that certain scents affected your mood. Mint wakes you up, and cinnamon makes you feel more alert. Chicken pot pie must qualify, she thought. The mouthwatering smell was already making her feel more cheerful.

In the kitchen the table was set for two, with the

chicken pie sitting in between. There was also a green salad.

Claire was at the sink, washing out some pans. She turned when Liza entered the room. "Everything's ready. Just take a seat. I put beets in the salad. They're also from the garden. I hope you like that."

"Sounds great," Liza said.

She sat down at her place, hoping she hadn't kept Claire waiting too long. She had lost track of time, fussing over her e-mails and office dramas. Claire was an employee, but for some reason, it didn't feel right treating her that way. Sometimes Liza couldn't help feeling that she was merely a guest in Claire's territory.

Claire sat down and then closed her eyes and bent her head for a moment. She was saying grace, Liza guessed. She waited until Claire was finished before she began eating her salad, which was a mixture of greens with icy cold thin slices of red beets on top and a sprinkling of goat's milk cheese.

"Delicious salad," Liza said between bites. "Is this cheese from the farm down the road?"

Claire nodded. "They started the business only a few years ago, but they're getting quite a reputation. They sell to a lot of stores and restaurants in the city."

"I want to pick up some lavender there to take home with me." Liza pictured her apartment, which could have been on another planet she felt so distant from it at the moment. Had she only been here two days?

"Lavender is wonderful stuff," Claire agreed. "Your aunt always had me spray the bed linens with lavender-scented water—for the guests and for herself, too. The scent helps you relax."

"I have been sleeping well here," Liza admitted. "Maybe that's it."

"The sea air helps. And all the hard work," Claire added. "How is your back?" she asked with concern.

"Much better, thanks. Walking was a good idea." Liza took another bite of the pot pie. The flaky crust just about melted in her mouth. "I met Reverend Lewis on the beach. He was surf casting."

"Oh yes, that's his hobby. He comes out here a lot with his rod and reel, though I've never seen him catch anything," Claire added with a smile.

"He told me he wasn't very good at it."

"There's more to surf casting than catching a fish for Reverend Ben," Claire said. "I think he needs the time alone with just his own thoughts and the ocean. It refreshes his spirit, you know?

"Daniel stopped by while you were down on the beach," Claire went on. "He left an envelope for you. I put it on the mail table."

"That's probably the estimate for the painting," Liza said. "Thanks. I'll take a look after dinner."

Liza was far more interested in talking about Daniel than about Reverend Ben's surf casting. She had a lot of questions about that man. But she didn't want to be too obvious.

"I guess I'd like to hire Daniel if his price is reasonable," she said carefully. "But I don't know much about him. Do you think he does good work?"

"Excellent work. He's very responsible and professional. He's more of a carpenter. But I'm sure he'll do a good job painting for you," Claire added.

"He seems to do a little of everything," Liza remarked, thinking of how he fixed the leaky pipe.

"You don't find too many specialists out here. A person needs to be flexible to earn a living, just to get by day-to-day."

Liza knew her aunt and uncle had been very self-sufficient, doing many jobs at the inn themselves when they were young and strong enough—painting, renovating rooms, ripping up rugs, and refinishing floors. At the time she thought they were just trying to save money. That may have been true, but it was also probably easier to do it themselves than to find someone to come out to the island.

"You have to be pretty self-reliant to live out here," Liza agreed. "It's not for the faint of heart, especially in the winter."

"The winters are hard. There's less work. And it

can be hard on the soul, all the solitude and quiet. For some people, I mean."

From her tone, Liza didn't think Claire counted herself among those who were disturbed by the solitude. She seemed so self-sufficient and had such equanimity. But Liza still wondered if she lived all alone. Wasn't there somebody in her life?

Was there someone in Daniel's life? That question seemed even more interesting to her right now.

"I imagine it's hard to support a family out here, even if both partners work." Liza paused. "What does Daniel's wife do?"

Claire looked up, her expression one of surprise. "Daniel isn't married. He doesn't have a wife."

Liza smothered a smile. "Really? I thought he mentioned something about a wife."

Okay, it was a bald-faced fib, but she couldn't help it. It had slipped out as she tried to cover her tracks.

"You must have misunderstood him."

"Yes, I must have," Liza agreed. She sensed that Claire knew she had fibbed but was too polite to call her on it.

So, the handsome jack-of-all-trades was single. But that didn't mean he was without a relationship. A man who looked like that *had to* be in a relationship. On this small island, he would have his pick of single women, Liza was sure. Or perhaps he liked playing the field and was the commitment-phobic type . . .

Liza caught herself, surprised by the direction of her thoughts. In the many months that she and Jeff had been separated and then finally divorced, she hadn't thought much at all about dating. No one had really caught her eye, though she had met a few single men through work and well-meaning friends who had dragged her out to restaurants and parties.

Liza knew she wasn't ready to take that step yet. She still felt attached to Jeff in a way. Not really married anymore—but not entirely separated either. That was more his doing than hers. It seemed he just couldn't let go, even though he was the one who ruined it for them.

"Care for some more chicken pie?" Claire's question broke into her rambling thoughts.

"No, thanks. It was perfect, though," Liza said, "just like Aunt Elizabeth's."

Claire seemed pleased by the compliment. "I'm sure it wasn't nearly as good. But thank you for saying that. There's some dessert if you'd like. A chocolate pudding pie. It's in the fridge."

Another one of her aunt's specialties. A graham cracker crust filled with rich chocolate pudding and covered with whipped cream. Easy to make, deadly to eat.

Liza sighed. "I'm going to put on twenty pounds if I don't watch out."

Claire glanced at her and laughed. "Even if you did, it would hardly show at all."

Not in the baggy sweats or jeans she had pulled from the charity bag to wear around the inn. But getting back into her sleek business suits and spandex gym clothes would be a challenge.

"I think I'll pass on dessert for now," she said finally. "Peter and Will will be here tomorrow. I'm sure that pie won't go to waste."

Liza helped Claire clear the table and clean up. There wasn't much to do. Claire was the type of cook who cleaned as she went and didn't leave a huge mess at the end. Unlike Liza, who couldn't manage to scramble an egg without using every pot and utensil she owned. Cooking had never been her forte.

Claire closed the dishwasher and turned it on. "Looks like we're all done. Thanks for the help."

"No problem. Thanks for dinner."

Claire nodded. "Do you need anything more?"

"I don't think so." Liza watched as Claire gathered her things, slipping on her down parka and taking a canvas tote from a hook behind the kitchen door.

"I'll be off then. See you tomorrow. I'm looking forward to meeting your brother and your nephew," she added.

"They're looking forward to coming here. Well, my brother is. I'm not so sure about Will."

Claire stood at the back door. "He'll be fine.

This place will do him good." She nodded to herself, then went out the door.

Liza hoped the prediction was true. Claire had a way of sounding so certain of things. Liza wondered where it came from, that sense of knowing, of certainty. She felt in awe of it—and suspicious of it.

Nobody could feel that grounded and sure of things, not with the way the world was these days. Her aunt, too, had had a touch of that inner certainty. Not as much as Claire, but more and more as she had grown older.

Where did this certainty come from? Liza only wished she knew. If she could bottle it, she'd make a million.

Chapter Four

L IZA woke to the sound of rain pounding against the building. The spring storms on the island could be fierce, but this one sounded like a hurricane.

She jumped out of bed and ran to the window—then realized she heard not only water but men and machinery. Outside the building, on the front lawn just below, she saw Daniel Merritt and a helper, both wearing big gloves and goggles. They were working with some sort of water equipment, with a hose and a pointed nozzle aimed at the house.

Power washing, she realized. The preparation for the painting had begun. Daniel certainly didn't waste time. She had called him back last night about the estimate. The price seemed reasonable and the timing fast enough. He had said he would start with power washing to strip off the old paint. But she had not understood that meant he would start before eight a.m., and it would sound and feel as if the house were under attack.

Liza took a fast shower and pulled on her jeans and a black turtleneck, a somewhat more attractive outfit than he had seen her in yesterday but not nice enough to look as if she had gone to any special trouble. She hoped.

Just to make sure, she pulled her hair back in a tight ponytail and left her face bare of makeup.

It was too early to call the office. No one important showed up before nine. She looked around for her BlackBerry. It was on the nightstand next to a seashell she had found in her pocket last night, one she had picked up during her walk on the beach.

Now she took a moment to look at the shell, turning it over in her hand. The spiral structure was so smooth and unified, so perfect. She could understand why certain artists, like Georgia O'Keeffe for instance, had been fascinated by spirals and other organic shapes found in nature.

A few moments later, she laid the shell down and picked up the BlackBerry, then slipped it into her back pocket.

There was a hot pot of coffee waiting in the kitchen. Liza saw Claire's parka and tote bag on a chair, but Claire wasn't in sight. Liza poured herself a full mug and sat at the table, where a copy of the local paper, *The Cape Light Messenger*, lay open.

She scanned the headlines. There was a photo of the island's mayor breaking ground for the new park on the island. "Mayor Joe Gilroy breaks ground for Lighthouse Park on Angel Island. Mayor Emily Warwick of Cape Light and Mayor Noah Simms of Newburyport stand by. The park will be built adjacent to Lighthouse Beach and recreation area, with direct ferry service from the town dock in Newburyport. Plans include a sports center with tennis and basketball courts, luxury locker rooms, and a café."

Luxury locker rooms? That sounded pretty high-end for this island. Changes were definitely coming.

A sharp rap on the window of the kitchen door roused her.

Liza got up, expecting to see Claire, and found herself looking at Daniel Merritt. At some point while she had been reading the paper the machinery sound had stopped, she realized.

She opened the door, wondering why her heart had started racing. Too much black coffee on an empty stomach, she told herself. But when Daniel greeted her with a wide smile, she knew that coffee was not the problem.

"So, you got an early start," she said as he walked in.

"Yep. We're about halfway done. Sorry for the noise."

"That's okay. I didn't want to hear myself think today anyway."

He smiled at her joke. "I know what you mean. Whenever I get in one of those moods, I just turn the thing on and give myself a splitting headache. That keeps me from thinking too much."

"That would do it," she agreed, wondering what sort of concerns he had weighing on his mind. "Would you like some coffee?" She gestured toward the pot and mugs on the countertop.

"Sure, thanks." He stepped over and poured a cup, then added milk and sugar—the complete opposite of the way she drank it. *I could live with that,* Liza decided with a secret grin. *Nobody's perfect.*

"Have a muffin," she said, pushing the dish toward him. "Claire made them this morning."

"In that case, I definitely will." He took a muffin on a napkin, then took a bite. "Banana. One of her best."

"She made oatmeal raisin yesterday. They were pretty amazing, too."

They sat for a moment without talking. Daniel noticed the newspaper. "Keeping up with current events?"

"Trying to," Liza said between bites. "There's a

lot of good news in here, especially compared to what you see in the Boston papers every day."

Daniel turned the paper to read the front-page story. "Oh, I don't know. I wouldn't call building an Olympic stadium on this island good news."

"You mean the sports center?" Liza asked just to clarify. He was getting a bit carried away, wasn't he?

"That's right. Whatever they want to call it, it's a huge waste of money. The county could put the funds to much better use. Or build it someplace else, where more people will have access. It will be underutilized out here."

Liza was not surprised by his reaction. He had already made his feeling about the development of the island clear.

"What about all the new visitors who are coming over on that ferry this summer? Won't they use it?"

Daniel shrugged. "People always came to this island because it didn't have places like that." He glanced at the article again. "Luxury locker rooms?"

She laughed at his expression. "I noticed that, too. It does sound a bit much."

"If you want luxury locker rooms, go to a country club or a fancy spa or something. Don't come out here. That's not the point of this place. Or it shouldn't be."

"I see your point," she said quietly. When Fran

Tulley first told her about the island's planned development, Liza thought it was a good thing, a lucky break that would make the inn more marketable. But now that she was back and had gotten to know the island again, with sand in her shoes and salt breezes tangling her hair, she wasn't so sure. She could see Daniel's side of it, too. Some things—some places—were meant to stay wild and rough. They didn't need to be "improved."

But who would stop it? The plan had already been set into motion. She gave herself a mental shake. She would be leaving in a little over a week. No sense getting all caught up in a battle she couldn't fight.

"So, when will you start painting?" she asked, changing the subject.

"The clapboard needs to dry out for about two days. And we have to do some prep work—scrape a bit more and fill in some cracks. You said you didn't want a perfect job, so we're not going to go crazy on that phase."

"That's right, just the minimum will be fine."

"One coat of primer, one coat of paint. It's all in the contract . . ." He reached into his back pocket and pulled out an envelope. "That's why I came in here in the first place. You made me lose track."

He smiled at her, and she knew that he hadn't meant it in a bad way.

Liza pulled open the envelope. The letterhead at the top of the page read "Merritt General

Contracting" in large bold letters. Very official sounding, considering it was just him and a helper.

She scanned the contract. Everything they had discussed over the phone seemed to be written down, and the price was the same as well. But she did need a few minutes to read it over carefully. Without him staring at her. That was definitely distracting.

"Do you need this back right away? I'd like to take a minute later and read it carefully."

"Sure, take your time. No rush." He sat back in his seat. "How is the clearing-out process going? Is Claire letting you throw anything away?"

Liza smiled at him. "We have a magic question. It helps a lot."

"A magic question. That sounds interesting. I could use one of those." He smiled curiously, looking extremely charming. "Can you disclose this magic question—or will that ruin the magic?"

Liza laughed. She knew she was flirting with him, pretty obviously now, but she couldn't help it.

"I don't think it will ruin the magic. I mean, I hope not. It's really pretty simple. Whenever we get stuck trying to decide what to do with something, one person asks the other, 'Save, discard, or give away?'"

"And the other person has to answer?"

Liza nodded. "That's right. It's sort of a game, I guess. It certainly makes the work go faster."

"That's a good thing, then. But I'd bet that Claire mostly answers 'save,'" he replied with a grin. "I do know she likes to hang on to things until they're just about falling apart in your hands. You should have seen the broom she handed me one day to sweep up some sawdust." He leaned closer, aware that the housekeeper might be around. Liza leaned closer, too, suddenly very conscious of his nearness. "It hardly had two straws left in it. I was standing there, sweeping the thin air."

She could picture it. Especially from what she'd seen yesterday. She laughed at the story, and he did, too.

"What are you two laughing about—something in the newspaper?" Claire came into the kitchen, and they quickly sat back and exchanged a look.

"It's Mayor Warwick," Daniel answered, quickly covering their tracks. "She's always running around, getting herself in the newspaper. Her daughter doesn't even work for the *Messenger* anymore, and she's still on the front page every day."

"She does a lot of good for the town of Cape Light," Claire replied, defending the mayor. "People will vote for her again if she runs next fall."

"For the tenth time, you mean?" Daniel teased her. "There are no term limits in Cape Light," he explained to Liza. "Emily Warwick will run until . . . well, until she's running in a walker, I guess."

"Oh, Daniel. That doesn't make any sense," Claire said, shaking her head. Liza, though, glanced at him and smiled.

"Well, back to work." He rose and took a long last sip from his mug. "Thanks for the coffee."

Liza also took a last sip, secretly appraising his appearance as he walked to the door. Today he wore a blue sweater under a dark red down vest, his long, lean legs covered in worn jeans. For a guy out power washing, he looked good. Very good.

And he was clever and charming. But he had to be in a relationship, she reminded herself. And she was just divorced and not ready to date anyone, especially some guy living on a remote island. So what was the point of even thinking about him?

"Do you want to continue working on the closets down here today?" Claire's question broke into Liza's thoughts.

"I guess so. There's so much more to sort out. We might as well stay focused."

"Little by little, we'll get through it," Claire promised. "Your aunt was a big saver, but she knew how to store her treasures in heaven, too— 'where moth and rust do not destroy.' "

Liza nodded. The bit of scripture was vaguely familiar—and surprisingly comforting. Claire was right. Her aunt and uncle were not really material-istic people. They had always lived with strong faith and spiritual values. While Liza struggled to sort out the collection of possessions that chronicled their earthly lives, she had to remember that they both lived on in spirit, in some better place.

Looking at it from that angle, the rest of the closets didn't seem nearly as overwhelming.

"All right, let's get to it then," Liza said. Then she remembered that she hadn't checked in with her office yet. She had gotten distracted talking to Daniel. Now it was nearly ten, and no one had heard from her. That wasn't going to look good.

"I just have to check messages from my office first," she said to Claire.

She pulled out the BlackBerry, dismayed to see she hadn't even turned it on. What was happening to her? Three days in this place and she was losing her edge! She pressed the Power button, relieved to see there was Internet service this morning.

Liza was hardly aware of the housekeeper leaving the room as she quickly scrolled down her new e-mails. A message from her boss immediately caught her eye. Subject: Shoe Paradise Logos.

Liza clicked it open, feeling an anxious knot in the pit of her stomach. But the e-mail wouldn't open. The screen froze. The Internet connection was gone.

"Again!" she muttered. "Does this thing *ever* work out here?" She hit the Phone button and speed-dialed the office, Eve's direct line.

Why did I ever come out here in the first place?

It was just not the right time. I should have just let this place fall down . . .

The phone rang five times before Eve finally picked up. Liza greeted her with what she hoped was a cheery tone.

"Hi, Liza," Eve said smoothly. "How's it going?"

"Just fine. The house is already on the market. The real estate agent thinks we can sell it very quickly. I might be back even sooner than I thought," she added, knowing that wasn't entirely true.

"Sounds like you got a lot done out there," Eve commended her. "I'm not surprised. You're always so efficient."

"Not always, but thanks." Liza hesitated, knowing she had to ask about the logo. "So you got the sketches the other day? You should have seen me trying to find a fax machine." Liza turned her frantic search into an amusing anecdote. "The new technology has definitely not caught on out here. My real estate agent finally took pity on me and sent the package from her office."

"You poor thing. What an ordeal." Eve laughed and Liza felt a sliver of optimism. Maybe this wasn't going to be bad news after all?

Liza took a breath. "So, what did you think?"

"About the logos? They were fine. A little rough, but I could see where you were going."

"Sorry about that. I didn't have time to find a graphics place to do a mock-up."

"Of course not," Eve cut in. "You could hardly find a fax machine. Don't worry about it. We were all able to visualize."

We? Who did that include exactly, Liza wondered?

Liza guessed there had been a meeting about the logos—a big meeting probably—and wondered if Charlie Reiger had been included. Had the client been there, too?

"So you had a meeting about it?" Liza tried for a casual tone but heard an anxious note slip in.

Why didn't they let her know? She could have been included by telephone. That wasn't any big deal.

"It was sort of impromptu," Eve explained. "Shoe Paradise wanted to see what we would do before they signed on. You know how it is."

"How did it go? Did they like any of my ideas?"

"They did like one or two. I liked them, too," Eve said. "But some other approaches seemed more in tune with the market they want to pull in. One concept in particular caught their eye, and we've sold them on a campaign built around it."

An entire campaign from one sketchy little logo? It must have been brilliant, Liza thought. And not her brilliance either.

"Well, that's great. That's terrific," she said, trying her best to sound like a team player.

"We're all very pleased. We lost a few big clients this year, and nobody's spending like they used to," Eve reminded her. "Charlie is going to

114

work with the shoe people," she added smoothly. "His ideas brought them over, and he had good rapport with their CEO."

Good rapport? Liza nearly dropped her phone. Charlie's "rapport" usually consisted of discussing the Red Sox's pitching staff. And she could have bet money that his ideas were borrowed from her. The little twerp was forever searching her old ad campaigns for his "new concepts." She had taught Charlie Reiger everything he knew. Of course, it was easy for him to win the account while she was out of town. That was like saying you set a record for swimming, but Michael Phelps wasn't in the pool.

"Liza, are you still there?" Eve asked.

"I'm here. Sorry. I got distracted a moment. So much going on." The power-washing machine roared right near the window, blowing water against the building at gale force. "Sounds like it all turned out for the best," Liza said, letting her boss off the hook. "I'm sure Charlie will do a good job."

"I'm sure he will. And you certainly don't need the headaches of a new account right now," Eve added.

Perhaps she meant it kindly, out of concern. But Liza heard another message: You're distracted and overwhelmed, letting your personal life interfere with your work and not doing a first-rate job around here anymore.

"You just do what you have to do out there," Eve continued. "Don't worry about us. This is a vacation break, too, right?"

"Not really," Liza corrected her. "I'm basically working long distance for a few days. That's all. I'm totally available to the office."

"All right. I'll remember that. You take care. See you soon."

They said good-bye, and Liza ended the call. Her heart sank.

Charlie had won this round. Was he angling to force her out entirely? The economy was awful, and Eve had said that the company had taken a hit. Liza had never thought her job was in jeopardy, but maybe she had been wrong.

Or maybe it hadn't been in jeopardy until she came out here.

She was fair game now, unable to defend herself. Who knew what would happen by the time she got back?

Eve had not mentioned the promotion, Liza noticed. Earlier, Eve had promised her that no decision would be made before she returned, and Liza trusted her. But she still worried. She had left a few days ago concerned about a promotion. Now she was wondering if she was losing her job.

Liza sighed and heaved herself up from the kitchen table. She walked to the sink and turned on the tap, hoping a cool glass of water would calm her down.

Back to battling the closets. At least that was a front she might win. There might even be some upside to all this anger if she could channel it productively. Maybe the closet question could calm her?

"Save, discard, give away," she chanted under her breath. "Save . . . discard . . . strangle Charlie Reiger . . ."

"What did you say?"

Liza spun around to find Daniel standing in the kitchen doorway, staring at her. "Save, discard . . . strangle somebody?"

She laughed self-consciously. "I was just . . . upset about . . . something. A phone call from my office," she confessed.

"That's the problem right there." He pointed to the BlackBerry still in her hand. "Don't you know those things are bad for your health? They definitely raise your blood pressure—and put you in a bad mood."

"Well, it did today," she admitted.

"A problem at work?"

"You might say that. A problematic person," she clarified, not knowing how much she wanted to confide.

"There usually is at least one of those in any office," he said sympathetically. "What do you do for a living, Liza? I don't think you mentioned it."

"I'm in advertising. An account executive."

His eyebrows rose a notch. "Nice. Very impressive."

She couldn't tell if he was teasing her or not. He didn't seem the type of guy who was impressed by fancy titles or big salaries. Was she trying to impress him? She wasn't sure.

How had he even snuck up on her like that? She heard the machine still running outside. But obviously, his helper was handling it alone right now. Daniel must have walked in the front door without her noticing.

"Do you need something?" Liza stared up at him, trying to act more businesslike.

"I just came in to tell you that a window on the third floor is open. Someone needs to go up and close it."

"All right. I'll take care of it," she said, hoping he would take the hint and leave her be. She just wanted to have a good sulk. Now she was getting all distracted by him again.

He looked about to say something to her, something more serious. The BlackBerry buzzed. Liza tried to check the number but Daniel was faster, snatching it out of her hand.

"Why don't you just shut this thing off for a while? You'll feel a lot better, honestly."

Liza tried to grab it from him. But he held it just out of her reach. Then he laughed at her. "I know it will be hard at first, but you can do it. I know you can."

She stared at him in disbelief. "Would you please give that back to me? It might be important—"

"I doubt it. Probably just another annoying person."

Liza couldn't argue with that. He was almost certainly right. But it was also annoying to be teased like this. "Fine," she said, pretending to give up. She started to walk away, then quickly whirled around and reached for the phone.

But he was quicker. "Whoa . . . nice move. You nearly got me."

"This is so . . . silly. And childish. Just give it back to me, Daniel."

He laughed at her again, and this time she started laughing, too, despite her efforts to look stern. This game was maddening! So why was she enjoying it?

The BlackBerry buzzed again and she pounced, grabbing his wrist so that she could finally see who was calling.

"It's Peter! Give it, give it . . . I have to speak to him. Right now!"

Daniel finally heeded her excited tone, and his hold on the phone went slack. Liza snatched it back.

"Who's Peter? Your boss?" He seemed genuinely interested in knowing—or was that just her imagination?

Liza quickly hit the Call Back button. "Peter's my older brother."

"I'll give you some privacy, then. I'll just run upstairs and close that window if you don't mind."

"Thanks. I don't mind at all." Liza met his dark glance a moment, then watched him leave the kitchen.

Daniel was likely right. These instant-communication devices were probably bad for your health and your mood. Luckily, there was a handsome home repairman around to put it all in perspective. The perfect antidote.

Peter's phone rang several times. Liza hoped she hadn't missed him. Finally, she heard him pick up and say hello.

"Hey, what's up?" Liza greeted him.

Please don't tell me you're not coming. I'll just scream.

"We're at Logan. We caught a flight late last night with a connection in Atlanta and just got in. We're waiting for the baggage to come down—"

"You're at Logan? That's terrific!" Liza nearly hopped up and down, she was so relieved.

"The car rental is set. We should be there in about two hours."

"Can't wait to see you. Drive carefully, okay? . . . You remember the way?"

"Couldn't forget it. See you soon." Her brother sounded tired but eager to get out to the island.

Liza felt something deep inside her relax. Thank goodness he was on the way. There were still so many questions to be resolved, so many memories to be untangled. If she really had to say good-bye to the inn, at least she wouldn't have to do it alone.

Chapter Five

ENERGIZED by the news of Peter's arrival, Liza whipped through the rest of the foyer closet, then moved on to the dining room.

Claire covered the long dining-room table with a soft old blanket, and they began sorting out china, piles of dinner plates, soup bowls, teacups, and saucers—placing them in three categories: save, discard, and give away. Liza had just finished one shelf of many when she heard a car pull up the gravel drive.

"I think they're here," she said to Claire.

Liza set down a flower-rimmed bowl and ran to a window that faced the drive. A small red hatchback pulled up next to her own car. Her brother, Peter, sat in the driver's seat, and an absolutely huge teenage boy sat beside him.

Was that her nephew, Will? She couldn't believe it.

She watched as they got out of the car and Peter opened the trunk. Will got out of his side and walked to the back of the car. He was as tall as his father now, maybe even taller; it was hard to tell with his thick pile of dark hair.

"Look at Will. He's so big, I didn't even recognize him," Liza said aloud. "I'll go out and see if they need any help."

Claire met her gaze and nodded with a gentle

smile. "Let me know if you need a hand," she said simply, then continued working on the china.

Liza ran out the front door and around to the drive. The cold air cut through the fine wool of her turtleneck, but she hardly missed a coat.

"Hey, you made it." She ran up to her brother and greeted him with a big hug.

Peter hugged her back. "All the way from Tucson to Angel Island. It feels like we've landed on another planet," he said.

Liza hadn't thought about that before, but her brother had been living out in the desert since he started college, almost twenty years now. It must feel strange to come back to this place surrounded by water.

She was eager to say hello to Will, but he stood with his back to her, gazing out at the ocean.

"Has Will ever seen the ocean before?" she asked Peter.

"Once or twice. We took some trips to California. But not since he was much younger."

Liza walked over to Will and touched his shoulder. "Hi, Will. It's good to see you."

"Hey, Aunt Liza." Will glanced at her, then looked back at the water. He had plugs in his ears, which led down to an iPod in his T-shirt pocket.

Liza wondered if he could even hear her but continued the conversation anyway. "You've gotten so tall. I hardly recognized you," she said with amazement.

He turned again and met her glance. "Everybody says that. Like I'm a giant freak or something."

"I didn't mean it that way," she said quickly. "You just look all grown-up, that's all."

"Yeah. I know." He sighed and looked over at his father. "Dad, I'm really hungry. Can we get something to eat?"

"Can you help with these bags, Will?" Peter ignored his son's question, his voice flat and tired. Liza didn't blame him. It was a long trip, and it sounded as if they had been traveling all night. Will rolled his eyes and walked back to the car.

Liza followed. "I can help," she offered. She grabbed a duffel out of the trunk right after Will did and gave her nephew a smile. Finally, he smiled back.

Peter took the last duffel and slung a backpack over his shoulder, then shut the trunk. Liza noticed his care with the pack and guessed he had camera equipment in there. Peter rarely traveled without a camera or three.

As they marched into the inn, Claire stood in the foyer near the staircase, her hands folded primly in front of her. She might have been a statue, Liza thought, except for the warm sparkle in her blue eyes.

"Welcome, Peter and . . . Will. Is that right?"

Peter put his bags down and extended a hand.

"You must be Claire North. It's nice to meet you. Liza's told me a lot about you."

A lot? She hadn't said a lot. Just a few significant details, Liza thought.

"It's good to meet you, Peter." Claire's voice was warm and sincere. She turned to greet Will, but he was fiddling with his iPod and seemed to be purposely ignoring the housekeeper.

"Why don't we just leave the bags down here for now?" Liza suggested. "Are you guys hungry? We'll make you some sandwiches or something—"

"I'll take a sandwich," Will cut in quickly.

"Please." his father suggested.

Will just stared at him, then shook his head and stomped toward the kitchen.

Peter rolled his eyes. "I've embarrassed him now. Gail says he's too old to be corrected in front of other people, but he doesn't have any manners."

Liza didn't have any kids and wasn't about to take sides, but she could see how Will wouldn't want to be corrected in front of her and Claire.

"Children that age will get embarrassed about anything," Claire put in. "Even the way you breathe annoys them."

Peter turned to Claire, looking validated. "He did say that to me once; I'm not kidding." Then he suddenly looked alarmed. "I'd better catch up to him," he said, "before he cleans out the refrigerator."

Liza and Claire followed Peter to the kitchen, where they found Will standing at the counter, polishing off the remains of the chicken pot pie.

"Will, what are you doing? We're guests here." Peter's voice was low and tense. He stepped over to Will and took the pie dish from his hand.

Will looked surprised, a bit of carrot hanging from his lip. "Dad, just chill. I'm just getting something to eat. You're, like, flipping out on me."

"It's all right," Liza said quickly. "We're family. He can help himself to anything he likes."

"I'm, like, starving here, and you're standing out there talking. I thought you said you owned half of this place," Will added in an accusing tone. "Doesn't that include the food?"

"It certainly does," Claire told Will. "But you really want to eat this warmed up. It has no flavor otherwise."

She stepped forward, took the pie dish, placed a piece of paper towel on top, and stuck it in the microwave. "Just wash your hands and take a seat over there." She pointed to the long table. "I'll bring this over to you when it's ready."

Will scowled at her, but her expression remained smooth and calm. "There's chocolate pudding pie for dessert. Interested?"

Will finally nodded. "Okay, I guess," he said, as if she had been working hard to persuade him.

He walked over to the sink and washed up. Peter

watched, then glanced at Liza. Liza didn't say anything, relieved that the conflict had been so easily smoothed over. By Claire, of course.

If this is a preview of the next ten days, I'd better fasten my seat belt, Liza thought.

It was going to be a bumpy ride.

WHILE Will was fed—and calmly tolerated—by Claire in the kitchen, Peter and Liza took some coffee out to the front porch. Liza had unwrapped a few chairs from their plastic coverings and set them near the front door. Peter settled down in one of the big Adirondack chairs, but Liza stood at the railing a moment and looked out at the patch of blue ocean and sky.

It felt good to get some fresh air after being in the house all day, dealing with dusty china—and her own chipped and cracked ambitions.

"You okay?" he asked her.

"Mostly," she answered, not wanting to go into her problems. "How about you?"

Peter zipped up his fleece pullover and stretched out his legs. The wooden Adirondack chair suited him. "Could be worse, I suppose."

She turned to face him. "What does that mean?"

Peter gave her a wry grin. "I'm telling myself it's not the end of the world. I mean, I'm healthy and Will is—well, a teenage boy. It's just that business has been awful lately, Liza. I know everyone is hurting these days, but I'm really limping along. Any cash reserves I had tucked away were eaten up by the divorce. I'm more or less winging it," he admitted. "I really do need the money from this house. I hope that real estate lady was telling the truth."

Liza had known her brother was eager to receive his share of the profits from the sale of the inn, but she hadn't realized money was so tight for him right now. And he had a kid to worry about, too.

"I don't think Fran Tulley was exaggerating," she said carefully. "People around here are pretty excited about the changes on the island. Though there's definitely a faction who don't want the changes," she added, thinking of Daniel.

Peter shrugged. "There will always be people like that, but they usually don't win."

"No, they don't," Liza agreed. Though she secretly thought that in some cases it would be better if the naysayers did win out and progress wasn't so inevitable.

"How soon can she bring buyers around?"

"Fran's coming by in a little while with a contract for us to sign," Liza told him, "an agreement with her agency for the right to sell the property. We can ask her then."

"Okay, I will. Good work setting all this up, Liza," he added. "I know I haven't been any help so far."

No, you haven't, Liza nearly answered. *And I definitely have more important things going on than dealing with this old place.*

But she didn't want to snipe at him. The delay in his arrival hadn't been his fault. Now that he was here, she knew he would pull his share of the weight. Maybe even Will would help.

"So, was it hard to get Will to come? How did you persuade him to give up the camping trip?"

Peter gave her an embarrassed look. "I had to bribe him."

"You bribed him? How?"

Peter shrugged. "He wants a new phone. An iPhone or something like that. It does everything but floss your teeth. I told him I'd get it for him, but he had to chip in part of the money," Peter hurried to add. "I know it's wrong to pay him off like that with material gifts, but I didn't know what else to do . . . You think I'm an awful father now, don't you?"

Liza shook her head. "Of course not. I think you're just caught in a tough situation. I'm not judging you, Peter. I don't have any children. What do I know?"

He didn't answer, just gazed out at the ocean beyond the open land across the road. "It's been difficult since the divorce. I hardly ever get to see him anymore. One night a week and alternate weekends. It's not enough time. He just starts letting down his guard and warming up to me, and it's time to go. We used to have a good relationship. Now everything I do is wrong. Or stupid. Or embarrassing."

"Isn't that pretty much expected for kids his age? Teenage angst and all that?"

Peter turned to her. "It's more than that. The problem is . . . well, it's really Gail," he said, finally mentioning his ex-wife. "She's brainwashed Will against me. I don't know who he thinks I am anymore. I've gone back to court for shared custody," he added. "I want Will to live with me half of the time so we won't have this threadbare, fractured relationship. He's going into high school next fall. Four short years and he'll be on his own. This is my last chance to be a real father to him, you know?"

"What are your chances to win shared custody?" Liza asked.

"Pretty good," he said hopefully. "Fathers have more rights in court these days. But Will has a lot of say in the situation now. He isn't a baby. So far . . . well, he just shrugs when I ask how he feels about living with me half of the time. Either he hasn't made up his mind, or he's afraid to give me the bad news."

Liza reached out and touched his arm. "When will the court decide?"

"There's a hearing in a few weeks, but I'm not even sure I'm going to keep pushing for it. Will seems so distant from me. I'm surprised he agreed to come here," he added in a quieter tone. "Even with the new phone thrown into the deal."

"Maybe that's a good sign."

Peter shrugged again. "Well, he did seem excited about the beach."

"And you'll be able to spend time with him here without Gail interfering," Liza pointed out.

"True. I guess I have to look at it more positively." Peter glanced at her. "Who knows? Maybe it will turn out to be a good thing that I had to drag him out here."

"I hope so," she said sincerely. "Besides, I'm looking forward to getting to know him again, too."

Peter got to his feet and gazed out at the surf breaking along the shore. "I haven't seen an ocean in ages. What a sight." He walked over to the porch rail. "I want to take some pictures of this place. The whole island, I mean, not just the inn. I wanted to show Will some photos before we left, and I couldn't find any. I guess I wasn't really into photography until we were older and I'd stopped coming out here so much."

"I think so," Liza agreed. "There's no lack of photos in that house, though. I feel as if I'm a curator in a photo archive. I've been going through boxes and boxes of them. It's sort of sad," she added, "seeing Aunt Elizabeth and Uncle Clive the way they looked when they just moved out here, younger than we are now."

"I guess they were. Though when we were kids, we thought they were old," he added with a laugh. "We had a lot of great times out here with them. They were so much fun to be around. Much more fun than Mom and Dad," he added.

"We had a lot more freedom out here. But they were strict, too," she reminded him. "Uncle Clive made you work with him in the garden, mow the lawns, and take care of the animals every day. Remember? They didn't just let us laze around."

"And listen to our iPods," he added. "Or whatever distractions we had back then. I do remember. But for some reason, we loved it. I would love to show Will Clive's old workshop. Is the shed still there?"

"Barely. One good wind will knock it over," Liza predicted. "I bet Uncle Clive's tools are all still there on his bench."

"Maybe I'll take a few back to Tucson with me as a remembrance," he added.

"I was thinking of taking some things, too. Some furniture. Aunt Elizabeth still had the piano," Liza added.

"I'm not surprised," Peter said quietly. "Would you really spend the money to move it to Boston? It's probably not worth the bother. And you don't even play."

"I know . . . but I think I'll take it anyway."

The piano was in bad shape. A few keys needed repair, and it had never really kept in tune in the damp, salty air. But Liza couldn't imagine leaving it here. That would be deserting an old friend.

"Well, we could have some sort of big tag sale," Peter suggested.

A tag sale? The thought of organizing all the odds and ends they didn't want into a tag sale was daunting. "I'm not sure there's enough worth selling to bother," Liza said.

"Of course, there's enough stuff. Are you kidding? There are some real antiques in there, quality furniture. And people will buy anything, Liza. You have no idea. Besides, there are companies who do all the work for you. They just take a percentage of the sale."

Liza thought it would still take time and care, even if a company was called in. Time that she desperately didn't have right now. If it were up to her, she would find a worthy cause with a pick-up service that would come haul everything away. But Liza didn't feel like arguing the fine points with Peter right now. He had practically just gotten here.

"I'll ask Fran Tulley about it. She would know," Liza said evenly.

She leaned on the porch rail and pushed her long hair to one side. Her ponytail had come undone sometime during the workday, and she hadn't bothered to find another hair tie.

Out in the driveway, Daniel was packing up his truck. He slammed the tailgate closed and waved to her. She waved back.

"Who's that?" Peter asked.

"The handyman, Daniel Merritt. He's going to paint the house. He just started today with the power washing."

Daniel turned the truck in the driveway, then drove past them on the way out. He slowed for a minute and met her gaze but didn't wave again.

"I'll introduce you tomorrow." Liza checked her watch. "It's not that late. We can do a little more work around here before dinner. Unless you're too tired from the flight."

"I'm all right. That's what I'm here for. Lead the way. I'd like to see the photos," Peter added. "You didn't throw them out, did you?"

"Of course not." Liza had been tempted to toss some of them. There were pictures of people she didn't recognize, relatives of Uncle Clive's, perhaps, or friends and neighbors. But Claire had encouraged her to save all the photos.

"I've got an idea." Liza slapped her brother on the shoulder. "I'm putting you in charge of the photo archives. You're certainly qualified for the job. Claire thinks the historical society in Cape Light might be interested in some of the older shots. We could get our names on a little plaque."

"I'd love my name on a little plaque," Peter replied. "A person has to have goals."

"Definitely," she agreed with a laugh.

It was good to have her brother here. She had, she realized, just plain missed him. With everyone gone now, their parents and Elizabeth and Clive, Peter was all the family she had left, him and Will. She hoped this visit would bring them all closer. That's what Aunt Elizabeth would have wanted. Liza knew that in her heart.

FIFTEEN minutes later, as Liza was showing Peter the boxes of photos, she heard a car on the road. She peered out the front window and recognized Fran Tulley's blue Camry. "It's the real estate agent," she said to Peter. She glanced at her watch. "Right on time."

Fran came to the door, and Liza introduced everyone, then led the way into the house.

"Someone's been busy around here," Fran said, as she gazed around the front parlor. "The room looks twice the size already."

"It will look even better when we move some of the furniture out," Peter said.

"Absolutely," Fran agreed. "You can store it in that shed or sell it. There's an antique store in Cape Light called the Bramble. Maybe they would buy it from you."

Fran took a glossy folder that read *"Bowman Realty"* on it from her bag. "Here's the contract," she continued, "a copy for each of you. I worked with our broker, Betty Bowman, on the asking price. Certainly, the final number is up to you. We've checked recent sales on the island and added in the bump in value due to the coming improve-

134

ments. We also considered the condition of the place and the fact that you want a quick sale."

"Of course," Liza said. Peter just studied the copy of the contract that Fran handed him. Liza's eyes went straight to the listing price on the bottom of the front page.

Fran waited a moment, giving them a chance to consider it.

"That's the asking price. I expect you would actually sell at about ten thousand under."

Liza scanned the contract. Of course, they also had to deduct the brokerage fee, but the bottom line would be a very decent profit, even split two ways. Liza hadn't realized the inn was worth so much, especially in its run-down condition.

Her brother, however, didn't seem as pleased. "I honestly expected it to be higher."

Fran didn't seem taken aback. She probably dealt with this reaction all the time, Liza realized.

"We do think it's market value. Certainly within range," she explained. "We could push it up another ten thousand or so, but I wouldn't go any higher than that if you want to sell quickly."

Peter didn't seem entirely happy with that reply, but he said, "All right. Let's try it. If anyone wants to make an offer, please let them know there's very little room for negotiation."

Fran nodded. "That sounds reasonable. I'll make that change on the contract, and we can all initial it."

The document wasn't long or complicated. Liza and Peter were able to read it through and sign on the spot.

"So, when will you start showing it?" Peter asked. "Do you have any clients who might be interested?"

"I do. I've already let them know that something in their price range was coming up," Fran replied with a small, tantalizing smile. "As soon as I get back to the office, I'll start lining up appointments."

"We're having it painted. Like you suggested. But we just had the power washing done today, and I guess it looks even worse with all the paint blown off," Liza said.

Fran stood up and grabbed her jacket from a nearby chair. "Don't worry, people can deal with that. Though the building will make a stronger impression once the painting is done," she added, glancing at her watch. "I've got to run. Nice meeting you, Peter. I'll call tomorrow and let you know if I'm bringing anyone over."

"So, what do you think?" Liza asked her brother once Fran was gone.

"She seems all right—competent, experienced. I'm not so sure about that price. Didn't you think it would be higher?"

"Honestly? No," Liza replied. "I mean, look at this place. We don't want to sit here, waiting forever for a buyer," she reminded him. "It's better to put it out a little lower than market value if you ask me. Who knows, we might even have some sort of auction if a lot of people get interested at once."

"There's an idea." He started toward the staircase. "We can suggest that to Fran tomorrow."

While Peter went up to his room to unpack, Liza returned to the dining room, where Claire continued to work in her quiet, steady way. She was wiping out the now-empty china cabinet with a soft cloth and lemon-scented furniture oil.

Over the past two days Liza had noticed that when Claire worked at any task, no matter how small or menial, she seemed calm and unhurried yet totally focused—giving it her entire attention, as if it were the most important job in the world. It was like watching the ocean waves wash in and out, Liza thought. Like watching a steady, reliable force of nature.

Liza went back to examining the pieces of china and placing them on different sections of the table. She would never have that sort of calm, unhurried air, she decided. You had to be born like that.

Will had gone upstairs right after his late lunch. He said he wanted to take a nap, Claire reported.

Or just be alone, away from the adults, Liza suspected.

When dinnertime rolled around, Peter was the first to come downstairs to the kitchen. "Will isn't hungry. Maybe he's still full from his late lunch."

137

"He did seem to enjoy his food," Claire said. "I'll save him a plate. He might be hungry later."

Liza didn't doubt it. Teenage boys were notorious for their appetites. But she also knew Will could have come downstairs just to say hello or get a glass of water. Maybe he was planning on hibernating, plugged into his iPod, for the entire trip?

"He likes to stay up late at night now and sleep late in the morning," Peter explained. "It's just his biological clock. If you hear someone roaming around later, don't be alarmed. The house isn't haunted."

"I like to stay up late myself," Liza said. "And I'm not afraid of ghosts either."

Her own late hours were not due to her biological clock but because she worried a lot lately. Though since coming to the inn, she had slept surprisingly well. All the physical work and ocean air, she suspected. Maybe it would be the same for Will.

Claire served the meal, a roast chicken dusted with herbs, string beans, and mashed potatoes. Liza suddenly noticed that there were only three places set on the table, just enough for herself, Peter, and Will.

She looked up just as Claire took off her apron and hung it on a hook behind the door, then reached for her tote bag and jacket that were hanging there. "I hope you enjoy your dinner.

Dessert's in the refrigerator when you're ready. I'll be going now. I need to leave for home a little early this evening."

"Sure," Liza said. "No problem."

"See you tomorrow, Claire. And thanks for all your help today with Will," Peter added.

"Don't mention it. Enjoy your evening. I'm sure you two have a lot of catching up to do." Then she said good night and headed out the back door.

Liza wondered what was calling Claire home early tonight. Again, she wondered where Claire actually lived. Liza had asked her while they were working on the closets the other day. Claire had been vague, saying only, "On the other side of the island."

Liza hadn't prodded further, and Claire had not volunteered any additional information. Was there someone waiting there for Claire tonight? Liza knew from her aunt that Claire wasn't married, but that didn't mean she was alone. Or maybe the housekeeper had simply been staying later than she usually did in order to keep Liza company?

"So what do you think of Claire North?" she asked her brother between bites of the perfectly roasted chicken.

"Well, I can see what you mean about her being sort of a cipher. She is very . . . unobtrusive."

"That's one way of putting it," Liza agreed.

"She doesn't bother me. I like her—what I've seen so far."

"I like her, too. More than I thought at first," Liza admitted. "She's been a great help. Not just with the work, but she's so calm and steady. So positive. She never seems stressed or over- whelmed. It calms me down, too."

"That's good. Then . . . what's the problem?"

Liza smiled and shrugged. "I don't know. There isn't one, really. She's just different than other people. She has this way of almost knowing what you're thinking or about to say. Sometimes it seems as if she's actually reading my mind."

Peter laughed and helped himself to another scoop of mashed potatoes. He had always been lean as a kid and could still eat whatever he wanted, she noticed. It was totally annoying.

"Reading your mind, huh? I know you've been under a lot of pressure lately, Liza, but maybe we should find someone for you to talk to about this."

He was making fun of her. She made a face at him. "Laugh if you like. Let's see what you say when it happens to you. It's probably very boring for her to be reading my mind, now that you men- tion it. She might as well be watching the Worry Channel."

She tried to make a joke about her situation, everything piling up on her at once—selling this house, her problems at work, and her divorce being finalized all at the same time.

Peter decided to ask about the last item on her list.

"So, what's going on with your divorce? Is it official yet?" he asked in a more serious tone.

"I got the final decree in the mail just two weeks ago. So did Jeff. But for some odd reason, he hasn't stopped calling me."

Peter didn't seem surprised. "Maybe now that it's really over, he's having second thoughts."

"I can't see why. He was the one who—" It was still hard for her to say the words *cheated on me.* Or even *had an affair.*

"He was the one who claimed to be unhappy and wanted out of the marriage," she said finally.

Peter gave her a thoughtful look. "Maybe he just wanted your attention? And now he knows he went about getting it the wrong way?"

"Definitely the wrong way. If that man's brain was put inside a bird, the bird would fly right into a wall."

Peter gave her a reluctant grin. "You've got a point there. But sounds to me like he hasn't moved on."

She winced. That was the last thing she wanted to hear.

"Well, that's too bad. It's too late for second thoughts," she said. The angry tone of her voice surprised her. "Jeff can't have things his way all the time. I'm not some . . . pull toy he can just yank around on a string."

"Of course not. I didn't mean that at all." Peter rested his hand on hers, slowing her down. "

know you're angry at him for what he did, Liza. It wasn't right and makes me angry, too, when I see how he hurt you," he added, sounding every inch her older brother. "But maybe he realizes now he made a mistake."

"He did make a mistake. A whopper. What am I supposed to do about that now? The marriage is over. I have the documents to prove it."

"Officially," Peter clarified. "But it sounds like you still have some unfinished emotional business. Don't be so quick to pull the trigger. I can see how it's easy to call it quits when you're angry, but that might not always be the right choice. Once you cool down and get things in perspective, you might see that the marriage doesn't have to end."

Liza sighed. In the rare moments she could forget her anger and hurt feelings, she wondered the same thing. Had she made a mistake insisting that they break up? Jeff had claimed that he was sorry countless times.

"I don't know if I'll ever get things in perspective about the way he betrayed me, Peter. I'm not sure I ever can," she said honestly. "So far, I haven't been able to move past my anger."

"You will someday. Gail and I still seem to have a lot to argue about," he admitted. "But I think I'm on my way to forgiving her and getting on with my life, seeing the positive side of our relationship as well as the negative. Sometimes I wish I had gotten to this point sooner. It might have saved Will a lot of pain if we could have managed to work things out."

Liza didn't doubt that. But Peter's experience was very different from hers. And he had a kid.

If she and Jeff had started a family when Jeff wanted to, maybe she would have stayed with him despite his infidelity. Or if they'd had a child as he had wanted, maybe he wouldn't have cheated on her.

It was impossible to say, but she couldn't help wondering.

They finished their dinner and cleared the table together. Liza wrapped the leftovers from dinner and left them in clear view on the top shelf of the fridge. "Tell Will there's some food left for him if he gets hungry later," she said.

"I suppose," Peter agreed. "But he shouldn't act so spoiled. He should come down and eat with everyone else."

"It's been a long day and a big time change. That's probably screwed him up a bit," she offered.

"He's just brooding. I hope he snaps out of it."

"Me, too."

They had a lot of work to do together the next few days, but Liza was hoping there was some way she could have fun with Will. She saw so little of him and didn't want their visit to feel like a punishment or complete drudgery.

"Well, I'm beat. Guess I'll go up," she told her brother.

"Sure, you get some rest. My body thinks it's two hours earlier. I'm going to check out those old photos for a while."

They said good night, and Peter headed for the front parlor. Liza headed upstairs to her room. She checked her BlackBerry one last time before she got into bed. Thankfully, there were no messages from the office. But there was another call from Jeff.

She stood by the window, listening to the message. "Hi, Liza. Me again. Hope you're okay out there. I just wanted you to know that I'm thinking of you. Let me know if I can help. I really mean that. I'm still here for you. Please remember that."

Liza sighed and put the phone aside. Jeff's soft, deep voice still tugged at her, she had to admit. Maybe Peter was right.

Maybe she had pulled the trigger too quickly. Was there still a chance for them? Was that what Jeff wanted?

Liza didn't know what she wanted anymore.

She just wanted . . . peace. A peaceful heart. She wanted to be tranquil and accepting of her life. The way Claire North seemed to be.

She stared out the window at the dark night sky. There were hundreds of stars. She had forgotten how it was out here.

If only she could squeeze her eyes shut and

make a wish and have everything that troubled her right now resolve in the blink of an eye—the conflict at her job, her defunct marriage, dealing with this old house.

It could never be that easy. *That's why they call it being a grown-up, Liza*, she reminded herself. Too bad this place made her wish she was just a little girl again, sitting on the back steps, letting her aunt comb the tangles from her hair.

If only Aunt Elizabeth were here now, to comb the tangles from her life.

Chapter Six

LIZA woke up very early the next day. She showered and dressed, then crept downstairs, trying not to disturb Peter and Will. The coffeemaker had been set up the night before—by Claire no doubt. With silent thanks, Liza took a cup and wandered into the front parlor, looking for her laptop. She still felt stung from being beaten out by Charlie on the shoe account and thought she might work on a few pitch ideas for new clients. She needed a few more sharp arrows in her quiver when she got back to the city. Liza settled herself at the antique secretary and opened the computer.

Then she stared out the big bay windows to gather her thoughts. It was a damp morning, with a foggy mist rising like smoke off the ground. She couldn't even see the ocean, just the blurry outlines of trees on top of the bluff. The mist made the landscape look magical, and even more fantastic when a strange sight came into view.

Liza blinked twice, then stood up from her chair and walked quickly to the window.

Was that a goat tiptoeing through the fog, munching the sparse weeds on the front lawn? Liza's eyes widened. Yes, it was. Most definitely. Not just one but two . . . no, three. Three little goats were having breakfast in the ethereal morning mist, right in front of the inn. One was silver gray, the other black with a white chest, and the third, which actually skipped across her field of vision, a creamy buff color.

Liza could not recall ever seeing goats this close. But she was pretty sure as to where they had come from. What to do about them was the question.

She grabbed her jacket and scarf off the coat tree, and stepped outside. She moved slowly, hoping she wouldn't startle them. She quietly shut the front door and noticed that they barely lifted their heads.

They were very cute, she thought. She had even heard that goats made good pets, though given the chance, she would prefer a dog.

She walked down the steps and held out her hand. "Hi, little goat. What are you up to?"

The buff-colored goat lifted its head and walked

over to her. Its horns looked very sharp close-up. Liza stood still as a statue as it bumped its head on her leg and nuzzled her hand. Looking for food, she guessed. She pulled her hand back quickly, but that didn't seem to insult the goat.

The edge of her scarf was dangling, and the goat nipped on the wool fringe with big white teeth.

"Hey . . . give that back. You can't eat my scarf!"

Liza tugged on one end of her scarf while the little goat tugged on the other.

I'm losing, she realized, feeling ridiculous—and desperate.

"Bette, bad girl!" Liza heard someone shout.

She looked up to see a woman dressed in baggy khaki pants and a red barn jacket hop over the stone fence that bordered the inn's property.

Her long dark red hair was tied low at the back of her head and streamed out behind her like a flag. Her cheeks were full and ruddy, practically matching her coat, and her feet were covered by dark green rubber boots. Suitable for wading through mud or a barnyard, Liza realized.

"Don't worry. I'll get them. They won't hurt you," she shouted at Liza.

Liza was so startled, she didn't answer. The goats were startled, too, Liza realized as the naughty Bette finally released the tasty scarf.

Then the goat stepped back and complained with a loud sound.

Ba-a-a-h!

"That's right. You let that go. I have something for you, don't worry."

The woman pulled a handful of brown feed from her pocket and let the little mischief-maker eat from her hand. As the goat gobbled, the woman grabbed the animal's collar and held it fast in her hand. Then she took a length of thin nylon rope from her pocket and tied it to the goat's collar.

"I'm so sorry. I don't know how they got away," she said with a laugh as she looked up at Liza. "I hope she didn't tear your scarf. I'd be happy to replace it."

"Oh, I think it's fine." Liza lifted the end of the scarf and took a look. It was a little stretched out and had a few teeth marks, but she was sure she could wash it out and pat it flat again. "Please don't worry about it."

"That's very nice of you . . . I'm Audrey Gilroy, by the way. My husband and I run the farm next door." She nodded her head toward her property.

"So I gathered," Liza said with a small laugh. "I'm Liza Martin. My aunt Elizabeth owned the inn."

"Yes, of course. Elizabeth Dunne, a wonderful woman. She was such a great help when we first came here. I don't know that we would have lasted without her. So lighthearted and encouraging."

"Yes, she was all of that," Liza agreed. It was gratifying to hear perfect strangers praise her aunt

148

so lavishly. But it still made her sad, poignantly conscious of her loss.

"I was so sorry to hear that she'd passed away. I'm very sorry for your loss," Audrey said sincerely.

Liza quietly thanked her.

"What will happen to the inn? If you don't mind me asking," Audrey added.

"My brother and I put it up for sale," Liza told her. "We both have our own careers, and it seems too much to take on."

Why did she feel guilty admitting their plans? Liza wondered. Why did she even bother making up some flimsy excuse? She and Peter had never considered keeping the inn and trying to run it at a distance. But for some reason, Liza felt she had to explain herself. Even to the goat lady, Audrey Gilroy.

"I see. That's too bad. It's such a lovely place. But maybe someone will buy it and take it over," Audrey said optimistically.

"I hope so," Liza answered. "It would be great if someone saw the potential in it. I'm afraid it's going to need a lot of loving care to restore it to its former glory."

The silver gray goat strolled over and butted Audrey's hip, trying to work its muzzle into her jacket pocket.

"This is Meryl. She's a little pickpocket," Audrey said.

She slipped another tether on Meryl's collar and gave her a little feed.

"What's the other goat's name?" Liza asked.

"That's George. He's the smart guy. The gang leader," Audrey explained.

"Interesting names."

"My husband and I are film buffs. We take turns naming the goats after our favorite movie stars—Bette Davis, Meryl Streep, George Clooney . . ."

Audrey suddenly handed Liza the leads for Bette and Meryl. "Here, hold these a minute for me."

Before Liza could reply, she was in charge of the two goats, while Audrey stalked George. The black-and-white goat was staring at them and looked a little tense as Audrey approached. She held out a hand full of feed, and he sniffed the air.

Then he suddenly leaped across the yard, trying to escape capture. Luckily, he was headed back toward the farm. Audrey pursued him, waving her hands. "That's right, go along. Go back home, now."

With a graceful bound, he cleared the low field-stone wall.

Audrey looked back and laughed. "He thinks he's so smart."

Meryl and Bette started wailing, suddenly tugging their leads. They wanted to follow George, and Liza was tugged along.

"I guess they're ready to go home, too."

"I guess so." Audrey ran back to help her. "Here, let me get Bette from you. I'll just tie her to a tree and take Meryl back first."

"Oh, I can help you," Liza said. "I'll take one, and you take the other."

"Are you sure?" Audrey sounded doubtful. "I think we've been enough bother."

"It's no trouble. Lead the way. A little goat herding in the morning is good exercise. It's either that or a jog around the island."

Audrey laughed, looking pleased by Liza's answer. Liza could tell she really didn't want to leave her goat. As much as she scolded them, she talked to the ornery creatures like babies.

From what Liza had seen so far, a goat tied to a tree would be pretty likely to chew through its tether before Audrey had a chance to come back.

Liza followed Audrey across the property and to a low spot on the wall. Liza's charge jumped over automatically, and Liza quickly followed, careful not to get her feet tangled up in the lead.

They brought the goats to a large pen, where there were quite a few others. The penned goats brayed up a storm as they saw Audrey and the escapees return.

"Oh, hush up now, all of you. We have a guest," Audrey told them. She glanced over her shoulder at Liza and smiled. "You've been such a good sport, I can't send you home without some goodies. Do you like goat cheese?"

"Love it," Liza admitted.

"You've come to the right place," Audrey said. They passed the barn with milking stalls. In the distance Liza saw a farmhouse, a beautiful old building that must have been there since the early 1800s. It had always been stark white with black shutters when she was growing up but had since been painted a charming shade of periwinkle blue, with dark purple shutters and a yellow door. The colors seemed to suit Audrey's personality, Liza thought.

Just past the barn they came to another wooden building, painted white, where Liza guessed the cheese was made. Audrey slipped through the red door, and Liza followed. The room inside was cool, as cool as outdoors. The cement floor was painted gray, and there was a drain in the middle. There was a huge stainless-steel tank, studded with dials, pipes, and faucet handles, in the middle of the room.

Both walls were covered by large stainless-steel refrigerators. Audrey pulled open a metal door and took out a large roll of cheese covered in herbs and wrapped in plastic. Then a chunk of what looked like fudge, also wrapped in plastic. She left the delicacies on a metal table that stood to one side of the front door, which also held a metal scale.

Then she walked over to a metal shelf on the far side of the room and returned with some bars of soap wrapped in floral paper and two small glass jars containing skin creams. She pulled down one of the baskets that were hanging from the ceiling and packed all the goat-milk-based goodies inside.

"We just started making skin products. Let me know what you think of them."

"That's too much," Liza protested. "You're being far too generous."

"Nonsense. You have a party with it or something. Need some recipes?" Audrey asked.

"No, thanks. I have a feeling Claire will know what to do with the cheese."

Audrey quickly wrapped the basket in a sheet of brown paper, then stepped away from the metal table. "One more thing . . . wait right here."

She left the room through another door and quickly returned, carrying a large bunch of dried lavender. "Here you go. The cheese is from the goats; that's from me."

Liza laughed, overwhelmed by the generosity. She'd been thinking about coming here for lavender. Now she had an armful. "Honestly, this isn't necessary . . ."

"Just trying to thank a neighbor. I appreciate your help. Someone else would have been calling animal control."

Maybe that was true, but Liza didn't think of herself as a real neighbor. She was just . . . passing through. Still, she loved the lavender and couldn't wait to try the cheese.

"Thank you, Audrey. I'm going to enjoy all these gifts. And I really liked meeting your goats."

"The feeling was mutual, believe me." Audrey smiled, and Liza had the uncanny feeling that, given the right circumstances, they could be friends. The goat-wrangling redhead was only a few years older than Liza was, she realized, and had a down-to-earth manner that Liza found refreshing.

She wondered about Audrey's story, what had brought her and her husband out here to start this unique enterprise. "How long have you been raising goats?" Liza asked curiously.

"Oh, about five years now. We started with ten goats, and now we're up to seventy. That's a good number for a farm like this one. We'll have to sell some off next year after the kids come. The mothers give birth from January to April, then they give milk until the fall," Audrey explained. "I was a nurse in my former life, so it helps with the vet bills—all those deliveries."

"I can't imagine it," Liza said honestly. "Did you always live on the island?" she asked, balancing the heavy basket on one hip.

Audrey shook her head. "We found this island by accident one summer. We came up to the area to go camping, and all the campgrounds we knew were filled. Someone told us to come out here to the beach. My husband and I just fell in love with the place. We kept coming back on vacation, and then when this farm came up for sale, we decided to make the big move. It was hard at first," she admitted. "But we've gotten used to it. I could never go back now. But I still do some nursing at the emergency medical clinic in the center."

"I noticed that place. Is it staffed by volunteers?"

"Completely. It's all islanders with medical experience. You must know Daniel Merritt. I saw his truck at your place the last few days. He drives an ambulance and is trained as a first responder."

"Somehow I can picture that," Liza said. Daniel seemed the type who would be calm under pressure, even in an emergency.

She could have talked longer with Audrey, but it was getting late. She had to get back to the inn. "Thanks again. I'd better go," she said.

"Need any help? I can give you a lift."

"No, I'm fine. I'll just go back the way I came," Liza said.

She stepped out of the small building, and Audrey followed. The sun had risen higher in the sky and burned off the mist, leaving a layer of frosty dew. Liza heard her shoes crunch on the brown grass as she headed for the field and stone wall.

Back at the inn, Liza walked around to the back door and came in through the kitchen. Claire stood at the stove, and Peter sat at the long table, a pile of pancakes on his plate. Thin and golden brown, the pancakes were covered with a layer of sautéed apples. Liza's mouth watered at the sight.

Peter's eyebrows rose as he saw the overloaded basket on her arm. "What is this? Little Red Riding Hood? I thought you were upstairs, sleeping late."

"Sleeping? I was herding goats while you were still in dreamland, pal." Liza stuck the cheese in the fridge and placed the lavender in a white vase she found on the sideboard.

Peter gave her a quizzical look. Claire laughed. "Did they get loose again? That George is a terror. He could chew his way through a cement wall."

"He's definitely the smartest. Bette is sweet. But she tried to eat my scarf," Liza added, checking the scarf again.

Claire brought her a cup of coffee and a plate of pancakes as Liza related her adventure. "Their farm is really lovely. You ought to walk over and see it sometime."

"Maybe I will. If I have time," Peter said, looking unconvinced that a goat farm could be so interesting.

In fact, he was staring at Liza as if she had imagined the entire thing. In a way, it felt as if she had, she realized. It was definitely a strange, almost dreamlike experience. And it had cast a certain spell.

"Maybe I'll get a goat as a pet," Liza teased him. "I hear they can be very affectionate."

"I'm sure your condo board will be interested to hear that." Peter wiped his mouth with a napkin. "You can try to win them over with some of that cheese."

"I probably could," Liza agreed. She was going to ask if he wanted some of the cheese to bring back to Tucson but was interrupted by a buzz from her BlackBerry.

The caller ID flashed, and Liza saw that it was Fran Tulley.

"Hi, Liza. Good news," Fran greeted her. "I have a couple in my office right now who are interested in seeing the inn. They drove out from Boston this morning to see some properties in the village, but when I told them about the island, they really wanted to see your place first."

"Oh . . . that's great." Liza knew there would be prospective buyers on the way, but she hadn't expected anyone to come this morning. Not this early anyway.

"Can I bring them over?" Fran asked.

"Sure, come right over. I'll try to straighten up a little if I can."

"Don't worry. They know the deal. We should be there in about twenty minutes or so. See you then."

Liza clicked off the call. Logically, she knew that many, many people might have to march through the inn before anyone wanted to buy it. But the idea of these first lookers seemed alarming.

She slipped her phone back into her pocket and looked up at her brother.

"Fran Tulley?" he guessed.

"That's right. And she's on her way over with hot prospects."

His mouth was full of food, and he quickly swallowed. "What should we do?"

"I don't know. All she said was, 'Don't worry, they know the deal.' I guess that means they know it's in need of improvements."

"I hope they don't think they're going to offer some ridiculously low price and whittle us down."

"Peter, they didn't even get here yet. Let's just let Fran do her job. We probably shouldn't even be here. We'll only get in her way."

Peter seemed alarmed at that suggestion. "I want to be here. I want to see how she handles herself, answers questions. We really don't know what kind of salesperson she is, Liza. She might be awful."

"I don't think she's going to be awful. She seems very experienced and competent. Besides, we signed a contract with her, remember? It's a little late to worry about all this now."

He frowned at her, and Liza sighed. Her brother was getting anxious. Not a good sign.

Liza heard a vehicle pull up and park at the back of the house, near the kitchen door. Was it Fran already? Did she take her clients around in a private jet?

She lifted the curtain on the window and saw Daniel's truck. He had arrived along with several helpers. He had told her he would need to hire a crew to keep the job moving along. She hoped the painters didn't distract the lookers. Then again, it might be a plus to see that improvements were going on.

Daniel was unloading a long ladder with the help of another man. He had on a gray hooded sweatshirt today, paint-spattered jeans, and worn running shoes. She wasn't sure how he managed to look as good as a guy in a five-hundred-dollar suit in that outfit, but somehow he did.

He suddenly turned to the window and smiled, but Liza acted as if she hadn't seen him and quickly let the curtain drop again. She was sure she looked a frizzy, frazzled mess after her goat-herding experience.

"I guess we ought to at least clean up the kitchen." Peter was standing at the sink, scrubbing the griddle. "Where did Claire go?" he asked in a cranky tone. "Isn't this her job?"

"She must be around somewhere. I don't keep her on a leash, Peter."

Liza never really asked Claire questions about her work or told her what to do. Claire seemed to know automatically what needed to be done and when to do it.

"Maybe she's upstairs, making the beds," Liza offered as she loaded the dishwasher.

"Yeah, she is," Will reported, stomping into the kitchen. "There's some painter dude staring through my window. Then she comes in and wants to make the bed . . ."

Will sat at the table, holding his head. His thick dark hair was sticking up on end, as if someone had been working on it with an eggbeater. He wore a huge baggy T-shirt and sweatpants, his feet bare. He hadn't reached his full height yet but had very large feet. Like a puppy with big paws.

"Want some breakfast?" Liza asked her nephew.

"Something simple. Don't let him make a big mess again," Peter said quickly. He wiped down the countertop with a large sponge and gave Liza a look. "Give him some yogurt or toast. Scratch that. No toast. Too many crumbs."

Liza knew that Claire had squirreled away a few pancakes for the boy but then decided not to make Peter crazy by warming them up now. Will would have to have the treat some other time—or figure out how to get up earlier and eat with everyone else.

"What is he all freaked out about?" Will strolled over to the refrigerator and took out a container of yogurt, then found a spoon on the table and began to eat it, standing up.

"The real estate agent is bringing a couple over to see the inn," Liza explained.

Will scratched his neck. "Like, they might buy it?"

Liza nodded. "Like, we hope so."

He grinned. "Me, too. Then we can get the heck out of here."

"Will," his father grumbled, "just eat something and go back upstairs and stay out of the way until these people are gone, okay?"

"It's no big deal," Liza said quickly. "You don't have to stay in your room all day, Will. It's really gorgeous out. You ought to go down to the beach or something."

"I'll take him to the beach," Peter cut in. "Later, when we're finished here with the realty agent."

"I don't care. I want to stay in my room." Will dumped his yogurt container in the trash, left the spoon in the sink, then headed for the hallway. "This place sucks. You'd have to be crazy to want to buy it."

Peter looked at Liza as if to say, "See what I mean?"

Liza sighed inwardly. Peter was convinced that Will was the problem, but from what Liza could see, Peter was at least half to blame; he kept pushing Will's buttons. She dearly hoped she wouldn't have to be the one to explain this to her brother.

Saved by the knocker, she thought, as the brass knocker sounded on the front door. "I guess they're here."

Peter quickly wiped his hands on a towel. "I'll get it," he volunteered.

"That's all right. I can go." Liza smoothed down her sweater and pushed her hair behind her ears. She hadn't put on a drop of makeup this morning, but it was too late now to worry about her appearance. The visitors weren't coming to see her, anyway. They were coming to look over the inn.

She wasn't sure why, but the realization gave her a sour feeling in the pit of her stomach.

She pulled open the door, fixing her face in a wide smile. "Hello, Fran. Come right in."

Fran quickly introduced the Nelsons, Alice and Ben. They were in their midthirties, Liza guessed, just a few years older than she was. She noticed Alice Nelson's designer handbag and leather boots, and Ben's supple suede jacket and the little polo-player logo on his baseball cap. Universal sign language that they had an impressive income. That was heartening, Liza thought.

Peter had run into the foyer right behind her and was now vigorously shaking Ben Nelson's hand.

"Why don't we start down here?" Fran said brightly. She had a sheaf of notes in hand, Liza noticed, that must have listed the specifics for the property.

Fran began her tour, and the Nelsons peered around.

"And in this room, there's stunning crown molding around the ceiling and bookcases. And these beautiful pocket doors." Fran demonstrated, pulling the doors in and out. "That's the original molding, and it is in excellent condition, as are these wide plank floors . . ."

The couple looked up at the molding, then down at the floors.

Fran seemed to have the situation totally under control, and Liza slipped away, planning to retreat to the kitchen. She paused in the foyer, glaring at her brother, sending him a silent message to do the same and leave the Nelsons alone with Fran.

He pursed his mouth and shook his head. Liza's heart sank.

No telling what he might say or do. She didn't want to see it.

She grabbed her down vest from the coat tree and headed out the kitchen door into the backyard. The irony of it all was that Peter was the one most eager for the sale, and now he was bound to interfere and possibly spoil it. There was nothing she could do about it, Liza reasoned. She decided to get a little work done outside while the house tour was going on.

Liza tramped through the backyard, realizing it was badly in need of attention. Now that the snow had melted, she could see that there were lots of old leaves and frost-damaged branches that needed cleaning up. Her aunt had taught her a bit about gardening, and Liza had always liked working with plants, but she had never had a chance to do much of it. None of her Boston apartments had had a yard, much less room for a garden.

She decided to grab a rake and at least get a start out here. Maybe Will would even help her later—if she asked him really nicely.

She went into the big shed to look for a rake but soon got distracted. The outbuilding had once been a horse stable and still had big swinging barnlike doors, a dirt floor, and two stalls inside.

Her uncle's workbench stood to one side near a large window. Practically all of his tools were still in place: the long band saws hanging on the wall, the rows of wrenches in graduated size, the screwdrivers and hammers, the big metal vise on the worktable that held wood steady while Clive shaped it or made a repair.

It looked just the same as when she was a child, Liza thought. As if Uncle Clive might step back to do some work at any minute.

A shadow crossed her line of sight, and Liza turned to see Daniel standing in the doorway.

"It's a regular tool museum in here," he said lightly. "I'd be careful, though. There are some Harry Potter–sized spiders."

The thought made Liza's skin crawl, but she wasn't about to let him see that. "I'm looking for a rake," she said. "Have you seen one around?"

"Over in the corner." Daniel pointed to the far left side of the barn. "I think there are a few propped next to the wall behind the bicycles."

"Bicycles?" Liza stared around. "I don't see any bicycles."

"Covered with that blue tarp. There are two or three. Your aunt kept them around for guests. She liked me to keep them in some sort of riding condition—though they're so ancient, it's a challenge, even with air in the tires."

Liza had loved biking when she was young but hadn't ridden in years. She walked over to the bikes and pulled off the tarp.

There were three of them, old-fashioned ten-speeds with curled handlebars and very hard-looking seats. They were stored upside down, so that the tires wouldn't get warped or deflated.

She reached out and spun a pedal, watching the rear wheel of the closest bike spin with a familiar clicking sound.

"Do you like to ride?" Daniel had sneaked up on her, his voice so close, she suddenly jumped.

"Oh . . . you scared me."

"Sorry. I didn't mean to."

"Of course not," she said quickly. She turned and looked up at him. He was so tall. She could hardly make out his expression in the dim light.

"I used to like to ride when I was younger," she admitted, "but I haven't been out on a bike in years. Maybe I'll take one of these for a spin sometime. Are they rideable?"

"They are. Unless you're training for the Tour de France."

"I decided to skip it this year. Too much going on around here," she answered, matching his dry tone.

"That makes sense. Well, if you do go for a spin, there are a few bike tools and an air pump in that box." He pointed to a wooden box near the bikes. "And some helmets, too."

"Okay, thanks." She turned to him and smiled.

"Are we still looking for the rake? Or going for a ride instead?"

Who is this "we" you're referring to? she wanted to ask.

Me, of course, his dark eyes seemed to answer her with a playful light. As if to say he wouldn't mind skipping work for a while and going for a ride with her.

Liza hesitated, wondering if she should suggest the idea. Then she quickly caught herself.

Are you out of your mind? Inviting the house-painter to go for a bike ride—in the middle of a workday?

Liza glanced at him and backed away from the bikes. "I can't go now," she said abruptly. "I have a lot to do."

"Right. Work. I almost forgot. I have a house to paint."

"Yeah, I think you do."

He walked away smiling, looking pleased that he'd gotten to her.

He did get to her. She wasn't sure why. He hardly treated her the way a contractor should be treating a customer. Somehow she stood for it—and even encouraged him.

Liza grabbed the old rake and got to work, gathering the dead leaves that littered the lawn. There were more under the bushes in the garden, but she decided to leave the garden for later. She pushed herself hard, deliberately trying to work up a sweat and burn off the ire from the latest in her office drama.

But for some reason, she wasn't really thinking about Charlie anymore. Her thoughts kept wandering back to Daniel Merritt, who was working nearby, up on a ladder at the back of the house. She raked industriously, never once glancing his way, yet for some reason totally conscious of his every movement.

The way she acted around him was silly, almost embarrassing, as if they were playing some dumb flirtation game. She was pretty rusty at that sport; she'd be the first to admit it.

Daniel Merritt, on the other hand, seemed a pro. He probably charmed lots of women he worked for. Out of sheer boredom, she guessed, from living around here. Liza knew she shouldn't make too much of it, especially since she would be leaving in just over a week. So what was the point of encouraging anything?

The pile of leaves and branches was growing bigger. Liza took a break to admire her progress and look for a new spot to attack with her rake. The kitchen door opened, and Will came out. Liza waved to him as he walked over, his hands dug deep in the front pockets of his jeans, the hood of his brown sweatshirt pulled up over his head though it was quite a mild day.

"Hey," he said.

"Hey, Will," Liza echoed his greeting. "Is the real estate agent still here?"

Will nodded. "She's, like, popping out of the woodwork, everywhere you turn. It's like a slasher movie or something. And my dad is, like, stalking them. It's really bizarre."

Liza had to laugh at the description. "Sounds about right. Want to help me rake?"

He shrugged. "I guess I could. It's so flipping boring here, there's nothing else to do."

She handed him her rake and started toward the shed to look for another. She turned around and called back to him over her shoulder. "I found some bikes. Maybe we could all go for a ride later. Your dad and I can show you the island."

He looked up at her, and she noticed a slight sign of interest in the flicker of an eyebrow. "What is there to see around here?"

"Lots of things. The beaches and some farms. There's a little bunch of shops not too far away. There are these amazing cliffs on the other side of the island that are shaped like wings. There's a legend about them."

Peter came out of the house then. He didn't look happy.

"Are the Nelsons gone?" Liza asked him.

He nodded quickly. "On their way to another appointment. Another big house on the island, though I don't think it's quite as large as this one or has a water view. I wish I knew where it was. I'd like to check out our competition."

He was getting obsessed. Liza let out a long breath, struggling for patience.

"I don't think we can really worry about that too much, Peter. What did Fran say?"

"She just said she would call us later. Very non-committal. I couldn't really tell if she had a feeling about them one way or the other."

"We can't expect the first people who look at the inn to buy it," Liza reminded him.

"Why not? Sometimes ballplayers hit the first pitch out of the park. It happens, you know."

Will, who had started raking, rolled his eyes so that only Liza could see. She struggled not to grin and give him away.

"Fran made a few mistakes when she was showing the place," Peter went on. "I had to correct her."

"What kind of mistakes?" Liza asked warily.

"Oh, little things. She said the house was built in 1895 for a sea captain. It was actually 1890. And she said the banister is oak when it's maple. We don't want to be inaccurate."

"No, we wouldn't want that," Liza muttered. She hoped Peter hadn't driven Fran Tulley crazy. Her brother could be so dense at times.

Liza's cell phone went off. She quickly pulled it from her back pocket and recognized Fran Tulley's number. Was Peter right? Were the Nelsons going to make an offer?

"Hello, Liza. It's Fran," the real estate agent began. "I'm out on another appointment, but I had a minute to call you."

"How did it go? Are they interested? Peter couldn't really tell."

"They liked the place, but I think the repairs that are needed scared them off. They're more the granite-kitchen, marble-bath type. It would be a lot of work to get the inn up to their standards."

"With those standards, yes, it would," Liza had to agree.

"I did want to tell you privately—and as diplomatically as I can—that it's difficult to show a property with the owner hovering and cutting into the conversation. That's why you hire someone like me. Because we have the knowledge and professional experience."

"I know exactly what you're saying, Fran. I was wondering about that myself," Liza replied quietly.

She noticed Peter walking quickly in her direction. He had obviously figured out that she was talking to Fran. He signaled to her, but she waved him away.

"Good. I'm glad we understand each other," Fran said. "No offense to your brother," she added. "I know you're both eager to sell. But his contributions are not helping that effort."

"I'll try to communicate that to him," Liza promised.

"I'd like to bring another couple by this afternoon. Would that be okay?"

"Fine with me. And we'll all try to stay out of your way," Liza said.

"Great. See you then."

Fran clicked off, and Liza turned to her brother, who was now hovering inches away.

"Was that Fran? What did she say?" he asked.

"She said the Nelsons liked the place, but they aren't interested in taking on significant renovations. They like granite kitchens and marble bathrooms. They don't want a fixer-upper."

"What else did she say? You were talking a long time."

This part was harder. Liza braced herself. "She said it was difficult for a sales agent to show a property if the owner was . . . hovering. It undermined her efforts."

"I was just trying to be helpful," Peter explained. "And I wanted to see how she handled buyers and showed the place . . ." He looked a little deflated. "I guess she didn't like that."

"She knows you were trying to help. But I don't think you would like it if someone was leaning over your shoulder, peering through the viewfinder, as you tried to do your job, would you?"

Peter didn't answer. But from his expression, she knew he had gotten her point.

"She's bringing more people today," Liza added, hoping that would cheer him up.

"Really? When?"

"This afternoon. But we won't be here, so you won't be tempted to butt in again."

Peter's face grew a little red. "Where will we be?"

"We're going to take a bike ride, you, me, and Will. We're going to show him the island. Right after we rake up all these leaves."

Will paused and leaned on his rake, waiting for his father's reaction.

Peter looked at the both of them. "Sounds like you have it all planned. Where do we get the bikes—rent them somewhere?"

"There are three perfectly good ones in the shed, oiled up and ready to go. A bit old," Liza added, "but I hear they work."

"What about that endless to-do list of yours?"

"It can wait a few hours. I promised Will a tour of the island," she answered. "It's a perfect day for it."

Peter turned to his son. "Do you want to go bike riding?"

Will shrugged. "I guess. It beats raking leaves."

"He's made some good progress," Liza said, pointing to the large pile Will had gathered. "Why don't we finish the job together and then go out for a ride? Maybe Claire can make us some lunch, and we'll eat on the beach."

"All right," Peter agreed. "The air is so clear around here; there's great light. I'll bring some cameras."

Liza fetched another rake from the shed and handed it to her brother. "Many hands make light work," she decided, was one proverb that was very true.

It was good to get this big job done, but she was looking forward to touring the island, too. She had always had such a strong work ethic, sticking to her responsibilities and duties no matter what. Never taking time for herself.

Well, today she was going to do something fun and not worry about it. So she tried not to feel too guilty about abandoning the inn and her long to-do list. It was important to spend time with Will.

Chapter Seven

"HOW are you doing?" Liza shouted to her brother.

When Peter briefly turned his head, his bike wobbled. He quickly looked straight ahead again before shouting back an answer. "That guy who said, 'Once you learn how to ride a bike, you never forget'? He didn't know what he was talking about."

Liza laughed and glanced at her nephew, who

rode just to her right. Will rolled his eyes. Of course, he was doing the best of all three of them and could have definitely raced ahead by about two miles by now.

"Hang in there, Peter. You're doing fine," Liza called.

"He'd better not fall off with his cameras; he'll flip out," Will told his aunt.

"Right after he strangles me for getting him out here in the first place," Liza confided, making Will spare a smile. "Let's think positively. I'm having fun so far. Aren't you?"

"It beats raking leaves," he said again.

After pumping up the bike tires, squirting the gears with three-in-one oil, and packing the food Claire assembled for their lunch—too much, Liza thought, for their modest trip—they finally mounted the bikes and headed down the main road toward the tiny island center.

They pedaled slowly at first, each getting accustomed to the various quirks of their machine, how the lower gears stuck on one and the seat twisted around on another. Luckily, Liza remembered to bring the little bag of bike tools, though she wasn't really sure how to use most of them.

They made slow progress, the inn eventually falling out of view behind them as they worked their way around the first curve in the road, then up a long, low incline.

When you were driving along in a car, Liza realized, the scenery just flew by and you wouldn't even notice a small bump in the road or a hole. Or even a hill like the one they were now riding on. But on a bike—especially having not ridden for years—the contours of the road registered on every part of your body.

The goat farm came into view, and Liza spotted Audrey Gilroy in the big meadow, wearing a field jacket and jeans. The flock of goats was clustered around, and she was checking the collars on the kids, petting them and giving them feed from the palm of her hand. She looked up at Liza and waved hello.

Liza waved back and slowed her bike. "There's Audrey Gilroy. You know, the goat-farm lady." She nearly said "my friend" but realized they weren't quite friends, yet. "We ought to stop and say hello," she told her brother. "It's fun to look around there. The goats are adorable."

Before her brother could answer, Will let out a loud groan. "Do we have to? What's so great about a bunch of dumb goats?"

Peter scowled at his son. "If your aunt wants to stop, that's what we'll do, Will. You don't have to argue with every little thing we say."

"I wanted to buy more of their cheese," Liza said, "but I guess it's better if I get it later. It might spoil," she told them, smoothing over the friction.

She waved back at Audrey one more time, then

pushed hard on her pedals to make her way up another hill. An expansive ocean view on the left side of the road was distracting enough to take her mind off her aches.

Distracting and refreshing, she thought. The blue sky was crystal clear, the waves topped with white foam crashing at the bottom of the cliffs. She knew logically the waves must be making a sound, but they were so far up above the shore-line, she couldn't hear a thing.

Even Will seemed mesmerized by the sight, his gaze fixed on the ocean, the expression on his young face eager and interested.

After a while, the road changed, and the ocean disappeared behind thick brush and trees. They glided down one long hill, which was totally exhilarating. Liza squeezed her brakes but still felt as if she were flying.

Of course, they had to pay for it at the bottom and work hard to get up the next rise. They rode on a few more minutes without anyone talking. Were Peter and Will getting tired already? Every once in a while, she would feel herself pedaling into a cool, salty breeze, but it never grew strong enough to really push them back.

The cycling had felt like hard work at first, but once she got her legs into the rhythm of pedaling and remembered how to use the gears again, a sudden wave of energy kicked in and she felt as if she could ride all day.

"Can we stop for lunch? I'm really hungry," Will called out.

Liza had guessed that was coming. They had already been riding at least . . . fifteen minutes.

"I thought we could eat at the cliffs, and your dad could take some photos there," Liza answered.

"Good idea," Peter said. "That's a great spot. You can get a cold drink at the General Store if you like, Will, then we'll go on to the cliffs. It's not too far."

Will scowled, looking like an angry bug for a moment under his bike helmet, but he didn't argue with them this time. He rose up and pushed hard on his pedals, suddenly breaking away from the adults. Just to show he could, Liza thought.

Peter was riding alongside her now. "Let's just let him go. He needs the exercise."

"I couldn't catch up to him now even if I wanted to," she confessed.

"Oh, I could. But I'm going to give him some space," he replied with a straight face.

"Right," she said, grinning at him.

They soon came to the little square with the fountain and the handful of shops, foremost among them the General Store.

"Holy mackerel . . . I'd forgotten all about this place." Peter parked his bike and swung off, gazing at the storefront wide-eyed. "I can't believe it's still here," he said to Liza.

"It's still here, still the same inside, too. Marion and Walter Doyle are still behind the counter."

"Wow, I've got to say hello to them." Peter turned to his son. "You've got to see this place, Will. It's like something out of an old movie. I want to introduce you to the old couple who owns it. I wonder if they remember me," he said vaguely, as he headed into the store. "Your aunt and I used to come here every day when we were kids."

That was true, and Liza knew the Doyles would remember Peter, even more clearly than they had remembered her. Peter had always been in charge of their money when they were kids. As the older sibling, he was the one who did all of the buying of their treats.

Peter was so excited about showing Will the store, Liza decided to wait outside while her brother gave Will the grand tour. It seemed like a good opportunity for some father-son quality time. Besides, it felt so good to be outdoors in the clear spring light.

It was hard to face it, but after this visit to the island, it was unlikely that she would ever return here. She hoped Peter took a lot of photos today on their bike trip. She wanted some for herself, so she could always remember these special places.

She walked across the road to the tea shop, curious to see if anyone was there today. As Liza peered through the dusty windows, she suddenly remembered the poem Daisy had thrust into her hands the other day—and that she had never read it.

Liza stuck her hand in her jacket pocket and found the balled-up scrap of paper. It was still there. She pulled it out and opened it.

If the sun and moon should doubt,
They'd immediately go out . . .

The bit of verse was not new to her. Her aunt and uncle had loved William Blake's poetry, and as Liza had grown older, the long, beautiful poem, "Auguries of Innocence," had grown on her. The verse was about faith. Mainly, faith in yourself, her aunt had once explained to her. "Sometimes you'll face a world of naysayers who make you doubt what you know is true, deep inside. You have to bear down, ignore them all, and believe in yourself. Guard that special light inside you."

Did she have that kind of faith in herself? Liza wondered. She wasn't sure. Lately, it seemed that all her goals were driven by a need to win the approval of her boss or clients or even her ex-husband.

She smoothed the paper with her hand, stared at it a moment, and then stuck it back into her pocket. It was something to think about.

By the time Peter and Will emerged, she had downed a bottle of cold water and was sitting cross-legged on a bench, eyes closed and face turned up to the sun.

She blinked, then reached for her pack as they approached. "So, how did you like it, Will?"

"It's okay," Will conceded. "They have, like, everything in the world in there." He took a big gulp from a bottle of blue sports drink.

"It's still the same," Peter reported. "So are Walter and Marion. And they did remember me. They gave me this for free, just to prove it."

He held up a package of Wing Dings, the gooey little chocolate cakes that used to be his all-time-favorite snack.

"Wing Dings, wow. I haven't seen those in a while. Can I have a bite?" she asked, just like when they were kids.

He held the package up above her head. "No, you can't. I'm saving them for later."

"I don't believe you, Peter. We're grown-ups now, remember? There are a ton of those things in the supermarket. You can at least give me a tiny bite!"

She started laughing—at him for regressing so totally and at herself for regressing just as much.

"I'll think about it," Peter replied in a serious tone. Then he smiled as he put the snack cakes in his pack and also slipped in the cameras. "I took a lot of photos inside. Will took some, too," he added, glancing at the boy. "I have this old digital for him to use. It's not the latest technology, but it has a good lens. It's a good camera to learn on."

"Do you like taking photos, Will?" Liza asked curiously.

Will met her glance a second, then nodded his head. Something about the shy way he answered told her that he did share this interest with his father, and it wasn't just foisted on him.

She wondered if he also shared his father's talent for it.

Feeling refreshed, they rode on, heading for the cliffs on the north side of the island. They passed a few large old houses, built in a style similar to the inn, and a few that were more rustic.

The view opened up, and the ocean and a rocky beach were once again revealed. Liza could tell by the terrain that they had almost reached the island's most famous landmark, and as they reached the top of the next hill, the cliffs came into view.

"Let's stop here a minute. I want to take some pictures."

They all parked their bikes on the side of the road. Peter took out the cameras, handing one to Will. Then the three of them hiked the short distance down a path that led to the beach below. They didn't go too far, though. Just enough so that the famous bluffs were in clear view.

"See what I meant, Will? They're shaped like two wings."

"Yeah, I see," Will replied, though he didn't

sound too impressed. He took a few shots of the bluffs, then turned his camera and took some photographs of the water below, where a flock of gulls were swooping down over large, glistening rocks.

"They must be feeding on something," Liza remarked.

"It's neat to watch them from up here, all swooping around in a bunch," Will said, gazing through the viewfinder.

He's really into it, Liza thought. Good for him.

When Peter finished with his photos, he snapped the lens cap back on his camera but kept it slung around his shoulder. "Should we try this path to the beach?" he asked Liza. "It looks a little steep."

"They're all steep now, Peter," Liza teased him. "I think when we were younger we just didn't notice it."

Peter and Will started down the path, and Liza went back to the bikes a moment and retrieved the pack that held their lunch.

Will hadn't complained again, but she was sure he was hungry by now. She was sure they all were.

They finally reached the beach. Will raced down the last few yards and ran at the water, shouting at the top of his lungs and waving his arms like a wild man.

"The ocean! The ocean! The big blue Atlantic Ocean!"

Peter watched him, his arm crossed over his chest. "I guess he likes it more than he let on."

"Yeah, I think so," Liza agreed with a smile. She felt like that about the ocean, too. Secretly, of course.

When Will was done venting his enthusiasm and his last bit of energy, he dragged himself back, panting, his head hanging to his chest. "Food, I need food," he gasped dramatically.

"I'm handing it out right now. Take a seat." She and Peter had already picked out boulders, and Peter sat on his, munching a sandwich.

Will took his sandwich and water bottle over to a rock nearby and began to eat. "So, we're here. What's the famous legend?" he asked his father. "Can you tell me now?"

Peter glanced at Liza. "Your aunt will tell you. She's a much better storyteller than I am."

Liza took a sip of water and settled herself. "Let's see, where should I start? You know that the village of Cape Light was founded in the 1600s, during the colonial era, right?" she asked her nephew.

"I guess I know now," he replied between huge bites of sandwich.

Liza ignored his snide tone and went on. "Well, during that time an illness spread among the colonists. They had no real medicine, of course, except for some herbal remedies. Nothing could cure the pox, and it was very contagious. So the sick and dying were separated from the rest of the colonists, and they were brought to this island."

"That's called a quarantine. Did you ever learn about that in school?" Peter asked him.

"I guess so. I don't know." Will made a face at his father, but he turned back to Liza with a curious expression and said, "So all the sick people were living here. I get it. Then what?"

"Well, it was very grim. There was little hope of them surviving out here, and very few people were brave enough or selfless enough to come out and help them. There would be weekly visits with food and water and other necessities but not much more than that. And if the land bridge was washed out, the help had to come by boat, and that was difficult, too—"

"Especially in the winter," Peter cut in. "The winters were brutal, and the island was practically inaccessible."

"I was about to get to that." Liza gave her brother a look. "Do you want to tell the story?"

"No, you go on," he said apologetically.

Liza turned back to Will. "The people in quarantine had very little help from the village—sometimes, none. And most of them were too weak to care for themselves. No one expected them to survive."

"Whoa, that's pretty nasty." Will looked shocked. Which was saying something, Liza thought. "They brought all these sick people out to this island and just dumped them here to die?"

"More or less," Liza said.

Will shook his head. "Then everybody was pretty horrible back then."

"It was different times, Will. It was hard to survive even if you were healthy. They didn't want to be uncaring, but they couldn't risk everyone in the village getting sick," Peter tried to explain.

Liza saw her nephew considering this idea. The story had finally captured his imagination.

"Well, the winter was long, and there were very few visits here," she went on. "Then a series of storms came, and no one could come at all. Finally, well into spring, a group of villagers were able to return. They came out to the island, not knowing what they would find . . ."

She purposely paused to draw out the suspense.

"Yeah? So? What did they find—a pile of bones?" Will said bluntly.

Liza shook her head. "Not at all. They found that everyone here had not only survived . . . they'd fully recovered. They were cured and healthy again."

"How?" Will made a disbelieving face at her. "You said they were dying and starving to death."

"They were. But the sick people on the island claimed that help had come from some other town. That a group of very able, gentle people had come and nursed them. Though no one could say exactly where these helping hands were from."

Will shrugged. "Some other town. You just said so yourself."

"Yeah, that's what they thought at first," Peter replied quickly. "But after they all returned to the village of Cape Light, a few of the people who had survived traveled around, looking for the ones who had rescued them, who had answered their prayers. But they could never find a nearby town or anyone who knew about the quarantine. Or who would admit to having gone there to help."

"That's pretty weird," Will said. He grinned at his father. "Maybe it was aliens or something."

"Funny you should say that," Liza answered. "Because many of the survivors said that the ones who had helped them were not people from another town. They claimed it was angels, who had come in human form, and that it was through their healing touch that the sick had been cured of the deadly disease."

"Angels? I like my idea about aliens better. It's more believable," Will told her.

Liza laughed. "Some people agreed with you. They didn't believe the healers were angels. But from that time on, the island was called Angel Island, and people would point to the cliffs that they say look like angel wings as proof that this bit of land was visited by the spiritual beings and that the island has certain . . . certain powers to heal people who are sick. Or even troubled," she added.

Liza gazed over at the cliffs. Some days, like today, they did look like huge, feathery wings.

Other days, she just couldn't see it. Perhaps it was more a person's state of mind than the actual topography.

"I think that angels could exist. Or something like them," Peter said, turning to look at Liza and Will. "I mean, why not? We certainly don't know everything there is to know about the universe. If there could be life on other planets, why not other dimensions? Or other types of beings right here?"

"Okay, Dad. If you say so." Will tilted his head and took a last bite of his sandwich. "Let me know if you ever get a picture, though. Okay?"

"I will, my boy. That one would be worth a million," Peter added with a laugh. "Right now, I'm going to take a walk down the beach and try for some pictures of seabirds. Want to come?"

Will nodded and hopped off the rock, camera in hand. Peter turned to Liza with a quizzical expression. "Aren't you coming with us?"

She thought about it for a moment, then shook her head. "You guys go ahead. I'm just going to hang out here awhile."

She watched them walk away toward the shoreline. Will seemed a little easier to deal with this afternoon, she thought, despite his sarcastic barbs. Maybe he just needed more time with his dad and more one-on-one attention?

Claire had packed a bountiful lunch for them, chicken sandwiches, apples, and homemade chocolate-chip cookies. Liza ate every crumb, deciding it was okay to eat her cookie since she was getting so much exercise.

She gathered up the trash and stuffed it into a plastic bag, then put the bag in her pack along with the empty water bottles.

The beach was pristine, and she wanted to leave it that way. Of course, no one ever came down here. She wondered how this beach would be once the ferry service started and all the tourists arrived. She could hardly imagine it. She wondered now if Daniel was right. Maybe the island should be left as a wild, rough place and the recreation centers reserved for those areas where there was already development.

She saw Peter and Will heading her way and slipped off her perch again. "How was the walk? Did you take any interesting pictures?"

"Yeah, I think we got some good shots," Peter said. He sounded a little winded but looked happy and relaxed.

"We found these amazing caves under the cliffs," Will reported. "I took a ton of pictures in there."

"Do you remember caves along this beach?" Peter asked. "They're carved right out of the stone by the rushing water."

"I'm not sure," Liza said honestly. "But every part of the island is different. Maybe we just never stopped here with Aunt Elizabeth and Uncle Clive. They used to take us to the beach near the inn mostly."

"Yes, they did," Peter agreed.

"Ready to head back?" she asked. She glanced at her watch. *All clear,* she thought. They had definitely missed Fran Tulley by now. One purpose of the outing had been accomplished.

"I'm ready. How about you, Will?"

Will nodded. He put the camera in his own pack this time instead of handing it back to his father.

"Don't forget to put the lens cap on tight," Peter told him. He glanced at Liza. "Will is going to keep that camera for himself. If he takes good care of it, maybe he'll get a better one for Christmas."

"Christmas?" Will sounded shocked. "How about waiting till I graduate from college, Dad? That's not so far off either."

Liza almost laughed but held it in.

"Your birthday is coming up in a few months. Let's see if you're still interested in photography by then," Peter told him as he mounted his bike.

Liza knew what Peter was saying. But she had a feeling Will would still be interested. She was almost willing to bet on it.

THEY took a different route on the way back, the Ice House Road, which ran north to south. The road had taken its name from the old ice house that stood on the large summer estate of some wealthy family. The family was so rich they had the ice blocks brought over on a boat in the winter and so generous that they let anyone who pleased come and help themselves to the frozen bounty. Which must have been a great treat during the hot summer months, Liza thought, as well as a necessary ingredient for making ice cream before refrigerators were invented.

The road had been built especially for the ice house and was a shortcut from the beach below the cliffs back to the island center, where the General Store stood.

Liza knew that the road would take them past the old cemetery, where her aunt and uncle had been buried. She had meant to come out and visit their graves ever since she arrived on the island but, so far, hadn't found the time. She considered asking Peter if he wanted to stop now, but then decided it was better to just keep going. She would return another time and bring flowers.

When they returned to the inn, Liza was surprised to see that Daniel's truck was still there, though he and his helpers were nowhere in sight. He had definitely made progress. All the shutters and doors had been removed, and the window frames scraped and sanded. The building itself had been scraped down and some broken steps on the porch repaired.

Peter noticed, too, looking the building over. "It's coming along. Daniel's pretty good so far."

"Yes, he is," Liza agreed.

They put their bikes back in the shed and went into the house together. Claire greeted them as they walked into the kitchen. Once again, she was cooking something that smelled incredibly delicious.

"Did you have a good ride?" Claire lifted the lid on a pot and peered inside.

"Yes, we did," Liza answered. "Better than I expected."

"Except that I ache all over and will probably feel even worse tomorrow," Peter predicted.

Claire shook her head. "A hot bath with some kelp crystals should help. Try the cabinet in the bathroom at the top of the stairs."

"I might try some of that, too." Liza sat down very carefully. She had been worried about good brakes initially but realized now she should have snatched the bike with the cushier seat.

"There's a surprise for you, Liza," Claire announced. "Just sit there, I'll get it."

A surprise, what could it be? Nothing from her office, Liza hoped. She'd had enough surprises from them this week.

Claire soon returned carrying a huge bouquet of roses in a tall clear vase.

Yellow roses, her favorite. There weren't too many people who knew that either.

Liza picked up the little envelope nestled in the flowers and hesitated. Claire had turned away, giving her some privacy, but Peter lingered in the doorway, waiting to find out who had sent the bouquet.

"Jeff," she said, without even opening the envelope. "Who else? He always goes for the grand gesture; I'll give him that."

"Read it," Peter said gently. "At least see what he says."

Liza pulled the card from the envelope and read. "He's been thinking about me, quote unquote, and hopes everything is going well out here." She looked at her brother. "He's left phone messages and e-mails every day since I got here, but I've hardly answered. I guess he's just trying to get my attention."

"Guess so. Though it might have been cheaper to hire a sky writer," Peter added. "Is that two dozen roses or three?"

Liza sighed and finally gave the abundant arrangement a careful look. "It's three. He likes to make a big impression."

"I remember." Peter gave her a thoughtful look. "You two have some unfinished business, Liza. That's all I have to say."

Liza let herself touch one of the velvety petals. The roses suddenly seemed to embody the very best days of her marriage, the bright, sunny, golden times when she felt close to Jeff and really loved him. Could she ever feel that way again? Roses on a bush fade and die, then new ones bloom to take their place. Maybe that's what marriage is about, having patience in the face of disappointment, waiting for loving feelings to bloom again.

But it was hard to let Jeff close again, close enough to start over. He had hurt her, and she didn't trust him. A houseful of yellow roses couldn't make her forget what he had done.

"I'm going to put the vase in the foyer," Liza announced, as she stood up from the table. "They'll brighten up the entrance. A nice touch for our prospective buyers?"

Peter nodded. "Fran will approve."

Liza stretched and rubbed her lower back. "Let me know when you're done with those bath salts, brother dear. I could use a dose."

She carried the roses out of the room, setting the vase on the small Eastlake-style table in the foyer. They looked perfect there, she thought. It was a beautiful, sweet-smelling bouquet, and she could hardly blame the flowers for her own muddled feelings toward the sender.

If only she could travel around the world on a bike from now on. She had been so focused on keeping her balance and pumping the pedals, there had been no space in her head to think about anything disturbing.

EVERYONE was very quiet during dinner, too tired to talk. Claire had cooked pot roast with noodles and a green salad on the side. Just like the night before, after she served them all dinner, she left the inn for her home.

All the exercise made Will even more ravenous

than usual. He ate quickly, wolfing down his food, then pushed himself back from the table, looking sleepy.

"I think I'm done. Can I go back up, Dad?"

Peter looked surprised and about to say no, then took a better look at his son and almost laughed. "You need to lie down before you fall down. Don't fall asleep here. You're way too big for me to carry you anymore."

The words brought a sweet image to Liza's mind. Will had been that small once. It was hard to believe now.

Will rose and carried his dish to the sink. "See you tomorrow," he mumbled over his shoulder.

"See you, Will," Liza said.

Peter waited until they heard Will's footsteps climb all the way up to the second floor. "He got some good shots out on the beach," Peter said quietly. "I might go into town tomorrow and print out a few."

"That's a great idea. I think he'd like that. By the way, Fran Tulley called. She said the people she brought by this afternoon had some interest."

"They do? Why didn't you tell me?"

"Well, for one thing you were taking a bath . . . and then a nap before dinner I think," Liza teased him.

"That's great news. We might unload this place pretty quickly after all."

"Yes, we might." Liza sat back and tilted her head to one side. "I have to admit, it does make me feel a little sad sometimes to give it up so quickly. When I was out in the shed this morning, just the way the light was slanting through the window, I could practically see Uncle Clive standing there, working on a fishing fly or fixing a broken chair."

"I know what you mean," Peter said. "This place is filled with memories. It's a memory museum, Liza. But what choice do we have? We have to sell it, and this is the perfect time."

"Yes, I know." She took a breath. "But not everyone around here agrees with that logic."

Peter looked confused. "Who do you mean?"

"Claire North. She doesn't say much, but I have a feeling she disapproves of us getting rid of the place like this."

"Has she told you that?"

Liza shrugged. "Not in so many words. But she doesn't have to say it. I can just tell. Besides, Claire's not the type to be so blunt. I just get this feeling from her sometimes that she doesn't think we should sell the inn so quickly. And"— Liza winced—"that she thinks I should have come out more often to see Aunt Elizabeth. Especially at the end."

There, she had said it. It had been hard to get the words out, but if anybody would understand, it would be Peter. Maybe he also had regrets at the way his relationship with Aunt Elizabeth had faded over the years.

He bowed his head a moment, then looked up

at her. "That *might be* what Claire's thinking," he said finally. "But maybe that's what *you* really feel, and you're projecting those opinions on her. Did you ever think of that?"

"That's possible," Liza conceded. "It's complicated."

She glanced at her brother but didn't say more. She wasn't sure he would understand. As much as she wanted to sell the inn and get back to Boston, there was a part of her that clung to this place. A part that couldn't accept or believe she'd never be able to come back here, to sit in this kitchen or lounge on the porch, gazing at the wide blue sky and endless sea.

Liza was just starting to see how this place was part of her, and giving it up was like slicing off a little piece of her soul.

Peter spoke about memories. But this was deeper. Did he feel that way at all?

She was about to ask him when he leaned over and patted her hand. "This is a difficult time for us, Liza. You're in a very emotional state."

"I can't argue with that," she admitted ruefully. "And I do like Claire. I don't know how I would have managed here an hour without her."

"She's been great. We'll have to do something special for her when we go."

Liza nodded. She knew he meant a gift of money, though with Peter's parsimonious streak, they would probably wind up arguing about the sum. She doubted Claire expected any sort of gift, money or anything else. She wasn't that kind of person. Liza wanted to give her something from the house that would have meaning to her. She just wasn't sure what that could be.

"I'll finish up here. Why don't you go up?" Peter got to his feet and picked up a few dirty cups and dishes from the table. "I think you could use some sleep. It's been a big day."

"They've all been big days lately. Is it just me, or have you noticed that, too?"

"Even more reason to get a good night's rest. We might get an offer on the inn tomorrow," he said optimistically. "That would be a big day."

"Yes, it would," Liza agreed. She might be able to leave here by Monday if that scenario played out.

Wouldn't Charlie Reiger be surprised to see her back? For some reason, the image didn't cheer her as much as it should have.

Liza said good night to her brother and went upstairs. As she entered her room, her laptop, sitting on the small table by the window, caught her eye. She really ought to thank Jeff for the flowers.

It wasn't late. But calling him seemed risky. She wasn't sure what to say if he picked up. She doubted she could maintain a calm, friendly distance. A safe distance. She had been touched by the gesture and felt confused about her feelings for him now. All things considered, it was probably best to send a note. A carefully worded e-mail that would express her gratitude for his thoughtful gesture yet leave no room for him to interpret that she had second thoughts about their divorce.

She didn't . . . did she? Liza sighed. She had acted pretty cool about the roses, but the gesture had gotten to her more than she wanted to admit. Maybe there *was* still unfinished business between her and Jeff.

Well, if there is, she told herself, *I'm going to finish it.* She thought for a moment, then typed out a quick e-mail:

Jeff,

Just wanted you to know I received the roses. It was thoughtful of you but very unnecessary. Peter is here, and everything is going well with selling the inn.
I know you mean well, but I'd appreciate it if you would stop calling and sending e-mails. I don't feel we have much to talk about, unless you have some issue with our divorce agreement. If so, please let my attorney know.
I'm sure we can work things out and move on with our lives.
That is my sincere hope. Take care of yourself. I wish you happiness.

Fondly,
Liza

Feeling satisfied with her message, Liza sent it off.

She turned off her laptop, climbed into bed, and shut off the light. It had been a long day, and she was very tired. By this time tomorrow, they might have an offer, and this entire ordeal might be over, she reminded herself. For better or for worse.

Chapter Eight

SUNDAY was a day of rest for most people, but not at the Angel Inn, Liza reminded herself. It was sunny and mild, and Peter and Will, who had run down to the beach to shoot some early morning photos, looked as if they wouldn't have minded hanging out at the beach until sunset. Liza quickly dished out the day's jobs along with the scrambled eggs and toast she had cooked for their breakfast.

"I've got a good one for you today, Peter. Take down the wallpaper in the bathroom on the second floor, the one next to your bedroom."

"Take it down? It's falling down."

"See, I gave you the easy job. It's half done already." Liza gave her brother an encouraging smile. "There's some solution to melt the glue somewhere. I found it in the basement with the painting supplies. You just rub it on, and the rest of the paper will peel right off. Then the walls need to be scraped and painted. Including the ceiling . . . mold spots," she snuck in quickly.

"Those need to be washed with bleach."

Liza was surprised. "So you do know what to do."

He shrugged. "Close enough."

She never thought of her brother as the handy type, but he did own a house and was economical. He must have learned a few home-repair tricks over the years.

"I'll start on the half bath down here," Liza told him. "It shouldn't take long. Claire found a pair of perfectly good curtains for the windows. She even ran them through the washer."

Peter glanced at Will, who had said hardly a word during breakfast. Liza could hear the hum of his iPod from across the table. The music volume and ear buds seemed to eliminate any possibility of conversation. Peter leaned over and gently tugged one from his ear.

Will looked startled. "Hey, what are you doing? You're going to ruin my earphones."

"You're going to ruin your ears. That music is way too loud, Will. Turn it down or I'm taking that thing away."

Will scowled but adjusted the volume. "Anything else?"

"Yeah. What about helping me paint the bath-room today?" Peter said.

"What about it?" Will echoed.

Liza saw Peter reach deeper for some patience. "I'd like you to help me. We were just talking about it, but I guess you missed the conversation."

"I heard you," Will cut in. "Take down the wallpaper. Mold spots on the ceiling."

"Sounds like a band," Liza said, trying to make a joke.

"Mold Spots on the Ceiling?" Will gave her a blank look. "Right," he said kindly.

She couldn't be faulted for trying. She did think that he secretly wanted to laugh but wouldn't give her the satisfaction. He hadn't argued about helping today, she realized. Maybe things were easing a bit between him and Peter. She hoped so. That would be one good thing coming out of this ordeal.

A short time later, the three-person crew was busy at work on their projects. Liza had found some perfectly good paint, robin's-egg blue, down in the basement and decided to use it. She had begun to play a game with herself, a challenge to be resourceful and use up what was in the house.

By the time Fran came by late that afternoon with a fresh set of "lookers," both Liza and Peter were too engrossed in their bathroom projects to be any bother. The real estate agent seemed very pleased with the progress.

"Kitchens and bathrooms make a big impression," she told Liza privately. "Even if they plan to renovate, they want the rooms to look fresh until they get around to their own repairs."

"I'm sure that's true," Liza replied. Unfortunately, there were two more bathrooms besides the two they were working on today, and one of them had a Grand Canyon–sized crack down the middle of the ceiling.

Maybe she could get Daniel's advice on that repair? It was definitely out of her league. He might help her fix it. Though the thought of working with him and a tub of spackle in such close quarters made her quickly nix the idea. It would definitely redefine the term *sticky situation*. She didn't need to complicate her short stay here even more, did she?

The truth was, though, that Daniel was the very nicest of all the complications so far. She did miss seeing him today, which was a secret she wouldn't have admitted to anyone.

Claire North didn't work on Sundays, and Liza definitely missed her, too. Even more than Daniel in some ways, she realized. Claire's presence balanced out the male energies in the house. But it was more than that. Claire was like the tiller on a sailboat, Liza decided. A solid, steadying force who helped Liza keep things on the right track. She was a good sounding board, even about small, silly questions—Which china cups should she keep or give away? What color should she paint the bathroom molding: stark white or cream?

Liza certainly didn't begrudge Claire her day off. She and Peter both knew they were lucky to have the housekeeper's indefatigable help these final weeks. It couldn't be easy for her, taking this place apart, Liza reflected. But she seemed so accepting, even cheerful at her work.

Liza wondered what Claire was up to today in her cottage on the other side of the island. She tried to picture the place. It wasn't like Daisy Winkler's ornate Victorian confection, she decided. It would be an old structure but far simpler. Did Claire entertain? Go out to visit friends? Or remain home alone for the day? Although she seemed completely at ease in her own company, everyone around here seemed to know Claire and think very highly of her. She probably had lots of friends.

Liza knew that Claire attended the church on the green in Cape Light, Reverend Ben Lewis's church. So she had probably gone there this morning. Liza recalled the church, the cool, dark interior and soft amber light from the stained-glass windows, the gentle music and quiet prayers. She pictured Claire sitting there, calmly taking in the sermon and service, and suddenly pictured herself there, too. Trying to absorb some of that soul-deep serenity. Perhaps church was the source of Claire's infallible inner calm.

But it doesn't work like that, Liza reminded herself. Going to church wasn't like soaking in a tub of warm water, easing out your spiritual aches and pains. You had to have faith. You had to believe in . . . in something to get the benefit. Didn't you? What was it that Reverend Ben had said about her aunt Elizabeth? That she was a woman of faith.

Distracted by her thoughts, Liza painted over the edge of the masking tape. "Oh . . . drat!" She quickly wiped the smear and stood back.

She had done enough for today, she decided. She was getting tired and messing up her work. It was time to make dinner anyway.

By the time Liza called Peter and Will to the dinner table, they both looked as if they might droop right into the dishes of pasta she had prepared. She had found a bottle of tomato sauce in the pantry, pepped it up with some sautéed mushrooms, and made a simple meal with bread and salad.

"This is pretty good," Peter said between mouthfuls. "But you have to admit, Claire's cooking is awesome."

"No argument there," Liza agreed. Claire was not a sophisticated cook, using the latest "hip" ingredients. Her dishes were comfort food, and yet too subtle and intricate to be called that either. Just like the woman herself, her cooking more or less defied definition.

"That may have been one of the reasons Aunt Elizabeth had so many return customers," Liza added. "It certainly wasn't the decor these last few years."

"Speaking of return customers, what did Fran say about the couple who came today?" Peter asked. "Any interest?"

"She called while I was cooking. They liked the place but are worried about energy costs," Liza reported. "Daniel already told me the building needs new windows and insulation. I guess that scared them off."

"Aunt Elizabeth managed. She would close off the third floor in the winter. Didn't Fran tell them that?"

"I'm not sure, but I don't think it would have made much difference. If people don't want the place, they don't want it."

Peter frowned at her a moment. "How about that couple who came yesterday while we were biking? The Hardys? Weren't they due back today?"

"They're coming back next week. They want to bring a friend, an architect."

"An architect?" His glum expression brightened. "That's a good sign. Why didn't you tell me that before?"

"Oh . . . I don't know." She shrugged and looked down at her plate. "An architect might say the place is falling down and not to bother."

"Always the positive view, Liza," he said sarcastically.

"I'm just being realistic," she defended herself. She didn't mean to raise her voice but realized too late that she had.

"I know that's what you think you're doing. But sometimes I wonder if you really want to sell this place," Peter retorted, his voice equally loud. "I'm starting to think that deep down inside, you don't want anyone to buy it. I'm afraid that if someone actually makes an offer, you'll point out reasons why they shouldn't."

Did she really sound like that? Liza rubbed the back of her neck, which was stiff from painting the bathroom ceiling. Peter's words had hit a nerve.

"Well, I guess I do have mixed feelings," she admitted. "The longer I stay here, the more I remember. Don't you?"

"Of course, I have memories, Liza. That's part of the territory. We both knew this wouldn't be easy." He wasn't exactly shouting, but his tone was hard, drawing a line.

It made Liza angry that he couldn't just step back a minute and look at the situation from another perspective.

"Of course, I knew it wouldn't be easy. But I didn't realize it would be so hard. You can't honestly tell me this isn't hard for you, can you?"

His expression darkened. "Are you getting cold feet on me? Is that it?"

Liza took a breath, then shook her head. "No . . . it's not that at all. I know we have to sell it. That's what we agreed."

And her melancholy feelings were irrelevant, she added silently.

"Maybe I wouldn't buy it myself because it's so run-down," she said finally. "So that's where I'm coming from."

"Maybe," Peter said quietly. "I'm just tired tonight. I'm sorry I yelled at you."

"I'm sorry I lost it, too. It's okay." Liza picked up some dirty dishes and patted her brother's shoulder as she passed him on her way to the sink.

Neither of them spoke for a while. Then she said, "There is one way you can make it up to me."

He turned and looked at her. "What?"

"I noticed that pack of Wing Dings the Doyles gave you just sitting in the refrigerator . . . and there's nothing around for dessert."

Peter laughed and shook his head. "Okay, I know when I'm beat. We'll share it. You deserve it for putting up with me."

Liza smiled in answer. She loved her brother, but she did deserve half of those Wing Dings. She knew it. And so did he.

ON Monday morning the inn was a beehive of activity. Peter, Will, and Liza continued their work on the bathrooms. Liza should have known they wouldn't whip through the rooms in one day. It would take more like two or three. Painting always took longer than you expected. But the results were so obvious and transforming, it was satisfying work.

As opposed to cleaning out closets or even sorting china. She had left those chores to Claire today, who carried on without Liza in her typical orderly way.

Daniel had arrived early with several assistants and another large contraption that sprayed paint onto the outside of the house. He had told her they would have to apply a coat of primer before the house paint went on, and that she and Peter needed to choose the colors.

"White with black shutters. Simple and saleable," Peter said at once. "Who could object to it?"

"I do," Liza argued. "It's so . . . boring."

Some old houses looked very good with that classic combination. But the inn had a whimsical spirit. You couldn't just smother the place with white paint and black shutters.

It would just seem so wrong.

After some discussion—and Peter realizing there was no extra charge for a real color—Liza won out with her choice, a soft, warm cream for the house, the same color the inn had been when they were growing up. She quickly ran to show Daniel the shade she had chosen on the paint sample wheel before Peter changed his mind.

"Good choice," Daniel noted. "That's just what I would have picked. We're on the same wavelength."

"About paint colors at least," she said quietly, without looking at him.

He smiled. "What about the shutters?"

"I'm not sure. Any ideas?"

"I have a few . . . but I don't want to rush you."

She met his playful glance, and a spark raced through her veins. Was she imagining this? These clever, double-edged exchanges?

Sometimes a paint chip is just a paint chip, Liza. You've just got a silly crush on him.

But something in Daniel's warm gaze belied that theory. There was definitely more than paint chips on his mind.

She smiled at him blandly and backed away, holding the color wheel. "I'll just take this with me and get back to you about the shutters."

"Take your time." Daniel smiled and nodded. He knew he had rattled her and seemed pleased about it.

She stalked off in a mild tizzy.

Yes, she was officially divorced. But it still seemed way too soon for this. Way too soon for someone like Daniel. She needed to start with someone far more boring and tame, she reasoned, as she retreated to the first-floor bathroom and set up her paint supplies. She needed to wade in the kiddy pool awhile. Daniel was the deep end. A leap off the high diving board in fact—and no life-guard on duty.

Liza decided her best course of action was to avoid him. She was working inside, and he was working out. It shouldn't be too hard, she kept telling herself, though it was tempting to peek out the window every time she heard him pass by.

Somewhere around lunchtime, she realized she needed to go out to the shed to find some sandpaper. There had to be a scrap or two on the workbench, she thought.

She heard the dull drone of the paint sprayer on the other side of the house and the men shouting instructions to one another. The coast was clear. *I'll just dash in and out of the shed without running into him,* Liza figured.

Wrong, she discovered too late. Daniel was in the yard, touching up the back wall of the house while his crew continued spraying the far side of the building. She nearly walked right into him before she realized it.

He turned and smiled at her. "Hey, how's it going? Doing some painting?"

"That's right." She nodded and lifted her chin. He seemed to find the idea of her painting amusing for some reason. "The half bath downstairs."

"Get any on the walls yet?" he asked in a serious tone.

"Very funny." She tried not to laugh, but she had practically coated herself with blue paint, shaking a can with a loose lid. "The lid on one of the cans wasn't closed properly. I'm actually a very neat painter," she defended herself. "I use lots of tape, and I hate a drippy job."

"I'm impressed. Maybe you can work for me sometime."

"Maybe," she replied, playing along with him. "Are you a good boss? Or do you shout a lot?"

He laughed. "Hey, aren't I supposed to be the one asking the questions?"

"I never said I was interested in the job," she clarified. "I'm just curious."

He smiled and held her gaze. "Good. Cause I'm curious about you, too."

Liza felt her stomach drop and suddenly looked away.

She had no idea what to say next and no idea what had gotten into her today. It had to be paint fumes making her light-headed. Staring off the end of the high diving board again . . .

Liza heard the BlackBerry in her sweatshirt pocket buzz, alerting her that a message had come in. She quickly reached for it. Daniel gave her a disapproving look, and for a moment she thought he might try to grab it away from her again. She quickly stepped out of his reach, just in case.

"I have to take a look at this. It's my office . . . excuse me," she said to Daniel.

"See you later."

"See you," she replied, her gaze lingering on him as he turned to join his crew.

Liza clicked open the e-mail. It was from her boss, Eve. She read it quickly, not liking what she saw.

Liza—

Harry Berlinger is being a total pain about those print ads, and now he's complaining about everything under the sun. I've told Charlie to hold his hand until you get back. We have to keep Harry happy. We can't afford to lose the account. I'm out of the office today at meetings. Talk to you soon.

—Eve

Great. Now Eve had just handed Charlie one of Liza's juiciest plums on a silver platter. What if Harry Berlinger no longer wanted Liza to handle his account by the time she came back? Then what?

Liza was fuming. She went back inside and started to paint again, but her hand was shaking, making a zigzag line. She tossed the roller down, sloshing it in the tray.

Should she call? No, not now. She was too upset. Eve was out of the office all day anyway. She wouldn't even reach her. Besides, what could she say? She could hardly tell Eve to yank Charlie from the account. Keeping clients happy was the priority, and she had to be a team player about this.

And what about the promotion now? Liza had thought she had it in the bag. Was Eve having second thoughts? If her boss was feeling even the slightest doubt, Liza was sure Charlie would fan that spark into a three-alarm blaze in no time.

And here she was, stuck on this island, unable to protect her own turf or defend herself.

Get a grip, Liza, she coached herself. *You're starting to get all crazy and paranoid. It's probably just as Eve said. Harry Berlinger is throwing temper tantrums, and you don't even have a fax machine out here. You'll just have to wait and see how this all plays out.*

Liza e-mailed a quick note back, saying she understood and that she would check in with Charlie to make sure things were going smoothly.

"I do have a few concerns however. Please give me a call when you get a chance," she added at the bottom of the note.

Liza thought it was better to be up front about her fears, even if they sounded silly. What was that old saying? "Just because you're paranoid, it doesn't mean they aren't out to get you." Maybe Eve trusted Charlie, but Liza knew better by now.

With that plan settled, Liza returned to her painting project. Painting might be messy, but it seemed gloriously simple and undemanding, especially when compared with the grueling emotional roller coaster of office politics.

I can always work for Daniel if the advertising career doesn't work out, she consoled herself.

At the moment, it didn't seem like such a bad alternative.

• • •

THE day passed quickly. Everyone reported in at dinner on their progress, tired but happy. Even Will seemed proud of his accomplishments. Peter had promoted him from a mere assistant to being in charge of his own job, the second-floor hallway.

"I didn't realize how dingy the hall looked until Will started with the fresh paint," Peter said, a touch of pride in his voice. "It really brightens up the space."

"It makes a huge difference," Liza agreed. She glanced at her nephew. "You're doing a great job, Will. I thought we'd have to skip that area; the hall is so long."

"He's got the energy, and he's stronger than he looks." Peter smiled at his son. "I didn't realize I'd be bringing so much extra man power."

Will looked embarrassed by their praise. "No big deal. I'm just hanging out. What else am I going to do?"

Stay up in your room with the door locked? Like you did the first few days? Liza replied silently.

But of course, she didn't say that. That phase seemed over with, thank goodness. And thank goodness Peter was starting to take a new tack and treat Will more like an adult. It was good for him to let go a little and see what Will could do on his own without grown-ups hovering over him.

Will did go up to his room right after dinner. Not pouting, though, as he sometimes did, but just because he was tired. Peter and Liza brought some coffee into the front parlor. Liza sat on the chintz love seat and worked on her to-do list.

Peter strolled over to the oak table that had become his work space. The photo albums were piled on one side, and he began rearranging several old shoe boxes he had labeled with white index cards.

"How are we doing?" Peter asked, glancing over her shoulder.

"Hard to say. Seems every time I cross one thing off, I have to add two more."

"There's something wrong with that system," he said. He walked over to the table, then handed her a book that looked much like the others, with a cracked binding and a dusty black leather cover. "Look what I found. One of your old sketchbooks . . . and look what was with it."

Liza's breath caught as she took the book from him, then a slim wooden box with a hinged lid. She looked over the box first. Her initials were carved on top, E.G.M.—Elizabeth Grace Martin. She traced them with a fingertip. She had been named after her aunt, her mother's sister, but everyone had always called her Liza while she was growing up. She rarely used her full name, except on legal documents.

"Uncle Clive made this for me, remember?"

Peter sat down at the table and nodded. "I remember. It was your birthday."

"That's right." She opened the top of the box, wondering if there was anything still inside. Soft drawing pencils and pieces of charcoal sat there, patiently waiting for her. She fingered them gently. They looked old and crumbly but were usable. When was the last time she had taken them out?

She opened the book next and found some of her old sketches. She glanced at Peter, feeling slightly self-conscious, as if looking through the sketch-book were a private act of some kind. But he seemed to be concentrating on the photos, not even aware of her in the room right now.

She turned the pages slowly, examining each drawing. A star-burst lily cut from the garden and tilted in a cup. Aunt Elizabeth's old gray cat, Cleopatra, sunning herself in the tall grass. A sketch of Liza's own hand and also her foot. Uncle Clive reading the newspaper. Aunt Elizabeth sitting on the back-porch steps, shelling peas.

Several more. The last few rough and unfinished.

Then the book went blank.

The same way her art career had trickled off and ended.

Liza sat back, holding the book in her lap. It was hard to look at sketches like these, made at a time in her life when she was young and hopeful, fully believing that if she worked hard, her talent would prevail and she would succeed.

As if hard work and a little talent were all it took. But, of course, it was much harder than that, and most who tried would never make it.

Jeff had always known that. Aunt Elizabeth had liked Jeff well enough, but Liza knew that her aunt didn't believe Jeff was a good match for her beloved niece.

Maybe she sensed that he wouldn't value or encourage Liza's career as an artist. That he would influence her to follow a different path, a safer, more conservative lifestyle. Was that how it had gone?

Looking back, Liza wasn't even sure now. She believed she had made those choices totally on her own. Jeff had been proud of her success and recognition, but he had never pressured her to accept promotions and move up the corporate ladder.

A ladder that looked more like a food chain in a jungle full of carnivores right now, Liza thought.

What was the use of even thinking about any of this anymore? Mulling this stuff over made no difference now. But wouldn't it be great to get up every day and know that all you had to do was draw or paint to make a living? Not face difficult clients, cutthroat colleagues, and a demanding boss all the time? What a fantasy . . .

It was too late now to go back and change anything in this picture. She had made her choices, and she was stuck with them.

Peter glanced up at her, then down at the sketch-book. "So, what do you think now?"

"Oh, they're dreadful. Hard to look at right after dinner," she said, trying to make a joke.

"Come on, Liza. They're not bad at all. They're very good, in fact."

"You've already looked at them?" Her voice rose in outrage.

He nodded. "I couldn't help it. I found the sketchbook, and before I knew it, I was flipping through the pages. I'd forgotten how good you were."

"I was . . . okay." Her brother was just being kind. But she was more realistic. "A marginal amount of talent. Certainly not enough to do more than grunt work at a drawing board in an art department somewhere."

"I think you're wrong," Peter said. "I bet if you picked up a pencil again, it would all come back to you. All that and more."

"Or all that and even less," Liza replied.

The truth was, the pad and box of pencils had given her the notion to try her hand again. But she was afraid of what she would see. To find that she had lost her eye and touch entirely would be very depressing.

"What difference does it make?" she asked. "The memories are sweet, I guess, but they also

218

make me sad. They make me remember that I was fooling myself to think I would ever make it as an artist."

"That's too bad." Her brother cast her a sympathetic look. "The thing is, it's not entirely about talent, Liza. It's more about persistence and even faith," he said quietly. "Faith in yourself. And how you define success, of course. I always thought Aunt Elizabeth was a great success because she hung in there and did her artwork and didn't give a darn what anyone thought of her work, good or bad."

Faith. There was that word again. Aunt Elizabeth had faith in herself. Liza couldn't argue with that. But how many people could be as sure of themselves as Aunt Elizabeth?

As for Peter—even if he was having financial problems, he never seemed to question his own gifts as an artist. From the first time he had held a camera, he had known he was meant to be a photographer.

She, on the other hand, had lost her faith in her talent. She had gotten distracted by a life path with a faster, more certain payout.

"Well," Liza said, "I think I'm going to turn in." She didn't want to take this conversation any further. "Are you going to stay up, sorting photos?"

"You did put me in charge of the photo archive," he reminded her.

"Right, but your duties as a bathroom painter

and head wallpaper remover do come first," she joked.

"I won't stay up too late, don't worry," he replied.

They said good night, and Liza headed to her room. What she told her brother had been honest. Looking at the sketches had stirred up something, regrets for the road not taken. But there was nothing to be done about it now. She had to focus on the road she had taken, her job at the agency.

Before she went to bed, she checked her messages for some further word from Eve, but there was none. There were also no e-mails or phone calls from Jeff. Had he finally gotten her message about letting go?

Liza felt a little stunned. She knew that would be a good thing, but if he was finally, really giving up, it was a kind of loss, too.

ON Tuesday the painting inside continued. Liza finished with the powder room and sized up another small bathroom on the third floor. The ceiling was slanted on the eave of the roof, and she needed a taller ladder and extension for her roller to get to it.

She considered taking a ride to the General Store or even to the village of Cape Light. Then she wondered if Daniel could lend her the equipment. He probably had everything she needed right in his truck.

All that and more, she taunted herself.

I know your tricks, Liza. You're just looking for some excuse to talk to him.

Well, that might be true. She hadn't seen him again yesterday after he had admitted he was curious about her.

And that was probably a good thing, Liza told herself. She didn't want to think about him too much, but that tiny admission had stuck in her mind. Along with a vision of his exceptional smile.

She quickly checked her appearance in the bathroom mirror: her long hair pulled back in a ponytail and covered by a Boston Red Sox baseball cap, her face bare of makeup, and dark shadows under her eyes from working hard and worrying.

Great. He'll think some sort of ghoul has come down from that attic.

Then she got annoyed at herself for even thinking about it. *I need a ladder, not a date,* she reminded herself. *Let him think whatever he likes. This thing between us is just plain . . . silly.*

Liza stomped down the stairs and was heading for the backyard when she heard voices in the second-floor bathroom. Peter and Daniel discussing some repair.

Liza poked her head in. The two men practically filled the space. "Hey," she said, not attempting to enter the room. If she did, she would feel like an extra sardine in a can.

"Daniel was just telling me how to seal the moldy spots with some spray," Peter explained. "He even gave me the right stuff."

Daniel had the right stuff. No doubt about that.

"Terrific . . . now I have a question for you," she told Daniel.

"Yes?" he asked with that curious, amused tone.

She tried to ignore the way he was looking at her—obviously happy to see her, as if he even liked the way she looked in her painting outfit.

"Can I borrow a ladder? The one I have isn't tall enough, and I also need an extension for the paint roller," she added.

"No problem. I thought you were going to ask me how to patch the crack in the ceiling up there."

"That was my next question, actually. How did you guess? You're going to have to charge a consulting fee."

"I'll keep that in mind," he said amiably. "Let me go down to the truck and get the ladder. I'll bring it up to you."

"That's all right, I'll carry it up." He had his own work to do. She didn't need him to wait on her.

She followed him down to the first floor, then they headed toward the back door in the kitchen. Claire stood by the stove, chopping an onion on a wooden board. She was putting up something for dinner in the slow cooker.

"Hello, Claire," Daniel greeted her. "What's for dinner tonight?"

"Short ribs," Claire answered. "Your favorite. Would you like a dish to take home? There'll be plenty."

"Thanks but . . . that's okay. Maybe next time."

How did Claire know his favorite dinner? He must have been invited by Aunt Elizabeth to join them from time to time. Aunt Elizabeth was a generous person and made friends easily. Liza could see how she would have enjoyed Daniel's easy company and his clever conversation.

Should she invite him to stay tonight for the short ribs? she wondered. Or was that crossing a line, sending some signal she wasn't yet ready to send?

He glanced at her, and she wondered if he was thinking the same thing—expecting her to pick up on this hint and extend an invitation.

Before she could figure out what to do, Claire's voice caught her attention. "I finally finished sorting the china," she said. "It's all in the dining room on the table and in boxes against the wall. I've put labels on everything, as you asked me to."

"Thanks, Claire. I'll take a look in a few minutes."

"What would you like me to start on next?" Claire asked.

"I'm not sure," Liza said honestly. "I'll check the list. But I need to run outside with Daniel for a minute. I'll be right back."

"No hurry." Claire looked at Liza and then at Daniel with a little smile that made Liza feel self-conscious. Then Claire turned back to the sauce she was making. "No hurry," she said again. "Some fresh air will do you good."

Liza ignored her, but she still felt . . . silly. Exactly like she did in sixth grade when a friend told the whole class that Liza had a crush on the most popular boy in the school.

Daniel could have been that boy, she thought, glancing at him. He would have certainly caught the eye of the girls in middle school.

Daniel politely pulled the door open for her. Liza was forced to endure another knowing glance from Claire as she brushed past him and stepped outside.

They walked over to his truck parked back near the shed. Bright green weeds were sprouting through the pebbles on the drive, Liza noticed. Another sign of spring and another job for the list. One for the new owner, she decided.

Daniel opened the gate on the truck and reached inside, moving things around.

"So, short ribs are your favorite dinner," she said, just to make some conversation.

"Yes, ma'am. One of my favorites. But only the way Claire makes them."

"Claire's such an amazing cook, everything she makes tastes the best," she agreed. "Did you come for dinner often when my aunt was alive?"

She wasn't sure that was a polite or appropriate question. But once again, she was curious.

"Fairly often. Your aunt was a great lady, and I enjoyed her company. I considered her a good friend."

Liza was silent for a moment. Daniel jumped down from the truck and faced her.

"She was a great lady," Liza agreed. "I miss her."

"I miss her, too." He looked down and met her gaze. "I'm sorry for your loss, Liza. I don't think I ever got to tell you that."

"Thanks for telling me now," she said quietly.

He nodded but didn't say more. He lightly touched her shoulder, and Liza looked up at him. But before she could say anything, her BlackBerry went off.

He smiled briefly at her, his hand dropping away.

She turned and fished in her back pocket for the phone, then checked the message. It was a call from Eve. Liza nearly groaned out loud.

"Sorry, I've got to take this," she told him. She stepped away while Daniel turned his attention back to the ladder, wrestling it out of the truck bed.

Liza took a breath and answered the call.

"Hello, Liza. I'm glad I was able to reach you," Eve said. "Hope I'm not interrupting anything?"

"Not at all. I've been wanting to speak with you," Liza said honestly.

225

"Good. I'd like to talk with you, too. Oh . . . can you hold on a minute, I just want to shut the door."

She was shutting the door? This was serious.

Daniel caught her eye. He had the ladder out and the roller extension. "I'll bring this inside for you," he soundlessly mouthed the words.

Liza nodded at him in a distracted way, her attention totally focused on the call. She couldn't tell yet from the tone of Eve's voice if the message was going to be good news or bad.

"So, Liza . . . your e-mail said you have some concerns about Charlie babysitting Berlinger. I think I can guess what they might be. You're afraid he'll steal the account from you?"

"Yes, to be perfectly honest, that's it exactly." Maybe Eve wasn't blind to Charlie's underhanded ways after all.

"I suppose that's possible," Eve conceded. "But you know, Liza, that wouldn't be the end of the world. It might not even matter that much who handles Berlinger in the big picture."

Liza didn't like that answer. And she didn't entirely understand what Eve was driving at. "In the big picture? You mean in regard to the agency as a whole?"

"That's right," Eve said quickly. "I'd like you to think of the big picture more often, Liza. There are going to be changes around here. Some big changes, very soon."

Sure that Eve was talking about the promotion

now, Liza's pulse quickened. So they had made a decision. Or were about to.

"It's hard for me to say this, Liza, but . . . I'll just be honest with you. You need to be less possessive about your accounts, less territorial. And you need to work out a better relationship with Charlie. You two will be working together more closely than ever. I know he came in as your assistant, but you need to turn that page," Eve warned her. "He's come a long way, and the new department structure won't work out if you can't recognize and respect his worth."

Liza's heart was beating wildly. Crucial that she get along with Charlie? What did this all mean?

"This is about the promotion, right?" Liza managed to ask.

Eve didn't answer right away, and Liza was sure her boss could hear her heart thudding through the phone line. "I'm not really at liberty to say. I'm sorry, Liza. I just want to give you a heads up. Things are going to change, and I hope you'll consider my advice. We'll talk when you get back. Listen, I've got a meeting. I have to run now."

"Okay. Thanks, Eve," Liza said, though she had no idea what she was thanking her for. She said good-bye and realized Eve had already hung up.

Liza felt stunned. Had Eve just told her, in a very cryptic way, that she was *not* getting the promotion? That it was going to Charlie, so she'd better be nicer to him? Was that what all the double-talk really meant?

Liza felt dizzy. Her head was spinning, and she thought she might faint. She felt like screaming but covered her face in her hands instead. She sat down hard on a chaise lounge, tears squeezing out of the corners of her eyes.

How could this have happened? It was a nightmare.

After all her hard work and dedication, she felt betrayed and exploited. So humiliated. It was exactly the way she felt the night she discovered Jeff's affair.

What an irony that her focus on her job may have even cost her that marriage. She definitely pushed aside Jeff's wish to start a family so she could advance in her career. And where had that gotten her? No baby, no marriage, and now, no promotion.

Why was life so unfair? Why was everything so hard? She didn't deserve this. She really didn't.

Chapter Nine

LIZA heard the back door slam and saw Peter marching toward her. "Liza, have you seen that wide scraper with the red handle? I need it for the . . ." His voice trailed off as he took in her expression. "Liza, what's the matter? What's happened?"

She looked up and shook her head. It was very hard to say it out loud.

"You don't look so good," he said gently. "Do you want to talk?"

"I'm all right," she said, but she knew she had to tell him. "I just spoke to my boss. That promotion I was going for? Sounds like they're giving it to someone else."

"No, that's impossible. You deserved that promotion. You work night and day for that company. They can't do this to you," Peter railed, sounding every inch the protective big brother. "And to tell you over the phone? That stinks."

"My boss didn't actually say it point-blank. When I asked her, she just said she would talk to me about it when I got back to the office. But I definitely think that's what she was trying to tell me. She was trying to prepare me for the bad news."

Peter gave her a thoughtful look. "Maybe it's not as bad as you think. Maybe you misunderstood?"

Liza met his gaze and sighed. "Maybe. But I don't think so."

Peter sat down next to her. "What if you went back to the office and claimed your territory? Boston's only a two-hour drive. You could go today. Meet with your boss and make her reconsider?"

Liza had thought of that and had finally rejected

229

the idea. "It's not just Eve's decision. And I don't think they'll change their minds and give it to me just because I stomped my feet and demanded it. Besides, Eve said she couldn't talk about it with me yet. Maybe the decision isn't final," she added, though she honestly felt that there was slim hope left.

Peter leaned over and put his arm around her shoulder. "I know this must really hurt. I wish there was something I could do for you."

Liza forced a small smile. "Thanks, pal. Just listening to me moan and groan helps. A little anyway."

"Why don't you take the rest of the day off? The painting can wait. You can take a ride somewhere, go into Cape Light or Newburyport? Get some distraction. Do you want me to come with you?"

Liza considered the offer. Both of those towns were perfect for an afternoon of walking around and browsing. But it would take more than window-shopping to cheer her up today. She felt so angry she was about to burst at the seams.

"I think I'll feel better if I just stay here and paint some more," she told him. "It will help keep my mind off it."

"All right. Whatever you say. If you change your mind and decide you want to go back to Boston and fight, you just go. I can take care of this place."

"I know you can, Peter. Thanks." She wiped her eyes with the back of her hand and stood up. "I just need a minute or two. I'll be in soon," she promised him.

"All right." Peter gave her a last look, then left her to get herself together.

Liza turned away from the house and looked at the shed and the garden and the property beyond.

The sun was high in the sky and felt strong today, warming the damp earth and calling forth the scents and sights of spring. Green shoots were pushing up from the soft ground, and the buds on the trees were swelling, about to burst into flower.

How could this be happening? Didn't the entire world realize she was sad and devastated?

Spring obviously didn't care. It was coming anyway. The seasons moved on, each day leading to the next. It was a comfort in one way and, in another way, offered her a humbling measure of perspective.

Liza worked diligently for the rest of the day, struggling to get her mind around the devastating news.

She wasn't sure if Peter had told anyone about her disappointment, but the rest of the house seemed to sense she was unhappy about something and stayed out of her way.

She didn't even come down for the special short ribs dinner that evening. Instead, she soaked in a hot bath, and once the coast was clear, she snuck down for a bowl of cold cereal that she ate in her room.

As tired as she was, Liza felt too riled up to fall asleep.

She lay in the dark, her eyes wide open, playing out scenarios in her mind. She would return to the office, confront Charlie Reiger, face down Eve Barkin, and give them both a piece of her mind.

But what good would any of that actually do? Unless she was willing to quit her job and walk out on all of them.

That would be satisfying, she thought. For a few minutes anyway.

But it was a terrible career move. It would be hard enough to find a new job in this economy without being branded as a nutcase or a hysteric. The story would hit the grapevine quickly, sealing her fate.

What will I do without that job? she wondered. *It's my entire life—even though I'm not sure I like it anymore. How pathetic is that?*

Well, I could always come back here and run the inn. Now there's a pleasant fantasy. She smiled to herself, amused at her own wild ideas.

It was a crazy notion. Crazy and impossible.

Too bad I'm so logical, Liza thought with a sigh. *People like me never have any fun.*

LIZA was the last one to come downstairs the next morning. Claire greeted her warmly. "Did you have a good rest?" she asked, as Liza poured herself a mug of coffee.

"Not bad, all things considered." She didn't feel as angry anymore at her situation, just deflated and sad.

Liza hadn't talked to Claire about her work situation, but Liza was sure the housekeeper had heard something from Peter. She seemed to be sending Liza silent waves of comfort, her sympathetic smile speaking volumes.

"A good night's sleep is a wonderful thing," Claire noted. "It heals your spirit and puts things in perspective, don't you think?"

Liza had to smile. "Yes, it does. A little, anyway."

"It's a beautiful day," Claire went on. "The weatherman said it was going to rain but no sign of it yet."

"Let's hope the clouds wait until tonight. I'd hate for Daniel to miss a day of work."

"Oh, he's out there," Claire assured her. "He was down a few men on his crew for some reason. Daniel asked Will to help him. And Peter volunteered, too," she added with a sly smile.

Claire looked down, continuing to wash out the griddle. "Though I'm not sure if he really needs all that help . . . if you know what I mean."

"Poor Daniel," Liza said with a smile. She poured herself more coffee and swiped a slice of whole wheat toast from a plate on the table. "Guess I should check this out. Nobody's come back inside yet screaming, right?"

"So far, so good," Claire assured her quietly.

Liza went out the back door and soon spotted her brother. He carried a large paintbrush and a bucket of yellow paint. "Hey, kid. How are you doing?" Peter greeted her.

"Hanging in. What's going on out here?"

"Daniel is short a helper or two today, and he asked Will if he wanted to step in." Liza detected a distinct note of pride in Peter's tone. "I might help myself. The outside is the priority, don't you think? The faster Daniel finishes, the better for us."

"Fran did say something like that," Liza agreed. Which reminded her—with all her own troubles, she had lost track of the real estate agent. She had to call Fran this morning and see when she was bringing the Hardys back.

"Maybe we should all work outside today," Peter said, sounding enthusiastic. "It would be great to have the front of the inn done before the Hardys come back. It could make all the difference. Curb appeal and all that?"

Peter had been reading too many "sell it yourself" articles on the Internet, Liza thought. Then again, working with Daniel for the day wouldn't exactly be a hardship.

"Sure," she told her brother. "I'll help paint the outside."

Maybe she was just volunteering so that she would have a good distraction from her worries, she realized. And maybe that wasn't the worst thing either.

. . .

A short time later, Liza stood on the porch, carefully applying cream-colored paint to the columns and railing. Daniel had not been delighted to hear that a band of amateurs insisted on painting with him, but they were his customers and, for various reasons, he was down several of the men on his regular crew today.

Since he knew they needed the job done as quickly as possible, he didn't refuse their help.

Liza liked working outside. It had gotten claustrophobic in the tiny bathroom yesterday, and she had dreaded facing that project again. But outside, with a blue sky above, the sun shining brightly, and a light breeze blowing, it was hard to be unhappy. All she had to do was glance out at the ocean, and the blue waters immediately washed away any negative thoughts.

"So, you've ended up working for me after all. Never say never." Daniel walked up behind her, the sound of his voice so close, she jumped up and hit her paintbrush on his knee.

"Sorry," she said. She looked up and smiled. "I should have expected that."

"Yeah, you should have. It will wash out, right?"

"Someday," he said lightly. He grabbed another brush and dipped it into the paint tray she was using, then started to paint the railing on the other side of the steps. Was he going to partner up with her on the porch? Liza wasn't sure she liked that idea. It made her too nervous. She was sure she would end up hitting him with the brush again. Or worse.

"We've been lucky with the weather," he said, seeming unmindful of her discomfort. "It usually rains a lot around here this time of year. That would have really slowed us down."

"It has been great weather," she agreed. Thinking back, the only rain she had seen out here had been the night she arrived.

She glanced over at him. It was funny how just talking about the weather seemed so . . . significant. She felt as if she were in high school or something, talking to a boy she had a crush on and not knowing what to say.

"So . . . are you a big Sox fan, or do you just like the hats and T-shirts?"

"A fan . . . and I wear the hats and T-shirts to prove it."

He laughed. "Think they're going to make it to the Series this year?"

"Of course I do. They have a great chance." She turned and looked at him. "I'm counting the days until the opening at Fenway. Then it's really spring."

Daniel laughed. "Wow, you are a fan."

Liza didn't say anything. She turned around and got back to the painting. Lots of men thought it was funny to meet a woman who liked baseball as much as she did. Amusing . . . or just plain odd.

She couldn't help it. She also liked opera. That was just who she was.

They continued working without talking. Liza didn't mind at all. It was an easy kind of silence between them, not tense or strained. She liked just being near him for some reason. It was exciting and somehow comfortable at the same time.

She was so focused on painting that she didn't hear the car coming up the drive until it had pulled all the way up to the house.

She looked up to see who it was and nearly dropped her brush. A silver Volvo convertible had arrived, and Jeff had jumped out of the driver's side.

"Liza, please don't be mad. I know you asked me not to come. But I can explain," he began, as he walked toward her.

Liza stood up and drew in a long breath. *What in the world?*

She glanced down at Daniel. He had stopped painting and was staring at her. "A friend of yours?" he asked quietly.

"Sort of," she murmured back. "My ex-husband."

He nodded and looked back at the porch rails. "I get it."

"Good. At least one of us does," she replied.

Jeff stood in front of her at the bottom of the steps. He stared up with an apologetic expression. "I'm sorry to bother you, Liza. But we really need to talk."

Talk? What did they have left to talk about? Liza walked down the steps to meet him. "Didn't you get my note about the roses?" she asked him quietly.

"I did." He reached out and touched her shoulder for a moment, then let his hand drop away. "That's when I realized that I needed to talk to you. Face-to-face."

Liza stared at him in disbelief. "I told you in no uncertain terms it was time for us both to let go and lead our own lives. What part of that message didn't you understand?"

"Liza—"

"No," she cut him off. "You shouldn't have come without calling first, Jeff."

"I know. But if I called and asked, I thought you would tell me not to come."

He was right about that. He smiled down at her and stuck his hands in the pockets of his leather jacket. He wore a fine-gauge-wool sweater over designer jeans. His light brown hair was freshly cut, and his blue eyes sparkled.

He was an attractive man, she noticed in some distant part of her brain, but she wasn't attracted to him anymore. Was she?

Why did he have to come back like this and get her all confused again?

"I'm sorry, Liza, but after I got that note, everything seemed so final. I realized our marriage was really over and—I just couldn't handle it."

238

"I felt a little shocked, too, when I finally got the decree in the mail," she said, trying to sound reasonable. "But we knew this was coming for a long time. It shouldn't be that much of a surprise."

"What can I say?" Jeff rubbed the back of his neck and gave her a wistful smile. "That very official letter was hard to handle, Liza. Then your note just blew me away."

Liza met his gaze and sighed. This was more than she had expected. Was he here to try to reconcile? Was there any chance at all of them getting back together? She would have said "no way" a few days ago. Now, though, it seemed as if she didn't have a clue about what was going to happen in her life anymore.

She noticed Daniel had left the porch and walked over to his truck. He seemed to be politely ignoring the little drama, but Liza was sure he could still hear every word.

Peter had also come around the side of the building with Will. They were both staring at Jeff as if he had descended from another planet.

"Can we go inside?" Jeff asked quietly. "I really have a lot to say to you."

He took a step closer and took hold of her hand. Liza felt herself freeze inside and pulled away.

"No, we can't go inside. We don't have anything to talk about, Jeff. I want you to go."

Jeff laughed nervously but was not put off. "Okay then, I'll tell you right here," he insisted.

"I'd rather talk about this privately . . . but what the heck. Let the whole world hear. I'm not ashamed of what I'm feeling."

Oh, no. This situation was getting worse by the second. Liza didn't know what to do. There seemed no way to stop him, and she knew if she took him into the house, it would be even harder to get rid of him. In spite of herself, she turned and caught Daniel's eye. *Well, I have this ex-husband who just won't let go. A slight problem in regard to starting any new relationships. But I'm working on it.*

Miraculously, Daniel seemed to understand and disappeared around the side of the house.

"All right," she said to Jeff. "Just tell me, please."

And then go, she added silently.

He smiled at her, cleared his throat, and stood up straight, shoulders back. "Here's the revelation that came to me, Liza. Yes, we're officially divorced and all that. But maybe that's what it took to make me see what you really mean to me. What our marriage means to me. I want you back, Liza. I made a big mistake, and I'm willing to do anything I have to do to make it up to you. I can see now that we shouldn't have given up so easily. If you'll just give me a chance, our relationship can be good again. We can get back together and finally start a family."

Liza blinked. Her eyes had filled with tears for some strange reason.

"Jeff . . . it's too late for all that . . ." Her voice sounded shaky, as though she were unsure of her words. Was she unsure? Had he got her thinking again about starting over?

"You don't have to answer me now, Liza. Give it a chance to sink in." He took her hand again, and this time, she didn't pull away. "The other night, when I read your note, I realized how much I still love you. I really do," he insisted. "I've made my mistakes. Nobody is perfect. If you'll just forgive me, it will be completely different this time, I promise . . . If we had a baby, it would all work out for us. It's the chance of a lifetime, Liza. I just don't want to miss it."

"Oh Jeff," she said sadly. "A child is not the answer." She was suddenly sure of that. "It never was," she told him. "Please, just go, will you? It was wrong of you to come here like this. I'm very . . . upset. Really."

"Liza, don't say that." He reached for her, and she pulled away.

Then she slipped past him and ran down the steps, tipping over the paint tray in the process.

Jeff tried to follow her. She heard his fast steps on the gravel. She turned and saw Peter step into Jeff's path and grab his arm, not roughly but firmly enough to stop him.

"Liza said she doesn't want to talk to you right now, Jeff. I think you should just respect her wishes and go."

Jeff glanced at his former brother-in-law but didn't struggle. He just stared at Liza, a pleading look in his eyes.

Liza saw a bike in the drive, leaning against a tree, and ran toward it. Will must have gone for a ride and left it there, lucky for her. She jumped on and started riding.

Jeff called after her, but she didn't turn around. She hoped he didn't try to follow her with his car. But she could go off the road onto a path and lose him easily while on the bike, she realized.

If only it were that easy to get him out of her life.

Liza rode fast but aimlessly. She climbed the hill on the main road and flew down the other side as if she were being pursued by a pack of hungry tigers. She passed through the island center and considered going into Daisy Winkler's tearoom, where she could hide away, read books, and sip mint tea all day. But that stop was too close to home. If Jeff pursued her, he would be sure to find her there.

She rode on and turned onto Ice House Road, the road that cut north to south on the island and ended up at the Angel Wing Cliffs.

Thick gray clouds had moved in, covering the sun, as if Jeff had brought the bad weather with him, she thought. There was a strong wind, too, that seemed to be blowing against her no matter which direction she rode. It made it much harder to pedal, especially uphill. Liza was glad she'd worn a heavy sweatshirt that morning for painting and that there was a fresh water bottle on the bike rack.

She thought she might ride up to the cliffs and sit there for a while. Hopefully, Peter would persuade Jeff to go back to the city. Quickly.

But as she rode along, she came to the old cemetery and decided to stop there. She parked her bike on the side of the road and walked in through the wrought-iron gate. Set on a hill and surrounded by a low stone wall, the cemetery was not very large.

There were headstones that dated back to the 1600s, when the first inhabitants of the island had arrived; the markers were old stone tablets, moss covered and practically worn away by the caress of salty winds and rain. And the simple passage of time.

Searching for the marker for her aunt and uncle, Liza saw quite a few gravestones marked with the surname *North*. Claire must be a native of the island, Liza realized, her family lineage dating back all the way to the earliest settlers. Somehow, Liza wasn't surprised.

Wandering down the narrow rows, she finally found the headstone marked Dunne and under that the names Clive and Elizabeth, and the dates of their births and deaths. She gazed down at it a moment. She had expected to find the spot bare. But someone had planted spring bulbs in a cluster at the bottom of the stone, and she could see that the earth had already been cleaned of weeds and turned, the green shoots making their way up toward the sun.

There would be flowers blooming here in a few weeks. Maybe sooner than that. The thought pleased her but also made her wonder who had been so careful and considerate, coming to this remote spot to plant flowers that no one would see.

It should have been me, Liza thought. *But I was too busy, as usual, doing my oh-so-important work for the agency. It must have been Claire,* she realized. Just a guess, but it seemed like something Claire would do.

Well, I'll come again and bring more flowers, Liza promised herself. There was plenty of time for that.

She sat down on the grass near the marker and read the inscription:

Two roads diverged . . .
I took the one less traveled by,
and that has made all the difference.
—Robert Frost

Frost was their favorite poet. Frost and Whitman. Liza had found their beloved, worn-out volumes of *Leaves of Grass* and Frost's collected works when she was cleaning out the bookcases.

She had put them aside to take home as mementos. Her aunt used to read passages from *Leaves of Grass* to her, but Liza had never read the entire collection of poems on her own. She would start it, she decided, maybe tonight. It had to be a more worthwhile pursuit than staring at a computer screen and trying to catch up on office work. Where had that gotten her?

Liza gazed at the gravestone, wondering what Aunt Elizabeth would have thought about the scene at the inn today. Would she have encouraged Liza to have more patience with Jeff and consider his hope to reconcile? Liza had a feeling her aunt wouldn't have encouraged that. Actually, she wouldn't have tried to push her one way or the other. "Listen to your heart, Liza, not your head," Aunt Elizabeth used to say.

Her heart was telling her that it was over with Jeff. That she was even fortunate they had never had children together. That would have been a big mistake, she could see it now very clearly. She would have children someday. But she wasn't ready.

"If you're not sure, give it time. The right answer will come to you," her aunt used to say. "Give it time."

That was her aunt's guiding principle. *Give things time.* That seemed to be Claire North's philosophy as well. Of course, it seemed that out on this island, there was an endless amount of time.

It was different back in Boston, in her own life.

Jeff had been pressuring her their whole married life. Liza could see that now. He had come this morning, trying to sweep her off her feet. But this time, she wouldn't be rushed.

Liza stood up and gazed at the grave again. She wished her aunt were around to talk to, to give her some advice about . . . about everything.

One thing suddenly seemed clear. If Aunt Elizabeth were around, she would probably be displeased with the way Liza and Peter were rushing to sell the inn. Aunt Elizabeth had given the best years of her life to that beautiful old building, and now they were just abandoning it. It made Liza feel sad and even ashamed of herself in some way.

Liza had been telling herself they had no other choice. But there were always other choices. That's what her aunt would have said. If you were daring and honest enough to look for them.

She felt a few raindrops and pulled up her hood, then felt around in her pocket for a tissue. She found a shell instead.

How had that gotten there? She must have picked it up on the beach at some point but didn't remember when.

She held it for a moment, then placed it near the headstone.

It was a very pretty shell and all she had to offer right now.

Her aunt would like it. She had always been pleased by original gifts, Liza recalled.

Liza closed her eyes a moment and said a prayer. It was not something she was used to doing, and the words slowly came to her. It was a prayer her aunt used to recite at night as she tucked Liza and her brother into bed.

Dearest Lord, teach me to be generous.
Teach me to serve You, as You deserve,
To give and not to count the cost,
To fight and not to seek for rest,
To labor and not to seek reward,
Save that of knowing that I do Thy will.

Finally she stepped away and said good-bye to her aunt and uncle. The rain was falling steadily now, and the wind was even stronger. It was time to return to the inn, whether Jeff was still there or not. She reached into her pocket again, looking for her cell phone. It wasn't there, and Liza stood in the rain, searching all her pockets, twice, before she faced the fact that she had somehow forgotten it back at the inn.

She almost started laughing. How ironic. After carrying her BlackBerry around everywhere, like an extra body part, she didn't have it handy when she needed it most. She shook her head, went and got her bike, and wheeled it onto the road. Nothing to do now but head home the same way she came.

Liza pedaled steadily but slowly through the rain. She wondered if a car or truck would pass and give her a ride back.

But nobody came along the old road going in her direction.

The sky grew even darker, and she heard a rumble of thunder, then saw a bolt of lightning strike out over the water. Daniel had been talking about the spring storms just this morning. Well, here they were, Liza realized. Right on time.

Maybe this one would knock down the inn, and they wouldn't have to worry about painting it, fixing it, or even selling it.

Liza felt her clothes getting waterlogged from the rain.

Her jeans stuck to her legs and made it hard to pedal. She finally got off the bike and began to push it as she walked on the shoulder of the road.

The entire situation suddenly made her laugh out loud. This was just a metaphor for her entire life, wasn't it? She could only imagine what she looked like, with her soaking wet clothes and her hair plastered to her head, pushing along the broken-down old bike. She had splashed through so many puddles her legs were covered with mud up to her knees. Her sweatshirt and jeans clung to her skin.

What was that saying she once heard? "Man plans, God laughs."

She had always been a very good planner. Her

life was organized and scheduled, every assignment, appointment, and deadline neatly noted in her daily diary. School, marriage, buying a condo, her promotions up the corporate food chain.

Now here she was. At her wit's end. Laughing like a crazy lady. Pushing a bike on a country road in a thunderstorm. She didn't remember noting this episode in the plan. God was getting a good laugh today, wasn't He?

Liza paused and turned her face up to the sky. "Pretty funny. I hope you're enjoying yourself!" she shouted.

She heard a car coming up behind her and quickly yanked the bike to the side of the road. She turned and saw a white pickup truck slowing to a stop.

It was raining so hard she couldn't trust her vision . . . Was that Daniel behind the wheel . . . or just her hopeful imagination?

The truck pulled up slowly alongside her, and the driver's side window came down. It was Daniel. He took her in from head to toe, looking like he wanted to laugh and was struggling to hold it in. "Want a lift?"

She stared at him a moment, trying to remember the last time she had been so happy to see someone.

"Thanks, but . . . I'll only get the inside of your truck soaking wet. And it's not that far now. I can walk the rest."

Daniel abruptly stopped the truck, got out, and grabbed the bike without even asking. He tossed it in the back of the pickup with one swift, easy motion. He was pretty strong, she realized.

"Would you like to ride in the cab? Or in back with the bike?"

Liza imagined herself hoisted up and thrown in the truck bed. He looked like he could do it, too.

"In the cab, thanks." Liza walked around to the passenger's side and got in. Daniel slipped behind the wheel and closed his door. "Put your belt on," he reminded her as he started the engine.

The wipers slapped at the rainy windshield, and the windows grew foggy despite the blower. She felt her shoulder brush Daniel's as the truck rolled along, hitting puddles and potholes in the old road. It felt very close and intimate in the truck cab. Daniel stared straight at the road. His thick, dark hair was slicked back, emphasizing his strong profile.

She pushed her wet hair back with her hand, knowing she looked a perfect mess. Like a drowned cat. No help for it, she decided. She wiped a little space on her window with her hand and noticed they were near the town center.

"So you were sent to hunt me down and bring me back? Dead or alive, is that it?"

Daniel laughed. "Something like that. I didn't have my loyal bloodhounds handy, but I volunteered anyway."

He had volunteered to come find her? That was ... interesting.

"What about my ex-husband?" she asked quietly. "Didn't he volunteer?"

"Yes, he did, now that you mention it. We decided to split up and look on different sides of the island. I drew a little map for him with some ... directions."

Liza glanced at him, detecting a small smile. She had a strong feeling Daniel's map would have Jeff driving in circles for days. But she didn't comment.

"He might have found his way back by now, though," he added, making her laugh. He glanced at her. "Are you worried that he's waiting for you?"

Liza shrugged. "I wouldn't say 'worried.' And I certainly wouldn't mind a cup of tea," she added, as Daisy Winkler's cottage came into view.

Daniel glanced over at her and smiled, quickly turning the truck toward the tearoom. "Funny, I was just thinking the same thing. And here we are, right in front of Daisy Winkler's."

"Yes, here we are. How convenient," she agreed, meeting his dark gaze for a moment. Then she opened her door and slipped out her side of the truck.

The rain came down steadily as they ran down the path to the front door of the cottage. Liza was closest to the door and rang the bell. Daniel stood behind her. He had opened his jacket and held the edges out over her, like a canopy.

"Get under," he urged her as they stood waiting for Daisy to come to the door.

She stepped back, her shoulders nearly touching his chest.

She felt her breath catch at his nearness and felt the warmth of his body, even through her wet clothes. She was glad that he couldn't see her face. She was sure her cheeks were bright pink.

Daisy finally came to the door. Her small face stared out at them quizzically.

"Hello, Daisy. Are you open today?" Daniel asked politely.

"Yes, of course. Come in, come in . . ." Daisy urged them forward. Liza stepped inside, then felt self-conscious as she dripped water all over the entranceway.

"Oh, my dear, it looks like you've been swimming. Did you fall off a boat?" Daisy inquired in a serious tone.

Liza smiled and shook her head. "I was out on my bike, and the rain started." She stared down at her mud-covered shoes. She looked as if she had just emerged from a swamp. "Oh, dear . . . I don't want to make a mess in here. Maybe this was a bad idea."

"Don't worry, dear. I'll get something for you." Daisy waved her hands in the air as she trotted off to some other room of the cottage.

Liza glanced at Daniel as Daisy disappeared. He was so tall, his head nearly grazed the low ceiling. "She must be getting a towel," he whispered. Liza nodded. Then he reached out and pushed a wet strand of hair off her cheek. His touch was gentle and startling at the same time. "You do look like you fell off a boat. You look like a drowned—"

"Don't say it," she warned him fiercely. But couldn't help smiling.

Before he could answer, Daisy reappeared. She carried a towel along with a load of clothes draped over one arm. "I picked out a few things that might fit you from the thrift rack in back."

Daisy had a thrift rack in here, too? Liza hadn't noticed that during her first visit, but she had only glanced inside and hadn't really looked around.

Daisy handed over the bundle of clothes. "There's a powder room right there." She pointed to a pink door in the short hallway that separated the tearoom from another large room. "You dry yourself off and put on some warm things. I'll get everything together for your tea."

Liza glanced down at the clothes as Daisy trotted off in the opposite direction. The clothes were very—Daisy-ish. "I can't wear this stuff. I'll look like a mannequin in a costume museum," she whispered to Daniel.

He picked up the edge of a sheer, frilly blouse. "This looks promising. Why don't you try this one?"

253

"Dream on, pal." Liza snatched it back, and he laughed.

She headed for the powder room, shut the door, then jumped back when she saw her reflection in the small, gilt-edged mirror. Daisy's offerings suddenly looked much better. Anything would be an improvement, she realized.

A few minutes later, Liza emerged feeling drier, warmer, and much more presentable. She had washed up, twisted her wet hair into a knot at the back of her head, and secured it with some bobby pins she found in the bathroom. From the pile of antique clothes, she had picked out a dark blue velvet blouse with long full sleeves and a row of tiny, shiny buttons down the front. The blouse came down below her hips and had a high neck with a pointed collar. It would have looked very modest—a great disappointment compared to the sheer frilly number Daniel had picked out—except that it was a little snug across her bust.

But that couldn't be helped, Liza thought. It was the only top that didn't make her look like a heroine in a gothic romance. Well, not completely.

She couldn't find anything suitable to replace her wet jeans, though Daisy had given her several long skirts. She managed to clean her pants off a bit and replaced her wet socks and sneakers with some thick, warm socks.

When she came back to the tearoom, Daniel was seated at a small table by a window at the front of the shop. The table was set for two with china teacups and plates. A teapot stood between the place settings, alongside a tiered tray of cakes and little sandwiches that made Liza instantly aware that she was starving.

Daniel was looking out the window and didn't notice her approach until she pulled out her chair. "Not much improvement, but I feel a bit dryer," she reported as she sat down.

His eyes widened, taking in her appearance. "You look great. I love that shirt . . . Here, have some tea. I think it's ready."

He leaned over and poured her a cup of tea, which was made with real leaves and had to be filtered with a silver strainer.

Liza felt a bit shaken by his compliments and was glad she didn't need to handle a warm teapot at that moment.

"Daisy recommended something called Lapsang Souchong. I hope you like that kind."

"It looks fine," she said agreeably. "I'm not very fussy about tea. I hardly know the differences between all the blends."

"Me either," he admitted. "This one smells nice," he noted, pouring himself a cup.

The tea did have a pleasant, flowery fragrance, Liza noticed. A sugar bowl held a selection of cubes, white and brown. Daisy also delivered paper-thin slices of lemon, a honey pot, and a small jug of cream. Liza added some honey to her cup, stirred, then took a sip.

Daniel fixed his tea with sugar and cream. The same way he liked his coffee, she noticed.

"So, you don't really seem the tearoom type. Do you come here often?" she asked.

"Only when I need a good book. Or find a pretty woman wandering in the rain."

Liza had been gazing at him but now looked away. His compliment made her blush. "I see . . . Does that happen often?"

"No, not often enough, come to think of it." He popped a tiny cake in his mouth and smiled at her. "Hmm, these are good. Poppy seed." He pointed one out on the tray. "You should try one."

Liza scanned the tray and picked out the cake he suggested and also took a tiny sandwich, which looked as though it had cucumber and cream cheese inside.

She placed both on her plate with the silver tongs Daisy had supplied.

"So, how long have you been divorced?" he asked suddenly.

"Oh, not long. About three weeks officially. Though we've been separated for months. Nearly a year now, I guess. The paperwork seemed to take forever. Jeff is a good guy," she added, "but we just want different things now."

She looked up at him. "You're not married or anything, are you?" Claire had told her Daniel was single, but Liza wanted to be sure.

"No, never been married. I was engaged once. It didn't work out," he replied quickly.

She wanted to ask why not but didn't feel comfortable pushing for the details. "How long have you lived on the island?" she asked instead.

"Oh, about five years now. I was living up in Maine before that. In Portland. I just wanted a change," he explained briefly.

Liza suspected there was more to that story, too, but she didn't want to sound as if she were interrogating him.

"Five years is a long time. It must have been the right choice for you."

"It was. So far, anyway," he added. "How about you, Liza? Do you ever think of making a change? Of staying here?"

Liza was sipping her tea and suddenly sat back. The question caught her by surprise. "I didn't at first. It was the furthest thing from my mind. But now . . . I'm not so sure. I'm wondering if we're selling the inn too quickly, not considering all the possibilities." She sighed and shook her head. "But my brother and I agreed to sell, and I don't want to go back on my word to him."

Daniel nodded. "I understand. Maybe he'll come around to your point of view."

"I doubt it. I've already tried to talk to him.

Peter's very set on selling. He needs the money for his business," she confided.

"I see. And I guess you want to get back to your office. You have a big job in advertising, right?"

"Not as big as I thought, apparently." She glanced at him. "I thought I was getting this great promotion. It was practically promised to me. But now it looks like it's going to someone else." Strangely, confessing that to Daniel wasn't hard. For some reason, she felt none of the pain and embarrassment she had felt the day before.

"Oh . . . that's too bad. That doesn't seem right." He offered her a sympathetic glance and poured more tea in her cup, then filled his own again. "You seem very devoted to your work."

"*Obsessive* is probably a better word to describe it," she admitted. "But now I'm beginning to wonder: What was the point? Sometimes I think I'd love to just quit that job. The problem is, I don't know what else I would do. I just sort of work, eat, sleep . . . I'm a pretty boring person," she added with a grin. "You ought to know that right up front."

"Now that you mention it, that was one of the first things I noticed about you." He met her glance and held it, his expression saying that he found her anything but.

"That's funny, I thought the same thing about you."

He smiled, then reached across the table and

took her hand. "Well, we're in agreement. No wonder we get along so well. You really ought to consider quitting your job and staying out here. Nothing much ever happens. It's perfect for people like you and me."

"I'll keep that in mind." Liza glanced up at him but couldn't manage any more of an answer. She savored the sensation of his warm, strong hand holding hers. She liked looking into his eyes and feeling the rest of the world just slip away. It did feel perfect being with him, sitting here, sipping tea, the rain beating on the windows.

But this wasn't real life, just a serendipitous moment.

"Actually, Audrey Gilroy tells me that you're a volunteer at the medical clinic. So you're not quite that boring after all. What do you do there?" she asked curiously.

"Oh, some EMS. Basic first-aid stuff." He shrugged. "If people need a real doctor, we get them over to Southport Hospital or air vac them out."

"Where did you learn to do EMS work? Did you drive an ambulance or something?"

"Back in college. It was a part-time job." He looked as if he were about to say more when Daisy came by.

She smiled down at them. "How is everything? Would you like another pot of tea?" she asked, noticing theirs was just about empty.

"I'm fine," Liza answered. She looked at Daniel. "We should probably get back to the inn," she added, glancing at her watch. "I've been gone awhile now. They might just send out the real bloodhounds."

"I guess so," he agreed. "Just the check please, Daisy."

Daisy smiled and produced a little order pad from the pocket of her apron. She tallied up their check and set it facedown on the table. Then she took another pad from a different pocket and tore off a sheet from that one, too.

"And here's your poem."

"Thank you, Daisy," Liza said sincerely. "I really enjoyed the last one you gave me. I never got to tell you."

"That's all right. My poems are like birds. They're meant to fly away and give other people pleasure with their song. Pass them on, dear. Pass them on."

"Okay, I will," Liza promised, liking the idea.

Daniel put some bills on the table and stood up. Liza did, too, and scooped up her pile of wet clothing. "What do I owe for the blouse?" she asked Daisy.

"Oh . . . you keep it as a gift. It looks perfect on you. I think it was just sitting here waiting for you. I wouldn't feel right taking anything for reuniting it with its rightful owner."

Daisy's logic was a bit pretzel shaped, Liza

thought, but the gesture was generous. Everyone around here seemed so generous in spirit, reaching out for connection. It was so different from the city.

"Thank you. That's very nice of you," Liza said, thinking she would find some way to make it up to Daisy before she left the island.

"It's nothing at all. Don't be silly."

Daisy walked them to the front door of the cottage. The rain still fell steadily but not quite as hard. Daisy handed them an umbrella. "You can borrow this. Drop it off sometime when you pass by."

"Thank you, Daisy." Daniel opened the umbrella and held it out with one hand. Then he slung his other arm around Liza's shoulders and pulled her close. "Ready to make a run for it?"

Liza nodded, his nearness leaving her a bit breathless before she'd even taken a step. They ran to the truck, and Daniel opened her door, sheltering her with the umbrella as she climbed in. Then he walked to his side and got in the driver's seat. Daisy waved and went into her cottage, closing the door.

Daniel put the keys in the ignition but didn't start the truck. "We never read Daisy's poem," he said.

"Right . . . well, here it is." Liza took the sheet of notebook paper out of her shirt pocket and unfolded it. She read the words aloud:

A little madness in the Spring
Is wholesome even for the King.
—Emily Dickinson

"Interesting." Daniel smiled briefly. "I'll have to think about that."

"Me, too," Liza agreed.

But she could guess what he was thinking. The same thing she was. She was having a little spring madness today—running off in the rain and hiding out with him in the tearoom. It had been perfectly out of character for her . . . and perfectly wonderful.

She reached over and tucked the poem in his shirt pocket. "Here, you keep this now. Daisy said to pass it on."

He touched her hand, holding it to his chest for a moment.

"Thanks."

"Thanks for the tea," she said quietly. "That was an adventure."

"I hope it wasn't too exciting for you."

She smiled and shook her head. "Nope, not at all. It was just right."

"Good. I'm happy to hear that." He started up the truck, swooped past the General Store, and turned toward the main road that led to the inn. Then he reached across the seat and took her hand. "We'll have to do it again sometime."

"I would like that," she said quietly. "Very much." She would love to spend time alone with Daniel again and get to know him better. But she wasn't sure when or how that would happen.

In a few days she would return to the city, and he would stay here. Not just distant in miles but in an entire way of living and thinking.

Starting up a relationship with Daniel didn't seem at all practical. But the touch of his hand on hers reminded Liza that it was too late to worry about that. A relationship had already begun.

Chapter Ten

DANIEL steered the truck up toward the inn and parked at the front door.

"Coming in?" Liza asked. Half of her wanted him to come inside, the other half didn't. She wanted to be alone awhile and savor their time together in secret. She didn't want to be with him right now around other people.

He thought about it a moment, then shook his head. "Thanks, but I'm going to get home now. I'll see you tomorrow," he said.

"Right. See you tomorrow." She sat very still, looking at him. He seemed about to lean over and kiss her when her brother burst out of the house and ran down the porch steps, coming to a stop at the passenger door of the truck.

"Liza, are you all right?" he called.

Daniel laughed. "I guess you'd better go. Your adoring fans await."

"Yes, I guess so," she said quietly. She glanced at him a moment, then opened the door and jumped out, practically landing in her brother's arms.

"I'm okay, honestly."

Peter stared at her, his brow furrowed with worry as they climbed the steps toward the house. "What is that you're wearing? You look like . . . the Little Prince."

Liza laughed. "I do look like the Little Prince. I couldn't quite figure it out. But that's exactly right."

Peter seemed puzzled at her cheerful answer and good mood. But before he could question her further, Claire stepped out onto the porch, holding a towel as big as a blanket. Liza, who was still damp and chilled, gratefully pulled the towel around her.

"Liza, we were worried about you," Peter said, as they paraded into the house. "Where have you been?"

"Oh . . . I didn't go too far," she insisted.

A lightning bolt lit up the sky, and their conversation was interrupted by the big boom that followed.

"Where's Jeff?" she asked, looking around.

"He and Daniel went out to look for you. Jeff came back after a while and waited around. But he finally left a few minutes ago," Peter reported.

"Good." Liza sighed, feeling relieved. "I'm going up to change my clothes."

"You ought to take a hot shower," Claire advised.

A hot shower was a great idea. A long hot shower.

"Where's Daniel? Isn't he coming in?" Peter opened the front door and looked out at the rain.

"He had to go home," Liza said.

Peter closed the door. "Why didn't he call and let us know you were all right?"

Liza paused at the bottom of the staircase. "We stopped at the tearoom in the town center. I guess we just forgot to call."

Peter frowned. "Just forgot? That wasn't very considerate. Daniel knew we were all worried about you," he added, sounding like an anxious father.

Liza didn't feel remotely like an errant teenager, but she didn't want to turn this into a fight. "I'm sorry, Peter. It was my fault. I was afraid Jeff was still here. I didn't want to see him."

"I thought that might be the problem," he said, his tone softening. "Daniel was a good sport to kill some time with you until the coast was clear."

"Yes, a very good sport." She started up the stairs, hoping her brother hadn't noticed the smile that stretched across her face.

Liza took a hot shower and changed into clean, dry sweats and thick socks. Down in the kitchen she found Peter sitting at the table with a mug of coffee. It was late afternoon, almost time for dinner.

"Would you like some hot soup or some tea?" Claire asked.

Despite the shower and all the tea she'd had with Daniel, Liza still felt chilled.

"Some tea would be great. Thanks, Claire."

"The water's all ready." Claire made the tea and set the mug down at her place, then lifted Liza's wet hair and slipped a fluffy towel around her shoulders. "You don't want to get your back all wet again," she said quietly.

Liza tilted her head up and smiled at the housekeeper. She was so tired from her ordeal, she didn't mind being waited on and fussed over.

The rain was falling steadily in gusty sheets that battered the house. Peter had been reading the paper and put it down after a particularly loud rumble of thunder. "I feel like I'm in the middle of the ocean on a boat," he said.

Liza smiled. "At least the house isn't rocking from side to side."

"Not yet," he replied, raising his eyebrows as another loud crack of lightning illuminated the sky. "I hope you aren't thinking of going home in this tonight," he said to Claire. "The roads will definitely be flooded."

"They were already pretty bad this afternoon," Liza said. "You really have to stay over, Claire."

"Yes, I'll stay the night," Claire agreed. "That's what my room on the third floor is for."

"Don't bother cooking a big dinner, Claire," Liza

added. "We'll just have sandwiches or leftovers."

Will came into the kitchen then, earbuds draped around his neck. "This storm is fierce," he said. "I tried to text Sawyer, but nothing's going through." Sawyer, Liza had learned, was one of Will's friends in Tucson. "Think it will be over in an hour?" he asked his dad.

Peter shook his head. "No, this isn't like a monsoon back home. The storms here can last for days."

Will shot him an alarmed look. "Days?"

Peter looked about to reply when a huge crack of lightning streaked across the sky. The entire room grew very bright for a long moment, then they heard the thunder, which seemed to shake the entire building.

They all held their breath as the lights in the house flickered . . . then went out.

"That did it," Peter grumbled, putting down his newspaper once and for all.

"The power's gone out," Claire said.

The room was completely black. Liza could barely see her hand.

"This is cool. Sort of like a fun house," Will declared.

"It's not going to be much fun if it stays this way," his father pointed out. "There's not a lot we can do in the dark."

"There's nothing to do around here anyway. What's the difference?" Will asked.

Sarcastic but true, Liza thought.

"We may be without electricity, but we're not without light," Claire said. "I've gathered some flashlights and candles." She made her way over to the kitchen counter behind Liza and picked up something. Liza heard metallic sounds. Then a powerful beam of light glowed. It was a large camping lantern. Claire set it in the middle of the table and then picked up a smaller flashlight, which she handed to Liza.

"Thanks, Claire," Liza said. "Good thing you thought ahead and had those handy."

"Okay, we have some flashlights. What now?" Peter asked.

Liza was about to answer, but before she could, a loud knock sounded on the door.

They all turned to look at one another.

"Who could that be?" Liza asked, wondering.

"I'd better get it." Peter rose and picked up one of the other flashlights on the counter.

"Can I come?" Will asked, rising in his chair.

"You stay here," his father commanded. "Let me see who it is first."

"Who do you think it is, Dad . . . Dracula?" Will asked.

"Very funny," Peter grumbled, as he checked the light and stalked off. Though from the expression on his face, Liza wondered if he did expect a scary visitor of some kind.

Then she heard Peter open the door and heard him talking to someone, a man's voice.

Maybe it's Daniel, she thought. Maybe the route back to his house was flooded, so he had to turn around and come back here.

She secretly readied herself for Daniel's appearance. But her heart soon flipped from unexpected cheer to unexpected dread. She did recognize the visitor's voice. It wasn't Daniel. And she might have welcomed Count Dracula more.

"Jeff is here," Peter called out from the foyer. "The bridge was flooded. He couldn't cross."

Liza walked into the hallway and stopped. Jeff stood at the front door, slipping out of his wet leather jacket. His hair and pants were wet, too. He glanced at her with a sheepish expression.

"I'm sorry. I rode around the island for a while after I left here, just to take a look."

Looking for me, Liza filled in silently. She was glad she had gone to the cemetery. Jeff would never have guessed she was there, even if he had driven right by. It almost felt as if her aunt had protected her from him out there.

"The rain started and I wasn't thinking," Jeff went on. "But by the time I got to the bridge, it was closed. I didn't realize that's how they run things here."

That wasn't how any group of people on the island ran things. It was the way nature ran things. But Liza didn't try to explain that to him.

Claire stepped past Liza and handed Jeff a towel.

"Thank you," Jeff said sincerely. He wiped his face, then rubbed his hair.

"Well, you might as well come in," Liza said finally. "I guess you'll have to stay awhile."

If not the entire night.

"How long does it take for the water to recede?" he asked.

Liza shrugged. "It all depends on the weather conditions and the tide."

"High tide is around nine tonight. I just read it in the paper," Peter said. "With all this rain and wind, I doubt the bridge will open until one or even two in the morning."

"We can call the gatehouse and find out," Claire said. "I have the phone number in the kitchen."

There was a chance that the water would clear up by midnight or so, Liza thought. But not much of a chance. It seemed like she was stuck with Jeff, whether she liked it or not.

A short time later, they all sat down to an early dinner by candlelight—sandwiches and more soup. Luckily, the gas range was not affected by the power outage, and the meal was perfect for the rainy night.

Jeff was on his best behavior, Liza noticed. He was pretty quiet and only spoke when spoken to. He was probably afraid that given the way things were going for him today, she might toss him out in the storm. She had given it a thought.

After dinner it was too early to go up to bed, though the storm still raged outside and there seemed no possibility of the power coming back.

Jeff called the gatehouse at the bridge from his cell phone, though they all knew it was a lost cause.

"Still closed. They doubt it will open until the morning."

"You have to stay over, I guess," Liza said. "It's all right, we have plenty of room."

"Thanks, I appreciate it." Jeff tried to catch her eye, but she looked away.

"I'll make up a room for you," Claire said.

"I'll help," Liza offered, looking for an excuse to go upstairs.

"That's all right. I just need to put sheets on a bed. Everything else is ready."

As if she had already guessed someone would be staying over tonight, Liza thought. How did Claire know these things? Liza decided that one day she would have to ask her.

"Why don't we play a board game or something?" Peter suggested. Will groaned and covered his face with his hand, but Peter ignored him. "I saw some in the parlor; I'll get them."

Liza felt uncomfortable once Peter left. But at least Will was still there.

Jeff smiled at her. "What a storm. It's like a full-blown hurricane."

"Not quite," Liza answered. "But the island is

out in the open. The storms in the spring hit very hard."

"I'm sorry I had to come back," he said. "I know you weren't happy to see me."

Liza shrugged. "You're here now. There's nothing we can do about it. Let's just get through the evening, okay?"

He nodded. "Okay, Liza. Whatever you say."

Peter returned with an armful of board games. After some debate, they decided to play Scrabble.

It took a round or two to identify the best players at the table. Liza was not bad but not exactly a top contender. Neither was Jeff, and after a short time, he excused himself and went upstairs with a flashlight, planning to read in his room.

Claire was very good, Liza noticed, the best at the table. While Peter and Will argued over the rules, she would sit quietly, fiddling with her tiles. And then when her turn came, she would invariably lay down a high-scoring word.

"Zydeco . . ." Claire said, carefully placing her tiles and racking up over thirty points in one blow.

As the game wound down, it was easy to see that Claire would win by a wide margin. Peter and Will continued to battle it out for second place with fierce, competitive energy that seemed distinctly male, Liza thought. Or perhaps it was some father-son dynamic.

She suddenly remembered why she hated playing board games with her brother. It wasn't just that he was older and usually more skillful than she was. It was that he took them so seriously and was so focused on winning. Will seemed to be putting up with it and even giving Peter some of his own medicine back. But Peter was gloating at every chance, and that could get on anyone's nerves after a while.

At first it was great to watch Will having fun, without the benefit of his iPod, cell phone, or computer. But as the game drew to a close and the tension level rose, he started to sink into a mood. Finally, her nephew and brother were down to one tile each, with Will several points ahead of Peter.

Will had a *K* and could find no spot to place it. Peter had an *S*, which was much easier to add to almost any word on the board. He soon found the perfect spot, at the end of one of Claire's doozies—the word *quip*. And the *S* just happened to land on a "double word score" square.

"Eureka! Got you, Will. I told you that your old man would beat you. Believe it, buddy." Peter stood up and made a great show of placing the winning consonant down. *"Quips. Q-U-I-P-S.* Double word score—I win!"

"Claire won, Peter," Liza reminded him. "You're in second place."

"Whatever," her brother said, undeterred from his victory.

Even in the dark, Liza could see Will's face grow red with indignation.

"Let me see that." He grabbed the board and twisted it around. "Quips? Are you sure that's a word? I've never heard of it."

Claire put a steadying hand on his shoulder. "It's a word, Will. But you did very well. Especially for someone who never plays this game. I was very impressed."

Will didn't answer. He just stared at the board, his face twisted in disappointment. "That stinks. *S-T-I-N-K-S*," he said finally.

"Hey, it's just a game. I won fair and square, Will. No need to be a sore loser," Peter told him.

Will tossed his head back. "Right. It's just a game, Dad. That's why you're hopping up and down. Totally dissing me." Will stood up and flipped the board over, scattering tiles in all directions. "Whoops," he said, in a tone that clearly communicated this was no accident. "Sorry about that."

Then he turned and disappeared into the darkness.

"Will, come back here! Where are you going?" Peter called after him.

"Up to bed. All that spelling gave me a headache," he called back.

"He needs to come back and clean this up," Peter said, his voice tense.

Liza glanced at Claire, who wore an expression somewhere between sympathy for Will and outright laughter. Peter had been laying it on pretty thick. Maybe he did deserve a little of this bad behavior.

"It's too dark to find the tiles tonight, Peter. He can clean it up tomorrow," Liza suggested. "I'm really tired. I'm heading up to bed."

"Me, too." Claire rose and picked up her flashlight. "Let's go up together, we'll have more light," she suggested.

They left the room, and Peter soon followed.

Up in her room, Liza quickly prepared for bed. It wasn't really late, but sitting in the dark for hours had made her sleepy. Or maybe it was all the bike riding in the rain.

As Liza changed into her nightgown, she heard footsteps in the hallway outside her room, going back and forth to the bathroom. Claire had given Jeff a room on the third floor, and Liza was grateful for that. It was bad enough to have him stay overnight. She didn't need him sleeping in close proximity.

By the time Liza shut off the light and got into bed, the storm seemed to have slowed down. Raindrops still fell against the big window in her room, but the wind seemed quieter. She had not quite fallen asleep when she heard a gentle tapping on her door.

She sat up in bed. "Who is it?"

"It's me, Jeff," her ex whispered. "Come to the door."

Liza sighed out loud. She knew he was going to

pull something like this. She had half a mind to make a big scene, but she didn't want to wake everyone.

"Okay, I'm coming." *But you're not coming in, pal,* she added silently.

Liza pulled on a bathrobe, tied the belt, then went to the door and opened it a crack. Jeff stood in the darkness waiting, still mostly dressed, she was relieved to see. He was barefoot but wearing a white T-shirt and jeans.

"What is it? Do you need a toothbrush or something?"

"I need to talk to you. Just for a minute," he said quietly.

Liza stared at him. He just wasn't going to give up, was he?

"It's late, Jeff. We can talk tomorrow. Before you go," she added.

"I'd rather talk now. When we can have some privacy. Just let me come in for a second. For goodness' sake, Liza. We were married for over seven years."

But we're not anymore, Liza nearly replied, *and you seem like a stranger to me now.*

She wasn't sure when that had happened. But she felt now as if she were seeing Jeff for the first time, from a great distance. And she wondered how and why she had ever married him.

"Please?" he asked.

"All right. We can talk. Just for a few minutes.

Let's go downstairs," she suggested. She quickly stepped out of the room without giving him time to debate. Turning on her flashlight, she headed for the stairs.

Jeff seemed surprised by this maneuver but soon followed her downstairs and then into the parlor.

She sat in an armchair, giving him no opportunity to get close. "All right, Jeff. Here we are. It's late, and I'd like to get some sleep."

"I tried to sleep, but I knew I couldn't. I want to apologize for what I did today. I was just so . . . so overwhelmed by my insight about our relationship," he explained, "I had to share it with you. But I shouldn't have come here without asking you first. I can see that now. I just want to apologize," he added in a humble tone.

Liza was surprised. She thought she was going to have to field another plea for reconciliation. She could handle this conversation.

"It's all right. I understand, I guess . . . Let's just get past it, okay?" She took a deep breath. "I've done some thinking today, too. I'm not sure we should have ever gotten married. We always got along well, we seemed to want the same things out of life . . . but I'm not sure the feelings were ever deep enough to last. On either side," she added, though it was painful to admit.

"Liza, please don't say that. You're still angry with me. About my—my mistake. The way I hurt you. And you have a perfect right to be."

"I'm not angry anymore," she said honestly. She didn't know when that had happened. Maybe the rainstorm had washed all the anger out of her. "In fact, I even understand how it could have happened. Really," she insisted. "When you came here today, I was upset. But I know I played a part in our breakup, Jeff. I can see that now. Getting back together just wouldn't work for me. There's nothing to build on anymore," she said quietly. "I'm not sure there ever was much solid ground."

His expression tightened with pain, and she felt sorry for what she had said. She hadn't meant to hurt him. She just wanted to be honest. Maybe for the very first time.

He was silent for a long while. At last he said, "So this is how you really feel?"

"Yes, that's it. I can finally put it into words. I hope you understand."

"I do," he answered, then let out a long sigh. "I don't agree, but I guess I have to accept this as your final answer."

"It is. I admit, I've been uncertain these past few months about what to do. Or if we should try again. But I feel really clear about things now. I'm sorry to hurt you, but sometime in the future, I think you'll see it was the right thing to do."

She believed that, too, finally. She could see now in the rubble of their relationship an opportunity for both of them to be happier, to find a deeper, more genuine connection.

Would her connection with Daniel grow to something more? It was much too soon to say. But Liza could see from the short time they had spent together that there were possibilities for her.

She wasn't pushing Jeff away for Daniel, but her time with him had helped her see that she had changed and Jeff just wasn't right for her anymore. She needed something different. Someone different. Jeff did, too.

"I hope so, Liza. It seems I have no choice, no matter how I feel right now. Part of me will always love you," he insisted.

He leaned down and gave her a hug. Liza didn't resist. She knew part of her would always love him, too, in a certain way.

Jeff stood up. "Good night. I'll see you in the morning."

"Good night, Jeff." Liza stood up, too, but didn't follow him to the stairway.

She heard him go upstairs, and she went to the window. There seemed to be a break in the storm, though she wondered if it had ended for good. The thick gray clouds had parted and scuttled across the sky, driven by the wind.

Behind the clouds the full moon shone bold and bright, finally having its say. Liza thought it was a beautiful sight. It made her feel calm and whole, reminding her of the endless cycles that hold the universe together. That held her life together.

Nothing really ended, not even a marriage. It evolved into something different, and life went on.

BACK in her room, Liza left her flashlight on the night table by her bed. She slipped under the covers and quickly fell asleep.

She was not sure how long she had been asleep or what time it was when she heard the storm build again, the wind and rain beating against the windowpanes and rooftop. She woke up for a moment and rolled to her side, the rumble of thunder seeming part of her dreams.

It was sometime later when a brilliant light filled her room, startling her from a deep sleep. She sat up in bed, wide-eyed. It seemed as if a huge beacon had been shining into the bedroom windows.

Then she heard the crackle of lightning and a huge boom. The entire house shook, feeling as if it were about to explode. A thunderous cracking sound came next, then a huge crash—right above her head. It sounded as if the house had been hit with a bomb.

Liza jumped out of bed and ran into the hallway, grabbing the flashlight as she pulled open her bedroom door. Peter was already in the hallway along with Will.

Her nephew ran to her, looking frightened. "What was that, Aunt Liza? I smell smoke."

"I do, too. Get a rain jacket and your shoes, Will, and wait in the foyer. We may have to leave the house."

She didn't think the house was on fire. There was no smoke alarm sounding. But she had no idea what had happened. It didn't hurt to be cautious.

Claire came down from the third floor in her bathrobe, followed by Jeff. They both carried flashlights, and the thin beams darted around in the darkness.

"The big tree on the drive, right next to the house, was hit by lightning," Claire reported. "A branch went through the roof."

"Oh, great . . ." Peter pushed past everyone and ran up the steps, two at a time. Liza followed. They came to the third floor, and he pulled open the door to the attic.

Liza felt a cold rush of air and heard the rain coming in. She followed Peter up the narrow stairs. Ahead of her, he went all the way into the attic. She poked her head up to see what was going on.

"I can't believe this," he moaned. "Look at this mess!"

A huge tree branch had crashed through the roof and left a big jagged hole where the night sky could be seen clearly. The wind-driven rain poured in, soaking everything nearby—boxes and furniture and stacks of her aunt's canvases that had been stored up there. Bits of shingles, tarpaper, the wooden beams of the roof, and pieces of the tree were also scattered all over. The branch itself sat heavy and immobile in the middle of everything. It looked like the tip of a big wooden arrow, Liza thought, that had been shot at their house by some angry giant.

"Let's pull some of this out of the way if we can." Liza didn't wait for help. She ran over to the wettest area and grabbed what she could—a large steamer trunk—dragging it to a dry spot. Then she ran back to rescue more.

Claire and Jeff came up into the attic, and eventually even Will joined them, and everyone worked together to clear the space under and around the huge branch.

"We need to put something over the hole," Claire said. "A tarp or a drop cloth or something."

"How will we do that?" Liza was grateful for the suggestion, spoken in such a cool, level-headed manner, but she didn't have the foggiest idea of how this remedy could be accomplished.

"We can use one of the ladders Daniel left and get up to the roof, then pull the tarp over. One person can stand up on the balcony on the third floor," Claire suggested.

"That might work," Liza reasoned aloud. "We have to try."

The rain was still falling hard and showed no sign of letting up anytime soon.

Liza ran downstairs and pulled on clothes, then ran out to the shed and found three large tarps. Luckily they had ropes dangling off grommets on the corners. That would help to pull them up, she thought.

Peter was already outside with Jeff, positioning the longest of the extension ladders. He took a deep breath, gave his sister a look from under the hood of his yellow rain jacket, then reached for the biggest tarp.

"Go up to the balcony on the third floor," he told Liza. "I'll toss you one corner of the tarp. If you pull on it, maybe it will cover the hole."

"We should tie a weight or something to one end, Dad," Will said. "Then we can fling it over the peak of the roof."

Liza looked at her nephew, who had come out into the rain with the rest of them. "Genius. Sheer genius. That's exactly what we need to do, or it probably won't reach." She had to shout to be heard over the wind.

Will grinned, then ran off and found a good-sized rock. He tied one end to one of the ropes attached to the tarp, and finally Peter started up the ladder.

"I'll hold the ladder steady," Jeff told his ex-brother-in-law. Liza was surprised that he had come outside and was trying to help. It was a nice gesture, all things considered.

Liza ran upstairs to the third-floor balcony,

where she waited for Peter to toss one end of the tarp over the roof to her.

After several attempts and some adjustments in their strategy, the hole was finally covered. Claire had come out on the balcony to help Liza while Jeff and Will shouted instructions to Peter from below.

The tarp was pulled tight and secured outside by tying down the ropes that hung from each corner with some large nails driven into the roof.

When the tarp finally seemed secure, they all went inside again. Jeff and Will headed for hot showers while Peter, Liza, and Claire went back up to the attic to make sure there was no more water leaking in.

It was still a disaster area to be sure. But they could see that the tarp covered the hole adequately, and only a small amount of rain still seeped through.

"It should hold for a while," Liza said. "At least until the rain ends."

"It'd better. I don't think we can do anything more tonight," Peter said wearily.

They were all exhausted and returned to their rooms. For the second time that day, Liza pulled off sopping wet clothes and put on a T-shirt and sweatpants, then dropped onto her bed. The clock read five minutes past five. She closed her eyes, hoping for a few hours of sleep before she had to get up and deal with this latest crisis.

What was going to happen to her next? She was afraid to even consider the question. One disaster at a time. That was her new motto.

LIZA managed to sleep for an hour or so but soon woke up, feeling anxious and worried. She went down to the kitchen and was surprised to find Claire already there, the scent of something baking filling the room with a buttery, sweet aroma.

The smell of coffee rose from a drip pot, and Liza helped herself to a cup. "The rain has stopped. At least for a while. Is the power on yet?"

"Not yet, that usually takes a few hours," Claire replied.

Liza sat with her coffee and took a sip. "Thanks for your quick thinking last night. I would have never thought of covering the roof like that. We would all be swimming around in a fishbowl right now," she joked.

"Oh, I'm not sure about that," Claire replied modestly. "You would have come up with some solution."

Maybe so, but Claire's cool head and resourcefulness had definitely saved the day. Liza was grateful to her. Not just for the roof, she realized, but for all the help she had so freely given ever since Liza had arrived.

"I guess we'll have to get the roof fixed before we can sell this place," Liza said, thinking out loud. "No one's going to buy it in this condition."

"That branch has tossed a monkey wrench into your plans," Claire agreed in a sympathetic tone. She opened the oven and peered inside. The cinnamon smell was incredibly delicious.

"Too bad for your brother, he seems to be counting on a quick sale."

"Yes, he is," Liza said. She had come here wanting a quick sale, too. But she felt differently about it now. Perhaps Claire sensed that. The next thing the housekeeper said made Liza think so.

"Did you ever hear that saying, 'When God closes one door, He always opens another'?" Claire asked.

"My aunt used to say that whenever I got frustrated—trying to make a sports team or missing out on some job situation."

Claire smiled. "Yes, it was one of her favorite sayings. She also used to say that the problem with most people is that they sit staring at the closed door so long, they never notice the open one."

Liza didn't recall that part of the proverb. A nice twist, she thought. Were she and Peter staring at the closed door right now, even with a huge branch poking right through it? Claire seemed to think so.

Funny how just yesterday when she visited the cemetery, she was thinking that her aunt would not have approved of such a rush sale, making such a big decision without taking their time, considering their choices. Looking for another open door. Looking at things . . . creatively.

Peter needed the money. He had made no secret of that. He was counting on it.

But I have money I can loan him or even give him, Liza realized. She and Jeff had sold their condo as a condition of their separation agreement. Liza had planned to buy a new property with her share, but the money was just sitting in the bank. Hers to do with as she pleased.

"Would you like a muffin?" Claire asked, setting a basket of hot muffins on the table.

Liza took one and put in on her plate. Then she peeled back the paper wrapper. "This looks great. What kind is it, carrot?"

"Not exactly. It's called Morning Glory."

Liza took a bite. "It's good. Really good," she said around a mouthful.

Claire looked pleased by her reaction. "It's an old recipe, but it comes out a little different every time. It all comes together in the end, though. If you relax and take your time."

Liza didn't cook much, but she had some idea of what Claire was talking about. That was the way she had always felt about her art. She would set out with some concept for what she wanted to capture in a sketch or painting, but then she always had to allow for the work to take on its own life, to speak with its own voice. For the unexpected to evolve. That was the fun of it, the magic.

Liza wanted to talk more to Claire about this notion, but Jeff was coming down the hall toward the kitchen, dressed and ready to go. "Well, I'm off," he said. "If the bridge isn't open yet, I'll just wait."

"I think it will be open by now," Claire said.

"Would you like some coffee before you go?" Liza asked. She and Jeff might not be a couple anymore, but they could be decent to each other.

He hesitated. "All right, just a quick cup."

Claire poured a mug of coffee and handed it to him. He didn't sit down but drank it standing.

"Thanks for helping out last night," Liza said. "It was all hands on deck."

"It was exciting. I sort of enjoyed it." Jeff glanced at her. "A memorable chapter in a memorable visit."

Liza didn't answer. She met his glance and looked away.

"How about a muffin—for the road? They're very good."

She held out the basket, a peace offering. He smiled finally and took a muffin, then wrapped it in a napkin. "For the road, then."

Jeff said good-bye to Claire and headed for the door.

Liza followed. "Good-bye, Jeff," she said. "Drive safely."

"Good-bye, Liza." He turned and briefly hugged her. "I hope you find whatever it is you're looking for," he said, as he stepped away.

"I hope so, too," Liza replied. Though she hadn't until that moment realized she was searching for anything special in her life. She just knew what she didn't want. But maybe that was the same thing, just viewed from a different angle.

She stepped out onto the porch. Jeff climbed into his car and drove away. She watched the car turn at the end of the drive, then disappear. An ordinary sight. Yet in this instance, it felt so final.

Liza stood on the porch, hugging her arms around her for warmth as she stared out at the ocean and the crystal clear sky.

Finding closure about her marriage and her disillusionment with her job had left a gaping hole in her life. Two focal points of her life had been wiped off the playing board. In the blink of an eye, it seemed.

Now there was just a big hole there. Like the one up in the roof. How would she fix it? What should she do?

It seemed like a huge disaster. But it had also opened a space where you could see the blue sky or the stars at night.

That was something to think about, too.

It was all in the way you looked at things, Liza realized. Out on this island, she seemed to be seeing everything from a very different perspective.

Chapter Eleven

L IZA leaned on the porch railing and took one last, lingering look at the water. She certainly wasn't going to answer these huge life questions right now. For one thing, she had more practical matters to focus on—figuring out how to fix the roof, for starters. She knew very well that the huge storm last night was just the first of many. She had to get a solid roof on the inn before the next storm hit.

I guess I should ask Daniel what to do. Even if he can't do the repair work, he probably knows a few carpenters or roofers who could.

Another opportunity to see him, she knew. But she wasn't just trumping up a phony reason. There was, after all, a huge hole in the roof . . .

Liza caught herself and felt annoyed that she was giving the situation so much thought. Then she had to smile as Daniel's truck came into view. As if her thoughts had summoned him.

The white pickup pulled into the drive and parked near the front door. Liza waited on the porch as Daniel got out of the truck and walked toward her. His wide smile and dark eyes made her pulse race, but she did her best to hide her reaction.

"So, you survived the storm, I see. The place is still standing," Daniel greeted her.

"Just barely." Liza pointed to the tree that had been struck by lightning. "That tree was hit, and a huge branch fell off and went right through our roof."

"Wow . . . close call. You were lucky."

"I guess we were." Liza hadn't thought of it that way before, but it was true. The house could have been hit by lightning and caught fire. Maybe a big hole was not so bad after all.

"How bad is it?" Daniel stepped closer, looking concerned.

Liza was suddenly having a hard time focusing on the damaged roof. All she could think about was being alone with him yesterday and how good that felt.

She forced her mind back to his question. "Well, the hole is sort of off to one side of the eave," she answered. "And there's this huge branch. I don't know how we'll ever move that, it's so heavy. It's hard to describe," she said finally, glancing up at him.

"Let's go up and take a look." He met her gaze and briefly touched her shoulder, then followed her to the front door.

Something between them felt different this morning. Some ineffable . . . something. They had crossed some sort of line yesterday, a line of intimacy. Their relationship had moved into some new territory, one that was a strange, foreign land to her after being married for so long.

291

And she had made a final break with Jeff last night, even more final than their divorce—which left her free to see Daniel in a new way.

They headed into the house, and Liza led the way up the first staircase. "Do you work on roofs, too?" she asked him.

"I might be able to work on this one. Let's just see what's going on."

They finally arrived in the dimly lit attic. Daniel surveyed the branch and hole from a few different angles. Then he looked over the surrounding beams and the fractured wood around the opening. "Hmm. That is a nasty hit."

"So, what's your prognosis, Doctor? Can this roof be saved?"

"I'll give it my best shot—though the emergency surgery will delay the paint job."

"Oh, right." Liza hadn't thought of that. They could probably find someone else to fix the roof while Daniel kept painting. But now that he had looked over the damage and said he could do it, she didn't feel right taking the project away from him.

"Well, it can't be helped, I guess. A hole in the house is a priority."

"I'd tend to agree with that, especially with more rain in the forecast. You're catching on to this renovation stuff pretty quickly."

She knew he was teasing her now. "Thanks. I do watch those home shows from time to time."

"I guessed that. Are you sure you really want to sell this place? I think you secretly enjoy it."

She was secretly enjoying something about these repair issues, that was for sure.

She caught his eye for an instant, then looked away. A few cartons marked "Christmas" caught her eye, and Liza rushed over to move them to a dry spot.

"I didn't see these last night. I hope the Christmas decorations didn't get ruined," she said over her shoulder. "Aunt Elizabeth had such beautiful ornaments and lights."

"Here, let me help you." Daniel stepped over and began moving the cartons with her. They worked together for a few minutes without speaking, yet Liza felt strangely connected to him, relaxed and easy in their partnership.

Finally, he stood up and brushed some dust off his hands. "Anything else you want to get out of the way?"

She stood up, too, and brushed a few stray strands of hair off her face. He reached down and helped her, smiling gently.

"Why do I always look like such a wreck when I see you?" she asked in a quiet, plaintive tone.

"I don't know. But I have to tell you, I've rarely seen such an unattractive woman. It's . . . alarming." The way he was staring at her in the hazy light and the smile in his warm brown eyes suggested he was more charmed than alarmed.

He cupped her face in his hand and leaned down and kissed her. Liza closed her eyes, feeling herself melt. Her arms slipped around his waist as he pulled her closer. Liza wasn't sure how long they stood there, how long the kiss lasted. She lost all track of time.

She heard someone coming up the stairs, and she quickly pulled away. What had come over her? What had come over him?

"Liza, are you up there?" Peter called, as he slowly climbed the narrow flight that led to the attic.

"Yes . . . I'm here with Daniel. We're just looking at the damage," she shouted back.

Sort of . . .

She glanced at Daniel. He looked as dazed as she felt. Which was some comfort. They shared a swift, secret smile. Then he put on his game face and walked toward the steps to greet Peter.

"So, what do you think? A total disaster, right?" Peter ran his hand through his hair. "What a thing to happen. What timing." He looked over at Liza before Daniel could reply. "Fran Tulley just called. The Hardys wanted to come back today, but I had to tell her about the roof. She's going to tell them and see what they want to do. She didn't sound too optimistic." Peter's tone was glum. "She thinks they may be scared off."

Liza glanced over at Daniel. "Daniel says he can fix it in a few days."

"A few days?" Peter turned to Daniel. "Will it really take that long?"

"Two days at least. Depending on the weather," Daniel told him.

Daniel began to explain the different stages of the repair, and Liza decided it was the perfect time to slip away and let her brother take over.

Liza yearned for a shower and a change of clothes. The situation would look better after that, she was sure of it.

She knew there was plenty of work to be done today, but for some reason, the hole in the roof had taken the pressure off. Like getting a flat tire on a road trip. You had no choice but to stop and wait. And appreciate your surroundings.

And think about being kissed in the attic by the most amazing man you've met in ages? a little voice chided her.

Yes . . . that, too, Liza silently acknowledged.

LIZA came out of her room a short time later, wearing jeans and one of her good sweaters, her hair pulled back in a ponytail. She heard noises up in the attic, the sound of a saw and hammers. Daniel didn't waste any time getting to work, that was for sure.

She also heard Claire talking with someone down in the foyer. It was Fran Tulley, she realized as she drew closer.

"Oh, there she is," Claire said, turning to watch

Liza come down the stairs. "Fran is here to see you, Liza. I'll leave you two to your business. I have something on the stove."

The housekeeper headed back toward the kitchen as Fran and Liza greeted each other.

"Hi, Fran, I didn't know you were going to stop by. Peter said he spoke to you this morning."

"I was in the neighborhood and thought I should see the roof firsthand. This way I can prepare people."

"Daniel Merritt just started working on it," Liza assured her.

"Oh, that's good. Very good." Fran followed Liza up the first flight of stairs toward the attic. "I'm afraid the Hardys have backed off," Fran reported. "For now at least. I told them the damage probably wasn't much and would be fixed quickly. But they got spooked. Some people feel superstitious about lightning."

"What do you mean?"

Fran shrugged. "There's a lot of magical thinking attached to lightning. It's so sudden and explosive and powerful. Some people believe it's some sort of sign from the heavens."

Liza didn't believe in that stuff. She didn't even think about it. Not usually.

As they climbed up the last narrow flight, they heard voices, and Liza realized that Peter and Will were in the attic with Daniel.

"Everyone's here," Fran said, sounding pleased

as they stepped into the attic. "Peter, Will, good to see you."

Daniel met Liza's glance, and she could tell that he was not nearly so pleased to have such a large audience.

"How's it going?" Fran said, walking over to him. "Looks like you've found another big project here."

"Or it found me," Daniel answered. He nodded toward the huge chunk of tree branch on the attic floor. There was sawdust all around, and Liza was relieved to see that everything nearby had been covered with drop cloths.

"Daniel's cutting up the branch. Then we'll lower it out the window to the ground with some ropes and pulleys," Peter explained.

So he did need some help, Liza realized. Or maybe he was just humoring her brother and making him feel as if he were doing something productive.

Will seemed to be the only one actually helping Daniel. He wore large gloves and a plastic eye guard. He held one end of the trunk as Daniel pre-pared to cut into it again.

"Be careful, Will. Don't get too close to that saw. I wish you'd let me do that part," Peter told his son.

"I'm okay, Dad. Just chill, will you?"

"No need for attitude, Will." Peter's voice rose. "This is serious."

"I know, I know. Give me a break. You're always criticizing. You know everything, right?" Will stepped back from the branch, glaring at Peter.

There was a momentary standoff until Daniel stepped in. "Will's doing a good job. Just let him handle this last part. He's already got the gear on," Daniel pointed out.

Peter curtly nodded and stood back. Daniel positioned the saw again, but this time Fran interrupted him.

"How long do you think it will take, Daniel?" she asked.

"A few days. If I can get this branch out of the way and get started."

Liza seemed to be the only one who caught his sarcasm. And Will, she noticed, who was quietly laughing.

"That's not so bad," Fran said, considering.

"Could you let the Hardys know that?" Peter asked. "Tell them we're fixing the roof."

"Of course I will," Fran assured him. Then she peered up at the hole again, frowning. "This is a setback, no way around it. I don't think we should bring anyone else to view the property until this repair is made. It's just going to throw people off. There's enough to overlook already."

No denying that, Liza knew. Even her brother couldn't argue the point.

Daniel held up his saw. "Just want to warn you

all. I'm going to count to five and start this up again. Ready, Will?"

Will adjusted his goggles and nodded.

"You don't have to tell me twice. What a racket." Fran quickly headed for the steps. "So long, Daniel. Good luck." She turned to Peter and Liza. "Keep me posted. And don't worry. Sometimes you just can't force these situations," she added. "You just have to sit tight and wait it out."

Liza glanced back at her brother as she headed down the steps, wondering how he was taking that piece of advice. Not well, she decided, not well at all.

LIZA walked Fran to the front door, then wandered into the front parlor. Claire was sorting out more clothing, heavy woolen coats and sweaters that she was going to bring to a local homeless shelter.

"The weather's getting warmer, so I guess they'll hold on to this stuff until next fall," she said, packing the last bag. "It will go to use though, either way."

"I'm sure Aunt Elizabeth would approve," Liza said. "Do you need any help putting that in your car?"

"Nah. This is the last bag. I'm fine." Claire tied the end of the black bag and stood up straight again. "What are you up to today? Outside or in?"

Liza shrugged. "Oh, I don't know. I might hang the curtains in the bathroom downstairs. But it seems too nice to stay inside."

"That's the best thing about a big spring storm. It makes the air so clear and sweet," Claire agreed.

So it had. The storm had left the air sparkling clear, and now the sun shone down brilliantly. It was far too beautiful to stay inside, but Liza couldn't think of any outside jobs she wanted to tackle either.

"Why don't you take a break from this house today, Liza?" the older woman suggested. "Maybe that lightning bolt was trying to tell you something," she added with a smile.

"You think so?" Liza asked, curious. "I can't imagine what that might be."

Claire shrugged. "I don't know exactly. Whenever I'm tired and confused, I take a nice long walk on the beach. That's where I feel calmer. And closest to God. That's what helps me sort things out."

Liza nodded. She respected—and even envied—Claire's strong faith, though she didn't come close to sharing it. Liza wasn't a church-goer, hadn't prayed for years. Well, maybe once or twice in some desperate crisis, after her parents had their accident, probably. Liza didn't think God felt very positively about people who only called in an emergency. But Claire was right about two things: Liza did feel tired and confused, and she did need some time away from the inn.

"Off I go. See you later." Claire picked up the big bag of clothes and headed out to her car.

Liza gazed out the bay window at the stretch of clear sky and blue-green ocean. A beach walk would do her good, she decided.

As Liza left the parlor, she saw her sketchbook and pencil box still sitting on the end table where she had left them the other night. They seemed to be waiting for her like dear old friends.

She picked up the art supplies and tucked them under her arm. She wasn't sure if she had the courage to start drawing again, but it would be nice to look over the sketches once more, she thought. The images brought back such happy memories.

Wearing her scarf and jacket, with an apple and a water bottle tucked in her pockets, Liza crossed the road in front of the inn. She felt as if she were sneaking away, on some secret errand. Behind her, the steady sound of hammering and the sound of the saw broke the perfect quiet of the clear morning.

No one will miss me, she thought. *Not for a while anyway.*

As she climbed down the steep hill that led to the beach, she felt her cares and concerns about the inn lifting. The sight of the beach after a storm was captivating. She had forgotten how beautiful it looked, with long ropes of reddish brown and green seaweed flung about like strange confetti, as if there had been a wild party there the night before. Shells and stones were scattered in patterns that marked the tides, and little cliffs and alcoves had been carved from the shoreline by the strong surf.

The waves were still rough today, rushing to the shoreline, one after the other, and crashing with a thunderous roar.

Liza walked against the wind, her hands dug in her pockets and her head down. She felt as if the salt air were practically blowing her cares away. Claire was right. She did feel closer to something vital and elemental here. Was it God? Well, that was one word for what she felt, she acknowledged. The rough, wild sea did seem like the very soul of the Earth, the source of life, the source of everything.

Liza walked until her legs felt weary, then sat in the sand, resting against a large flat rock. She leaned her head back and closed her eyes, feeling the sun on her skin.

It was warmer here today than she had expected. She felt herself slowing down, almost getting drowsy. But the cackling and calls of seabirds nearby wouldn't let her drift off completely.

She opened her eyes and watched a flock of small birds—terns maybe? Or maybe herring gulls? Her uncle Clive had been a big birder. He knew the proper names of all the species common to the area. There were eighty-seven species of gulls alone, Liza recalled, though only a few lived locally.

Neither Liza nor Peter shared Clive's avian passion, though Liza loved to watch the seabirds feed and fly along the shore like this. Of all the creatures on earth, birds had such graceful lines and eloquent expression in their smallest gesture, the tilt of their heads, the gaze of bright eyes, or the arch of a delicate wing.

Without giving it much thought, she opened her sketchbook, took out a soft pencil, and began to sketch the flock. After a few minutes, she rose from her spot and crept up slowly to observe them at closer range.

One or two of the birds looked up inquisitively at her but soon returned to pecking at mounds of seaweed, searching for tasty bits of broken crabs or other delicacies in the sand.

Liza's hand moved awkwardly at first. Her fingers felt so clumsy. She couldn't draw a decent line. Frustrated, she tore off page after page. But finally, she stuck with a sketch and saw a tiny bit of improvement. She finished one drawing, flipped the page, and moved on to another.

The birds were fast, never staying in one pose very long. Which was a good thing, she thought. A lot like the fast-sketching sessions she was forced to do in art school. A model would hold a position for no more than three minutes, then switch to a new one. Students would rush to capture the pose in bold, swift lines.

"Don't think, just draw," was her favorite teacher's motto.

Liza could almost hear her professor's voice, shouting at her over her shoulder. The impulse had to flow from the eye to the hand, bypassing a certain analytical, editorial part of the brain that always made a muddle of things.

Maybe that's my problem lately, Liza mused. *I'm thinking too much.* "Don't think . . . just live," she adapted her art teacher's counsel.

Liza wasn't sure how long she sat there, drawing her small, winged models. Her drawing hand began to cramp, and she stopped to stretch her fingers. Suddenly, for no apparent reason, the entire flock of birds took to the air.

The birds hovered over the shoreline and rolling waves. The gulls formed a soft white cloud, swooping and flying as one. Then they sailed off down the beach and disappeared, searching for some fresh feeding ground, she guessed.

Liza sat back and looked over the drawings. A few weren't half bad, she conceded. It had been fun to try her hand again. She had been afraid of what might happen. Afraid that she'd lost her eye, her talent.

But maybe that never really goes away, she realized. It's like riding a bike. The equipment is a little rusty and clunky at first, but little by little, you get it all rolling along again.

Could she ever really quit her job and stay on this island?

Run the inn and return to her artwork?

Liza had joked about the possibility yesterday with Daniel. But hadn't she been a tiny bit serious, too? Hadn't she wished she had the courage to strike out on her own like that? To choose the road less traveled, the way her aunt and uncle had?

Liza sighed and put the sketchbook aside. Perhaps it was better to just stick with the plan. Sell the inn, return to Boston. Take her lumps at work or look for a new job. Draw a little in her spare time if she liked. Take an art class again.

Time was running out. Her two weeks away from the office were almost over. They expected her back next Monday. If she wanted a longer leave from work, she would have to call Eve before the weekend, either tonight or tomorrow.

Liza didn't know what to do. She'd had so little sleep last night, it was hard to make any decisions right now. Liza bunched up her scarf under her head and lay back on the sand.

She closed her eyes and took a few deep breaths. *God, I'm not too good at prayers,* she began silently. *I don't have much practice, but I just feel the need to talk to You. I'm so confused. I don't know what to do. Should we sell the inn? Should we wait? Should I stay here or go? If I could just have a sign, I'd be ever so grateful . . . You don't need to send another lightning bolt. A less dramatic sign would be fine.*

Liza wasn't sure how long she slept. The sun had traveled across the sky, and the air felt cooler. She sat up quickly and looked down. There was something in her lap, stuck to her jacket—a thick white feather. She picked it up and examined it. It was a long, silky plume. Very pure and clean.

She didn't think it had come from the flock of birds she had been drawing; they were mostly gray. She glanced around, but there were no birds in sight.

Staring down at the feather, Liza had an odd feeling. It seemed to be a sign, wordless approval of her artistic efforts for the day and also an answer to her question.

Liza stood up, brushed herself off, then carefully tucked the feather into her jacket pocket. She set off for the inn, knowing this was something she couldn't explain to anyone. Well, maybe Claire North would understand. It seemed to Liza that her rambling, desperate prayer had been heard. Heard and even answered.

PETER didn't seem to mind that Liza had taken a day off from house repairs. He didn't say anything about it at dinner. He had helped Daniel with the roof repairs for most of the day and was eager for Liza to see their progress.

After they cleaned up the kitchen, Liza followed her brother and Will upstairs, heading for the attic. But when they reached the second floor, Will headed to his room instead.

Liza was surprised. "I guess you're tired from all the work you did today."

"Yeah, I guess," the boy mumbled, avoiding her glance.

"Well, thanks for pitching in. I'm sure Daniel appreciated the extra help."

"Yeah, well at least somebody did." Will gave his father a dark look, then turned toward his room.

Will's door closed, and Liza looked over at her brother. "Did you and Will have another fight today?"

Peter shrugged. "Oh, he's just in a snit. That work was dangerous. I didn't want him getting hurt. Was that so wrong? I didn't feel like carrying his fingers in a plastic bag of ice to some emergency room and—"

"I get your point," Liza quickly cut in.

Poor Daniel. Had he played referee all day between them?

Peter shook his head. "Let's go up and look at the roof. I'll try to make it up to Will tomorrow," he added in a tired tone.

Moments later they were standing in the attic. The branch had disappeared, and the jagged hole had been cleaned up. Fresh beams of wood crossed over the hole, which was covered on the outside tonight by a sheet of canvas.

"Not bad," Liza said. "It's coming along quickly."

"I thought so. But Daniel thinks it needs at least two more days. At this rate, it will be Labor Day before we sell this place."

"I've been thinking, Peter, maybe this delay isn't such a bad thing?" He turned and looked at her, but she rushed on before he could interrupt. "Right before the storm, when I ran off on the bike, you know where I ended up? At the cemetery. I went to look for Aunt Elizabeth and Uncle Clive's headstone."

"I guess I should visit, too, before I go," Peter said. "Maybe I'll take Will."

"Maybe you should. I was so upset about Jeff and about my job, about a lot of things. I just sat there for a long time, thinking. I got this feeling that if Aunt Elizabeth were here, she wouldn't like the way we're handling things—rushing to sell this place to the first person who has a pulse and enough credit to get a mortgage."

Peter laughed, a sharp, surprised sound. "What other credentials should we be looking for, do you think?"

"You know what I mean." Liza walked over to a pile of her aunt's canvases that were stacked against the wall. One had fallen, and she bent to pick it up. Some of these should be framed, she thought. They would look great in the bedrooms and hallways.

She dusted her hands off and looked at her brother. "I know the roof repair is an annoyance and a speed bump. But it's also an opportunity. Maybe we should just slow down and consider our options."

Peter laughed. "Oh, no. Don't tell me. You think that lightning bolt was 'a sign' or something now, too?"

Liza wasn't entirely sure what she thought about the lightning bolt. Maybe it was a sign of some kind. Who could say either way? She wasn't willing to go down that road with him right now. It was beside the point anyway.

"Let's just say we've been forced to stop and take stock. We have no choice. So why not look at all the possibilities?"

"What possibilities?" Peter folded his arms across his chest, his expression not quite angry but tense. Still, she had to persist, get this out in the open while she had a chance.

"There are choices we've never discussed," Liza said carefully. "Like holding on to the place as an investment. Once the island gets more active, the property is bound to increase in value. Maybe we could find someone to run the inn, and we could be absentee owners."

"Liza, please. Don't do this to me. Not now." Peter shook his head. "I don't want to be an absentee owner of a run-down money pit. And how would we find anyone to manage this place for us? Anyone we could trust? And what about the cost of renovating? Aunt Elizabeth had her regular customers who didn't expect much, but you're talking about a wave of tourists with far different expectations . . . And why am I even getting into this discussion in the first place? Honestly, Liza. This is the last thing I expected. I'm really not in the mood to argue with you tonight."

"I'm only pointing out some possibilities," Liza said quietly.

Then she stopped talking. She didn't want to argue either, and she didn't have answers to his questions. But now that Peter had mentioned it, Liza did think Claire North would be the perfect person to run the inn. She was definitely someone they could trust.

"You know I need my share of the money," her brother continued. "I thought this was all settled between us. Why are you backtracking?"

Liza sighed. "It's hard to explain. It's just that my feelings have changed since I've gotten here. I've started to feel differently, and I can see some interesting alternatives to selling. Can't you?"

"To be perfectly honest, I've felt relieved knowing I won't be stuck with this place. It's practically falling down. Or haven't you noticed?"

Liza didn't think the condition of the building

was quite that bad. Though the repairs needed were definitely daunting.

Peter's expression remained tight and grim. She could see that she wasn't making any headway.

"If it's a matter of money, I have some savings I can loan you, Peter. I'd be happy to help you. Honestly."

Peter stared at her, then let out a long frustrated sigh. "It's not just the money, Liza. It's the whole idea of it. I own half of this property," he reminded her. "It's not just about your feelings, which seem to change day to day."

"I can't help it. I've had a change of heart."

"You've had a lot going on in your life, too. Everything at your office and your divorce. Jeff surprising you here—"

"What are you trying to say?" she asked warily.

"Only that you're going through a lot of change and loss, a lot of emotional upheaval. Maybe changing your mind about selling the inn is some sort of reaction to all that. That's all I mean."

What he meant was that she was upset and confused right now and that she shouldn't trust her own feelings or impulses.

"I don't think that's it," she said finally. "But I'll think about it. If you'll think about what I said."

"All right. Fair enough. I'll try."

"Let's just get the roof fixed and get our bearings," Liza said. "We have to delay showing the place that long anyway."

"Fran Tulley certainly thinks so," Peter grumbled. He stood up and stretched, then rubbed his lower back. "I'm turning in. See you tomorrow."

"Good night, Peter."

She knew that she ought to go downstairs, too, but somehow she didn't feel like leaving the attic space so quickly. She wandered around, peering into boxes to check for water damage.

She came to the boxes of Christmas decorations and thought about the kiss she had shared with Daniel in the shadows at that very spot. The episode seemed like a dream. Like some wild fantasy. How seriously should she take it? Another question to add to her growing list.

Most likely it was just a fluke, not the start of anything real, she told herself. She would be foolish to let things go any further if she wasn't going to stay here.

It was funny how all the pressing questions seemed tangled together now, one sticky thread twisted with another.

Clearing out this old house had become a process of clearing out the cobwebs in her own life, Liza realized. Cobwebs she hadn't even known were there.

Chapter Twelve

D ANIEL started working on the roof very early the next morning. Liza heard heavy footsteps pass her bedroom door, then tramp up the next flight toward the attic. Hammering soon followed, making it impossible to get back to sleep. With a sigh, she got out of bed and quickly dressed.

Down in the kitchen, Peter and Will had already eaten breakfast and looked ready to start their workday.

"Daniel wants us to help his man with the exterior house painting today," Peter said. "He's concerned about falling behind schedule."

Liza thought Daniel was probably concerned about having Peter and Will up in the tiny attic again, breathing down his neck as he hurried to fix the roof. But his diplomatic solution seemed to solve two problems at once.

"I'll come outside and paint, too," Liza offered. "It's a perfect day. We can get a lot done."

"My thought exactly." Peter took one last sip of his coffee and left the mug in the sink. He seemed in a better mood today.

Liza quickly downed some yogurt and a mug of coffee, then took out her BlackBerry. She had woken up certain that she wanted to stay on the island a week more, or even longer. Now she needed to tell Eve she wasn't coming back on Monday.

But when she called the office, she got bounced to Eve's voice mail. Though she would have preferred to tell Eve directly, she decided to leave a message. "Hi, Eve, it's Liza. We've had some setbacks here. A branch went through the roof during a storm, and we need to make a lot of repairs. Everything is taking longer than I expected, actually. So I do need to take some more time here. A week at least. Possibly more. You can call me if you'd like, or I'll try you again on Monday."

Liza ended the call and put her phone away. She had been anxious about asking for more time. But after the call she felt relieved, certain that it was the right decision.

She stepped through the back door and was greeted by the warm sunshine. The day was clear and very mild. Spring had arrived. She could actually smell it in the sweet air and damp, earthy scent of the garden. Even the sunlight seemed brighter and stronger.

She found Peter and Will at the side of the house, choosing from a selection of paints and brushes spread out on a canvas. A man from Daniel's crew had started to spray a coat of paint on the building with a special machine.

"Let's put you to work," Peter greeted her cheerfully, talking above the noise.

"We need to follow with the brushes, Dad.

Before it dries." Will, holding a thick brush and a bucket of ivory paint, walked toward the clapboard.

"Hold your horses. Just wait until I show you," Peter said firmly.

"Daniel showed me the other day," Will insisted. "It's not exactly brain surgery."

Peter reached out and took Will's brush away. "I asked you to wait. Now just calm down."

Will scowled and stomped off into the house, slamming the door behind him.

"That went well," Liza observed. Her brother arched an eyebrow at her. "We're not restoring the Sistine Chapel, Peter. Let him paint with you."

"I want him to paint. But there's a right way to do this, Liza. You don't want the house to look like a big mess when we show it, do you?"

"Of course not," she replied. Though she thought Will had been painting pretty well so far. Maybe even better than Peter, who was so painfully slow and meticulous, he could have been doing brain surgery.

"I was working on the porch before the rainstorm. I'll just keep going on it," Liza told her brother. She was happy to have that territory staked out for herself. She didn't need to be back here, in the middle of Peter and Will all day.

With a paint can in one hand and brushes and a tray in the other, she marched off toward the front of the house.

315

If you ran an inn, this is what you would be doing most of the time, she reminded herself, *painting and repairing. You couldn't call Daniel for every little thing.*

Though she'd definitely want to.

Liza set her equipment on the porch, climbed halfway up the ladder, and started to paint the window trim in the bright sea green her aunt and uncle had used. She had always loved this color; it seemed so much a part of the island and the inn.

As she worked, her thoughts drifted. Eve might not like it, but Liza was glad she had asked for more time off. It hurt all over again to think about how she had been pushed aside. So much had been going on the past few days, she had been distracted. Now it all came rushing back. She felt so awful about the situation that she hadn't checked her e-mails or messages in two days. That was saying something.

Maybe once more time had passed, she would see things differently. But right now there didn't seem anything left for her at the agency. It was hard to imagine returning to her job. In two more weeks. Or ever . . .

"Whoa there, lady. . . . You don't need to paint the windows. I don't think the customer would like that."

Liza turned suddenly at the sound of Daniel's voice—and smacked him on the side of the head with her paint tray.

"Daniel! For goodness' sake . . . I'm so sorry . . ."
She hustled down the ladder, sloshing green paint
off the tray in all directions, drips falling on both
of them. He stepped back, then sat down on the
top of the porch steps, holding the side of his head
with his hand.

"It's all right. I have a hard head, but you are
dangerous. Don't even look at the electric saw."

He was right. She was dangerous with a paintbrush. Around him anyway. She took a step closer
and tried not to laugh.

"Let me see your head. Take your hand away. Is
there a bump?"

When he wouldn't cooperate, she reached out
and moved his hand with her own. His hand was
wide and calloused, covered with sawdust and
now some paint. Which was also on his face and
in his hair.

"I'm so sorry. Let me wipe that off your head at
least."

Before he could answer, she grabbed a clean wet
rag she had stashed in her back pocket and gently
wiped the smear of paint from his skin and hair.
He sat very still, tilting his head toward her.

It felt odd touching him so personally, despite
the fact that he had kissed her. This was different
somehow. She felt as if she were taking care of
him.

"I see something, a little red spot where the tray
nicked you." She reached out with her fingertips

and felt a small bump on his forehead near his hairline. Her fingers yearned to touch his thick dark hair again, but she quickly drew her hand back.

He stared up at her, and she forgot what she wanted to say.

"I'll go inside . . . and get some ice," she finally managed.

"That's okay. I'll be fine. Sit down. Take a break. Talk to me a little."

He reached out and took hold of her wrist, tugging her down to sit on the step next to him.

Liza sat and stared straight ahead. He was very close, though they weren't quite touching.

"Are you sure you're okay?" she asked again. "Head injuries can be tricky. You don't have a headache or anything?"

He laughed. "It was a paint tray, Liza, not a bowling ball." He turned to look at her. "I guess I would have to wear some protective headgear, though, if we ever go bowling."

Was he thinking of asking her out on a date? She hated bowling. But she would put up with the hardship if necessary.

"How's the roof coming along?" She half dreaded hearing his answer, knowing fast progress meant less time to work on Peter.

"The hole is nearly patched. We still have to do the shingles. Fran can bring lookers around, I guess."

"All right. I'll tell her that if she calls."

He studied her with a curious expression. "You don't want to call her?"

Liza shrugged. "I'm busy now. Maybe later."

"Your brother would call her in a heartbeat," Daniel pointed out.

"Yes, he probably would."

"Have you talked to him at all about your doubts?"

She looked away, wondering if she should confide in him.

It felt a bit disloyal to Peter. This was their private business, family business. But for some reason, she wanted to tell Daniel what was going on.

"We talked about it last night. I asked him to just slow down and try to consider the possibilities—keeping the place and having someone run it for us. Or letting me stay."

"Some good ideas. Especially the second idea," he said quietly. "What did he say?"

She turned to him, surprised to find that his face was so close to her own. Their shoulders were practically brushing. Had he moved closer at some point? Had she moved closer to him without realizing it?

"He said he would think about it. But I think he was just placating me. He still seems very intent on our original plan." She swallowed hard and looked back at the ocean in the distance. "I just want to look at all the options and not rush into anything."

Daniel nodded. "That sounds reasonable."

"Not according to Peter. He's annoyed at me for changing my mind. He thinks I'm just being emotional, overwhelmed by everything. And who knows, he may be right. Maybe it is just pie in the sky to even consider it. This place needs a ton of work that will cost a ton of money—doesn't it?"

Daniel considered the question a moment. "The place needs work, no question. But you could do the basics first, then manage the rest over time. Your aunt didn't rent out all the rooms, you know. She just had a few on the ocean side ready for guests and the one large bathroom on the second floor. Renovating a big house like this is usually done in stages."

"That makes sense." Some of the rooms were in much better condition than others, and it wouldn't take much to bring them up to quality standards. But there were certainly other concerns, beyond wallpaper and new curtains.

"What about the plumbing and electricity and the furnace? All the stuff you can't see—and that I don't know anything about?"

"Your aunt kept up with those repairs. You might need a new water heater and a new roof in a year or two. And new windows and insulation would save a lot of money on heating bills in the winter."

He had told her that before. They were all important, costly changes, but there was nothing that was a big emergency.

"Hey, guys. What's up?" Peter came around the corner of the house.

Liza suddenly stood up, feeling guilty, though she wasn't sure why. "I was just taking a break with Daniel. I hit him in the head with the paint tray," she explained.

"No major damage," Daniel added. "But you should watch out for her."

Was Daniel going to tell Peter that they'd been talking about the inn? She glanced at him. No, he wasn't.

Peter still looked at them curiously. Did he suspect something? He probably just thought they were flirting, Liza decided. Which was partly true.

"How's the porch coming, Liza?" Peter asked.

"Slowly but surely," Liza said. "That's more or less my painting style."

"Slowly but deadly, more like," Daniel murmured, making her smile.

"Where's Will?" she asked Peter.

"Still sulking in the house. He's probably on his computer."

"Maybe I can lure him downstairs with some lunch," Liza suggested. "I'm about ready to go in for a bite."

"Me, too," Peter quickly agreed. He said goodbye to Daniel and headed through the front door.

Liza lingered a moment with Daniel. "Would you like to have lunch with us?"

He didn't answer right away. Then he shook his head. "Thanks. I'm okay. I'd better get back to the roof. I'll see you later." He started down the steps and headed to his truck.

Liza watched him a moment before going into the house. It was probably better that he didn't take a break with them, she decided. Peter might initiate some conversation about selling the inn and realize that she had turned to Daniel for advice.

No telling what might happen then.

THEY finished painting a little before five o'clock. Liza felt bone tired but forced herself to rally. They had promised Will a trip into Cape Light tonight, and she didn't want to disappoint him.

She took a quick shower and dressed in clean jeans and a plum V-neck sweater. She had a feeling that they would end up at the Clam Box for dinner, so there was no need to dress up.

There was never any need to dress up out here, Liza realized. Over the past two weeks, she had grown accustomed to not giving a thought to how she looked. It was a relief after life in the city, where she strategized every outfit, especially if she had a big meeting or was giving a presentation to a client.

She had never even realized how much time and money she wasted working on her image—always needing the right clothes, shoes, briefcase, handbag—not to mention the time she spent clothes shopping and at the gym and the hairstylist and getting facials and manicures. Personal maintenance was nearly a second job. It was so different out here. She glanced at her nails—a few were broken, the polish was chipped, all evidence that they had ever been manicured was gone. And that was fine. She needed so much less to get by.

She met Will and Peter down in the parlor, and they soon piled into Liza's SUV and set off for the village. It was not quite six o'clock, and the sun was setting quickly. Will had never driven over the land bridge late in the day and found that part of the outing a big adventure.

"It's like the road is practically floating on the water," he said, staring out his window. "And the sky looks really neat, too. You should take some pictures, Dad," he told Peter.

Peter seemed surprised by the suggestion but also pleased.

"I think this would make a great photo, Will. Why don't you try it?"

Ever since they were kids, Peter had rarely left the house without some kind of camera. So Liza wasn't surprised to see him take a small silver point-and-shoot out of his jacket pocket and hand it back to his son.

"I really can't stop the car here, Will. There's not much of a shoulder," Liza told her nephew.

"That's okay. I'll just open the window. It might look more interesting with stuff blurred," he added.

Peter glanced at Liza and smiled. She could see he was pleased at his son's growing interest in photography, and Liza was pleased about it, too. It might create a new bond for them, something to help smooth over the rough patches.

Will found more interesting sights to photograph in the village. They walked down to the harbor and village green. Will ran out on the dock to take pictures. Peter and Liza stayed on the green, giving him some small measure of independence.

Liza noticed the old stone church. "I met up with Reverend Ben on the beach one day before you came," she told Peter. "We had a good talk."

"Really? What did you talk about?"

"About Aunt Elizabeth mostly." Liza paused. It was still hard to talk about her aunt, even to Peter. "I asked him how it was with her, toward the end. I felt so bad that I never came out to visit last winter."

Peter's expression grew thoughtful. She sensed he felt the same way, but he lived so far away, he had a better excuse. "What did Reverend Ben say?"

"That she was always very positive and

peaceful. She was satisfied with her life, the choices she made. And that she had great faith," Liza added.

"We should all be so lucky, eh?"

Liza glanced at him and nodded. She did agree her aunt was fortunate, but she also knew it wasn't a matter of luck. It was more a matter of Aunt Elizabeth knowing what she needed to make herself happy and sticking to her principles.

Will ran back to them, looking excited. "I think I got some really good shots of the harbor. Those big chunks of ice that are partly melted and the reflection of the water and the sunset . . ."

Peter looked impressed. "Wow, that sounds great. Can I take a look later when we get inside?"

"Sure. If you want," Will said with a shrug.

Liza smiled. Will was obviously eager for his father to see the photos but couldn't risk being uncool and actually showing that enthusiasm. It wasn't easy being fourteen.

As she expected, they ended up at the Clam Box for dinner.

They all ordered the same meal, a cup of chowder and the clam roll with fries.

"This place is exactly the same," she said to her brother. "They haven't changed a thing."

"For better or worse. Even the menu is the same," he noticed. "I guess that Otto Bates has passed on by now, though. I think his son runs it."

"What do you think, Will?" Liza asked him.

"It's pretty cool. Sort of retro," Will said.

"Very retro," Peter echoed. "And I'll bet they don't even mean to be."

After dinner they walked up the street to the movie theater.

There was a movie playing that Will wanted to see—a sci-fi plot about a deadly virus sent by aliens who wanted to take over Earth and a small band of survivors who fight off the space creatures and find a cure.

Liza was sure most of the movie would have her either cringing or snoozing, but she happily agreed to her nephew's choice. *Who knows, I might learn something . . . about aliens.*

There was time before the movie, so they bought ice-cream cones and walked down Main Street. "Look, there's that antique store Claire keeps mentioning, the Bramble. Let's look in the window, okay?"

Peter agreed, and Will followed without comment. The store was on the first floor of a Victorian house, painted pale yellow with white trim and dark purple shutters. Liza could see that in the warmer months there was a garden in front. She stepped up on the porch and peeked through the windows. The shop was crammed with antiques, from furniture and quilts to china teacups.

"Wow, this place is stocked," Peter said. "Claire's right. They'll probably take some stuff we want to sell. Maybe we don't need an estate sale after all."

That *he* wanted to sell, Liza nearly corrected him.

But she stopped herself. No need to get into all that tonight. She turned away from the window and headed back down the steps. "I'll call them tomorrow. Maybe someone will come out and take a look at what we've got. I want to keep a few pieces from the inn for my new apartment. I'm tired of all the modern stuff I picked out with Jeff. I'd really love to redecorate with antiques."

Peter glanced at her. "That's fine with me. I guess there are one or two things I'd like to take back to Arizona."

Liza stood at the end of the walk and looked back at the Bramble. "I love the way this place is painted. Maybe we should try a different paint scheme. Wouldn't the shutters on the inn look great with that color?"

"It's not just the paint," Peter pointed out. He gestured at the rest of the street, at the row of beautifully kept nineteenth-century buildings. "It's the way all these Victorians have been maintained."

"The inn could look like that again, given half a chance," Liza argued.

"And half a million dollars," Peter added.

"Oh, not that much." Liza started walking down the street and took a lick of her ice-cream cone.

Will ran up ahead, taking photos of the old-fashioned streetlamps.

When Peter didn't answer, she said, "Daniel says the building is pretty sound—the electricity and plumbing and all that. A lot of the work is just cosmetic."

"You were talking to Daniel about this?" Peter's tone sharpened.

Liza took a breath. She hadn't meant for that to slip out, but now that it had, she wasn't sorry. "I did talk to him a little. It just . . . came up."

"I thought we were in this together, not pulling in different directions. Of course Daniel is going to tell you there are no big problems. That inn has been a gravy train for him. It probably supplies most of his income. Of course, he doesn't want to see a stranger take it over, someone who might not hire him."

Liza didn't think that was true. She doubted Daniel would lie to her for that reason. Or any reason, for that matter.

But she did understand why her brother was upset.

"I'm sorry, Peter. I didn't mean to go behind your back. I just wanted his opinion. He knows the building inside and out. It doesn't hurt to ask, does it?"

"It does if you think it will change my mind about selling the place," Peter said bluntly.

He had her there. Liza felt a lump of the cold ice

cream stick in her throat. She swallowed it down, telling herself to remain calm.

"I'm trying to figure out the very best thing for us to do," she explained. "I know you're concerned about money, but the inn could make money for us. In the long run. Much more than we would get from selling it now, especially when it's such a mess."

Peter took one last lick of his ice cream and dumped the rest in a trash can. "Liza, what you're saying might be true. The problem is, I need money now. Not five or even ten years from now. And even if we did keep the place and make a big investment, fixing it up enough to bring in guests again, we just come back to the same questions. How would we run it long distance? Who would manage the place for us?"

Liza had been thinking about this, too. More than she wanted to admit. "I think Claire North could do it. She would probably be happy to stay. And I know we can trust her."

And I could help run it, she added silently. *I could take the summers off. Or even quit my job and work as a freelance graphic artist and designer again.*

Peter stared at her, his mouth twisted to one side. "Liza, I know you're still upset about your job. You definitely deserved better. But don't toss the baby out with the bathwater."

"What do you mean by that?"

"I mean, I think you're fantasizing about quitting your job, some showdown scene with your boss that will give you a lot of satisfaction—for the moment, anyway."

Liza glanced at him, then looked away. Well, that much was true. She did have a fantasy of returning to the office just to quit and tell Eve what she really thought of her.

"Of course you want to escape from your life. To run away and try something completely different. Anybody would," he added in a kinder tone. "But a week or two more on that island and you'll be dying to get back to work. I know you. You should use your extra time off to look for a new job, and then you'll really show them."

"I already thought of that. I don't want a new job. It will just be more of the same. I'll be working my tail off and dealing with the same old office politics. Another Charlie Reiger—or Charlene—will be out to get me."

All she wanted to think about now was the inn, how she could improve it and open it again.

Peter sighed and put his arm around her shoulder. "I'm sorry. I know you're going through a lot right now, and I want to help you. I really do," he insisted. "But I just don't think you're being realistic."

"Hey, I think it's time for the movie," Will called out to them, as he ran back up the street. "I heard the opening is totally awesome. The aliens, like, land on the Pentagon in these huge pods."

"That does sound awesome," Liza said. "I definitely don't want to miss that."

Just as they reached the theater, she felt her BlackBerry vibrating in her pocket. She pulled it out and checked the caller ID.

"Fran Tulley?" Peter asked eagerly.

"No, it's Eve, my boss. I'd better take this. You guys go ahead."

"Okay, we'll save you a seat." Peter and Will went into the theater, and Liza took a few steps away from the entrance for some privacy.

"Hi, Liza, I'm glad I caught you," Eve greeted her. "Is this a bad time?"

"No, not at all. Did you get my message about needing to stay here longer?" Liza asked.

"Yes, I did. Sorry about the roof. What a mess. You really didn't need that on top of everything else, did you?"

"No, we didn't. It's almost fixed, but it's slowed things down a lot."

"I understand," Eve said in a surprisingly patient tone. "It's fine if you need to stay longer. But there's something I wanted to talk to you about. It really can't wait."

"Is there some problem?" Liza asked, suddenly feeling anxious.

"Not at all. It's about the promotion," Eve replied.

Liza felt like a fly that was about to be hit by a

giant swatter. She could barely focus on Eve's words.

"I'd rather give you this news in person, but we've made a decision, and I need to talk to you about it. We're promoting you to vice president, Liza. This will be effective on the first of the month. There's a substantial raise in salary, of course"—Eve gave her a figure, which was even more than Liza had expected—"as well as more vacation time and additional benefits."

"Oh, my goodness," Liza said. She knew that sounded ridiculous, but it was all she could manage. "I—I thought Charlie was getting the promotion."

"Charlie? What in the world made you think that? This was yours all along, Liza. I thought you knew that."

"The last time we spoke, you said something about big changes and getting along with Charlie better. Letting go of my accounts?" Liza rambled, trying to explain. "I thought you were trying to tell me that he was going to be promoted, and I would be reporting to him," she confessed.

"Oh, Liza. You had it all backward. Charlie will be reporting to you, along with some other account execs. You will need to trim your client list, however, so that's what you should start thinking about. You'll be managing a big staff now and playing a bigger role in decision making. That's what I meant to say. I just wasn't allowed to tell you yet," Eve explained.

"I see." Liza took a deep, steadying breath. She couldn't get her mind around this. A few short days ago, this conversation would have sent her jumping and shouting with joy. But now she just felt stunned. And confused.

"I know this is a lot to spring on you," Eve went on in her usual brisk tone. "Why don't we talk on Monday, and I'll give you more details, okay?"

"Um, sure. I—"

But Eve had already clicked off. She was probably speed-dialing her next power phone call.

Liza put her phone away and stood for a moment, staring at Cape Light's quiet Main Street. People passed, making their way to the movie theater. She hardly noticed.

Had this really happened? Liza still couldn't believe it. She had gotten the promotion after all. That should have smoothed out all the wrinkles in her life, untangled all the knots. She and Peter could sell the inn to anyone who offered, and she could return to Boston in triumph.

Was this the sign she had asked for—telling her to give up on the inn and return to the city?

Clearly, that's what she should do. As Will would say, this was a total no-brainer. She had worked years for this promotion, sacrificed everything. How could she even consider giving it up? And for what? A broken-down house and a faded sketchbook? A fledgling relationship with a carpenter?

Eve hadn't asked *if* Liza wanted the job. She assumed that Liza would take the promotion, that she would be back in Boston in a matter of weeks to become a vice president of Barkin & Carr, one of Boston's most prestigious ad agencies. And why wouldn't she?

Because something was stopping her. Something was holding her back.

All this rushing, she heard her aunt say. *Everyone is rushing and rushing and not getting anywhere. Ever notice?*

Eve would call back on Monday. The decision could wait until then, Liza decided.

This was too important a choice to be rushed. A life-altering fork in the road. Liza stared down both paths—and had no idea which way to go.

Chapter Thirteen

"THAT was Fran," Peter announced on Saturday morning, snapping his cell phone shut. "The Hardys will be here around eleven with their architect in tow. Fran is some sales agent. I can't believe she talked them into coming back."

"Maybe they looked around at other old houses on the market and decided this place was still a better bet, lightning bolts and all," Liza said.

She lifted one end of a rolled-up rug while he hoisted the other. Peter had called the Bramble Antique Shop right after breakfast, and Grace

334

Hegman, the owner, agreed to see some pieces of furniture. They had picked out a few chairs, a large mirror, and some small items and begun packing Liza's SUV.

"It's practically impossible for lightning to strike twice in the same spot," Peter pointed out. "I mean, statistically and all that stuff. Maybe Fran reminded them of that. Maybe they'll make an offer."

"Maybe." Liza forced a positive note into her voice, one she didn't really feel.

Lost in his happy thoughts, Peter took no notice of Liza's mood or the fact that she was not pleased by the call from Fran.

Just as well, Liza thought. She hadn't told her brother her big news about the promotion yet. She knew that if she told Peter, he would immediately assume she was happily returning to her job and accepting the new spot. Liza guessed that if she even dared to hint at her doubts, he would tell her she was crazy, then bombard her with reasons why she had to accept the offer.

Liza didn't want to hear any of it. She wanted to sit with her questions for a while. Her questions and confusion. The news about the Hardys returning should have tipped the scales in favor of accepting the promotion, she thought. But she still wasn't convinced that selling the inn and going back to the city was the right thing to do.

Working together, the two of them managed to

push the rolled-up rug onto the roof of the car. Peter secured it with some bungee cords and nylon twine, then headed into the house for more furniture.

Liza stayed out on the porch, her hands pressed to the small of her back where it ached a bit. She gazed out at the ocean, squinting at the sunlight.

Was this how it was going to wind up after all? She had been here nearly two weeks and only three couples had come to see the property. Now, suddenly, the Hardys would return and make an offer. And that would be that.

No more arguing with Peter. No need to imagine how this room or that room would look with fresh paint or new curtains. No more fantasizing about living here and running the place.

If this were a movie, I'd be really disappointed at the ending, Liza realized.

But it wasn't a movie, it was her real life. Just like returning to her job at the agency was her real life. But another voice inside her spoke, and it quoted one of Aunt Elizabeth's favorite sayings, *"If you keep doing what you've always done, you'll keep getting what you've already got."*

Which Liza had always taken to mean that a person couldn't expect anything different in life if he or she kept sticking to the same old game plan. Wasn't that the question she was wrestling with right now? Whether or not to stick to the straight and narrow—or take a detour into unknown and even frightening territory?

"Guess I'll bring this old lamp. It needs to be rewired, but maybe she'll take it. It looks like real brass." Peter's appraisal interrupted her thoughts. He tramped out onto the porch again, carrying a pole lamp, the frazzled cord dragging. "By the way, Fran thinks it would be better if we weren't here when the Hardys come," he added as he passed by. "So they can look around without anybody getting in the way."

Fran dreaded the thought of Peter hovering and ruining her sale, Liza suspected. But she couldn't tell her brother that.

"Okay, I'll make sure I'm not underfoot."

Peter stood at the bottom of the steps, looking up at her.

"Do you want to come into Cape Light with me?"

She considered the offer, then shook her head. "I don't think so. I'll work around here awhile, then maybe go down to the beach or take a bike ride."

"All right. I think I've got the best of the lot. If Grace Hegman takes this load, I can always come back for more, right?"

"Absolutely," Liza agreed, though she wondered what he had actually packed. She hadn't been watching very closely, she realized. There were a number of items she didn't want to part with, including some chipped china dishes and broken lamps. Had he taken any of those? Then she decided she just didn't care.

What was the sense of haggling? It felt as if this place were slipping away from her, like grains of sand sifting through her fingers, and she just couldn't hang on to any of it.

Peter had pulled out his cell and begun texting someone. He stared at the phone and released an impatient sigh.

"Do you believe this? I've been reduced to texting my son while he's under the very same roof. What is the world coming to?"

Liza would have laughed if her brother hadn't seemed so distressed. "Why don't you just go up and knock on his door?"

Peter's mouth grew tight. "Tried that, he won't answer. He's pretending that he's sleeping, but I know he's awake in there."

"What's the matter? Did you argue?" Liza hadn't witnessed any squabbles last night, but emotional weather between father and son had been unstable the last few days.

"He got a message from a friend last night that the camping trip was great, and now he's mad at me for missing it."

"Oh, that's too bad," Liza replied. "I thought he was enjoying the island—at least, he seemed to be into painting and repairing the place."

"He'd probably tell you it is 'okay,'" Peter said.

"Maybe it is. But I bet it doesn't compare to an

outdoor adventure with his friends. I remember what it was like at that age to feel like you missed out."

"Well, that's the way it goes sometimes. Life isn't fair. The sooner he figures that out, the better," Peter muttered. "There will be other camping trips. I'll take him myself next school break."

"Good idea. You ought to tell him that," Liza replied.

"If he ever comes out of his room, I will. Guess I have to drag him out."

Peter shook his head, then pulled open the door and went inside. Liza followed, dreading the scene to come. Luckily, Will was coming down the stairs just as they reached the foyer.

"There you are. It's about time," Peter greeted him.

Will gave a long, dramatic yawn. "What's up?"

"We're going to town to that antique store, remember? I need your help unloading things."

Will rolled his eyes. "More grunt work. This is child labor, you know. And I'm not getting paid a dime."

Peter's expression tightened. "You're getting an iPhone out of the deal, as I recall. Or you *might* get it if you stop giving me so much attitude."

Will's mouth dropped open. "What do you mean, *might*?"

"I mean, your smart mouth is putting that agreement in jeopardy," Peter said evenly.

"I can't believe you! You said it was a done deal. All I had to do was get on the plane," Will reminded his father in an outraged whine. "No way! That totally stinks!"

Peter's face grew bright red. "That's it, Will! One more word out of you, pal, and no new phone. And the one you have will be turned off." Peter paused, letting his words sink in. "Now, go outside and get into Aunt Liza's car."

Will stared at Peter defiantly. He looked like he was going to mouth off again, then just blinked, his eyes bright and glassy. With an angry sigh, he stomped down the stairs, brushed past the adults, yanked open the front door, then slammed it on his way out.

Peter let out a long, shaky breath. "Another cheerful outing with my boy. What a joy," he said drily.

"Peter . . . I know you have to set some boundaries for his behavior, but put yourself in his place. This visit hasn't been much fun for him. I think he's been a pretty good sport most of the time. I bet his friend just rubbed it in about the trip, and that's what got him all upset."

"I know that. But he's got to figure out that he can't blame me for everything that goes amiss in the universe either." Peter scratched his head, looking baffled by the mysteries of fatherhood. "Don't worry, he'll cool off. We'll work it out somehow. I think once he gets hungry for lunch,

he'll decide to acknowledge my presence again."
He offered Liza a small smile. "Let's just hope
there's some good news later about the Hardys,
right?"

Liza nodded quickly, even though her idea of
good news and Peter's were two different headlines.

Peter and Will set off for Cape Light, and Liza
went up to her room. She glanced at the laptop on
the table by the window but didn't open it.
Instead, she drew the shade and lay down on her
bed. She rarely napped during the day, not unless
she was sick. But she did feel off today in a way—
not exactly sick but not completely well either.

She noticed the white feather on her nightstand
and picked it up, twirling it in the dim light. It was
so pure and silky. As if it had fallen from an
angel's wing, she thought, instead of some ordinary bird.

Maybe a sign from above was not like a fortune
cookie, predicting your future, but more like a
marker in the road, an arrow, pointing out a new
direction, saying, "You can go this way if you
choose. Didn't you notice?"

Liza considered all that had happened and
decided the feather was telling her she could continue with her artwork if she chose to do so. It
was not too late to follow her bliss, her heart's
desire.

Liza resolved that was what she would do, no

matter what happened with the Hardys. She closed her eyes and felt herself drift off to sleep.

The next thing she knew, a gust of wind blew through the curtains and caused the shade to flap like a bird's wing. She opened her eyes and glanced at her watch. She had only slept for a few minutes but felt much better. Refreshed and ready to start her day again, she got up and walked over to the window and raised the shade.

A small blue ceramic pot sat on the windowsill. She hadn't noticed it before. It was filled with white pebbles and bulbs. Small green shoots pushed themselves up from the center of the wrinkled brown orbs. Liza wondered what type of flowers would bloom from the bulbs—paper whites or daffodils? Her aunt used to force bulbs in the late winter, to lend the house some fresh flowers before the spring. Liza had never learned the knack or had the patience.

This had to be Claire's handiwork, she realized.

Liza took a closer look and noticed the pot was handmade, one of her aunt's creations, probably unearthed during the clearing out of closets.

Aunt Elizabeth had finished the pot with a blue glaze and a bright green stripe. She had also inscribed a saying along the rim. Liza lifted it up to read the words.

And we know that all things work together for good to them that love God.

Liza couldn't recall the last time she had been inside a church, not counting her aunt's memorial service. But she easily recognized one of Aunt Elizabeth's favorite bits of scripture. The words helped her feel calmer. No telling what the day— or the Hardys' visit—would bring. Liza decided she would try to take a page from her aunt's book and hold on to the view that no matter what, all would work out for the best.

She glanced at her laptop again but the cool, fresh air and fair weather distracted her, calling her outdoors. This could be her last day on the island, she realized. Or close to it. It might be her last chance to get out and enjoy herself here. There didn't seem to be any sense in staying indoors to do any sort of work.

Liza grabbed her sweater and down vest, then went downstairs, where she scavenged the kitchen for a few snacks and her refillable water bottle. She stowed her necessities in a small, light pack, along with her sketch pad and cell phone, and slung it over her shoulder.

There was a note from Claire on the kitchen table, written in even, square handwriting. The housekeeper had gone up to the General Store for some vegetables to make soup and would be back soon.

Liza wrote a note back, explaining that she was going out for a while but noting that Fran Tulley would be by with some clients around eleven.

"Thank you for the pot of bulbs I found in my room," she added at the bottom. "That was very thoughtful." *As always,* Liza added to herself.

She headed out the back door, suddenly aware of just how much she would miss Claire when she left here. It had only been two weeks, but she'd grown accustomed to the older woman's calm, steady ways—and her incredible cooking.

What would Claire do if they sold this place? She seemed so attached to the inn, an integral part of it. While Liza was sure that Claire could find work easily, it was hard to picture her working anywhere else. Claire seemed to belong here, Liza mused.

Liza found the bike she preferred in the shed, hooked the helmet to the handlebars, and tugged the bike outside.

She wondered where Daniel was this morning. She'd seen his truck and heard men working outside earlier, but it was quiet now.

If things worked out with the Hardys, she wouldn't be seeing him anymore either, she realized. She would miss him, too—or maybe just miss what might have been.

She slipped on her helmet and started off on the bike. She had no plan in mind, just to ride long enough to make her too tired to think. The Angel Wing Cliffs should do it, she decided, and headed off in that direction.

Liza rode for about an hour along the main road,

which offered an ocean view most of the time. By the time she reached the cliffs, she was more than ready to take a break.

She stopped on the side of the road near a large smooth boulder, where the cliffs were in full view and the shoreline stretched out below. They had stopped at this very spot the day she and Peter had come out here with Will. The weather had been chillier then. It felt more like spring today, and there were more signs of the season. The brush and trees scattered on the cliff top looked as if they had been touched with an artist's brush, tipped in bright green paint.

The sun was high in the clear sky, beaming down on the empty road. She rolled the bike over to a shady spot under a tree. The tree was still bare of leaves, but she could see small green buds on the branches, nearly ready to burst.

Tired from riding, Liza took off her helmet, then took a bottle of water from her pack. The water was still cool and tasted wonderful. Such a simple pleasure, she realized, cold water when you're tired and thirsty.

She sat on the side of the road and gazed around. She hadn't seen a car or another biker, or even anyone walking on the road since she started the ride. She felt as if she were suddenly the only person left on the island. It wasn't a bad feeling either.

It was so very quiet. She heard the sound of the

waves dashing on the shoreline far below and the breeze rustling the branches of bushes and trees. A flock of birds hopped among the brush, chirping and squawking at one another before growing silent again.

Liza took out the food she'd brought—an apple and a wedge of cheddar cheese and a few whole grain crackers—and ate every bite. The snack revived her, but she wasn't quite ready to get back on her bike. Stowing her trash in the pack, she noticed her sketch pad and took it out.

It was open to a sketch of the seabirds on the shoreline that she had drawn the other day. Liza looked at it for a moment, then flipped to a fresh page. She took out her soft umber pencil and started to sketch the view before her, the Angel Wing Cliffs and the shoreline below.

Perhaps it was a trick of the sunlight at this time of day, but Liza could see the cliffs clearly as wings today. The rugged white cliffs seemed both solid and gently yielding, almost ready to expand and lift off the earth. It was really an inexplicable sight, impossible to describe in words, and Liza struggled to capture some small sense of it in her drawing.

Her aunt had painted this same view of the cliffs in watercolors and oils. Many famous painters were fascinated with a particular land-scape, painting it over and over in all types of light, in different seasons, and with different techniques. Van Gogh and the haystacks. Monet and the water lilies. Aunt Elizabeth had been that way about the cliffs, and Liza had seen many versions of this landscape among the paintings in the attic. Of course, lots of people who came to the island chose this spot to paint or photograph. But it made Liza suddenly feel close to her aunt, in touch with Elizabeth's spirit, to recall those efforts and work at that vision herself.

After she filled a few pages, the light and the wind shifted, subtly changing the scene. Liza felt she was ready to close her sketchbook but sat with it in her lap a moment and ran her finger along the edge of the binding.

She had practically laughed at the sketchbook the night Peter had handed it to her. Her old efforts seemed so amateur, even embarrassing. But now, she held them in her lap like a treasure, a glimpse into her past, a touchstone she had lost and forgotten about but now rediscovered. An important part of herself she had pushed aside but now embraced.

With her eyes closed against the sunlight and the rhythmic echo of the waves below in tune with her own heartbeat, Liza felt as if the entire world had very slowly come to a full stop. A sense of complete and utter calm filled her like a white light. She felt part of something larger, connected to the ocean waves and blue sky, the rocks and sand, the trees and birds.

It was a rare and indescribable feeling. Even as she experienced it, she knew she could never explain it to anyone. For the first time in a long time, she felt whole. And certain. As she slowly opened her eyes and looked at the world around her, her surroundings somehow looked different and new. Or perhaps she was the one who felt different deep within.

She wasn't sure exactly. But she was sure of one thing. She knew what she had to do.

Liza returned to the inn in the late afternoon. Peter was sitting on the porch in an Adirondack chair. She left her bike on the gravel drive and walked up to him.

"How's it going? Did the Bramble take anything?"

"One or two items. That woman who owns the place, Grace Hegman? She's very fussy and drives a hard bargain. You wouldn't think so from that display in her window."

Liza could tell that Peter was out of sorts. Was he just annoyed after dealing with Grace Hegman? Or was it something more? She walked onto the porch and sat in a chair next to him.

"I called Fran Tulley," he reported. "She said the Hardys were here a long time, but we shouldn't expect any word until tomorrow. Maybe even Monday," he added glumly. "They need to review their information and figure things out. I hate all this waiting."

"I know," Liza said sympathetically. But what she was thinking was, no news is good news. From her point of view anyway.

She stared out at the ocean, realizing that she had fully expected to return here and be facing a firm offer from the Hardys. The delay in their reply seemed an amazing, eleventh-hour reprieve. *Thank You, God.* She offered up a silent prayer without even realizing it.

"I guess it won't be the end of the world if they don't make us a good offer," Peter said, though his tone belied his words. "I just wish we had this settled."

"I do, too," Liza began. "But even the fact that they're so interested is a good sign. I mean, at least it shows the property is a good investment." She turned to face him, gathering her courage. "It's nice to see all the hearsay confirmed, don't you think?"

"There was never much question of that."

"I know, but I've been thinking . . ." Liza leaned back. "Why hand over this great investment to some stranger and never get to reap the long-term benefits? I'm sure Aunt Elizabeth knew about the changes on the island. Maybe she just assumed we would be smart enough to hang on to the property until the value went up. By the time we're ready to retire, this place could be worth a fortune."

Peter moaned and covered his face with his hands. "Don't tell me you're going off on me again, Liza. It's been a hard day. I'm not sure I can take it."

"Peter . . . please . . . just listen a minute. I felt awful all day, thinking someone might buy the inn. I just feel it in my heart that selling it is the wrong thing to do. I've had time to think about this, and I'm very certain that I don't want to go back to my job. Not in two weeks, not ever."

He had taken his hands off his face, and she saw that he was about to interrupt.

"And this is not about losing that promotion," she quickly added before he could speak. "I never got to tell you about the call from my boss on Friday night. Right before we went into the movie. She called to tell me that . . . that I did get the VP spot. It seems I totally misunderstood what she said last week and tortured myself for no reason."

But maybe that misunderstanding had turned out to be a good thing, Liza realized now. It had forced her to look at her life from a new perspective and see alternatives beyond her job at the agency.

Peter shook his head in confusion. "I don't get it. You got the promotion—and now you don't want it?"

She nodded. "Yeah, that's it. I guess I feel gratified by the offer. But I know now it's not for me. Having a bigger office, a big title, even making more money. It's just not going to get me where I really want to go."

"And where is that, Liza? Do you know?"

"Yes, I do," she insisted. "I want to stay here and run the inn." She paused, giving the words a chance to sink in. "I know that's the last thing you want to hear, Peter, but that is the honest and entire truth. I know for sure, this is what I really want to do."

"Liza, don't you realize what you'd be throwing away? Everything you worked for. Your entire reputation in the business. You can't just wake up one morning and say, 'Heck, I'm going to chuck my entire career out the window.' I can't let you do that."

Liza held on to her patience. "It's not your decision to make, Peter. It's mine. I've lived my entire life doing what I thought I should do to make other people happy or approve of me. Or to be considered a success on their terms. I don't want to do that anymore. I simply won't," she stated flatly. "Even if you don't agree to let me take over here, I'm not going back to the agency. I'll start freelancing as a graphic artist or do some consulting. And I'll get back to my own artwork. If I don't do it now, while I feel motivated, I probably never will. You're the one who told me I should," she reminded him.

"Yes, but I didn't say for you to blow up your entire life doing it," he shot back.

Liza ignored his irate tone and pale, shocked expression. "If I stay out here, I can work independently to bring in money until the inn turns a profit again. I know it will be hard at first, but I have so many contacts in the business. Even Barkin & Carr will give me work. I know you were expecting money from the sale," she rushed on, before he could argue again, "but I could easily loan you money for your business. Couldn't you just give me a chance and see if I can make it work out? Maybe just a year or so? The inn might be worth more by then, too, if we still need to sell it."

Peter looked about to answer, then just let out a long, exasperated breath. He rose and shook his head, pacing back and forth on the porch.

"Liza . . . please. Don't press me for an answer on this right now. It's a lot to think about, a lot to consider. And it's definitely not a good moment to back me into a corner. Your timing is just terrible."

Liza's heart sank. "Why is it terrible? Has something happened that I don't know about?"

"I had a call from Gail today—another big argument about Will. She won't agree to the joint custody. We had a terrible fight, then Will got on the phone and told her that he doesn't want to live with me half of the time. He has one more week off from school for the spring break, but he told his mother he wanted to go home tomorrow."

"Oh, Peter . . . that is terrible. I thought you were making some progress with him. Except for the past day or so," she added.

352

"I thought so, too. I know this place isn't as exciting as a trek into the mountains, but I thought he was having some fun. And we were getting a bit closer again."

Peter sat back down and covered his face with his hands. It had been a bad day for him. First, a battle with his ex-wife, then rejection from his son, and finally a hard sell from his sister.

Liza could understand why her brother wanted to be free of the inn. It was just one more thing to worry about in his overly complicated life.

She knelt by his chair and rubbed his shoulders. "I'm so sorry. I didn't mean to pressure you. I'm sorry about Will. Maybe he didn't mean what he said about living with you. Were you two still arguing over the cell phone?"

"We smoothed that one over right before lunch at the Clam Box, as I predicted," he added with a small smile. "Afterward, we were walking around town and he wanted to use my camera. He had forgotten the one I gave him and wasn't even sure where he had put it. So that got me annoyed. I only had my Nikon, the one I use for work. I didn't want him to fool around with it. So he was mad at me all over again when Gail called."

"That might have been it right there. He was just trying to get back at you," Liza pointed out. "He probably didn't mean it."

"Maybe. But that doesn't help my case with Gail. She heard him say that and will use it against me in some deposition or in court. Even if he denies it later." Peter let out a long sigh. "I don't know. Maybe I should just give up and see him every other weekend. Or just when she decides I can. Maybe that's the way he really wants it, too."

"Listen," Liza said, "I'm no expert on kids, but I think it's clear that you shouldn't give up. You're his father, Peter. You shouldn't be kept away from your son. He's in a difficult stage right now, and the divorce has made it worse. But when he gets older, he'll appreciate that you fought to be with him. I know he will."

"You think so?" he asked hopefully.

"I do," she said.

Peter looked somewhat calmer, comforted by her words. "Thanks, Liza. I appreciate you listening to me. Sometimes I feel so alone. I don't have many people I can talk to."

"Me, too." She smiled at him. "But we still have each other, right?"

"Yes, we do." He smiled back and patted her hand. "I'm sorry we're arguing about the inn. It sounds as if coming back here has really affected you."

"It has," she said quietly. "I'm not sure why, but I can't deny it. I really dreaded coming back here, but now . . . I just feel really different. And really grateful."

He looked into her eyes, seeming surprised at

what he saw there. "I've been so busy with my own problems, I didn't even notice what was going on with you. I'm sorry," he added sincerely. "Why don't you give me a little time to think things over? I need more time with Will, too—that is, if I can persuade him to stay for a few more days." Peter shook his head. "I know the inn is important to you. But to me Will is more important, the most important thing in my life. The divorce taught me that."

"I understand," Liza said. "I think he does, too. Let's just put it aside for a while and come back to it when we feel ready." Liza went inside, satisfied that her brother had finally heard her. He understood how she felt about the inn and what she wanted. There was no need to discuss it further right now.

She also felt an inner certainty that the right thing would happen, one way or the other. She wasn't sure how or where this feeling had come from, but the intuition was strong and unmistakable, lending her a sense of calm in the midst of her confusion.

She only hoped that she could hang on to this fragile peace of mind, come what may.

ON Sunday morning, Peter and Will were up and dressed and had already eaten breakfast by the time Liza came downstairs. They were getting ready to go someplace, she noticed, some special

355

destination by the look of the belongings gathered for the outing.

They weren't going back to Tucson, were they? Liza felt a prick of alarm. Her brother would have said something last night if that was his plan. But you never knew. Peter's moods changed as quickly as the weather sometimes.

"Good morning, guys. Heading out somewhere?" she asked, as she walked into the kitchen.

"Will wants to do a whale watch. There's a boat out of Newburyport, but we have to hustle to catch the morning sail."

"That's a great idea. You'd better bring warm clothes. It can be cold on the water this time of year," Liza reminded her brother.

"We're bringing a ton of stuff. Sweatshirts, hats, extra socks, sunblock, water bottles, snacks—" He glanced at Will who continued the list.

"Tripods, iPods, binoculars, at least three cameras."

Peter nodded in approval. "Check. And double check."

Will nearly gagged. "Dad, that's so dorky."

Peter just laughed and pulled on a Red Sox cap, turned backward. "Is that better?" he asked his son.

Will rolled his eyes, and Liza laughed, feeling relieved to see that her brother and nephew were on better terms today.

Liza saw a loaf of Claire's freshly baked bread

on the counter and dropped a slice in the toaster. "Do you want some sandwiches? I think there's plenty of stuff in the fridge."

"We'll be fine," Peter assured her. "We really need to go. I'll call you later. We might stay in Newburyport for dinner," he added.

"Have fun," Liza called after them. She watched Peter head out the door with Will close behind. Her nephew slung an orange backpack over his shoulder, then turned and waved. She smiled and waved back at him. Will looked excited. He seemed to have forgotten he needed to look bored and cool.

A short time later, Liza headed out to the shed to find some gardening tools and gloves. Everything she needed was neatly stored on the potting bench, not far from her uncle's workbench. She piled what she needed in a wheelbarrow and pushed it out to the garden, then began the slow but necessary job of cleaning out the dead leaves stuck under the flowerbeds and tugging out anything that looked like a weed.

Maybe she wouldn't be here to see flowers bloom, but she could clear the way for them and make the garden presentable for the next owner, whoever that might be.

She had been working for a while and had accumulated an impressive pile in the wheelbarrow when a shadow fell over her.

Liza turned and looked up. It was Daniel. Even

though it was Sunday, she had a feeling he would come by.

"That looks like slow going," he said.

"It's even slower for me since I'm not sure what's a weed and what's a flower," she confessed. "I have to stop and really think about it."

"When in doubt, don't pull it out," he advised her with a grin.

"That's a pretty safe philosophy." Liza stood up and pulled off her garden gloves. She looked a perfect mess, wearing a pair of her aunt's cast-off overalls and a huge misshapen sweater. But for some reason, Daniel was smiling at her as if she were dressed for the red carpet in an evening gown and jewels.

"So," she began, "you're almost done with the painting. Is that why you came over today, to finish up?"

He gazed at her a moment, almost smiling but not quite.

Then he shook his head. "Oh, I didn't come here to work. I just stopped by to grab the color wheel." He held it up for her to see. "I left it on your porch and need to drop it off with another client."

He did look a little more dressed up than usual, in an oxford-cloth shirt, neatly pressed jeans, and a leather jacket. His shirt was an unlikely shade of pink. Liza had never guessed a man could look so good in that color, but there you were. You learned something new every day around here, didn't you?

Still, a certain light in his eyes made her wonder if he had really needed that color wheel or if it was just a convenient excuse.

Don't flatter yourself, Liza, a little voice inside her warned.

Liza smiled to herself, blithely dismissing the warning.

"Right, I didn't notice it out there," she said lightly. "You have other clients?" She put on an indignant tone, teasing him. "I thought I was the only one."

He laughed and stepped closer. "You're my favorite," he admitted, teasing her back. But when he caught her gaze and held it, it didn't feel like teasing anymore.

"The paint job looks wonderful," she said, needing to break the suddenly serious mood. "You've done a great job."

She meant it, too. Daniel had definitely gone the extra mile to make the inn look refreshed and elegant again, repairing steps, loose clapboards, and even the broken shutters and windows. Liza was almost certain that they weren't paying him enough for this painstaking attention.

"Thanks. I like this old place. I did my best under the circumstances. We should be done in a day or two," he reported. "How's it going with your brother? Does he still want to sell?"

Daniel cut right to the chase, as usual. But she was almost getting used to it.

"Yes, Peter still wants to sell. But I've persuaded him to at least think about holding on to the place and letting me run it."

"That's something . . . What about your job?"

"I've decided to quit my job, no matter what happens," she told him. "I'm going to look for freelance work and try my own artwork again."

She did feel sure this was the right thing to do, but saying it out loud made it seem very real. And frightening.

A big smile spread across Daniel's handsome face, warming Liza like pure sunshine. He looked so happy at the news, you would have thought he had just been told he had won a prize of some kind. Daniel Merritt had a way of making her feel special—and right somehow.

"Sounds like a good plan to me. You have it all figured out, don't you?"

"A little. Not all of it. Not by a long shot." She let out a long breath but couldn't help smiling again. "I started in the art department. So I figured I could go back to that, design work, graphics. That sort of thing."

"I'm not surprised. You seem the arty type."

"I do?" Liza was surprised and pleased by his comment. Was he just saying that to get on her good side? He was already on her good side. That was for sure.

"Well . . . thanks. I don't know anything about running an inn. That's going to be the hard part— a pretty steep learning curve, I imagine."

"You watched your aunt all those years. Something must have sunk in."

"That's true." Liza hadn't thought of it that way. "I guess I did learn a lot from her."

"I'm sure you did," Daniel said evenly. "I'm sure you'll do an amazing job here if your brother gives you the chance. I hope he does. It seems to me the right thing to do," he added in a serious voice.

He reached out and touched her shoulder. She felt the warmth and strength of his hand and leaned toward him, appreciating his encouragement and support. His touch seemed to calm her worries. It felt good just to be near him.

He turned and looked at the house again. "Guess I'd better get going. See you tomorrow."

Liza nodded. "Sure, see you."

She watched Daniel walk down the drive to his truck. His brief visit had been a bright spot in her day, giving a boost to her flagging energy and tamping down a few stray doubts.

Their conversation had made her feel hopeful again. Maybe Peter would give her a chance here. And maybe she really could run this place. What an amazing change of course that would be in her life's path. Setting off for a new place, to be sure. But not exactly. In a way, it would be more like traveling back to her origins, her center.

• • •

IT was late afternoon when Liza finally decided to come indoors again. The sun was low in the sky, and the shadows in the garden had deepened. Her back ached a bit, and her hands were a mess, despite her gloves. But the garden looked terrific, as if she had given the grounds a giant haircut. She could hardly stop admiring her handiwork, looking at it from the kitchen windows.

Her aunt had possessed a genuine green thumb. Liza had never believed she inherited the trait, but she had never had a chance to work in a real garden before either. It was possible that she had a knack for growing things, too, she thought. She certainly enjoyed it.

Liza washed her hands in the sink, then searched the fridge for something to eat. She hadn't even stopped for a real lunch today and felt very hungry. There was no telling what time Peter and Will would be back, so she wasn't going to wait.

Claire had cooked a large pot of chicken soup the day before, and Liza found the leftovers in a white plastic container. She dumped the soup in a pot and waited by the stove until it came to a simmer.

Fixing herself a steaming bowl, Liza set it on the table. The broth was thick, filled with chunks of chicken, herbs, and noodles. Liza forced herself to eat slowly, but she was so hungry and the soup was so good, she could hardly hold herself back.

Finally, spooning up the last drop, she sat back from the table, feeling full and sleepy and thinking that a hot shower and a nap were next on her agenda.

But before she could budge, her BlackBerry buzzed. Liza quickly checked the ID. Fran Tulley. Liza felt the dozy, contented feeling vanish as her heartbeat accelerated. She answered quickly and greeted Fran in a wary tone.

"Hi, Liza, glad I caught you. Guess what? Good news. The Hardys called in. They made an offer. A very nice one, considering."

"An offer?" Liza sat up. Was this really happening?

It felt like a bad dream. "What's the offer?" she asked quietly.

Fran eagerly told her the figure. "That's just the opening bid. They'll probably go higher if we push a bit," she added.

The opening bid was substantial, more than they expected. Peter, she knew, would be pleased.

"Their architect was very helpful. He seemed to think the property was perfect for the house they have in mind."

"The house they have in mind? A new house, you mean?"

"Yes, new construction. They love the location and the views."

Liza felt her soup coming back up. "They want to knock the building down? The entire inn?"

363

"Yes, that's right." Fran's voice slowed considerably.

"Did you and your brother figure out if you're willing to sell in that situation? I just assumed you would be, since you both seemed in a hurry to sell."

They had spoken about it a little, but had they ever come to an agreement? Liza couldn't remember. Though she could guess which side each of them would take on the question.

"We didn't really talk it out completely," Liza told Fran.

"Well, it seems the time has come to crack that nut," Fran advised. "Why don't the two of you talk it over tonight and get back to me tomorrow morning? I should be in around nine."

"Okay, Fran. We'll do that. And thanks," Liza added, remembering her manners. Fran had put in a lot of time showing the house. Liza couldn't be mad at her. They had, after all, hired Fran to sell the inn.

Liza hung up the phone and sighed. She did think Peter was finally giving some serious thought to her request. But once he heard this offer from the Hardys, Liza had a feeling that her plans and wishes would be quickly brushed aside. There wasn't much she could do except argue— and Liza wasn't sure she had the energy left for that conversation.

After a hot shower, Liza pulled on some sweats

and stretched out on her bed. All that hard work on the garden today, and now a bulldozer would plow it all under.

Despite her aches and anxious thoughts, she fell into a deep sleep. When she woke up, the room was dark. She had no idea what time it was. She looked at the clock on the nightstand. Half past nine. She couldn't believe she had slept that long.

She got up and went downstairs. The rooms were dark. She turned on the lamp in the foyer that sat on the Eastlake table, then walked into the front parlor and turned on a light by the love seat and the small Tiffany lamp on the piano.

The room looked cozy and warm. She sat in the middle of the love seat, savoring the silence. The calm before the storm, she thought, knowing Peter and Will would soon be back.

She hadn't taken much notice of Peter's photo-sorting project lately, but now she could see four albums piled on the tiger-oak table where he had been working. She walked over and opened the one on top. She saw a Post-it with her name on it. The other albums were also marked. One with Peter's name and one with Will's. And a smaller one, with Claire's.

It looked as though her brother had made each of them an album full of photos, as a keepsake. She opened up hers and looked through the pages. It started with old pictures and worked up to the present day, a chronicle of their aunt's and uncle's lives on the island and the summers Liza and Peter had spent with them.

Liza opened the albums Peter had made for himself and Will, and realized they were much the same. There were similar photos, taken at the same occasions. Peter had taken the time and care to sort them all out and arrange them.

It gave her a good feeling. Peter did care for the inn in his own way, more than he liked to show. Maybe he wouldn't agree to destroy it. Maybe there was some hope here.

Before Liza could look much further, she heard a key in the front door. She walked out to the foyer just as Will and Peter came through the doorway. They both looked tired and windblown. And angry.

Will stalked into the house without acknowledging her. He bolted up the stairs, and Liza heard a door slam. Peter stood staring after him, a grim look on his face.

"Are you okay? What's wrong?" Liza asked, as he shed his down jacket.

"Everything's wrong. That's what wrong," Peter answered curtly. "It's no use. I've tried and tried. Will and I are going back to Arizona tomorrow. I'm wasting my time here with that kid of mine."

"You had a bad day," Liza said quietly.

"Yes, we did. A very bad day. I've made up my mind about a few things, though. No more fooling around. Not with Gail or Will . . . or with you,

Liza. I want to sell this house, as we agreed. I'm going to call Fran Tulley tonight. If the Hardys don't want it, maybe she can set up an auction. There's got to be a way to sell it faster."

Liza let out a long sigh. She had to tell him. She had to be honest. She had hoped they would have a chance to sort this out calmly and rationally, but that's not how the pieces were falling.

"I have some news—if you could slow down long enough to listen," she finally said.

"Okay, I'm listening." He gave her a hard look.

"The Hardys made an offer."

"An offer? That's great! When did you hear?"

"A few hours ago. I guess it was around five."

He looked surprised. "Why didn't you call me?"

"Oh, you were out on the boat. I didn't think your phone would work. And I didn't have the heart," she admitted. "They want to knock the place down, Peter. That's the deal. They just want the land so they can build a new house. That's why they had the architect with them."

Peter stared at her, and she wished she could read his thoughts. Did it bother him at all that the inn would be destroyed?

"What are they offering? Is it a good number?"

Liza told him the figure.

"Nice." He nodded, looking pleased. "And that's just a first offer. I expect we could get them to go higher."

Fran had said the same thing, but Liza wasn't about to mention that.

"Look, why don't we go inside and talk this over a little?" she suggested. "Did you have anything to eat? I could heat up some of Claire's soup. It's really delicious." She was hoping the good food would get him in a better mood, a more receptive mood.

"I'm not hungry, thanks." He glanced at his watch. "I suppose it's too late to call Fran back. I'm going up to bed. We'll call her tomorrow, first thing."

She didn't answer. Peter brushed past her and headed up the stairs. "Good night, Liza. Tomorrow is a big day. You ought to get some sleep yourself."

Liza didn't answer. Tomorrow would be a big day. A sad day, she expected. She wished it would never come.

Chapter Fourteen

LIZA woke up slowly, a few minutes before her alarm clock sounded. She felt as if something had woken her, but as she opened her eyes, all she could see was early morning light sifting through the sheer curtains. The blue ceramic flower pot on the windowsill was just as she left it yesterday. The windows were open a little, and a cool ocean breeze filled the room.

She had slept well and felt full of energy, ready to tackle whatever dirty job the day tossed her way.

Then she remembered . . . The offer from the Hardys . . . Calling Fran Tulley to accept . . . Total strangers coming here to demolish the inn.

Was that really happening? As she rose from bed, she felt her heart sink. She dressed quickly, then went downstairs.

Crossing the foyer, she heard Peter's and Claire's familiar voices talking in the kitchen. Her brother had probably popped out of bed at the crack of dawn, wondering if it was too early to call Fran Tulley.

Had he told Claire what was happening? Liza felt a little pang in her chest. She had felt bad enough about telling Claire the inn would be sold when she first arrived and hardly knew her. But now . . . well, they had been through a lot together during the past two weeks, sifting through all of her aunt's belongings, even being struck by lightning. Telling the housekeeper the place was sold and would be knocked down seemed a very hard task to face. Practically impossible.

Peter was the one pushing for this scenario; let him tell her, Liza thought. She hated giving in to her anger and frustration, but she couldn't help it. Not when she thought about Claire.

Peter was sitting at the kitchen table, reading the local paper. He looked up with a sheepish smile. "Morning, Liza. Sleep well?"

"Not bad, all things considered." Liza poured herself a cup of coffee.

Claire stood at the stove, cooking scrambled eggs. She turned to Liza and smiled. "I'm sure you were tired enough. After all the work you did out in the garden. When I looked out the window this morning, I could hardly believe my eyes. I bet the plants will double in size by the end of the week."

Liza felt embarrassed by her praise. Yes, she had cleaned up the garden. For a bulldozer to plow it under.

Liza took a seat at the table. There was a basket of cranberry scones next to her plate. They looked tempting, but she didn't feel hungry. Her nerves had stolen her appetite today.

"I think you may have inherited your aunt's green thumb," Claire said, as she brought a platter of eggs to the table and placed it between Liza and Peter. "She was quite a force of nature out there."

"She definitely was," Liza agreed. Aunt Elizabeth seemed to have an intuitive sense for helping plants thrive. Liza knew she would be lucky to have half that ability. *Though I'll never know now if I do, will I?* she mused.

Peter closed his newspaper with a snap, folded it, and set it down by his plate. "It's a quarter past eight," he announced, checking his watch. "Too early to check in with Fran, do you think?"

Liza nodded, forcing herself not to laugh. "I

think so. She's probably still at home with her family. I don't think she gets in to her office until at least nine, Peter."

He checked his watch again and sighed. "Guess you're right. I was thinking of calling her cell, but that might seem a little too eager. We do want to bargain a bit if we can."

Liza sipped her coffee without answering. She glanced at Claire and got the feeling that Peter hadn't told her anything.

"We had an offer on the inn," she told Claire quietly. "From that couple who came a while ago, the Hardys."

Claire nodded. "I remember them. They were scared off by the lightning but came back Saturday."

"Yes, that's them. They made a good offer, and we have to talk to Fran about it," she explained. She glanced at Peter, thinking, *Jump in anytime, brother dear.*

He met her glance, then quickly looked away and rose from his chair. "I'd better try to wake up Will. I don't want him to sleep until noon again."

Liza watched him go, leaving her holding the bag. Well, at least Peter seemed to have a few pangs of conscience about the situation. That was something.

She looked back at Claire. She didn't have to tell her that the Hardys were knocking down the inn. That didn't really pertain to her. Claire would lose her job, one way or the other, Liza reasoned. But Liza knew that Claire deserved to hear all of it. It just seemed right. In some ways, the inn seemed to belong to Claire more than anyone. Or maybe it was just that she seemed so much a part of this place.

Liza sighed and took another sip of coffee. "Well, we have to catch up to Fran and talk over the offer," she said again.

"Don't worry about me, Liza. I'll find other work," Claire said. She brought a cup of tea to the table and sat down nearby.

Liza looked across the table at her. "I am concerned for you, Claire. But it's not just that. I don't really want to sell the inn. I've been thinking a lot about it, and I want to stay here and run it."

"Yes, I thought something like that was going on," Claire admitted. "But I wasn't sure."

Though her arguments with Peter had mostly been private, Liza realized that Claire must have overhead or just sensed some of the friction between them.

"Peter does want to sell, and this is a good offer," she repeated. "He's got a lot going on right now. He just wants to settle this situation and get back to Arizona," she added, trying to defend her brother.

"Understandable," Claire said calmly. "It is a pity, though, that he won't give you a chance. I can see it. I can see you taking your aunt's place here." Claire smiled over at her. "You are so much like her, Liza. I see it more and more every day."

Liza was deeply touched. Claire could not have given her a greater compliment.

"Thank you, Claire, for saying that . . . I wish I were more like my aunt. If I was, maybe I could persuade Peter to let me stay—and keep the Hardys from knocking this place down."

Claire's expression fell. "Is that what they plan to do?"

Liza nodded bleakly. She hadn't meant to tell Claire this way but felt relieved now that the whole truth was out. "They want to build a new house. It's awful, isn't it?"

Liza heard the tremble in her voice and felt embarrassed for a moment. Then realized she hadn't confided her true feelings about this to anyone. It felt good to talk to Claire, the one person who would completely understand.

"It is awful . . . but it hasn't happened yet," Claire pointed out. "I know it looks bleak. But if you're meant to stay here, God will clear a path, Liza," she promised. "Trust in Him to show you the way." She met Liza's gaze for a long moment, then reached over and patted Liza's hand.

Liza took Claire's hand in her own and gave it a gentle squeeze. "Thanks, Claire. I'll try," she promised quietly. Before she could say anything more, Peter ran into the kitchen, his face pale.

"Have either of you seen Will? Did he come down here?"

"I haven't seen him this morning," Claire said.

"Me either," Liza added. "He's not up in his room?"

Peter swallowed hard. "No, he's not. I knocked and knocked, and he wouldn't answer. I thought he was just being stubborn. But when I finally walked in, his bed was empty. First I thought he was taking a shower. Or maybe he had gone up to the attic for some reason . . ." Peter took a breath. "When I went back to his room, I realized that some of his stuff is gone. His down jacket, his pack, his shoes . . . I looked in all the rooms upstairs. He's gone somewhere. Without telling anyone."

"Maybe he got up early and went down to the beach," Liza suggested, "or walked up to the General Store. Are you sure he didn't leave a note?"

"I looked around his room. No note. And there was nothing down here. I'm sure one of us would have seen it," he said, glancing around the kitchen.

"I'll go check in the foyer and the parlor. Maybe he left a note out there," Claire said, "on the desk or something."

"Good idea," Liza replied. "Maybe he left a message on your cell phone," she said to her brother. "Did you check yet?"

Peter pulled out his cell and checked the messages. "Nothing. How about you?"

Liza doubted that Will would have left a message on her phone, but you never know what kids are thinking. She checked her pockets and realized her BlackBerry was still upstairs in her room. At some point during her stay here, she had fallen out of the habit of keeping it close. She would have to tell Daniel.

"It's upstairs, I'll run up and check." She ran up to her room and found her phone. No message from Will appeared on the list of new calls. She felt a pang of worry but refused to give in to it. Will hadn't been gone very long. He probably just needed some time to himself after arguing with his dad the night before.

She walked down the hallway to the stairs, passing Will's room on the way. She paused and peeked in. His bed was a tumble of sheets and blankets, the pillow still dented with the imprint of his head. His big sneakers, which normally took up half of the floor, were conspicuously absent, as were the parka and sweatshirt that were normally draped over an armchair. His carry-on duffel was still on the floor near the closet, with clothes spilling over onto the floor. That was a good sign, Liza thought. Maybe they were worrying for no reason. Maybe he hadn't gone far at all.

As she headed downstairs, she took out her

phone again and auto-dialed her nephew's number. Will's phone rang a few times, but he didn't answer. "Will, it's Aunt Liza. Please call me or your dad when you get this message. We don't know where you are. It's very important that you call us," she said, trying not to sound too upset.

When she got to the kitchen, she saw Peter had his phone out, too, and was busily sending a text message.

"I just tried calling him," she said. "He didn't pick up, but I left a message."

"I left a voice message, too. And now a text." Peter looked up at her. "I don't like this, Liza. I have a bad feeling."

"Let's not get too worried yet," Liza said in what she hoped was a calming tone. "Will's not a little boy. He knows how to take care of himself. He must have just gone out for a walk or something and forgotten to let us know."

Claire returned to the kitchen. "I looked all over. I didn't find any notes, sorry."

"I didn't think you would," Peter admitted. "But thanks for your help, Claire." He drummed his fingers on the table, then said, "You're right, Liza. It's too soon to panic. Let's give him a few hours."

Liza and Peter had breakfast, then they busied themselves around the inn, each hoping that Will would walk in at any moment.

Well before noon, Liza and Peter met up in the kitchen where Claire was starting another pot of soup. Peter looked ready to jump out of his skin. "I still haven't heard a thing from Will," he told Liza. "Maybe I'm overreacting, but I can't just sit here, being patient. After that argument we had last night, who knows—"

A knock sounded on the kitchen door, and they all turned at once. But it was Daniel peeking through the glass, not Will.

Liza quickly ran over to open the door. For some reason, the mere sight of Daniel was a great relief.

"Good morning, everyone," he said brightly, though his gaze was fixed on Liza. "How's it going?"

"We have a situation," Liza told him. "Well . . . we hope it's not a situation, just a misunderstanding. Will's gone out somewhere and he didn't leave a note."

"And he's not answering our messages," Peter added in a far more anxious tone. "He's been gone all morning. I think I'd better go look for him. I'm getting worried."

"He could have gone out for a walk or a bike ride," Daniel said. "Did you check the bikes? Are any missing?"

"I should have thought of that," Peter said. He ran out the back door and headed to the shed, with Liza, Daniel, and Claire following behind him.

"Okay, one bike is gone," Peter reported, as he emerged from the shed. "So Will probably isn't just taking a walk on the beach."

"That gives us something to go on," Daniel replied. "Why don't we split up and look for him? It's not a very big island. He couldn't have gone far."

"Unless he decided to head for the mainland," Peter said. "For all I know, he's on his way to Logan—"

"Let's hope not," Liza cut in, trying to tamp down her brother's panic. "We ought to at least take a quick ride around before we jump to that conclusion."

"I'll call the gatehouse and ask if they've seen a boy pass on a bicycle," Claire said. "I'll make a few calls around to the neighbors, too. Maybe someone has seen him."

"Good idea, Claire." Liza followed her toward the house, knowing she needed to grab a jacket and her car keys.

"Let's go inside a minute and look over a map, so we don't duplicate our efforts," Daniel suggested.

Peter nodded grimly. Liza reached out and touched his arm. "Don't worry. I'm sure he's all right," she said quietly.

"I hope so," Peter answered.

A short time later they had figured out a plan, and each took a different section of the island to search. Claire had already called the gatehouse at the bridge. The gatekeeper had been on duty there since five that morning and did not recall seeing a boy on a bike heading for the mainland.

"I doubt he would have left before five," Peter conceded, "considering how late he normally sleeps."

"That's good news, then. He's got to be around somewhere," Daniel said. "Keep calling, Claire. Maybe someone has seen him."

"That's what I plan to do," she said, dialing the phone again. Claire knew everyone on the island, Liza reasoned. She was the perfect person for this job.

"Should we call the police?" Peter said finally.

"I suppose you could. There's no police department out here, but Cape Light might send someone to help," Daniel replied.

"I'll take care of that," Claire offered. "I'll call your cell phone, Peter, and tell you what the police say. You go on and start looking. Who knows, you might find him right away."

"We might. I just hope he's all right." Peter led the way out the back door. Liza and Daniel followed.

The section of the island that Liza had been assigned covered an area close to the inn. She drove along the road slowly, keeping her eye out for Will and also just for the bike. If Will had gone down to the beach to explore, he would have had to leave the bike up on the road, she reasoned.

She came to the goat farm and spotted Audrey's two black-and-white herding dogs, darting in circles around the braying goats. Audrey was nowhere in sight, and Liza wondered if she should drive in and ask if anyone there had seen Will this morning. But Claire would call the farm, she remembered. It was important to keep going and not lose time.

She drove on and came to the island center. She decided to check in the General Store. It seemed a logical place for Will to stop.

"Why hello there," Marion Doyle greeted her. "Can I help you?"

"I hope so," Liza replied. She quickly explained that she was looking for Will. Walter Doyle had come around his side of the counter and listened with interest.

"Oh, dear. That doesn't sound good," Marion replied with concern.

"You know kids, they just don't think sometimes," her husband added.

"No, they don't," Liza agreed. "Has he been by this morning?"

Marion frowned, carefully considering the question, then shook her head. "No, dear. I don't remember seeing him. How about you, Walter?" She turned to her husband. "You remember Peter Martin's boy? They were in here about a week ago."

"Sure, I do. But I didn't see him this morning."

"Let me give you my cell number," Liza said, "just in case he does come in."

"Good idea," Marion said, handing her a pencil and a small brown paper bag to write on.

"Who's gone out looking?" Walter asked.

"It's three of us—me, my brother, and Daniel Merritt. He's been painting the inn and offered to help."

Walter quickly untied his apron and laid it on the counter. "I'll help you. I know some places where a boy might want to explore—or hide."

Liza was surprised by his generous offer. Everyone on the island knew Walter and Marion Doyle, but they had no special relationship with her aunt. Not as far as Liza knew.

"That's very nice of you. Are you sure you don't need to stay in the store?"

"Marion can handle it," Walter assured her. "I'm in her way most of the time."

"He'll just worry anyway," Marion explained. "He needs to help. It's just our way out here. We all pull together."

Liza nodded. Audrey had told her the same thing. "Thank you. Thank you so much."

Walter had grabbed a red and black plaid jacket and a big black cap with ear flaps off a hook by the door. There was a map of the island on the wall nearby, and Liza showed him the places that they were all covering and also exchanged cell phone numbers with him, just in case he found Will.

"Okeydokey, let's go. See you later, Marion," he called over his shoulder, and headed for his truck.

Liza felt good knowing someone else had

joined the search. She walked over to Daisy Winkler's shop and knocked, but there was no one there. Liza left a note, asking Daisy to call the inn if she had seen Will or if he turned up at the tearoom. Unlikely, but possible.

Liza walked over to the building that housed the environmental office and the village hall. It was dark and the door looked locked. Liza tried it just in case.

Just as she turned away, a man in a small open Jeep drove up and parked. He climbed out and walked toward her with a purposeful stride.

"Can I help you with something?" he asked. He stood back and looked down at her curiously. He wasn't that tall, only a few inches taller than Liza, but he had an athletic build and the wind-blown look of someone who spent a lot of time outdoors. He wore jeans and a flannel shirt under a dark green nylon jacket with an official-looking emblem on the sleeve.

"I'm looking for my fourteen-year-old nephew, Will," Liza explained. "He and my brother have been staying with me at the Angel Inn, down the road. Will seems to have left the house early this morning without telling anyone or leaving a note. He took a bike," she added. "We're pretty sure he hasn't left the island, but we can't be positive."

The man listened with a serious expression. "I was working down at the beach near the inn and a little farther south. I didn't see any cyclists on the road this morning. Or any teenage boys on the beach," he added. "But I'd be happy to help you look. I'm Eric Hatcher, by the way." He held out his hand. "I work for the environmental office."

"I figured that," Liza replied. She took his hand and shook it. "I'm Liza Martin. You may have known my aunt Elizabeth Dunne. She ran the inn."

He nodded. "I did know her a little. Lovely lady." He smiled briefly. "Is there anyone else out looking for your nephew? Or are you on your own?"

Liza explained the search group and the areas they were covering. Eric listened without interrupting her.

Then he said, "Sounds like you could use more help on the far side of the island near the fishing cottages. There's some marshy land out there. It's not smart to walk around there unless you know your way."

He didn't add, it could be dangerous. He didn't need to. Liza already knew the dangers of getting lost in the marshes in that area of the island. Her aunt and uncle had warned them each summer and never let them go there. She hoped Will hadn't been reckless enough to go exploring in that direction.

A few minutes later, Liza and Eric climbed into their vehicles. Eric set off for the south side of the island. Liza sat in her SUV a moment, getting her bearings. Her phone rang, and she answered it at once.

"Any news?" her brother asked.

"I'm afraid not. No one has seen him. But two people have offered to help us look, Walter Doyle and a man named Eric Hatcher. He works for the environmental office and said he's going to look in the marshes down by the fishing cottages."

"I didn't even think of that," Peter said. "I just spoke to Claire. She's been calling all over. The people who own the goat farm—the Gilroys? They've gone out to look, and the Cape Light police force is sending two officers to help us. I'm going over the bridge to meet them."

Liza wasn't surprised. She had a feeling that Audrey would jump in to help once she knew what was going on.

"The more people out looking, the better," Liza said.

"Right. I keep calling and calling, but he won't answer his phone. I think he may have just gone out for a short bike ride and forgotten to leave a note. But I'm scared that something has happened to him," Peter confessed. "He could have been hit by a car or gotten stuck somewhere . . . Anything could have happened . . . I'm really worried, Liza."

"Of course you are." She took a deep breath, pushing back her own fears. "But let's try to stay calm and keep searching. We have a lot more help now. Someone will find him. He's going to be okay," she promised.

Peter just sighed. "I see the police cars. I've got to go."

Liza hung up, too. She put the keys in the ignition but didn't start the engine. It suddenly occurred to her that Eve was going to call today, expecting her to take the promotion. And it seemed completely absurd that she had ever worried about it at all.

Liza sent a quick text:

Sorry but can't talk today. Family emergency. I'll be in touch soon.

Will's disappearance put everything in perspective: All the job drama, losing the inn, even allowing the building to be knocked down—none of that was important now.

LIZA had always thought of the island as very small, tiny even. But trying to search the roadside, inch by inch, ditch by roadside ditch, it didn't seem small at all. It seemed endless. After she drove around her assigned territory twice and carefully combed the roadside, she consulted again with Peter and Daniel by phone.

Still no sign of Will, they both reported.

"I spoke to a guy who thought he saw a bike rider early this morning on the Ice House Road,"

Daniel told her. "But he wasn't sure. I went up and down the road in both directions. I didn't see any sign of him."

"He's got to be somewhere. The gatehouse is watching for him now. He can't get past them," Liza replied.

"Let's just hope he didn't get past them already without them realizing it."

She headed off again on the same roads, this time stopping every hundred yards or so to check the area off the roadside, any place where she saw a path into the woods or one that led down to the water. She even walked up and down the hillsides, searching along various stretches of the beach that weren't visible from above.

She didn't find a thing. Not even a water bottle or a candy wrapper. The boy could not have disappeared into thin air, she reasoned. But at the moment it seemed that was exactly what he had done.

Liza squeezed her eyes shut and whispered a short prayer. "Dear God . . . please let Will be all right. I don't care about keeping the inn. I don't care about anything. Just let him be found safe and sound. Please . . ."

THE search went on until the late afternoon. Darkness was falling when Liza, Peter, and Daniel finally agreed to return to the inn. Peter had wanted to join the police, who had called for more men and were going to continue to search the island and the town of Cape Light. But Liza finally talked him into coming back to the inn, at least for a little while, to rest and have something to eat.

She parked her SUV near the front of the house, then walked slowly to the porch. It had gotten much colder as the sun went down, she noticed. It was going to be a chilly night, and Will was still out there somewhere.

It was hard to believe that they hadn't found him yet. When they started off that morning, Liza was sure they would find him easily. Nearly eight hours later, there was still no sign of him.

She wasn't sure what she would say to Peter, but she knew she had to help him through this. Even before this crisis, she had come to see that she and her brother needed each other. They had to stay close and support each other—not just in an emergency but all the time.

Something about coming back to the island had helped her see that life was about connection, to the people you loved and the places and the work that had meaning for you. She had spent so much of the past years disconnected. From her brother and nephew . . . from her heart's own desires.

Even if she lost the inn, she had learned something important here, she realized. The priority was finding Will. Her heart twisted with the hope that he was safe somewhere, just unable, or unwilling, to find his way home.

She walked into the front parlor and found Peter, Daniel, and Claire waiting for her. Peter was on the phone, finishing up a call. "Thank you, Officer Tulley. I appreciate the news. I'll be in touch in an hour or so."

He closed the phone and looked up. "That was the police, Officer Tulley, Fran's husband," he explained. "They found Will's cell phone, but there's still no sign of the bike—or Will."

"No wonder he didn't answer your calls," Claire said. "He probably didn't even realize he lost his phone."

"Where did they find it?" Liza asked, dropping down on the love seat.

"In the old cemetery. I wonder what he was doing there." Peter leaned forward and held his head in his hands. "I'm a terrible father. Of course he ran away. I was too hard on him, always nagging him about something, dragging him out here, trying to force him into living with me half of the time . . . He doesn't want to live with me at all. He hates me. That's why he ran away."

"You're a good father," Claire assured him. "You're fighting for time with him because you love him. Anyone can see that. I think even Will knows that."

"All parents have some conflict with kids this age. That's part of growing up, Peter," Liza reminded him. "We both acted out at his age."

"And teenagers can be very dramatic," Daniel pointed out.

"Daniel's right," Liza said. "Will can be dramatic and emotional. You can't blame yourself, Peter," she added. "Please don't do that to yourself."

Peter took a long breath but didn't seem convinced. "I used to stay out all day wandering the island when I was his age. But at least Elizabeth and Clive had some idea of where I was. I wasn't trying to run away from them . . ."

They sat silently. No one knew what else to say.

The truth was, they didn't even know for sure that Will had run away, Liza thought. He could be stuck someplace, hurt and unable to return. Which was an awful thought, one she didn't want to think about or talk about right now.

"There was this place I would go," Peter went on. "The caves under the Angel Wing Cliffs. I loved that spot. I even camped out there once with Uncle Clive, remember Liza?"

"I remember. I had no interest in that adventure. I was terrified of bats," she admitted.

"Did you look down there?" Daniel suddenly asked.

Peter nodded. "I checked this morning. That was one of the first places I thought I might find him. I showed him the caves when we were out biking."

Liza remembered. It was one of the sights on the island that had impressed her nephew.

Daniel glanced out the window. "Maybe we ought to go back and check again. It's dark and cold out now. Will might be looking for some shelter if he's really trying to stay away."

Peter considered the idea a moment. "You know, that makes sense. It's worth a try." He glanced at Daniel and then at Liza. "I can't sit around here any longer. I want to get out there and keep looking."

"I'll come with you," Daniel offered. "You might need some help."

"Me, too," Liza said. She turned to Claire. "Can you let us know if anyone calls?"

"Of course I will," Claire promised. "You ought to take some blankets. He'll be chilled." She walked into the hallway and opened a few boxes that were stacked there, then took out two big wool blankets and handed them to Liza.

Peter had already gone out, but Daniel waited by the door with a large flashlight. Moments later they stepped outside, only to see the taillights of Peter's rental car disappearing down the drive. "I guess he couldn't wait," Liza said.

"Understandable," Daniel replied. "Come on, let's catch up."

He rested his hand lightly on her back as they walked over to his truck. Liza climbed in her side and fastened the seatbelt. Daniel did the same, quickly started the engine, and pulled out.

"At least it's not raining." Liza stared out at the

dark, velvety blue sky, studded with thousands of stars. "Do you think we'll find him?" she asked quietly.

"I did at first . . . Now I don't know what to think." He glanced over at her with a serious expression, and Liza felt a pang of dread.

She stared straight ahead, watching the narrow road fly by in the beam of the truck's headlights. It was so dark out there.

No houses or lamps on the road to light the way. If Will was all alone out here tonight, he had to be cold, hungry, and scared by now. She hoped they would find him soon.

The trip to the cliffs seemed longer than usual, though Daniel was driving as fast as he dared. Finally they reached the spot. He pulled over to the side of the road and parked behind Peter's car. He shut off the engine and grabbed the flashlight as he got out. Liza jumped out her side and ran over to her brother, who stood at the edge of the road, waiting for them, holding his own light.

"I don't see the bike around, but I'd rather not waste time looking," Peter said. "I'm just going to climb down there and look in the caves. I think I can remember my way around, even if he's gone deep inside."

Liza really hoped that was not the case. "You start down. We'll follow," she told her brother.

"Right, go ahead. I have a strong light for me and Liza," Daniel said.

Peter started down the side of the cliff. It was hard enough to climb down in broad daylight and very tricky in the dark. But Liza didn't complain. She followed Daniel, who was holding out the light for them.

Just a few yards down, her foot caught on a root, and she lost her balance. Daniel turned and caught her with his arm around her waist. "Are you all right?"

Liza nodded quickly, caught off balance now by his nearness.

"I'm fine. My foot caught on something."

"Here, hold my hand." Without waiting for her answer, he took her hand in his in a warm, steady grip, holding the light out for them with the other.

They started down the hill again. Daniel's strong hold on her hand helped to steady her steps and also steadied her nerves. She trusted him, she realized.

Down on the beach, they were greeted by the crashing sound of the waves on the shoreline. The tide was coming in, almost at its peak. Sea foam swept up to the big rocks at the bottom of the path, filling their shoes with cold, salty water.

The same beach that looked so inviting in the sunlight now looked ominous in the dark.

They were a few yards from the entrance to the caves, and Liza silently sent up another prayer. *Dear God, please let us find him.*

"There's Peter." Daniel pointed farther up the

beach to where Peter stood waving his flashlight near the entrance to the caves. They ran over to meet him.

"Let's go in this one. It's the most obvious place," Peter said. He started in to the largest of the caves, and they followed.

Liza quickly remembered to pull up the hood on her jacket. She knew most bats were harmless but still hated the idea of one even brushing by.

They entered the first chamber and walked in a few feet. Peter cupped his hands around his mouth and called for his son. "Will? Are you in here? Answer me, please . . ."

His voice echoed off the stone walls. They stood very still and listened for an answer—but only heard the sound of water dripping into puddles.

"Will? Please . . . if you're in here, please answer," Liza called. She had meant to leave it all up to Peter but found she couldn't help herself.

Daniel gazed down at her with a sympathetic look and put his arm around her shoulders.

A few tense moments of silence passed. Liza sensed her brother's optimistic hopes quickly fading, and her heart went out to him. It was dreadful to see him in so much pain.

"Let's walk a little farther," Daniel suggested.

They walked deeper into the caves, ducking their heads to cross into another chamber. The ceiling of the second cave was higher than the first, and Daniel flashed his light around curiously. Then they suddenly heard the furious flap of wings.

Everyone ducked and covered their heads.

Daniel leaned over and shielded Liza with his body. She pressed her head to his chest and squeezed her eyes closed. His embrace lasted just a moment but somehow gave her back the bit of hope she had nearly lost.

"Will? Are you in here?" Peter shouted again. "If you can hear me, please answer." He paused. "Nobody's mad at you, Will. We just want you to come home. You're not in trouble, honest," he said in a more desperate tone.

They stood very still, listening again. Liza didn't even dare breathe. But once again, only the sounds of the falling water and the ocean surf out in the distance could be heard.

Peter caught her gaze. His face looked drawn in the dim light. "I guess I was wrong. I guess he's not in here," he said quietly. "Just wishful thinking."

"Maybe," Liza said, not wanting to agree. She felt so sad for him. "There's got to be something we—"

But before she could finish her thought, she heard a scraping sound nearby. She jumped, moving closer to Daniel. He quickly swung the light in the direction of the sound. Liza expected to see some creepy, nocturnal animal emerging.

Instead, she saw her nephew, standing in the opening that led to the next cave.

Dirty, wet, and sheepish-looking, Will came toward them and then just stood there. His head slowly lifted, and he looked at his father first, then at Liza and Daniel.

"Hey, guys . . . What's up?"

Chapter Fifteen

PETER gasped. "Will! Thank God!"

He seemed so overcome, Liza thought he might faint. He staggered toward his son and wrapped his arms around the boy.

"Will," Liza said, hardly able to speak. "Thank goodness you're all right . . . You are, aren't you?"

"I'm okay," he said. He glanced at his father. "I'm sorry, Dad. I—"

Peter hushed him. "That's okay. We'll talk about it later. Don't worry, everything is going to be fine. As long as you're all right."

With his arm around Will's shoulder, Peter led him out of the caves and back up the hill. Liza was glad she had brought the blankets and quickly ran to Daniel's truck to retrieve them. She carried them over to Peter's car, where Will sat shivering in the front seat.

Daniel was giving the boy a quick examination to determine whether he needed to go to a hospital.

A few moments later, he said, "Well, he's chilled and a bit dehydrated, but I don't think he's been overexposed. If we get him home and get him warm, give him plenty of fluids and some food tonight, he should be fine."

"Good. I don't really want to take him to a hospital," Peter admitted. "I don't want to let him out of my sight."

Liza leaned into the car and covered Will with the blankets, wrapping one around his legs and another around his shoulders.

"I—I can't seem to stop shivering," her nephew said, sounding embarrassed.

"You will," Liza said. "I promise."

A few feet away she heard Peter on the phone, calling the police officers first and then Claire, sharing the good news.

PETER ushered Will from the car into the house, adjusting the blankets that clung to the boy's shoulders. Liza got out of the truck, and Daniel walked around from the other side to meet her.

Liza saw Claire standing in the doorway at the top of the steps, her sturdy silhouette outlined by the warm light from within. As Will came closer, Claire stepped out to meet him, then smothered the boy in a comforting embrace, one that briefly took in Peter as well.

As they walked into the house together, Liza remembered how Claire had been waiting there the first night she returned. Even then, not knowing her at all, Claire had been ready to welcome her home. Just as she was there now for all of them.

Liza began to head for the house, then noticed that Daniel hung back. "Guess I'll say good night," he said.

"Aren't you coming in?"

Daniel looked down at her and stuck his hands in his pockets. "Thanks, but it's late. And it's going to be hard enough for Peter and you to talk to Will without strangers around."

"You're not exactly a stranger," she replied. "But I know what you mean. Thanks . . . Thanks for everything. We really appreciated your help today."

He shook his head. "It was nothing. I was glad I could help. At least there's a happy ending to the story, right?"

"Yes, to this one," she said, thinking of the Hardys. Now that Will's little drama had concluded, she and Peter would have to return to the dilemma of what to do with the inn. What had Claire told her to remember? Worry not.

Daniel gave her a curious look. She was tempted to tell him about the Hardys . . . to tell him everything. But they had all had enough stress for one day. It was best left for tomorrow.

Instead she asked, "Will you be back to work?"

"Bright and early. Tomorrow could be my last day."

She didn't like hearing that but nodded. "Okay. See you then."

He looked about to walk away, then stopped. "Is there something on your mind, Liza?" he asked quietly.

"Um . . . no. It can wait."

"Okay . . . but there's something on my mind."

He stepped closer and put his hands on her waist. Then he lowered his head and kissed her. Liza leaned into him, feeling his warmth and strength. Savoring the sensation of his lips on hers.

Liza felt breathless when they parted. She slowly stepped back and gazed up at him.

"Good night," he said quietly. "I'll see you tomorrow."

She smiled, unable to speak for a moment. "Good night, Daniel," she said finally.

He turned and walked back to his truck, and Liza headed for the house, feeling a bit light-headed and glowing with happiness, as if a low, steady flame had been lit somewhere deep in her heart.

She simply loved being with him. It didn't seem to matter where they were or what they were doing. It was all good, as Will would say. She was going to miss Daniel so much when she left. But she didn't dare think about that now.

LIZA found Peter and Claire in the kitchen, fussing over Will. The boy sat at the head of the table, still wrapped in the blankets but practically inhaling a bowl of soup and a big sandwich. Claire stood at the counter, fixing more food for him.

Peter sat at Will's side, just staring at his son. "Now you're sure you don't need to see a doctor? Nothing hurts? You don't feel dizzy or weak?"

"I'm okay, Dad. Honest," Will managed between mouthfuls.

Peter nodded. "All right. You get a good night's sleep, and we'll see how you feel in the morning. Daniel said you need to drink a lot of liquids. You might be dehydrated."

"He did? How does he know stuff like that?"

"He's trained as a first responder, EMS," Liza said. She walked over to Will and slung her arm around his shoulder, then planted a big kiss on the top of his head. She dropped down in the seat on his other side, across from her brother.

"You scared us to death, Will. The Cape Light bloodhounds were out, trying to sniff down your trail."

Will's eyes widened in surprise. "They were?"

Liza laughed. "Not quite . . . but almost."

"We were worried sick," Peter cut in. "Where were you all day, Will? We didn't know what had happened to you."

"I don't know. Just riding the bike around." Will shrugged. "It's a pretty small island, I'm surprised you didn't see me."

Liza's gaze narrowed, recalling how she had searched her assigned area for hours, even on foot.

"It's hard to find somebody who doesn't want to be found, even in a place as small as this."

"How did you end up in the cave?" Peter asked. "Were you hiding down there all day? I checked in the morning. We didn't see you."

"I didn't go down there until it got dark. I got a flat on the bike, and I left it on the side of the road behind some bushes. I was near the caves and felt pretty cold, so I thought it would be a good place to stay for the night."

"Was it?" Peter asked, meeting his son's gaze.

Will smirked. "It was pretty creepy. All the bats and spiders and stuff."

A good story to tell his friends though, Liza realized. A tale to swap when they boasted about their camping trip.

"So, why did you do it, Will?" Peter asked, his tone almost pleading. "Can you just tell me that?"

Liza sat back and looked at her nephew. He had stopped eating and was staring at the table, avoiding his father's gaze.

Peter just waited, and Liza gave him points for patience.

Will shrugged. "I don't know . . . I just felt like it."

Peter let out a frustrated sigh. "You just felt like it? That's all the answer I get? After what you put us through today?"

Liza gave Peter a quick look and shook her head. It wasn't going to help if he went off the deep end and lost it.

"It must have been more than that, Will," she said. "Can you just try to tell us how you're feeling, what you're thinking about right now? We were terribly worried, but we're not mad, honestly."

"We just want to understand," Peter told his son.

"We really do," Claire chimed in. "How can we help if you don't tell us what's wrong?"

Will slowly raised his head. He looked around at all of them. "I . . . I don't want you to be mad at me."

"I won't be. I promise. Just tell us," Peter said quickly.

Will looked at him, seeming doubtful. But then he stared straight ahead and said, "I don't want to go back to Tucson. I want to stay here."

Peter sat back as if someone had slapped him. "You want to stay here. Because you don't want to come live with me half of the time, is that it?"

Liza saw him struggling to keep an even tone.

Will shook his head. "That's not it. That's not it at all. I would come live with you part of the time, but I just hate the way you and Mom are always fighting about it. Fighting over me. You're so angry all the time. You make me feel like it's all my fault."

Peter looked shocked. "Of course it's not your fault, Will. Your mom and I breaking up had nothing to do with you. We both love you very much."

401

Liza felt Peter's frustration, but she understood what Will was saying, too. Maybe he even understood intellectually that his parents' divorce had not been because of him. But he didn't feel that way deep inside. And almost two years later, they were still fighting about his living arrangements.

"I can just give up, Will," Peter said softly. "I can just agree to let your mom have custody, and I'd visit you every other weekend. Is that what you want?"

Will shook his head. "Not really. I wouldn't mind living with you, Dad . . . if you could be the way you are here."

Peter looked puzzled. "The way I am here? On the island, you mean?"

Will nodded. "Yeah, like more fun and stuff. The way you were that day we went bike riding and when we took photographs together. The way you used to be before the divorce . . . Not all wound up and crazy and fighting with Mom over every little thing."

Peter took in a long breath. He held Will's gaze but didn't answer for what seemed like a long time. Finally, he said. "Okay. I'm glad you told me what's on your mind, Will. I need to think about this. It's pretty serious stuff. We can talk more tomorrow after we've all had some rest. Is that all right with you?"

Will nodded. "I feel pretty tired. Like I'm going to nod off into my soup."

"That would be . . . messy," Liza said with a smile.

"Why don't you finish your supper and take a hot shower?" Claire suggested. "I bet you fall asleep tonight before your head even hits the pillow."

"I bet we all do," Peter said. He looked over at Liza and sighed.

She wondered how he felt now about Will, and even about selling the inn. But she didn't want to press him. Not tonight.

WHEN Liza got up the next morning, she thought she would be the first one downstairs, so she was surprised to find her brother in the front parlor. He sat at the oak table with the photo albums and a mug of coffee.

"Did you recover from the search and rescue mission?" he asked, as she took a seat at the table.

"I think I recovered when we first spotted Will down in that cave. It was brilliant of you to think of that, Peter."

He shrugged and smiled. "And of Daniel to suggest going back there a second time. I'd say we were lucky. But I did get to thinking about that last night and realized that it was almost as if my happy memories of this place led us to him in some strange way. If I hadn't been sitting here, reminiscing about my own adventures, I wouldn't have thought of it."

Liza smiled, charmed by the idea. "That might be true."

"I feel it is true, Liza," Peter said, with more emotion that he usually showed. "I do feel differently here, just like Will said. Maybe getting back in touch with a happier time in your life does that. I can see it's happened for you," he added.

"Yes, something has happened to me here. Something . . . important," she said quietly. "You know, when I first came and started cleaning out the closets with Claire, I was surprised at how hard it was. I don't mean physically. Emotionally," she explained. "And Claire said, 'Of course it's hard. This is your past. It's your family. It's part of you.'" She looked up at her brother. "It's part of you, too, Peter."

He sipped at his coffee and nodded. "Yes, you're right. I can see that now."

"This old, broken-down house is the only link left to our past, our family," Liza continued. "For me, it put me back in touch with some part of myself that I lost along the way. Maybe that's why I feel so strongly about staying here, staying connected to that more hopeful, optimistic version of myself. It gives me a way to go back and start over," she tried to explain.

"I understand," he said quietly. "I mean, I really didn't before, but I get it now, Liza." He sighed. "I've been feeling the same thing but fighting it," he admitted. "It's definitely more than nostalgia. I got in touch with some buried part of myself, too. Some better version of me. Isn't that what Will was trying to say last night?" Without waiting for her answer, he continued, "This place is a touchstone—all we have left of our folks, and of Elizabeth and Clive. I was wrong to think we could let someone come here and knock it down. Or even sell it," he said finally. "The inn and the island are important to both of us. To all of us. I want Will to know this place and share it, too."

Liza stared at him in disbelief. "Are you serious? You really mean that?"

"I do," he said quickly. "You should stay here. You need this chance to start over, more than I need the money. We can figure that out. I want you to have a chance to center yourself and figure things out. I can see you've gotten in touch with something out here that's been dormant a long time. I couldn't take that from you now, Liza. What kind of a brother would I be to do that to you?"

Liza felt so overwhelmed with relief and gratitude that for a moment she couldn't speak at all. "Thank you, Peter," she said at last. "Thank you for understanding and for changing your mind."

"Will likes it here, more than he ever thought. He doesn't want us to sell it either. He wants to be able to come back here. He told me last night before he went to sleep. I think he really meant it, too."

"I think he did," Liza agreed, sending up a silent prayer of thanks for Will's influence over his father and for Peter's amazing change of heart.

"Someone is going to have to tell Fran Tulley," Liza said quietly, trying to hide the grin that threatened to break out across her face, ear to ear.

"Yes . . . someone is. Someone named Peter Martin, I think," her brother said with a resigned sigh. "Poor Fran. She worked so hard the last two weeks and finally reeled in a big fish for us. We'll have to make it up to her somehow. Send her some flowers or something."

"A free weekend at the Inn at Angel Island, our deluxe suite."

"Our deluxe suite?" Peter gave her a look. "You have big plans, don't you?"

"I do," Liza said in a soft but firm voice. "I definitely do."

For the first time in a long time, she felt very sure of things, what she wanted and where her life was going.

CLAIRE had arrived while they were talking in the parlor. Liza hadn't even heard her come in but realized she was there when the warm, delicious smell of something baking beckoned.

"Something smells good." Peter sniffed the air. "Shall we go investigate?"

Liza followed her brother to the kitchen. Claire

stood by the open oven, checking a pan of dark brown muffins that smelled incredibly good.

"What are those made of? Nectar of the gods?" Peter asked, teasing her.

Claire laughed. "Not quite. It's a lot of good things, though, in the recipe. They're called Morning Glory Muffins. Just let them cool a minute and you can try one."

"I can't wait," Peter admitted, taking a seat at the table.

Liza glanced at him, and he seemed to read her mind. "We have some good news, Claire," he began. "We've decided to keep the inn."

Claire turned and looked at them each in turn, casting them a warm smile. "That *is* good news. Wonderful news. I'm very happy to hear it."

"I'm going to stay here and run it," Liza added. "I hope you'll stay and help me, Claire. I don't think I could do it without you."

Claire met her glance. "Of course I'll stay. I don't think you could get rid of me now . . . short of knocking the place down."

Liza laughed. She'd never heard Claire make a joke before—and actually, from the sparkle in the housekeeper's blue eyes, Liza wasn't entirely sure that Claire was joking.

Liza watched Claire beat some eggs in a bowl, working in her steady, competent way, and felt so utterly grateful for her friendship and loyalty. It felt like a gift. And maybe it was, she realized.

A final gift from her dear aunt, who was always looking out for her, trying to guide her and help her grow.

Liza impulsively leaned over and gave the housekeeper a quick, fierce hug. "Thank you, Claire. Thank you for everything."

Claire stepped back from the stove and hugged Liza back, then patted her arm. "I had a feeling it would all work out. I had a feeling your prayers would be answered," she added.

Liza had never told Claire that she had prayed about the inn. But she didn't question that Claire had guessed this and somehow knew.

Will appeared in the doorway, his thick dark hair tousled and his eyes still puffy from sleep.

"Hey, Will, what's up?" his father said cheerfully, for once beating his son to the famous question.

Liza walked over to her nephew and slung her arm around his shoulder. "Going for any big bike rides today?" she teased.

He gave her a sheepish grin and shook his head. "I don't think so . . . My butt is pretty sore. I can barely sit down."

They all laughed. Even Claire, who tried not to but couldn't help it.

"Well, eat your food standing up, then," she said, handing him a muffin. Will took a huge bite, putting practically half in his mouth at once. "Mmm . . . that's really good."

"It's a great day. Maybe we can go out to the beach and take some pictures," Peter said to Will. "And we can talk some more," he added. "Would you like to do that?"

Will gave his father a serious look for a moment, then nodded.

"I'm glad you guys aren't leaving for Arizona today," Liza said. "Now that everything's settled, maybe you can stay a little longer and just enjoy the island."

"That'd be okay," Will said, grinning at his dad.

Peter grinned back, then glanced out the window. He suddenly put down his coffee and rose from his seat. "There's Daniel. I never got to thank him." He walked to the back door and pulled it open. "Daniel, come in for some coffee?"

Liza felt her heart quicken at the mere mention of his name.

She watched for him at the doorway and met his glance. Their eyes locked, and she smiled. It was only a moment, but it was more than enough.

"Good morning," Daniel said, as he walked into the kitchen. "Hey, Will. How are you this morning?"

"I'm okay. Except certain parts of me."

Peter laughed. "Don't ask," he told Daniel. "I just wanted to thank you for all your help yesterday. You didn't have to go out of your way like that. I really appreciate it."

"That's all right. I'm just glad this crazy kid was found safe and sound," he added, glancing at Will.

"So are we all," Peter replied.

"There's some news, Daniel," Claire said. She turned and winked at Liza.

"Some news?" Daniel looked around curiously. "What kind of news?"

"Peter and I agree we're not going to sell the inn. I'm going to stay here and run it for a while. We've decided to keep it in the family. It's important to us."

"Wow . . . that is news." Daniel cast a warm, wide smile in her direction. Liza felt herself starting to blush and quickly looked away. She could tell that Peter knew something was going on between her and Daniel, and was grateful that he hadn't asked her about it. Yet.

"Congratulations, Liza," Daniel said. "This place will keep you busy. But I think you're up to the challenge," he added.

"I hope so," she said.

"You'll be great. But you'll get sick of seeing me," he predicted.

I sincerely doubt that, Liza nearly said aloud. Sick of hearing hammers and power tools, maybe. Looking at him?

Not likely.

"Oh, we'll see about that," she said quietly. "There is a lot to do."

"One step at a time," Peter said. "We've made some good progress the past two weeks. You might even be ready for guests this summer."

"Yes, we might be. It's a good goal," she agreed, feeling excited and even a little scared at the idea. But she could do it with Claire's help, and Daniel's. And even the ephemeral support of her aunt Elizabeth, whom she often felt hovering nearby.

It was a beautiful day, the warmest so far, and Liza felt no pressure now to clean out closets or tackle any new repair jobs on her to-do list. There would be time enough for that, she knew. Peter and Will now planned to stay a few more days to visit with her, and she felt their time together was precious. They decided to take a long walk on the beach. But not before a few necessary phone calls. One to Fran Tulley, explaining that they had taken the inn off the market and thanking her for her hard work.

Fran was disappointed but understood the situation, Peter told Liza later. "She even sounded pleased that the building wouldn't be knocked down after all and that you were staying here to keep the inn open," he added. "She's been a pretty good sport," Peter added.

"Yes, she has been," Liza agreed. A good sport and a good neighbor.

After Peter called Fran, Liza steeled herself and called her boss, Eve Barkin. It was a difficult task to face.

She had to turn down the promotion—and quit her job. Eve was completely shocked. She asked

Liza if she wanted to take more time to think the situation through.

But Liza felt sure of her decision. As sure as she had ever been in her life. Finally, Eve accepted her resignation and wished her luck. "Thank you, Eve. I wish you luck, too . . . and please tell Charlie Reiger the same," she added graciously.

Charlie would doubtless get the promotion now, Liza knew. And somehow that, too, seemed just as it ought to be.

As she ran down the hill with Peter and Will, the ocean came into full view. Her brother and nephew ran ahead, chasing each other in some crazy game of seaweed tag they had just invented, darting in and out of the lapping waves on the shoreline.

Liza fell back, walking alone at her own pace. She felt as if the cares and questions that had weighed so heavily for so long had just floated away, like the puffy white clouds on the horizon.

It wasn't as if she didn't have responsibilities now. Far from it. In a way, she had even more. But they were not the worries and concerns over clients and office power plays. It was a whole new ball game.

A whole new life. The realization was positively . . . stunning. How had this happened? She had no idea.

But it was wonderful. A new path she'd never imagined, opening up before her.

Liza closed her eyes against the sunlight and said a silent prayer, asking for help to live up to her promises and to make the inn thrive again. For help to create not just a successful enterprise but one that fulfilled the promise of the island and the traditions of her own family.

A haven for travelers searching for a place to refresh their spirit and find a new start. Just as she had.

This was the true legacy her aunt had left to her, Liza realized, and the one she hoped to pass on.

Here's one of Claire's favorite recipes, which never fails to make smiles bloom around the breakfast table. The ingredients and spices are varied, and Claire claims there's no reason to worry if you don't have everything on hand. Just improvise. The muffins never come out the same way twice but are always delicious . . . and could be called Vanishing Muffins, since they disappear so quickly.

Morning Glory Muffins
MAKES 16 MUFFINS

Ingredients
2¼ cups unbleached all-purpose flour
2 teaspoons baking soda
¾ cup brown sugar, lightly packed (light or dark)
¾ cup white sugar
2 tablespoons cinnamon
1 teaspoon ground ginger
½ teaspoon allspice
2 cups grated carrots
1 cup (8 ounces) crushed pineapple, packed in juice and drained
¾ cup raisins (golden preferred)
½ cup shredded coconut
½ cup chopped walnuts or pecans
3 large eggs
1 teaspoon vanilla extract
1 cup canola oil

Directions

Preheat the oven to 350 degrees F with a rack in the lower third.

Line muffin tins with paper cups.

In a large bowl, mix together the flour, baking soda, sugar, cinnamon, ginger, and allspice. Add the carrots, pineapple, raisins, coconut, and nuts, and mix thoroughly.

In a separate bowl, whisk the eggs with the vanilla and then the oil. Pour egg mixture into the dry ingredients in thirds and blend well. (Do not overmix or muffins will turn out tough.)

Fill muffin cups to the brim. Bake for 30–35 minutes or until a toothpick or sharp, thin knife inserted in the middle of a muffin comes out clean. Allow to cool for 10–15 minutes and remove from tins.

Center Point Publishing
600 Brooks Road ● PO Box 1
Thorndike ME 04986-0001 USA

(207) 568-3717

US & Canada:
1 800 929-9108
www.centerpointlargeprint.com